THE
ANTEATER

A Novel by Edan Benn Epstein

The following story is fiction. Any resemblance to real events or people is purely coincidental.

PROLOGUE
After the Storm

He runs naked through the middle of the street. Limbs move with shocking ease, far beyond their given strength. He runs through sickly yellow light, over cracked sidewalks, past the mean and windowless warehouse walls. He runs and there is his car and he lays down heavily, bruising and scraping. Adrenalin courses through him, so he still feels warm and he doesn't care much about anything, not even whether he ever awakens at all. Inside his dream world he hears the sound of a man shouting the name of the one that they say is the Lord, over and over, and his head touches the damp, blunt pavement. It might be real. Suddenly, the shouting ceases and all that takes its place is the uneven rattle of a shopping cart carrying its despised cargo of rotten newspapers and rags, and that much he knows is certainly real. He hears the quiet steps that come for him.

BOOK ONE – Before the Storm

1. September, 1985

Attracted to the desert red bluffs and the endless sky, Andy lingers in New Mexico, at home in his pick-up. He sleeps at lonely road sides and he awakens in thoughtless moments of not needing to be anywhere, noticing the rugged smallness of the day. Late one afternoon he pulls into a filling station with its tiny wooden store. He studies the racks of chips and crackers, tins of sausage and sardines. He rattles some change in his pockets and he imagines he's inside a crappy little satellite floating in endless space. The air conditioning, the smallness and the isolation tingle the back of his neck. An unlikely dolorous alto sings a somber song. The cashier reads a worn and greasy paperback. She has a long sharp nose which gives her face an inquisitive aspect. Andy brings a half gallon of water and a pack of Pop Tarts to her for purchase. "These and a couple of incense sticks."

"How many?"

"Five, I guess. And some matches."

"Cinnamon Delight or Passion Nights?"

"I don't care. Cinnamon."

"No passion?"

"No. I guess not."

"Three twenty nine." Her voice is small. Andy pulls a crumpled, faded ten from his wallet and hands it to her. She sighs as if to suggest impatience with unkempt money. "You want a bag?"

"Sure. What's that music?

"Mahler."

"Who?"

"Gustav Mahler. One of his Kindertotenlieder."

"Kinder…"

"Kindertotenlieder."

"What's that?"

"Songs for Dead Children." she says evenly.

"….It's beautiful. And unexpected."

"It is."

"Who is Mahler?"

She rises and Andy assumes the conversation is over. He is startled to see that she walks with a limp and a cane, like an old woman. The girl turns down the music and rifles through some objects on the back shelf. She returns and holds something out to him. "Here," she says. "Listen to this while you're driving to L.A. Mahler's Tenth Symphony."

"How did you know I'm going to L.A.?"

"Your truck's pointed that way," she says, looking out. "That's where most people are headed."

"I'm moving there."

"Why?"

"To play music. Sell records."

"If you like the Kindertotenlieder, this here will really put you in your place," she says pointing to the cassette in his hand "What's your music like?"

"I can get you a tape out of my truck."

"Get it." He hurries out and brings her a cassette, green and gold oddly melded designs on the cover.

"I recorded it....Do you play music?"

"Piano."

"Great. You got a piano?"

"I have three," she says archly. "No lie." She smiles and she looks at his cassette and she turns off the dead children and puts in his cassette instead. She grins as the cassette begins and they speak about their music and the music of others that sustains them. She loves Stravinsky, Miles Davis, Screaming Jay Hawkins, Woody Guthrie, Siouxsie and The Banshees. She writes bad poetry and sings a bit. Poorly, she says. He likes Coltrane, Debussy, King Crimson, Balinese Gamelan, Pink Floyd.

"I'm Andy," he finally says, putting out his hand

"I'm Maggie," she replies, keeping her hands to herself. "I'm here all day, Wednesday through Sunday. But you're leaving this shit hole the minute you walk out the door."

"Looks like it. But you never know."

"Thanks for the tape," she says, and she smiles and she lets it play.

2.

The little man with the long blond hair talks to himself, bug eyed with thick glasses and a purple bruise around his left eye. Addressing no one in particular, he acts as if trying to sound reasonable. "I'll tell you what. There's no gays here in Gary, New Mexico. That's right..... No gays. This is a family place. So everyone can just relax. You know?" The man looks squarely now at Andy. "Just relax. Cause there's no gays. I mean faggots! Faggots. I meant to say faggots, of course. Isn't that the politically correct term now?" Andy nods his head at the man. "But, I'll tell you. There are at least a few men, perfectly straight, perfectly straight, who don't mind," he hiccups, "who I say do not mind receiving a nice…fine….blow job. A *nice* blow job! That does not mean you're gay. Or a faggot. So I'm told." Andy continues to nod and the man continues, "You know how real men act when they meet a gay man. A faggot. You want to know? I mean a real man. A He man. You want to know?" Andy nods that he wants to know. The man makes a vicious gesture like a cartoon creature holding his hands above his head like cartoon claws. "They say, 'hey, look at the faggot. Let's *fuck* that faggot in the ass!'"

"That's enough now," the bartender tells him, trying to restrain a laugh. "Get on out already with that trash talk."

"This is a family place, right?" the little man says.

Someone stands, a large man, shirt untucked. Andy inwardly cringes; he realizes he's hopelessly rooting for the little man. The bartender speaks. "I got this," he says, "But *you* had better go now."

The little man grabs something that resembles a long, thin brief case. "If you insist. You know what's in *here*, though?"

"Just go."

"I got something that I could use to *blow* you all away!"

"I'm gonna count to three."

"I know you can do it," the little man says.

"If you're still here when I get to three, I'm gonna let Dennis over here escort you out."

"Goodie!"

"One."

"But I really have to be going."

"Two." The man called Dennis stands up again and the little man scrambles away, stumbling out of the room. "Three!"

The little man is already gone. Dennis and the bartender bust out laughing. Someone says, What'd you have to go threatening him for? "I was tired of his bullshit. Weren't you?" I thought he was a bit downright entertaining. Yeah, I love a bit of a show. That piss ant is harmless. "If I'd knowed that it was good for business, I might have let him stay." More laughter. What the hell he have in that case anyways? "Who the hell knows?" Andy thinks he has a pretty good idea. He takes a last gulp of his beer, gets up and he steps outside with the half-hearted intention of finding the little man. But despite the nothingness of the short empty endless street he sees no one at all.

That night, Andy sleeps in his truck in the back of the supermarket lot. Early the next morning he heads west once more. Not more than five minutes out is the first hitchhiker he has seen in days. He thinks of his mother's warning. The little man with the long blond hair and the purple shiner stands with his thumb out, wearing a worn looking backpack and holding his saxophone case with his other hand. They make eye contact, though Andy is certain that the little man does not recognize him.

3.

He arrives in the early sea green morning hours after listening all night in the desert to tapes of Hank Williams and Charles Ives. He ends up in the San Gabriel foothills and sleeps until noon in the truck. After eating at a diner in Pasadena he idles with the want ads and watches the restaurant diners turn over and over. He finds a motel in Sunland and he plops down on the clean but creaky double bed with the thin crenulated spread. He opens up the drawers to distract himself. The television fails to entertain him and he turns it off and turns on the air conditioner instead and he listens intently to it. He tries to find its tones and chords on his guitar. The next day, Andy looks for work in recording studios and radio stations, hoping to turn his experience in producing his own records into a paycheck. After a week of this, Andy begins to notice that there are far more homeless men and women than he ever imagined and not so far from his motel. Many are neatly dressed and washed. Maybe they shower at a YMCA. They wear the same clothes and they walk the same streets and their skin is dark and heavily creased. Already he wonders if he will have to live like them as well. Andy begins to notice listing after listing in the paper for messenger driver. Something about the idea of driving his truck for a living appeals to him. The first two places he applies won't hire him because he confesses he has lived in the city for only a week. A third only hires motorcycle drivers. He needs a job so the next interview has to be different.

4

Tom Hagen of ZZZZAP Messenger in Culver City wears a square face, oiled hair, and a tan blazer. His hands are fat and pink. Andy decides that this is where he will end up working. Because of the name. ZZZZAP! Messenger. It's a silly, stupid name and Andy likes it very much. What kinds of people would seriously entrust a company named ZZZZAP! with their business? Andy decides he wants to find out. "You don't forget that name do you! There are hundreds of messenger companies in Los Angeles. Hundreds! So we have to stand out. We have to live up to our name. Do you have any idea how competitive this business is? I have people out there who depend on us for their daily bread, their very livelihood. Every day we carry bids for construction companies upon which thousands of dollars depend. We deliver depositions and filings for attorneys upon which *millions* of dollars and maybe even somebody's freedom might depend." He leans forward, face flushed, as he continues. "That's not all, Andy. People's very *lives* depend on us. Our drivers are bonded and licensed to carry specimens of blood for clinics and research labs. Blood we carry. Everything is carefully vacuum sealed, of course, completely professional. But we carry it. And not just blood, but sperm, urine, and even feces. Feces, Andy. Think of it. That's a sacred trust I think you'll agree."

"I completely agree!"

Hagen, impervious to sarcastic enthusiasm, reels from the desk and runs his hand across his slick black hair. "It's my damn job to get the clients and it's yours to keep them. If we screw up, the client can fire us like nothing."

"Like zap!" Andy says, astonished at his own impudence, but Hagen seems to agree.

"That's right. Can you handle pressure?!"

"Yes." A strange city with no job and dwindling funds. Sperm. Blood. Feces. "I can handle that."

Hagen winks, "It's time to introduce you to Mikros"

The dispatcher eats Pad Thai amongst stacks of papers. Small, scruffy, and hirsute, a single bushy brow dominates his black bean eyes inside his bottle thick glasses. "Have a seat," the man says.

"Thanks." Andy glances about the room, an airy corner office featuring two enormous couches, upholstery bulging and bursting from its grimy casings. Andy sinks into its benign clutches. Behind Mikros is a large wall clock with its relentless red second hand and below that an enormous white-board, filled with hand printed names, places, times, and arrows. After wiping his mouth with a napkin, Mikros turns to Andy.

"You really want to work for this company?"

"Sure."

"You need a job?

"Well yeah," Andy doesn't understand the point of such a question.

"I want people who want to work."

"I want to work."

"Why do you want to work here? This is a *shit* company. Messenger is a shit job."

"Yeah. I've heard that," Andy says, thinking of Hagen and his sacred feces. "Well I need a job and I want to work. I just moved to L.A."

"You just moved here? Ahh! Wonderful. Now they send me someone who doesn't know shit about the streets? How can you find your way around?"

Andy winces at his own stupidity. "Ouch. You're right. I guess you want someone who knows the city already. I mean, I could learn. I like driving." Mikros chews and stares at him. "Look, there's no need to get upset. I don't want to waste any more of your time." He stands up.

"Where are you going? I thought you wanted to work."

"Yeah. I do."

"What kind of car you drive?"

"Chevy pick-up."

"A truck? Good. New?"

"Ten years old."

"Better. A good shit car. You'll make money with that."

"Really?" Andy envisions himself hoisting huge vats of sloshing sperm and steaming coils of excrement into the haul of his truck.

"Do you know how to read a Thomas Guide?"

"I don't know what that is."

"It's a map! It's a fucking map. Do you know how to read city maps?"

"Yeah. Sure."

"Do you have any common sense?"

"Sure," I'm a broke and homeless musician who wants to work as a messenger in a strange city.

"Do you have a brain?"

Andy sighs, "Yes."

"Can you get along with people?"

"Sure."

"Sit down. Please," Andy sits back down on the couch. "This is not brain surgery. It doesn't take much to learn the job. To do it well you just have to pay attention." He points around the empty room. "This is when I like *my* job. When everyone's here, all people do is fight over who gets this and who gets that. Too many egos, too many babies. Fighting. Over nothing. Over shit. You understand? That's what I do *not* want. I do not want anyone to make my job any more difficult. Just get the package there. Get a signature. Don't break anything. Be nice. Call us when you're paged. Wear your pager and keep it on. Yes, we have pagers and a toll free number. This is a fucking backwards ass wipe company. No radios, no nothing."

"I see."

"You want to work?"

"Yes! I want to work."

"All right. You're hired. Buy yourself a Thomas Guide. Fifteen dollars. Any big drug store. You get minimum. Plus thirty cents a mile. That's where you make your money. Are you an American citizen?"

"Yes."

"Fine, you start tomorrow! Eight o'clock! Now go see Sandy to fill out some bullshit paperwork!"

5. First Tuesday in November:
16 days before the storm

Andy wears his brand new shirt, a short sleeve, white pull over with a blue collar and "ZZZZAP! Messenger Express" written in bold blue lettering across his heart. He feels slightly displaced as if his own shirt had suffered a grave accident and that this is the only thing he can wear in the interim. "We do a hundred deliveries a day with just six drivers. So you're seven. Sometimes, I send Sandy out. Mr. Hagen, too. We never say No to a customer. If we have to do the impossible, we do the impossible. How do you do the impossible? You can't but that's what we do. You have to be smart, not stupid. Today you'll learn from another driver. He is the best."

"Is he the fastest?"

"He's a psycho is what he is. Eugene. He can make it from here to downtown or the airport in less than fifteen minutes, whereas some of these idiots take nearly an hour." As he speaks, another driver clocks in. The man is dark skinned and sinewy, with high cheek bones and thick, greased black hair combed straight across his head. Like all drivers who will follow, he also wears the company shirt. "This is Perry. Perry never gives me any trouble at all."

"Good morning," Perry says quietly. Andy takes an instant liking to him and introduces himself. There is a rustle in the other room. Andy watches as Mikros tenses and then relaxes again as he watches the door. Perry greets the newcomer. "Hello Max." Max has the downy, complexion of one who never needs to shave. His head seems larger than normal. He wears a cheerful blankness. The phones begin to ring. Mikros looks thoughtfully at his whiteboard, clucking his tongue.

Another man enters, perhaps in his sixties, taking it upon himself to turn on the light in the outer office. The man has large, deep set gray eyes. He looks vaguely familiar though Andy is certain the man is a stranger. He has a crown of white hair around the side of his otherwise bald and bulbous head. He smells of cigarettes and has a discreet paunch. In one hand he carries two envelopes and he places them on the counter near Mikros, rapping his knuckles as he does so. In the other hand he carries a clipboard. Walking towards the couch he asks, "Has Sandy come in yet?"

"You can see very well she has not?"

"Are we startin' in already on another one of *those* days?"

"We have two rooms here, plus Hagen's office. If you don't see her, why do you ask me if she is here? When do you ever see her here before nine o'clock?

"Yup. I guess so. Just one more of those days, all right," he says, smiling dangerously, sighing and rubbing his chin.

"You will get your check, don't worry."

"I ain't worried," he says walking towards Andy. "Don't get up," he says with a wave of his hand which he then extends to Andy, who shakes it. "Tim Langham," he says, breathing hard.

"I'm Andy."

"That's the new guy," Mikros adds

Tim laughs his joyless laugh still looking at Andy, "Next you'll be telling me that two times two is four," he says, jangling his keys. He sits down heavily, rubbing his face and tapping his foot and he greets Perry and Max, inquiring of Perry's family.

"Good morning, gentlemen!" a voice booms. The voice belongs to a handsome, athletic blond in his early thirties; sparkling eyes and bushy blond brows. His ZZZZAP! shirt is untucked over a pair of khaki shorts and tennis shoes. He bristles, his face full of mischief and mockery. Like Tim, he places several envelopes on the counter. "Good morning my little Mikros," he says in a loud stage whisper, bending near the dispatcher, who is on the phone, "Are you sending me to Diamond Bar this morning? Or maybe Anaheim?" And he puts his hand out as if to pat Mikros on his curly head but Mikros sharply recoils and turns his back.

"Oh yeah," Tim mutters to no one in particular. "We're off and running."

The nameless driver laughs. "Timmy!" he shouts, "My best friend in the world. You're still here. They still haven't fired you?"

Tim shakes his head like an agitated animal. "I'm just minding my own business. You just try minding your own, if you're capable of that."

"Please. Minding your own business? That's the last thing you know how to do. Ask Mikros. He's going to send you running around Culver City today." Andy gathers that some cities like Anaheim are good, because they're far, while others, like Culver City, which is where their office is located, are bad because you make no money from mileage.

"Rolfe! I am on the phone with a customer!" Mikros says, his hand covering the phone. Rolfe kowtows before Mikros, holding his finger to his lips, shushing the room loudly. He tiptoes about the room and shamelessly looks through papers on Mikros' desk with mock astonishment. Then he looks over at Andy.

"So you're going to work for this shit company?"

Andy does not know how to answer. "Yes," he finally says.

"What's your name?"

"Andy."

"Rolfe." He walks over and shakes Andy's hand.

Another driver arrives, also in his sixties, tall, exceedingly thin, and intense, leathery skin, spectacles, a wooly beard and a mop of thick brown, tangled hair. Andy thinks that no one could look less like a messenger driver. "Good morning," the man says, before dropping upon the couch next to Andy.

Rolfe, still standing, hails the hairy man. "Welcome, Professor Samuel," He gives Perry a casual salute. Then he stops in front of Max. Andy's stomach tightens. "Good morning my little Mr. Pathetic. How are you today?"

Max shrugs. "Fine."

"You know, Ralph, maybe he doesn't like being called Mr. Pathetic," Tim growls from the couch.

"He can speak for himself. And maybe he *does* like it!" Rolfe says, smiling at Max. "And maybe I don't like being called Ralph, either, *Timmy?*"

"I really loathe you Ralph. You're really not at all a nice man."

"Ahh. Timmy just put me in my place!"

"Nothing's ever good enough for you. All you do is brag and complain, even though you still get the best runs from your little girl friend over here."

"Do not refer to me in this way!" Mikros objects.

"Gentlemen, please," Samuel said. "I really am getting a most unpleasant sensation of deja vu, here."

"You may run a little bit faster than someone like me or Samuel, but you aint no faster overall. Everyone here does it all just the same."

"Please, Tim. Even Mr. Pathetic is faster than you."

"His name is Max. Max. And you ain't nothin special. Understand?" Rolfe stares at Tim with his warped smile dismissing him with a wave.

Samuel shakes his wooly head and turns to Andy. "You are obviously the new man here. I'm Samuel." Andy introduces himself.

Tim turns to Max, "Doesn't it bother you that he calls you that?"

"I don't say it to be mean," Rolphe clarifies.

"Max?" Tim persists. Andy watches.

"No," Max finally says.

"No?" Tim said. "You're saying it doesn't bother you?"

Max half smiles, purses his lips, and says, "I *am* pathetic."

"Max is a good man," Perry says mildly.

"I think so, too," says Rolfe.

"Why, Max?" Tim says softly. "Why do you say that?"

"Leave him alone," Rolfe says, almost gently.

Max put up his hands as if to shrug again, "I come to work, I work, and then I go home and I sit there until I go to bed. That's what I do."

"You sit there?" Tim said, squinting. "Whaddaya mean?"

"I have a little couch and I sit in it in my room. I like to watch TV. Mostly, that's what I do."

"That's what you do, too, Timmy," Rolfe says, "only you won't admit it. Max is not ashamed or defensive. Only you are."

"Please, Rolfe," Tim says quietly, looking at Max, "Just this once. Be quiet."

6. Thursday, the night before the storm - Rolfe

He hoists himself, chin abreast with the thick angry, high grade piping, wearing only shorts and shoes. For a long second he hangs and dangles from the pipe, sweat stinging his eyes, pretending to hang without a care from a great height. Finally he lets himself drop. He stretches while holding a baseball bat behind his arms. He takes a few practice swings, mouthing words of admiration from the bleachers. He heads back, shirtless in the cool night air as he bounds up the steps to his apartment. "Tanya!" he calls.

"I'm on the phone."

"Fine. Fine," he says again, this time to himself. He flops on their white couch, his fingers tapping. A baleful whining approaches. "Taxi! Taxi! Come on boy," he calls out to the unseen feline. "Bring me a coat hanger. Would you bring me a coat hanger?" A lean gray cat appears grasping a severely chewed paper hanger tube, bereft of its wire, clutched in its teeth. The cat brays some more and lays the hanger down about six feet away from Rolfe. It sits there staring slit eyed, content with itself. "Hey, you stupid beast. Can't you actually bring it all the way to me? What are you doing over there?" He laughs and walks to the refrigerator to get a beer. "Where are you going, cat?" he asks as the feline seems to aimlessly wander about the living room. He flops back on the couch and opens his beer.

Tanya, still on the phone, sits on the back of the couch running her fingers through Rolfe's hair. He admires his lean young wife in her leotard top and cut-off jeans, cascades of curly black hair. "This is a shit cat," he coos affectionately, and he lifts the long suffering beast over his head, then lowers it pretending to put Taxi's entire head into Rolfe's mouth.

She gets off the call. "Are you torturing my baby again?"

"I love this thing," he says, lifting Taxi with one hand. "He makes a great bar bell."

"He's not a thing. He's our baby."

"We have to fatten him up though. I can't eat him like this."

"If Taxi were a child, would you talk about eating him?"

"Of course I would. Kids love that. But Taxi's not a child you know. You do realize he's a cat."

"That was my friend Angie from work. She just got through complaining about how *immature* her boyfriend is, always acting *stupid*, and how she could never marry him."

"Angie!" he sneers, still looking at Taxi, while walking the cat on his hind legs, holding him up and manipulating him by his shoulders. "She's lucky any man will stay with her at all, she's so annoying." Rolfe lets the cat down and strokes him. It manages to leap to its escape. He turns to his wife. "Did she really say that? About her immature boyfriend?"

"Not just now, no. But she has."

"You think I'm immature." Rolfe winks at her.

"Of course not, dear. Let's see you put Taxi's head in your mouth."

"I will one day. It will be glorious."

"Angie was telling me that she's going back to school."

"Yeah?"

"You know that what I want to do."

"That's what I want to do, too."

"You're too busy putting the cat's head in your mouth to go back to school."

"We don't have the money, Tanya."

"We could take out a loan."

"A loan? What would we put up for a loan?"

"Some kind of student loan."

"Oh a *student* loan," he says with mock enthusiasm. "We can't both go back to school."

"I want to be a physical therapist. I don't want to just work in an office or sweat on a bike in front of some creepy guys at the gym."

He scoots over and places an arm around her waist. "If you didn't know me and you saw me come to one of your classes, would you think I was creepy?"

"I already know you're creepy," she says falling playfully over onto the couch, her head on his lap. "Are you going to try to put my entire head in your mouth now?"

"I wasn't exactly thinking of your head, my dear." Tanya laughs. He has a *hot* wife he thinks, almost angrily. He even loves her weak chin, which forever gave her a look of naughty surprise and vulnerability and makes her perhaps slightly less attractive to other men. He hopes.

"But I'm not done talking with you about serious stuff."

"You won't answer my question?"

"What question? Oh my god, you're serious. You mean about whether I'd find you creepy?"

"Of course."

She smiles. "You already know. I had to make you all mine the moment you smiled at me."

"That was my thought, too."

"You wanted to make yourself all yours? That's what you thought when you looked at me? You're so in love with yourself?"

"Ah. That's very funny. Extremely funny."

"But true!" she protested. "You are totally in love with yourself."

"Please," he frowned, impatient to seduce her again. "Now you're going to go there again."

"Tell me it's not true."

"Sometimes I don't even like myself. OK? I don't always love myself."

"I didn't say you loved yourself, Rolfie." She sits up now and faces him, sitting cross legged on the couch. "I said you were *in love* with yourself. That's completely different."

"All right. All right. Very funny."

"I *was* trying to be funny. But now I'm serious."

"I *know* you're serious. You're always serious these days," he says, raising his voice.

She looks at him. "Just now I wanted to talk about school and you completely dismissed me, Rolfe. I don't like it when you do that."

"I didn't dismiss you. We can't afford it."

"Right. And why? Because I'm a secretary working at a real estate development company. How long are you going to drive a car for a living while all you do for your career is to tinker with the apartment plumbing and build and paint sheds and pull weeds for rich people?"

Rolfe leaps off the couch and paces the floor. "Here we go."

"I'm not trying to sound mean."

He turns to her. "You're not mean, Tani. You're right. But I do work and I am try to do something better. You always sound so dismissive of all that. Speaking of being 'dismissive'."

"I'm frustrated that you won't even consider talking to Frank." Rolfe grimaces at the mention of the name, 'Frank'. "He can get you a good job. Real estate development! Buildings! We put up all kinds of buildings. Real buildings. Yes? You can be a part of that."

"I don't even like the fact that you work there, Tanya. You know that."

"But I have to work somewhere Rolfe. We have bills to pay and we can't live even on just your little messenger job. I have a good job."

"First of all, my job is not that little. It's a shit company, it's true, but I can make more money than you. Second, you can work anywhere as a receptionist. Why do you have to work in the same firm as him?"

"I have benefits there."

"Of course you do."

"Oh what is that? You know what I mean. They're your benefits, too."

"You can get the same somewhere else."

"It's not so easy. And what about you? You have nothing but car expenses. And how many times are we going to argue about this? I don't even work in the same department as Frank. It's a big company. I actually rarely even see him and he never seeks me out and I have zero interest in him. Plus, he's got a girlfriend that he's probably going to marry."

"Oh great! I should feel secure because Frank Giambi has a girlfriend? Is that what you're saying?"

They look at each other and it seems to Rolfe as if she is tearing up. "Listen to me, Rolfe. I want to say this to you and I want this to really sink in. You're my husband. You're my love. I love and want only you. For anyone I may have been with before you, it's as if I was never with anyone at all. It's like you're the first. Do you understand?" Rolfe bites his lip. He hates himself at this moment. "What else can I say to you?" He sits down heavily next to her, leans back and puts his hand on her knee.

"I know it's stupid. I just don't like the idea that you work there."

"Maybe you can work there, too. You can check up on me," she says coyly.

"I'll check up on Frank."

"Come on. Don't get me started on all of your ex-girlfriends and one night stands."

"I don't work with or have any contact with any of them."

"Rolfie, will you stop already? I hardly have any contact with Frank, either. I just told you."

"I know."

"But I want *you* to have contact with Frank. He likes you. I don't know even know why. I told you, he's even asked about you."

"I thought you said you never see him."

"Uggghhh!" and she slaps him - hard – on his shoulder. "You're impossible sometimes, you know that? Every few weeks I pass him in the hallway or the lobby. For a minute or less. OK?"

He turns to her. "Are you saying I should go work for Frank Giambi? Seriously?"

"It's a big company," she begins to rub his shoulder, the one she had just slapped. "They do all kinds of construction, design, whatever. You should be doing something with that. Instead of driving a car."

"You're right," he says, flatly.

"Let me get you his phone number."

"Maybe instead of working for Frank, I could work for his boss."

"Aye, you're giving yourself a promotion already?"

"I've seen her."

"Who have you seen?"

"Frank's boss. Or one of them. I've dropped off at the firm before. Some young hot shot. I pay attention to these things whenever I'm out. I don't just drive in a fog. I'm trying to learn."

"A woman?"

"Yeah. Mayra Granger . Some kind of sales and marketing person."

"Do you know her?"

"No."

"Well you know *Frank*. And if you worked there, we could have lunch together every day. Maybe. Unless you're too busy for me."

"He'll put me out on a construction site. You won't see me."

"Will you whistle and hoot at me when I walk by?"

"Fine. I'll talk to him."

"You will? Oh good! I'll just give you his number. I don't even need to speak to him."

"Maybe."

"Maybe you'll even become good friends." she says archly.

He playfully slaps her on the thigh. "Very funny."

"I want to call Yuri now."

"You know that's what's going to ruin us, you making all these overseas calls every month." He stands up again, straightening his shorts.

"I won't be long. I still have friends back home as well as here."

"Back home? Did you say, 'Back home' to me?"

"I just meant where my family is and you know it. My blood family. The *rest* of my family," Tanya adds. "How does that sound?"

"Fine. I'll take a shower and go for a drive."

"You want to go for a drive? Again? You drive all day and you want to go for a drive? That costs money too, you know."

"You talk to your friend. You always talk all night to your friends half way across the world. Maybe I'll even go see a friend of my own."

"Do you even have any friends, Rolfie? I never hear you talk about them anymore"

"Maybe. Go call Yuri."

7. Thursday Night before the Storm- Max

The building is a pea green two story walk up with a gate and simple small apartments facing each other across a little courtyard. On the ground floor in the corner lives Max, number three, a single room. Partially hidden by the bushes, an air conditioning unit hums along. Max sits on a little couch in his corner, wearing a clean white t-shirt, a little pudge of belly beneath his shirt peeping over his belt line, his thin, pale arm, shooting down from his shoulder sleeves. He watches re-runs of MASH, All in the Family, Get Smart, Star Trek, or his favorite, Bugs Bunny and Daffy Duck. Nothing in the world is funnier than Daffy's duck bill being shot off after which he stares at the audience as if to say, 'Oh the indignity.' What if Max could live in a cartoon and be friends with Daffy? Then again, it was an extremely violent world all the same, with neither death nor any kind of relief, filled with hyper, neurotic beasts.

The day has fallen and night overtakes. Max sits with a hardback book, filled with worn edges and photographs of wild animals in their native habitats.

He likes the electric looking Zebras and the gentle giant Elephants. The Rhinoceroses, fiercely ugly, are secretly shy herbivores and stunningly beautiful in their pure, primeval way, reminiscent of the great Triceratops from a disappeared magical world. Max loves and dreams as well of the exotic herbivores of South America; llamas, alpacas, tapirs, and best of all, the peculiar and wonderful Anteater. Shaggy with its bizarrely narrow head and its dangling proboscis, it is perfectly designed for its sole purpose of foraging for and eating ants. They never cease to enchant him with, their intense and outcast beauty, noble and at peace with their place in the world. Perfectly content, Max projects himself into the heart of the beast, seeing the world through its eyes, so that he fails to hear the sound of rapid steps of someone approaching. The door explodes with a fist knocking at his door. Max starts and puts the book down as if he had been doing something wrong. A familiar voice calls out his name. Max gingerly approaches the door. "Hello?"

"Max. Maxie!"

"Who is it?"

"Maximillian. MaxaBillion!"

"Rolfe? Is that you, Rolfe?"

"Of course it's me. Can I come in? I want to talk to you."

He opens the door and smiles. Rolfe smiles back; khaki slacks and a black pullover. Max has never seen Rolfe without his ZZZAP! shirt before. "Thanks, Maxie. May I come in?"

"Yes. Please. Would you like to sit on the couch?"

Rolfe immediately sees that the couch is the only place to sit. "I'll sit on the carpet. Should I take my shoes off?"

"You can if you want."

"Maxie. Nice little place. So this is the maxie pad." Rolfe sits down himself on the carpet against the wall, but he keeps his shoes on. "You keep it clean."

"How do you know where I live?"

"I'm a genius, Maxie!"

Max seems to consider this. "You know, it makes me nervous when you call me Maxie. Please call me Max."

"Good for you, Max. This is your place. Here, at least, we play by your rules."

"How did you know where I live?" he repeats.

"I saw some papers the other day on Mikros' desk."

"I see. Why are you here?"

"Let me ask you. Does it bother you when I call you Mr. Pathetic?"

"I wouldn't want you to call me that here."

"No, no. It's Max, while we're here at your place."

"Do you really want to talk to me about something?"

"Or did I just come to bother you, Max? Yes, I really do want to talk to you."

Max looks carefully into Rolfe's face. "Are you OK?"

"I will be….. You want to know something, Max. I respect you. I do. I know you don't think so. It's true, I once thought you were too stupid to live. But I like you. I appreciate you now, Max. I used to think that understanding you was the easiest thing in the world. But it isn't. You're fucking complicated."

"I am?"

"You are. I don't want to be like you, Max. But sometimes I do. Do you know why?" Max slowly shakes his head, wide eyed. "Because you always seem content." Max says nothing, but gives a little shrug. "Are you?" Max says nothing. "Are you happy, Max?" Max cocks his head. Rolfe runs his hand impatiently up his forehead and through his hair as if attempting to wipe away something burdensome from his face. "I don't blame you for not answering. It's a rude question, isn't it"

"What do you want?"

"I just want to talk with you. That's all."

"No, I mean what do you want to make you happy?"

Rolfe speaks as if to himself. "I want to build things and to do things. I want to live. I want to conquer."

"What do you mean? What do you want to conquer?"

"Like… build a business, build a building, make lots of money, really do something. You know? Ah. Clearly you don't." Rolfe shakes his head. "You, Maxie. You have nothing. And you seem to want nothing. And yet you seem happy." Rolfe began to pick at something on his pant leg. "You seem happy. Well I'm not."

"I know."

Rolfe looks at him. "You know?"

"You never seemed happy to me."

"Yeah? Well, it's only been a day or so that I knew."

"You never seemed happy."

"You don't know anything Max. But you knew *that*." He shakes his head with a half-smile. "So how did you know?"

"That you're not happy?"

"Of course that's what I mean."

"You're always angry."

"Always? Even when I'm joking around?"

Max's eyes grow soft. "*Especially* when you're joking around, Rolfe. And you're *always* joking around."

Rolfe smiles and looks away. "I don't like to hear that," he mutters as if to himself. "But this is exactly why I came, I suppose. You understand perfectly." He turns to Max again. "Everything pisses me off. Everything."

"That sounds miserable."

"Is it?"

"Yes."

"So I should be like you?"

"No."

"This little closet of yours is depressing me already." He looks up at the ceiling. "You have a water stain up there. You should tell the landlord to check the plumbing."

"Is it nice being married?"

Rolfe sniffs. "Is it what? Yeah. It's real nice. Sometimes."

"Is she nice?"

"My wife. She's nice. Mostly."

"What's her name?"

"Tanya."

"Tanya. That's a nice name."

"Have you ever been married?"

"No."

"Of course, not. How old are you, Max?"

"Thirty three."

"You're three years older than I am. ….. Have you ever had a girlfriend?"

"No."

"Have you ever kissed a girl?"

"On the cheek."

"On the cheek. Well. We have to do something about that."

"Do what?"

"Something. It's not enough, Max. Just watching this?" and he reaches up and wraps on the side of the television with his knuckles.

"I have a book?" Max said.

"A book. *A* book? Is that the way to be happy, Max? Just not think about anything?"

"I don't know. Maybe not."

"Do you like being a messenger, Max? A driver?"

"I like it very much. Sometimes it's hard, though."

"I like driving, too. It's the easiest fucking job imaginable. No offense. But I want more. "

"How much more?"

"Max, is there anything else you want to be? You want to be a driver all your life?"

"I don't know."

"What do you to be in your life, Max?"

"You'll laugh."

"Tell me what Max wants. You won't get it if you don't tell people."

"You'll laugh."

"So what. I'm an asshole. If it's your dream, though, who cares. Besides I won't laugh."

"I know it's not real."

"Well what is it?"

"I know it's not real."

"You said that. What is it, Max?"

"I'd like to be an anteater."

8. Thursday Night - Eugene

Shortly after eight o'clock at night, a short pudgy man with curly hair and thick glasses climbs the stairs from his dark basement room and emerges into the cool night air on his way to have his second dinner for the evening. He lives in the basement of a three bedroom wood shingled house near the corner of Hill and Highland Avenue. Six months have passed since he moved away from his aunt, his only local living relative. He had responded to a line item in the classifieds of a local paper. In the main house live three young men all of whom are in their twenties, vital and easy going, casual and sinewy. They tolerate him for he always pays on time, always in cash, and almost always stays in the basement except when he uses the bathroom in the pantry. Though none of the residents own the house, he pays the rent to Thomas, a pale skinny platinum blonde with long, shaggy braids. "Eugene, I can let you live in the basement for a rock bottom price," intending no doubt, Eugene realizes to be funny, but worse than that, intending to be clever. Thomas is arrogant and precious, rigid and narrow minded, for all his hippy trappings. But if he could only live there and be left alone, Eugene reasons he could be happy enough for now. For his birthday, he went back to his aunt's house for a dinner of Salisbury steak with green beans.

To reach the bathroom at night, Eugene is obliged to climb the staircase from his basement and enter the pantry where there is a toilet and shower that he considers his own, but which is often used by others. More than once, he must clear the shower drain of a viscous rat like menace of soap scum, body hair, and semen. Oft times the sink is peppered with beard shavings and rime of shaving cream. He finds slimy, depleted condoms that rudely missed the waste bin. One day he finds a pair of women's lacy pink panties hanging from the shower rail. With thumb and forefinger, he inspects them, even sniffing them, scared and hopeful that he might experience the scent and funk of a young woman. Another time, he finds an orange bikini, along with a man's soiled tube socks and a thin, gritty layer of sand and foot print shaped filth marks in his shower. Gritting his teeth, Eugene seizes both of these and though barefoot he proceeds out the back door and down the scabrous driveway to fling them both in the trash. Furiously washing his hands, he looks down and sees that his own feet stand in shallow inky black puddles of his own filth. Eugene lets forth a short, choking scream of puny rage. He begins to sweat and feel filthy all over.

Weekdays, Eugene drives for ZZZZAP! He takes pride in being the best driver. It is the first and only time he has ever been the best at something. A month after moving out from his aunt's, he obtains a second job on the weekends working in the stock room at a large hardware and home improvement store. While at the store, Eugene could care less about being the best. He thinks he takes the second job to ensure he has enough money to pay his bills and entertainment. But the truth is that he simply does not know what to do with himself on the weekends.   There is simply far too much time to sleep and masturbate and cruise the streets. He has to keep himself busy enough so that he might look forward to something, even these barren, solitary habits.

For reasons that he neither understands nor questions, he enters into a special fantasy world whenever eating at fast food restaurants. In his secret world he is a bureaucrat who works for the National Bureau of Administrations. Eugene doesn't know what a bureaucrat actually is. He imagines that a bureaucrat is someone who thinks he is important, but who in fact does quite little. I could do that, he thinks. He carries his tray, eyes darting, and he sits in the corner, clean though smelling of ketchup. Generic food in colorful Styrofoam containers. National Bureau of Administrations. In the world of his own making, Eugene wears a long gray trench coat and outside there are always thunderous looking gray clouds. His desk sits in the basement of a great hulk of a stone and iron building.   The walls are piss yellow and snot green and the floors are endless scuffed linoleum. Everything is imposing yet utterly mediocre. Great brooding stacks of official papers in triplicate await his stamp or seal or signature or shuffling. This is his private office but the hallway outside his door leads past dozens of doors, some of which open up onto hundreds of such desks. Shrieking elevators with fake wood panels and greasy buttons churn restlessly up and down hundreds of similar floors all day long, every day. He has never shared about this world with another human being. No one had to know.
Eugene has other secrets as well that he never discusses with other human beings.

One day he spots two young girls jutting their thumbs out for a ride in the middle of the day. What was this all about? Eugene was working so he dared not stop. But a week later while coming back from dinner, he sees another young woman with her thumb out as well. Suddenly realizing that there are hitchhikers available to ride in his car, to keep him company for short periods of time, Eugene decides to seek them out. Up and down the street he drives, past tired looking store fronts and diners, looking for hitchhikers. He is frightened of women who resemble prostitutes. They are hard and flippant, garishly dressed and made up. He much prefers to pretend that women are just hanging out hugging themselves with nothing to do, lonely like himself. One night he picks up an unusually nice looking woman whose dress suit and make up makes her look like she could be a bank manager. She asks him, "What do you need?"

"Where would you like to go?" he asks, feigning naivety.

"Did you need anything?"

"I'm going as far south as Washington. But you know, I have the time, I could take you further if you want."

"I'm not going anywhere, except right back where I was." And she starts to undo her seat belt.

"We could just talk for a bit. Or drive around."

"I'm working. Are you gonna pay me what I ask to drive around and talk?"

"Pay? You need money? Me too."

"What?"

"I don't really have any money."

"I don't believe this," and she opens the door and flings herself out. "I should have had this conversation from out there."

"Are you sure I can't take you anywhere?"

"Asshole!" she calls out to him from the sidewalk.

"Be safe," he says. And he slowly drives away. Eugene considers the irony that had he asked her bluntly to suck his penis for a price, she would have done so without a fuss. But to offer to take her to coffee or give her a lift; that had earned him an insult, to be labeled a sphincter, a shit hole. He puts his car in gear and slowly drives away.

9. The previous Sunday:
5 Days before the storm - Tim

He never cared for the way that Jack Rohmer eats with his mouth open. Throughout the years, Tim says nothing about it. He just sighs and sees Jack less and less frequently. Jack Rohmer is the only friend he has kept in contact with from his days in the army, a time he holds no special fondness for. Neither one of them had ever gone overseas. Jack had worked in the motor pool. Later he became a successful used car dealer.

Jack breathes heavily, a burly chested man, craggy broad face and a thin layer of red hair greased back. His thick hands look like they can crack walnut shells with a firm squeeze, even in his sixties. Tim secretly envies the man's persistent vigor.

"I don't approve, Jack. Don't expect me to approve."

"So who needs your approval? I'm just telling you. As a friend."

"It's as a friend I'm telling you I don't approve. Alice is a helluva gal. She's put up with you all these years."

"She is not easy to live with, I guarantee you. And she's let herself go. A lot."

"She's been ill and had those surgeries. No?"

"Even so. She's all cut up and she's as big as a house. Tim, I thought you'd understand. Being with Sophia gives me what I need to stick with Alice, to stay married. Alright?" But Jack had been cheating on Alice since before they were even married thirty three years ago.

"You should show your wife more respect."

"Listen to you. You're big on respect aren't you? I'm still with her, right? We're together and I take care of her, don't I? And Alice doesn't even know about Sophia."

"Or any of them?"

"There's only Sophia," Jack says, lifting the coffee to his lips.

"You mean right now. I've known you a long time."

"Hey. How's the job?"

"It's a buck. I don't mind," Tim says, and he sucks his teeth. "I just don't care for the dispatcher who plays favorites. I like his girlfriend even less, this Nazi prick who gets in my face."

"Nazi! You mean that German guy?"

Tim rubs his eyes. "Hey Jack, you know what? I'm out of line. He's no Nazi. I just made a stupid comment because I can't stand the guy. He's arrogant, he's a bully, and the dispatcher gives him all the best runs, but that don't make him a National Socialist."

Jack laughs. "I don't care for Germans. We fought against them too long. They still think they're better than us."

"We? We fought the war from a mess hall at Travis. Good thing for us it ended when it did."

"We Americans. That's the we I'm talking about."

"As I recall, you clocked some cracker in Biloxi. Now that was fighting the good fight. I'll give you that."

"I don't remember too good."

"You were drunk."

"Are you gonna go back to what you were doing?"

"Doing? Doing when?"

"The print shop stuff."

"I'm out of the union. There's no jobs anyway for guys like me anymore."

"You wanna keep driving?"

"It's alright. I aggravate myself, but the work is OK. What am I gonna do? Soon I can retire. Except I can't."

"You know why you can't get a job working in a print shop these days?"

26

"The business changed. I didn't."

"It's because all the shops are owned by Iranians who hire only Mexicans to work there."

"You don't say."

"I just did. Look around you."

"I look around, alright. Maybe there *are* a lot of Iranians running these shops. So what. Good for them."

"We got a flood of them now, ever since their own revolutions. They're all coming here. And the Mexicans. Please."

"So!"

"So…. They take all the jobs. I gotta spell it out? Then they complain about how rough it is here."

"Well I guess you could say we been having trouble with these foreigners since our great granddaddies came off the boat. Right? Them Indian chiefs is the worst, right? "

"They're not so bad."

"We *killed* them all!"

"You should come work for me, Tim."

"And do what? Sell cars?"

"Why not? You can sell a load of horse crap. Maybe you should be able to sell some horse power."

Tim smiles and shrugs. "No thanks."

"You're stubborn."

"Cause I don't want to sell cars?"

"You'd rather drive them instead. Crappy ones. All day long."

"Just my own piece a crap." Tim sips his coffee. He realizes he could care less about defending Mexicans and Iranians. But it makes him feel just a bit smarter than a well off blow hard like Jack Roehmer. "Thanks for the thought." They each stare into their cups.

"You still haven't heard from her?"

"No."

"How long has it been now? A couple a years?"

"Six,"

"Jeez." Tim just shrugs and stares off somewhere. "Come round tomorrow and I'll make us some steaks. Maybe I'll even invite Alice seeing as how you're so sweet on her and all."

"I don't know….Sure." Tim agrees slumping slightly in his seat. "Yeah. Invite Alice since she's your wife after all," he adds, sucking his teeth again.

"Who knows? Maybe Alice has a girlfriend she can invite over. We can all get a little drunk together."

"Ah, I don't know. Like a set up? Nah, let's leave that."

"Why not?"

"I don't think so."

"When's the last time you went out on a date? Had any fun?"

"Jack. Leave it. Thanks, but no thanks."

"Just a little female company."

Tim squirms in his seat, rubs his hands lightly on the table. "I don't know, Jack. I can barely stand being around you."

"So this will take your mind off a that."

Tim chuckles. "Maybe. Try not to burn the steak." He thinks about Alice when he first knew her. She was a lively one. Great smile, great curves. She had a laugh that could fill the night and turn every head; bold and promising.

10. Sunday - Five Days Before the Storm – Andy

Andy sits at a coffee shop booth, poring over two papers, both of them scavenged from other tables. He has a job, enough to pay the relatively high rent of this cheap motel, but not enough cash to stake to a security deposit or a last month's rent - about $300 to $600 it seems - on a half way decent apartment for himself. Or perhaps a half way decent promotional demo on something up and coming called a compact disc, though he has no idea how much this latter venture might really cost.

He considers seeking a sublet room but the roommate prospects seem undesirably exotic. The very last thing he wants - and the main feature being advertised – is a roommate into body shavings and "mutual servicing" which he presumes is diaphanous code for giving and receiving fellatio. Andy guffaws out loud at the ludicrous nature of this repeated theme. Adjacent to the roommate ads are photos of young women posing in pouty contemplation of their own bosoms or looking out over their shoulder at their own buttocks perched outwards. Nominally, these were ads for "healing massage" coupled with modeling sessions. Could there possibly be thinner conceivable code, Andy muses, for flat out prostitution? Andy's smile slowly fades as he takes in something beneath the humor and titillation; something aching and wounded.

11. Saturday - Six Days Before the Storm - Perry

"Hand me the three-quarter, will ya? Do you think you can find that one, buddy?" Murray Head seems headless, ducking behind the cooling tank. Perry's eyes glaze over and he feels himself break out yet again into an oily sweat. Three-quarter. *Three-quarter.* A wrench. He picks it up and places into Murray's thick calloused hand. Apparently it is the right tool. At last. Murray raises his sweat drenched ragged melon head, plastered tentacles of thin black hair cleaving to the sides of his rosy scalp. "That's the one. Alright. So you follow what's doin' here? See the gauge?" To Perry it is all a blur. Murray winks. "We're gonna seal this sonovabitch up. Comprende? You with me?"

"Seal the sonovabitch," Perry pipes up brightly.

"That's right." Moments later he turns to Perry. "Look. Let's take a little break right here. "

"OK."

They walk out of the furnace room and back into the long cool hallway before stepping outside. Perry stares at Murray's sagging jeans to take his mind off of what is likely coming next. They step outside. Perry squints at the balmy afternoon glare. Murray dons his sunglasses, thick as goggles, dark and plastic. "Let's get a coke." Three buildings down, they enter a liquor store. "Here you go," Murray says, twisting the cap off. Perry had wanted a bottle of water but chooses not to say anything. "Cold enough in there?" he says, nodding to the store. "They take care of their A/C don't they? Let's sit over there." They walk to the empty bus stop and sit. Perry considers his own cringing reflection in Murray's sunglasses. "You're a good guy, Perry."

Perry nods. "Thank you."

"How you likin' this?"

"Excuse me?"

"How you likin' this? This. All this we're doin' here," Murray gestures. "This kind a work."

"Yes. I'm liking it."

"Yeah?"

"Yes. Very much."

"That's good. That's good," he repeats. "But…I gotta tell you – it don't seem like you're pickin' up on it too good. I mean, most of the time you couldn't even hand me the right tool. Other stuff, too. I figured by now, you'd be doin' some of the repairs yourself with me lookin' on of course, but instead you're still just watchin' my ass all the time and handin' me the wrong tool."

"I'm sorry," is all Perry can say.

"I know you are. But you don't need to be sorry, Per. I just gotta move on and find someone else real quick."

"I can do better. I can do better. I promise."

"Yeah, well maybe you can do better if given enough time which I ain't got enough for to give you no more anyhow."

"Oh." But Perry feels relieved that it is over at least. He won't have to feel like he's failing Murray Head any longer, he tells himself. "Thank you, Mr. Murray."

"Stop calling me that. It's Murray. Come on."

"OK. Sorry. Thank you for all of your help. I wish I had done better."

"Don't take it too hard. Hey, maybe it's the way I speak English." He winks.

"I want to repair air conditioners."

"I know. But maybe it ain't your thing."

"I guess not today."

"Maybe not today. Right. I love it. But look at me. Right? Do I look someone you want to be like?"

Perry smiles. "I'm sorry, Mr. Murray."

"I tell you what. I like you, Perry. I do. I need people I can trust. You're solid and you're willing and maybe you just need more time, like you say. Right now, I just need people who already got this. But if I ever get a big job where we need a lot of people fast - like clean up and all that - and I don't think you're gonna kill yourself or anyone else, well, I'll keep your number. Maybe I can teach you more then. Anyway, I'll still pay you for the whole four hours. Cash. Alright? Just go home now to your family and take the last hour for yourself." Perry imagines Lorena and her worried, disappointed face.

He stands on his porch staring out at the pastel evening, the muted colors laced with smog. His narrow cracked driveway turns steeply down to the tiny curb. A tiny white fence barely surrounds a dubious patch of discolored and useless weeds and grass. There seems nothing to be done with it, Perry observes; too steep to play on, too expensive to landscape. He collects his son's toys, his eye falling upon the squalor of what resembles an abandoned house across the way. He shakes his head and walks back inside. A warm, close smell of baked bread and sour milk and raw onions greets him as he walks through the tiny unlit front room, scattered with toys and stray socks. Past the bedroom and through the back screen door, he blinks at the pale evening light and the stale, sweet, rank smell of a cigarette. Paco, his brother-in-law sits on the stoop, beside a transistor radio smaller than his own hand, the while looking in the general direction of a boy of about four years of age, quietly sitting in the grassy dirt, playing with a number of inch high plastic soldiers hiding from two and three inch colored plastic dinosaurs. Sometimes the boy softly murmurs as if talking or singing to himself; then suddenly he simulates an explosion in slow motion at the roof of his mouth, while the dinosaur pounces and pummels one of the soldiers. The sky is streaked with high, thin, lonely blade like clouds. Perry squats near Paco.

"Hi Guillaume," he greets his son with that sweetness reserved for small children and pets. "Que haces, mijo?" What are you doing, my little son? The boy remains deeply absorbed inside the world of his own creation.

"Playing with his soldiers and dinosaurs," Paco adds without looking up. Perry ignores him. Paco is in his early twenties, lighter skinned than his sister, lounging in a black t-shirt and black jeans. He leans back on his hands, a lit cigarette clinging from his mouth, a can of beer beside him. He sits upright now and seems to count what appear to be blue pills in his hand.

"I told you not to smoke around here."

Paco says nothing at first. He holds up a finger and finishes counting his pills, putting them into a small plastic bag. He takes a final drag from his ebbing cigarette and discards the nub and grinds it out with his shoe on the narrow strip of pavement below the step. Smoke cascades through his half open mouth and nostrils. He rubs his hands on his jeans and says, "There. And you told me not to smoke *in* the house."

"The back hallway smells of smoke. My son is breathing in your smoke. You cannot smoke here at all."

"OK."

"And who's supposed to pick up your filthy butt?"

"I'll pick it up."

Perry leans against the raw, wooden beam of his back porch. He sits on the step next to his brother-in-law. "Did you look for work today?"

"It's Saturday."

"So. Hotels. Stores. Restaurants. They're all open today. This is when they need people."

"But they don't actually *hire* anyone on Saturday. They're too busy."

"How do you know this?"

Paco turns and spits beneath the low bushes next to him, beside the porch. "Everyone knows that."

"You will look on Monday, then."

"Sure."

"It's been over two months."

"I'll get a job," Paco assures and he takes some tobacco out of his pocket and cigarette paper and prepares the contents for rolling. "It takes time."

"What are you doing?" Perry observes.

"Just getting it ready. For later." Paco turns to him. "That OK with you?"

"Fine."

They sit in silence, Paco focused on his cigarette; he shakes his head and raises a single eyebrow. "So. What were you up to today?"

"Working!" Perry says with emphasis.

"Today? Why?"

"To pay for the food my brother-in-law eats."

31

"But it's Saturday."

"Customers need help on Saturday, too. You keep eating."

"More driving?"

"No. I'm training to be an air conditioning man."

"Yeah?" Paco studies his cigarette. "That's cool….Hey," he brightens. "That's 'cool', huh, repairing air conditioning. Cool! Get it?"

"Yes. It's cool," Perry agrees, glumly.

"So how's it going? Air conditioning."

Perry looks at his shoes, then at his son. "I got fired." He gets up to go sit with his son on the grass. He talks softly to the boy, admiring the fierceness of the little dinosaurs. Guillaume responds by walking a little blue triceratops up Perry's arm. "Oh my, he's coming to get me."

"He's climbing, papa," Guillaume explains, as if to explain that Perry isn't being attacked. He's just a mountain to be climbed.

"Sorry, man," Paco says, standing up, hands in his pockets. "I'm gonna go out." Perry doesn't respond but continues to lean over and smile at his son, running his fingers slowly through the boy's black hair. "Lorena just took Eva to the store is all. They should be back soon."

"OK," Perry returns on a slightly sing-song note. He's still smiling at Guillaume, rubbing lightly the boy's little back. Paco fingers his cigarette and steps back through the little house. Guillaume produces a T-Rex and excitedly romps it up Perry's chest. He falls into his father's arms and giggles before he can complete his assault.

12.   Same Saturday - Samuel

As the cart squeaks and rolls along the dun colored linoleum, Samuel's mind wanders upon a lyrical, icy passage from the same symphony he always wanders upon; the lonely land, pastures and forests, gazing upon the glaciered mountain, the forgotten, wistful mystery land. The left front wheel rivets and drags, forcing him to stop every fifty feet it seems to make an adjustment. He wears a set of loose fitting scrubs, tops and bottoms, wearing a t-shirt unlike most of his colleagues who don't seem to mind baring their chest hairs or tattooed breasts. Most of the doors to patient rooms are flung wide open, the better for nurses and other staffers to move in and out. The patients are oblivious to the endless rattle and buzz of carts, alarms, phones, and staff casually shouting at each other; unaware of their own shouting and moaning, as one nurse once pointed out to him. It was grimly comforting for him to know that many patients were oblivious to their own suffering. Many sleep but almost no one looks peaceful; instead, quite a few have simply passed out, mouths open, brows clenched, bodies frozen in twisted poses, as if they had all fallen from great heights and lay as they landed, or worse, had happened upon some deeply disturbing revelation and were now impaled upon that singular thought forever. Samuel cannot help staring at their physical degradation. He reflects that he won't have to wait so long before he knows for himself what goes on inside their wracked and mortal coils.

"You got my chux for me with your linens tonight? Samuel? Hey baby. I know you not standin' there ignorin' me." Samuel turns, startled, and looks over at Virginia, the ponderous black ward clerk. She leans back in her chair, mobile on wheels, far too small for her girth, and she stares at him over her glasses, short gray hair stretching perpendicular away from her neck as if trying to escape from her, her arms folded upon her great belly and ponderous breasts.

"Hello, Virginia. Sorry." and he reels his cart towards her, presenting his wares for her inspection. She hoists herself up, using the counter to brace herself, putting her hands in and out of the bins and drawers, crinkling sounds of freshly wrapped syringes, needles, and rubber tubings. "The chux are over here," he says, pointing to a bin below.

"I know where they are. Or where they should be." She nods in satisfaction, feeling what needs to be felt. She peers in as an afterthought. "You got my req, baby?" holding her hand out without looking back at Samuel. He places the paper in her hand. She squints while looking at it and grabs the pen hanging from her great neck. Finally she turns and eases herself down again. "I don't worry 'bout you, baby, but I gotta look at whatever body brings. Don't think too hard tonight."

Two tiny ancient looking Filipina nurses return to their work stations, looking at notes from their rounds taken on small scraps of paper and even upon the palms of their hands. They wearily begin to transcribe into patient charts set out in great giant binders. The floor is quiet tonight. But Samuel can see from the set of their jaws that most likely they are working short a nurse or an assistant. He halloos them both but neither seems to take any notice of him. So he rolls his cart to their storage area and slowly, carefully puts everything in its right place.

"Hey old man."

"Hello Carter," returns Samuel. The lead technician sits leafing through a magazine, sucking his teeth in the dull, unadorned room out of an early morning dream, windowless and stillborn in boredom. Yet he rather likes it. Quiet and untouchable. A glass coffee pot sits empty and stained. Metal chairs sag around a gray plastic table. Samuel doesn't mind Roland Carter calling him, 'Old Man', even though Samuel is only five or ten years older than him. Carter is still a robust specimen. He picks at his fingernails through jaundiced, blood laced eyeballs; then he rubs his perfectly shaped malt ball of a great head. Carter's fingers, to Samuel, resemble mahogany carvings, dusty looking knuckles and thick pink palms, powerful enough to effortlessly crush a dissipated, wrinkled old cornhusk like himself, a trampled, obscenely hirsute bag of watery bones.

"Take a load off, Samuel. I'll send you off to the storeroom in five. Maybe ten." No one bothers Samuel in the storeroom. Nice and quiet. He can play Vaughan Williams in his head all he likes. He can visit his sad, neglected, exquisite landscape. The bins and shelves in the store room recall the order and sanctuary of a library. No tired and hardened nurses. No shell shocked family members. No withered, dying patients. No holy ground at all.

13. Thursday - The night before the storm - Eugene

Hungry and bored, Eugene pulls over and parks. A lone figure stands in the unlit corner of the building, wrapped in shadow. Eugene pushes himself out the door, his underwear clinging, sticking sweaty cleaved half between his buttocks, stiff from too much sitting and gripping the wheel. Impatiently, he files through the store, grabbing his Cheetos, Baby Ruth's, then to buy a can; no – two cans of cherry soda. He pays the indifferent clerk. Laden with plastic bags, he loses his grip as he pushes out the door and the contents spill from the bag and to the ground. "Ahhh!" he shouts, "God damnit!"

"Oops!" she says.

Eugene snaps his head. The shadowy stranger is a homeless woman. She smiles at him. She might be pretty. "Stupid," he says, shaking his head. She shrugs. He stands. The woman, barely past adolescence, stands serenely by herself, hands in her sweat shirt pockets, her top a lumpy gray. Eugene's gaze snags upon the girl's bare feet, flat upon the oily pavement. "Well...have a good evening." He feels himself redden.

"You too," she says. He hesitates and fusses with his bag, angry that he has to turn and leave.

"You like Cheetos?" she says.

He turns and smiles. "Yeah. I like 'em a lot."

"Yeah? Me too."

"I love that crunchy, cheesy....taste."

"Sure. Me too." And she smiles.

"You want some?" he blurts.

"Yes, please."

And he walks towards her. To his chagrin, the girl towers over him. She puts her thick calloused gray hand towards the bag, and he panics at the filthy sight of it so he pulls the bag away saying, "Here! Hold out your hands and I'll give you a bunch." She cups her hands. He pours. Out come bright orange arthritic knuckles pulsing in the depleted halogen light.

"Whoa, that's too many," she laughs. "I won't be able to hold them and eat them."

"It's OK," he says. They both stand by, quietly munching.

"Thanks," she says. Her hair looks uncombed. Clean enough, he supposes. Straight and pretty and blonde.

"Hey. You want a cherry coke? I got two."

"Sure."

Proudly, Eugene pulls the cokes from the bag, puts one down, holds out the can to her, and with a flourish, pops the tab. The can seethes and spits a vomit colored tongue of foam that catches the girl's hands and sleeves. "Oh goddamnit! Shit!" he curses.

She ducks her head and laughs. Suddenly, Eugene laughs himself, a sickly throttled warble, like a sea lion in distress. "I'm sorry. I got you pretty good, huh."

"That'll cost you," she says with a smile, wiping her hands on her pants.

"It will?"

"Maybe. If you want to make it up to me."

"I have a candy bar. Do you want a candy bar?"

"What kind?"

"It's a Baby Ruth."

"OK. I'll take it."

He reaches down, grabs the bag, and hands the candy bar to her. She tears it open, winks, and happily begins munching. "Thank you," she says deeply.

"Do you want anything else? Are you still hungry?"

She chews and speaks. "Yes. But I still want my cherry coke."

"Fine." He hands her the other can.

"No," she laughs. "Of course, that's going to explode, too." She has a slight accent which he cannot identify. "Will you buy me a new one?"

"Yes."

"And some hot dogs?"

"Hot dogs. And more Cheetos."

"And doughnuts. I like powdered ones. It'll be a real party."

"Do you want me to give you a ride somewhere?"

"We'll talk after you buy the food. Go on," she urges, smiling at him. How pretty she is, he thinks. He buys the food, counting prices in his head as he grabs the items, including a large bottle of cherry coke that he wants to share with her - as if that would be a step towards kissing her. Eugene blushes at the thought. Another big bag of Cheetos. Four hotdogs. Two six packs of baby powdered doughnuts. He imagines her getting powder all over herself.

"I have the stuff," he announces upon his return, relieved to find her still there.

"Goodie!" she says, stepping towards the plastic bags he holds in his hand. She looks in and helps herself to a hotdog.

"Can I drive you somewhere?"

"Drive me? Where do you want to drive me?"

"We could go to the beach? Would you like to go to the beach? We could eat our food over there."

"We can eat over here, too."

"Yeah. Well. OK. I just thought maybe you'd like to go the beach."

"What's your name?"

"I'm Eugene." He tells her this, as if slightly embarrassed about his name.

"Hi Eugene. I'm Caroline."

"Hi Caroline."

"Eugene, why do you want to take me to the beach?"

"I don't know."

"You don't know? If you don't know, I don't know."

"Well."

"Yes?"

"I just wanted to be with a friend tonight." And it occurs to him that this is the truth.

"A friend? Are we friends?"

"Maybe we could be friends. We both like Cheetos." He looks at his shoes.

"Will you bring me back here later?"

Eugene looks up. "Yeah. Sure."

"Promise?"

"Of course. I promise."

"Alright. I'm hungry. Can I eat in the car?"

"Yeah, sure. But just give me a quick minute. I want to clean it up a bit."

"OK. But you don't have to." Eugene fusses with tossing Styrofoam, candy wrappers, and other discarded husks of hurried meals, and he flings these things in the back seat, placing an old t-shirt loosely over them, to try and mute their presence. He pulls himself carefully out of the car to avoid banging his head. Caroline stands there looking at him. She disrupts into giggles. Eugene smiles back. She gets in.

14.   Andy -
The Tuesday 16 Days Before the Storm

The interior of the Obsidian can fit inside his mother's modest living room in Indiana; half a dozen tiny black tables and stools, a faux black leather couch in one corner. Mobiles hang from the ceiling and haunt the walls. The floor is scuffed white and black checkerboard, giant squares. An espresso machine whirs unseen. He enters and calls out. Again. Finally a razorous, pale little man languidly approaches. His pasty, pock marked face is bluish and unshaven and his clothing is rumpled as if extracted from the bottom of a busy hamper. "We don't open for another hour," he murmurs in a thin velvet feminine voice. "Would you like to come back then?"

"You're not open?" Andy wonders why the glass front door is wide open but decides he is not going to ask that. "Can I just ask you a quick question?"

"Sure."

"You have live, original music here?"

"Almost every night. Tonight at nine we have three bands. Velvet Gravy, Pinot Noir, and Kettle Brain.   Five dollar cover is all."

"Terrific. Well," and Andy takes a breath. Five dollars is more than he can really afford. He swallows, realizing he is actually anxious before this strange little being. "I'm Andy. Andy Toben. And I'd like to play here as well. I play guitar."

"Ah yes, of course," he seems to purr. "Another musician. Another who wants to play."

"Who could I speak to about that? About auditioning."

"Well, you could speak to me. I'm the assistant owner."

"The assistant *owner*?"

"Yes. But now is not a good time. We're very busy right now."

Andy furtively glances at the empty room. "When would be a good time? A better time."

"I'm always here."

"Good. Well when might be a better time than now?"

"Just come anytime."

"I'm sorry, what was your name?"

"I'm Henry," and Henry half raises his hand. Andy puts his hand out and Henry grasps his fingers in a clammy squeeze. "What was your name again?"

"Andy. Andy Toben."

"I should tell you, Andy Toben that we're not really auditioning. We usually only book by referral only. Do you have a band?"

"No. Just me and a guitar."

"Is that very interesting?"

"It could be. I have a mixer. I sample sounds and play against them live."

"So you play with yourself?"

"That's correct. I play on my own, yes."

"Well, as I said before, we're not really auditioning right now. We have a long list of bands that want to play here. You know? We do things a little differently here at the Obsidian. And we're looking for bands that are completely unique, not just someone playing with himself." Andy reckons he could easily reach out and clutch Henry's blue chicken neck and whistle as Henry turns even bluer and drops like a mess of old rags silently to the floor.

"You know, I wouldn't mind playing with other people. I'm actually new here. Do you have any suggestions - Henry - about where I could meet other musicians?"

"Well it depends on what you're looking for. But if you come back here when the bands are playing, you might be able to meet some of them then."

15. This Thursday
(the night before the storm)

Rolfe stares at Max. Finally, he slaps his thigh, smiles and calls out. "Nice, Maxie. You're a funny guy, after all."

"I am?"

"You just told me you want to be an anteater. What does that mean?"

Max gets a puzzled look on his face. "It means. Well, it means that I want to be an anteater. I told you that you would laugh."

"I told you I want to be an architect. You tell me you want to be a goddamn anteater."

"I guess that's hard to understand."

"I think it's very easy to understand. It's just impossible to actually do."

"Of course," Max admits, "Of course I know that. It's just a dream. That's what you asked me."

"Yeah? Well maybe that does make sense. I mean, I guess you wouldn't have to be *you*, Max or wonder what to do with your pathetic life if you were just an anteater."

"That's true."

"You admit it."

"They look so strange. Yet they're peaceful, even though they are so awkward. They're who they are. They don't worry about anything."

"You're already an anteater. All you do is watch television and look at your picture book."

"Anteaters are really very industrious, the way they forage for ants."

"So what are you going to do with your little life?"

Max's lower lip trembles slightly. "Why do I have to answer that? You seem angry, Rolfe. I don't understand."

Mildly, Rolfe explains, "Because you're a stupid idiot?"

"So why does that make you angry?"

"You really don't know?"

"No, I don't. And neither do you. I was just looking at my picture book before you came. I was just sitting here, minding my own business, being nice. I didn't invite you. I don't mind. But I don't know why you're here or what you want from me."

"Maybe I don't know either. Do you want me to go?"

"If you are going to be angry then I would prefer that you leave."

"I can't argue with that," Rolfe admits. But Rolfe doesn't move.

"Do you want to be angry?"

"Do I *want* to be angry?" Ralph asks. "Come off it, Max! *Please.*"

"Maybe you do need to go now. I thought I was clear," Max tells him in a voice that is even and calm. "I don't want your anger, Rolfe. Not here."

"Fine. Fine already. Yes!"

"Yes?"

"Yes, I want to be angry. Yes. You're right. That's what I want."

"But why?"

"….Because when I'm angry……I feel in control."

"You feel in control?"

"Yes."

"What do you want to control?"

"Life. Everything. The world. My feelings. My desires. My emotions. OK?"

"That's a lot."

"Yes, it's a goddamn lot."

"It's everything."

"I want to do and be so many things. And you don't want to do anything. But you're happy and I'm not and that pisses me off."

"You sound like you'd be happier as an anteater."

"Maybe I'll go now."

"Well, I hope you get to do and build all the things you want."

"Yeah, sure. I hope you get to become a fucking anteater."

"Will you be happy when you build your first building?"

"Maybe," Rolfe says distractedly, tapping his toe, looking out the blinds now.

"Or maybe when you build you second building?"

39

"My second building?"

"I was just wondering when you would be happy," Max says thoughtfully. He shrugs.

"There's more to life you know, Maxie then being happy. All right? There's doing something with your life. I don't really see that going on in here," he says, waving at the room in general.

"That makes sense. Well, I hope you do everything you want to do. And I hope that makes you happy. If that's what you want."

"You know what, Maxie." Rolfe smiles. "You know what you little bastard. I'm going to get happy right now. You are, too."

"Really?"

"I'm going out and you're coming with me. And together, we're going to find happiness. How about that."

"Really. Where are we going?"

"To a magical land, Maxie. Where everyone is happy all the time."

"I don't believe you," Max grins. "But I'll come if you want me to."

"Yeah, whatever you're doing now you can do every day. Come out with me and experience something of life, Maxie."

"It's Max."

"Only until we get out the door and then I call you whatever I want. And you can call me whatever you want as well. Just bring your coat; you don't need to bring your wallet or any money."

16. This Tuesday (3 days before the storm)

Samuel's two little rooms on the third floor of the Piedmont stand flush with the speedway. When he opens his windows the sound deluges the mealy chittering of his radio. It drowns out the orchestra in his head. It submerges his plans to escape and the counting and recounting in his head of his meager savings. It even deluges the image of his youngest daughter. Tomorrow is her birthday. Eighteen. No more Mahler now. No more Vaughan Williams in his head. No more Joanne. The motorcycles especially, grind like a chainsaw cutting cleanly through his mind before receding violently away. Through dull and brute acceptance, he learns to hear the din like a river. When the windows are closed, the air is sour, the traffic is muted, yet there remain more insidious intruders. Televisions blast dissonance, neighbors fight and fuck. And sometimes his only escape is to open wide his windows once more and invite the chaos beyond to spirit its way unanimously inside, to wash and wave away what still cloys and seeps within.

17. Last Saturday

Perry sits on the bed watching his wife undress. However shapeless she seems in her hospital scrubs, underneath she is wildly curvy, breasts and buttocks planted in thick set muscular legs. He adores her. All day long he drives past sidewalks of young, skinny white girls on west side streets, like little boys, made up dolls, shapeless, empty and anemic looking. Lorena dons her camisole, arms up, the fabric falling lightly, straps upon her brown shoulders. She tosses her head forward and begins to fluff and fuss at her chains of curls. "Do you remember?"

He wriggles his toes. "Do I remember what?"

"I have to work tomorrow."

"You're working tomorrow? On a Sunday?"

"Ay!" She lightly taps his leg with her brush. "I told you. Do you listen to me?"

"I remember now."

"I have to work. So you're taking Emma and Guillaume to the park. And to church."

"You're not going to church?"

"I just told you. I'm working."

"Why are you working on a Sunday?"

"I work in a hospital. There's always sick people. But I made food for tomorrow's lunch. Just heat it up. You can give them cereal and toast for breakfast, can't you?"

"But you've never missed church before."

"I know, Perry. I'll have to pray as I mop the floor."

"What kind of a way is that to pray?"

She had been teasing out knots in her hair, always brushing it before bed. "I can pray anywhere.   But I only work in the hospital."

"You never worked Sunday before."

"So this will be my first time then. Somebody called out sick."

"Alright," he says glumly.

"We were lucky before. I guess."

"So anytime someone is out sick you have to go work on family day?"

"Please Perry, stop fussing with me now. Guess what. I'm making a lot of extra money for working on a Sunday. OK?" She attempts a playful smile, but it looks sad to him. "Are you going to survive without me?"

"Yes."

"You pray for me first," she winks at him. "Remember, Emma has a birthday party at two. Her friend, Lisa? You remember where that is?"

"Leave me the address. I can find it on the map."

"Of course you can, my love. That's what you do."

"I can do more."

She puts her hand on his arm and inches closer to him. "I know. Don't worry about today. There'll be something else."

"Yes. Something else," he repeats, looking depleted.

"So. Maybe things worked out. No? You might have had to work tomorrow."

"For a lot of money."

"Ay! So you can miss church if the money's good? No?"

"No…it's…" he smiles. "I'll miss you tomorrow."

"I know baby. Me too. Take Paco with you."

"He won't come. When will he get a job, Lorena?"

"Ask my brother. But he's not going to find one tomorrow, anyway."

"He's like a ghost, Lorena," he hears himself say, feeling the heat suddenly rise in his face. "He doesn't do anything. Except smoke. And eat. And shit and sleep and stare into space."

Lorena looks down, clears her throat, hand still softly on his arm. "OK, baby. Maybe we'll talk about this tomorrow night."

"Now he brings pills into the house. Did you know that? Blue pills that he counts while he smokes in front of my house."

"So. He takes vitamins."

"Please. I'm not so sure that that's all they are."

"I said let's talk about it tomorrow," she pronounces, eyes fixed hard. She softens. "I'm tired, baby. And I have to get up real early again. Turn out the light. OK? And just hold me."

18. This Wednesday (Two days before the storm)

After his encounter with Henry, Andy loses interest in the Obsidian. But the idea of connecting with fellow musicians sticks with him. So he decides to seek out a venue with no cover charge, and no Henry. After several tedious and unsatisfactory forays to venues by turns harsh and callow, Andy arrives at the The Blue Aztec Lounge, pulsing with flesh and ice blue lighting lunging from shadowy walls. He sits in the corner, sipping on a cherry lime rickey. The band arrives, a four piece jazz lavender Mobius strip of pure virtuosity. Andy sips his drink. Happy. Wanting to play amongst them, he forgets himself and lets their genius wash upon him.

19.   This Thursday (just before the storm)

Tonight he gets to work in the pediatric ward, enjoying a brief escape from the withered flesh of the cancer ward. Mobiles, colored crepe paper and thick cardboard cut outs of cartoon creations festoon the walls and hang from the ceiling while plush toy mascots peer out in crazed stupors. Donna, the stolid charge nurse, uncharacteristically on her feet, speaks softly and at close quarters with a familiar looking housekeeping attendant, young, plump, and lovely. She is crying. Donna no doubt is full of dry comfort, Samuel thinks, for the emotionally bleeding woman. He feigns absorption at the supply closet.

"Samuel," Donna shouts. "Come over here and talk to Lorena, please."

"Good evening, Donna. Hello, ma'am," he says, nodding to the housekeeper.

"Samuel, do you know Lorena?"

She gives him a faint smile and brushes back a curl of hair. "I may have seen you on the floor here and there. I'm Samuel."

"We all call him Professor Samuel."

"Please, Donna, I am no professor. I am merely an errand boy. A dispenser of sundries."

"Sam, Do you have a minute? Can you just put your 'sundries' down and just sit with her and her family for a bit, will you please? I've already told her that her boy's gonna be OK. He had a seizure."

"Oh, I'm sorry to hear that. How could I be helpful, though?"

"Do you have children?" Lorena asks.

"They're all grown," he says, softly.

"Just listen, Samuel." Donna raises her eyebrows at him. Evidently she wants me to spend a little time with the family so she, Donna, can focus on the rest of her work. Or take a break, perhaps.

"Very well. With pleasure," he pronounces, throat dry. It's merely time he would idle in the break room, re-reading his precious Dostoyevsky. "So where is your little boy? And what is his name?"

"Guillaume. We're over here," Lorena says, and she leads him to room 2055 just a few feet away.

20. Thursday night

The sound of the ocean rises and the lone street lamp mutes the darkness. "This is my favorite beach."

"I've never been here before."

"You'll like it," he says, feeling pride in showing her something new. "We can enter through there," he says, pointing to an unseen gap in a rickety wooden fence.

"Don't forget the food," she reminds him. "I'll get it," she adds. Eugene feels light, insubstantial. Stars multiply and the ocean raises its distant roar. His eyes adjust. "I love the smell," she says, breathing deeply.

Eugene cannot smell a thing. "Through here," he says. They plod up the sandy, mild slope, laced with hard scrub, stray pebbles, dog turds, and trash. He remembers her bare feet, but she says nothing. Then he hesitates. "It should be right here." Eugene stands gazing at the blackened telephone poles.

"Over here," Caroline shouts. Snarling irritably, Eugene slogs after Caroline.

"I know," he calls out breathlessly. "I know." He picks his way over low rubbery ice plants and he hears her giggle right before colliding with her. A jolt of fire lights through him. His fingers tingle with a longing to embrace; warm, solid, a faceless woman in the dark.

"Come on," she whispers, mirth quivering in her voice. She strides ahead. "Take your shoes off. It feels so nice." He stops to comply, sitting down heavily to yank off his shoes and socks. The sand indeed feels pleasant, cool, and safe. He feels stronger, like an animal, prowling in the dark. Where's Caroline? The beach is long, a measureless flat dune. He pads along.

"Caroline," he calls, his voice sounding thin and effete. At last he smells the ocean. The sand falls away before him and the glimmering moon slides across the surface of an endless lead plane beyond a crashing edge of foam. An utterly lost sensation thrills through him. "Caroline!"

"Over here." He spots her seated not ten paces away. "Where were you?"

"Where was I? I was looking for you?"

"Well I'm here. Sit down." He plops down alongside of her. "Have some candy," she offers from the bag. "And don't litter." She leans into him. Just for a moment. A thin, rank vapor carries from her. Somehow he hadn't noticed it before. Her clothes. He imagines her large, young face, which he can barely see, untouched blue eyes. She tells him, "I love coming to the ocean at night. It makes me feel clean." A wave crashes and seethes, foaming within a few feet of where they sit. Eugene recoils. "Relax," she tells him. "You won't get wet."

The sand feels damp and cold to him, "I know," is all he says, wrapping his arms about himself.

44

"Are you cold?" she asks.

"No."

"Liar," she giggles.

"I'm OK." And they both inch their way a little closer to each other for warmth.

"Can I tell you a fantasy of mine?"

"Sure!" He perks up.

"I'm in a giant bubble bath in a pink room. Warm, warm water. So I'm clean, clean, clean, and I'm warm but not in a bad sort of way like on a hot day and you don't know what to do with yourself. The room is bright and pink and soft and I'm in this huge white, white tub up to my neck and bubbles, foamy bubbles pile up everywhere." She looks at Eugene as if expecting a response.

He shrugs. "Everywhere?"

"Everywhere. Yes. Everywhere in the tub. Not on the floor or the ceiling, stupid, just in the tub. Nice?" And she smiles at him as if she were proud of the bathtub she had merely dreamed up. She pulls a bag of Cheetos, opens it and begins munching happily.

"That's real nice," Eugene admits.

"And...I would have lots of towels and a fluffy robe and there'd be perfume and powder and all that. There'd be lots of powder puffs, soft and all different colors. Have you ever seen those powder puffs?"

"I don't know."

"My grandmother used to have some. I'd play with them when I was little. She didn't like that very much. But I'd have lots of my own powder puffs hidden away because they kept me company. Anyway, so I'm out of the bath and I wear soft slippers or maybe I just walk barefoot on the carpet because it's really thick and it's white or pink and my feet would be warm and really clean and the bedroom would be warm and there'd be a huge bed. Huge! Bigger than a king. What is that? What's bigger than a king bed?"

"A dictator bed?" Eugene offers.

"Not a dictator bed. God's bed, maybe. I don't know. But it's huge and there's lots of really soft blankets and they're thick and they're furry. Very furry. But it's not real fur, you know. Because that's not nice. And there'd be a million furry soft pillows and I'd roll naked on top of them all and I'd be so warm and clean that I'd sleep naked beneath all of that, and it would be really, really dark when I turned out the lights, but I wouldn't be scared." Eugene straightens up at the lovely inviting image of Caroline naked and rolling upon furry blankets, clean and pink, big and voluptuous and curvy and beautiful. "I'd just feel all that fur and those clean sheets and blankets and pillows and I'd know I was safe and protected and maybe it would get purple outside but not quite bright and daylight because if it did, maybe I'd have to leave and my time would be over. So I'd just stay forever in that peaceful twilight. So it wouldn't be night, it would be early morning, but it would always be early and I would always have more time there."

"Dawn. I think it would be dawn, not twilight."

"Yeah. But there'd be a huge tray of food on the table and the table would have a white cloth and it's really clean. And there would be lots of delicious hot food." He sees her watching intently her imaginary world, her hands gently conducting the proceedings, proud and protective of her invented world.

"Food? Like Cheetos?"

"Cheetos?" She eats a few and talks over her munching. "Like warm roast lamb. Like big juicy red steaks with what lots of fat and with, what do they call it? Horseradish. Lots of fat. And roast potatoes with garlic and all the ice cream I can eat with hot chocolate syrup. And my hands and fingers are covered in chocolate sauce and the fat and juice from the steaks and the lamb and it gets all over me, and I rub it in but it's OK because I can just get back in my bubble bath and get clean whenever I want. And yes, I think you can eat an animal but you can't wear it. OK? What do you think?"

Eugene shrugs uncomfortably, intense desire and nausea struggling within him. "I like it. It sounds fun. Wonderful, really."

"It's cozy and safe. So you like it?"

"A lot."

"Want to go there?"

"Hell yeah."

"You don't look happy."

"I'm cold." The edge of the sea sizzles up to within a foot or two of their toes.

"Cummere. I'll keep you warm." She puts her arm, funky sweatshirt and all, around his shoulder and he sidles up against her. He wishes he could just feel glad, but he feels awkward and unsettled.

"I wish we were in that bubble bath together right now," he says.

"Yes. I would let you join me. For sure. And you and I could eat steak and bacon and lobster, with lots and lots of dripping butter. And then we'd drink champagne and eat donuts and ice cream together. And corn on the cob, too. And then we could hide together, warm beneath all those furry covers, Eugene, and we'd be nice and safe, and no one would come for us."

They sit in the presence of the ocean's churning. He shivers and he hears himself tell her, "I'm sad." He cannot recall ever saying that before out loud.

"You're sad?"

"I guess so."

She seems to think about this. "Well why?"

"Because we can never really go there. I'd like to go there."

"Maybe we will go there."

"But it's just your fantasy."

"Well. And why not? Stop talking like that. Or I may not like you anymore."

46

He looks at her in a panic. "How about a shower? I could get you a shower if you wanted one?"

"It doesn't make me feel bad, you know. I only think about it when I feel OK. Like when I'm eating Cheetos."

"What about when you're cold? What about when you're hungry?"

Caroline shrugs. "I think about it then, too. So what?"

"What about a shower? Would you like to take a shower? A warm shower. Would you like that?"

"You don't understand."

"I mean right now. For real. You said you want to be clean."

"I want to feel safe and warm and nice. You don't understand," she says.

Eugene thinks about this for a moment. A cold breeze worries his bare forearms. "But I do. I want to be there, too. With all the pillows. And the food and all. And the bubbles and all that kind of stuff." He knows it's pointless; that she'll remain dirty and cold and hungry and vulnerable. As if sensing his thoughts, she turns to him.

"Isn't there some place you go to or think about that makes you happy, like when you're eating Cheetos or something like that?"

He rubs his arms hugging himself. "I don't know."

"That means there is a place. Tell me."

"Maybe," he says. "Maybe," he repeats.

"Maybe what?"

"All right. There is a place I think of. A made up place."

"Don't call it made up. Is it your place?"

"Yes. It's mine. But it's stupid."

"Stupid?"

"Yeah."

"You think mine is stupid?"

"No. No, I don't. I think it's really nice. I wish I could go there, I like it. With the bubbles and the bed and the food. But I can't go there. I'm sorry."

"Don't be sorry. Just tell me about your place."

"I told you. It's stupid."

"Why do you say that?"

"Because it is."

"Why is it stupid?"

"Because it *is* stupid."

She thinks about this for a moment. "That's not a reason."

"Because *I'm* stupid."

"Don't say that."

"I am."

"Stop it."

"Well, I feel that way."

"Does your place make you happy?"

47

"No."

"No?"

"No, it doesn't."

"It doesn't make you happy?"

"It doesn't make me happy."

"Well. I don't understand that"

"Well I don't either. I told you it was stupid."

"Ah. Does it make you unhappy?"

He thinks about this. "No. No it doesn't."

"Why do you think about it?"

"I don't know. I like to think about it when I'm eating a cheeseburger."

"Ah! Just like with the Cheetos."

"Yes," he smiles.

"Tell me what it is already."

"I've never told anyone."

"Then I will be your first." she starts to laugh. He can feel her smile. He imagines it's beautiful.

"I'm telling you. It's really stupid."

"Stop saying that. Anyway, I think you want to tell me."

"I work in an office. In my fantasy. I wear a long gray coat."

"Is it a beautiful coat?" she asks.

Eugene sighs. "No. It's drab, but it's long. Like a trench coat."

"I'd like a trench coat. I think they're beautiful. And very warm."

"I'd like one, too. I'm cold," he shivers. "But this coat. Yeah, it's warm. But it's stained and ugly."

"What? Why is it stained? Don't you like it?"

"This is my fantasy. It just came to me like this. I work in this office. By myself. But....it's a big building. Huge. Big, big building."

"Yes. A beautiful, tall, shiny glass building?"

"No! No it's not like that at all. It's like a gargantuan iron filing cabinet."

"What?"

"It's hideous."

Caroline stares at Eugene. He feels a red surge of resentment and shame. Suddenly she bursts out laughing. But she puts a hand on his arm. "I'm sorry. You're right. It is stupid. But I don't care. It's amazing and I want to hear it anyway."

Eugene smiles and without really thinking about it, his hand falls into hers, all too rough, but dry. He leaves it there and she squeezes it. "It's a horrible place, really. But I like to think about it, anyway. Filing cabinets everywhere and piles of papers all over the place and there's thousands of offices and hundreds of floors and they're all the same. And it's gray everywhere, and it's always cloudy all the time and it rains a lot. And people are afraid of me."

48

"Ah, Eugene," she says and she squeezes his hand. "How strange."

"And I don't like them very much either. I walk alone in my trench coat across a big bridge over this gray river. And there's a big empty square and stony buildings all around. And the streets don't have no names. There's not many people, though. I mean, there's people everywhere, but it's a huge city full of tall, unpainted concrete buildings, but it's not very crowded. You can at least find a back street where there's no one else."

"What else, Eugene? Is there anything nice about this place?"

"I don't know."

"Well what about the people. Tell me more about them."

"There's not much to tell. People wear gray and black trench coats and they all kind of look alike. I've always thought of the word 'people' like that. Kind of generic people without a face, short black hair, and trench coats. That's what people are to me. I don't know why."

"No faces? How could they have no faces?"

"They don't really have faces, or maybe they do but you just don't notice them. And...and everyone's alone anyway. Nobody talks to each other. They all walk by themselves, heads down and their hands in their pockets and all. And their...their collars are up. Everyone is deep into whatever they're thinking. Or maybe they're not thinking of anything at all. And sometimes the wind blows. That's why their collars are up. There's wind and rain and sometimes a lot of fog. And the wind sometimes blows the trash around, mostly old papers. Forms or whatever, maybe advertisements, flyers for things that probably don't exist. Just blowing in the wind."

"How do people know where they're going if there are no street names?"

"I don't know. I don't know where they're going."

"Are there cars to take them anywhere? Do people drive?"

Eugene ponders this. "I see a rusty scooter now and then. Even a bicycle. But no cars. But there are trains, big iron ones. Old trains. And they ride right through the middle of the street all the time. And that's the only noise you hear. The rushing of trains. And their horns. Those long, strange horn sounds."

"My God, where are they going, these trains? Are they leaving this place?"

Eugene is hunkered down against the salty breeze. He looks down at his hands holding Caroline's. He shivers. "I don't know where the train is going."

"What a terrible place."

"I don't know. I don't mind it. No one bothers you."

"You don't mind? Is that because everyone there is sad and alone like you?"

"It's because I kind of feel important there...and what you just said, too."

"What do you do in the office?"

"I don't know. Mostly I shuffle papers. Maybe stamp forms. I forget to stamp some and I stamp others. They're actually important but I kind of get to do what I want. I'm sort of important, but not really. I guess it doesn't really matter what I do there."

She laughs again. "Maybe this place is just like the real world."

"No. This place is better."

"Which place? Your fantasy or real life." A mutant wave explodes on the sand and sprays them with water. Eugene curses, but Caroline holds tight his hands. "Answer me," she shouts above the ocean.

"Fantasy. I like the other place better with the papers and the train and the tower. It's gray and cool and no one bothers you."

"Tower?"

"There's an enormous tower on the edge of town. It's made of metal. Iron. Anyway, no one ever sees the top of it because there's always fog at the top. I've never actually been there. I'm a little scared of it."

"You're a strange guy, Eugene," she says, squeezing his hands. She says it softly as if merely curious, simply observing a remarkable fact. "I think I like that. You're kind of safe though. And sad."

"We should get you a pair of shoes." Maybe she's smiling. It's hard to tell in the celestial light and the dim echo of halogen from the distant street. "For your feet," he adds, needlessly.

Caroline giggles and snorts, her thumbs rubbing slowly on his hand. "I'd like some shoes. I have tough feet though."

"I can get you shoes first thing tomorrow, downtown. Not expensive you know, but nice. Good shoes."

"And socks? I'd really like some socks."

"I can get you some socks tonight. I have extra socks. Clean. All washed." Eugene shudders at the desperation and cruelty behind stealing shoes from a homeless girl. No one would ever do that in his fantasy world. "I could take you to where I'm staying. To where I live. I don't have a bath though. But we have a shower."

"You'll take me now?"

"I'll take you now, if you like. I have roommates, but they're upstairs."

"Is it warm?"

Eugene had never really thought about it. "It's warm. Or if it's not, I can turn on the heater, that's no problem. I'll get you some socks. Are you OK with that?"

"Do you have any slippers? I like slippers."

"Maybe. I'll look for some for you." He thinks of the many young co-eds who are constantly leaving something, maybe a pair of poofy slippers in his bathroom or his pantry. Suddenly Caroline leans over and kisses Eugene on the mouth. It happens quickly and then it's over. It was barely even like a kiss at all and it frightens him at first, her face against his. He looks at her. It seems she is smiling. "We have a washing machine too." The ocean roars.

21. That same Thursday Morning

The drivers take notice of the smiling, bespectacled, young woman in the room in her tight fitting Zzzzap! shirt. Hagen speaks. "Gentlemen, I know you're never thrilled about meeting here all together. You'd rather be out there on the road making money. That's good! So just a few minutes of our time. In a moment, I'll be introducing our latest addition to the team, Ms. Maureen Tafolinado. But first off, starting tomorrow, we take on our biggest account yet. By far. Ever hear of Triangle Title and Construction?" Everyone looks blankly at him.

Rolfe speaks up. "Yeah, sure. They're huge."

"That's right. They're huge. Huge! And they're ours; starting tomorrow. They expect the best; the best service, the most reliable, and the most professional, courteous, and competent drivers. And the most enthusiastic, too!" Mikros appears stony and distant. "You're going to be very, very busy, zzzapping throughout town, making lots and lots of money for yourself and for ZZZZap! Messenger." He smiles and winks at them. "It's a big deal. Huge! You might be interested to know that they are located not only in L.A. but also in Diamond Bar, Newhall, Riverside, and Anaheim, and we will be picking up and delivering to all of them, every day. *Ah*, do I have your attention *now*, gentlemen?" Mikros shakes his head. "So…" Hagen clears his throat, "We will need more drivers, some of whom will actually be living out in these areas. Shaking your heads? Do you expect me to pay you to drive out to Riverside at three in the afternoon to take something to Moreno Valley? Trust me, you'll be going long plenty often, but I'm gonna to need some options here. I'm not going to pay you to drive all afternoon for a five or ten mile job! At any rate, for now, you'll be pleased to know that this young lady sitting near me, Maureen Tafolindao, a nursing student at L.A City College, is going to help us out with all of our local pick-ups and hand-offs, and maybe even with our twice daily Cal Trans runs."

"All right!" Rolfe declares, genuinely pleased. Maureen smiles, exposing her considerable teeth and gums- bare arms ropy and muscular – fuchsia streaked brown hair. Ralph nudges Andy. "You like her?" Andy glances at him but cannot tell whether he is being ironic or not.

"Mr. Hagen," Samuel speaks up. "I for one am glad of the extra help. It is curious we are starting tomorrow. You are aware that a major storm is expected. The first of the season and the roads will be quite troublesome."

"So should we stop our business because of a little rain, Samuel?"

"No, of course not."

"Shall we call our clients and say, can you hold off on making money please, because our drivers don't feel like driving in the rain?"

Samuel discreetly chuckles. "Touché, sir!" And he sighs.

"Just be careful out there. Rolfe! You want to share some important information with the rest of us?" Hagen asks.

"Yes *sir!* I know our new driver will need training. And I think Andy would be a perfect person to do it."

"Thank you for volunteering him," Hagen replies, his mouth twisted wryly. "I was thinking of someone with a little more experience, like Perry or Tim. Perhaps yourself."

"Ah, but it's good to get the experience of someone who remembers what it's like to be new. Be a better more patient teacher. And Andy knows what he's doing already."

"That's fine with me. I'll do it," Andy hears himself say.

"All right," Hagen continues. "Works for me. We'll keep you local to train Maureen. We'll put you with Tim in the afternoon. Mikros?"

"Hmmm?"

"Just see what you can do."

"I'm sorry?"

"See what you can do to switch Maureen out with a different driver this afternoon - like Tim - so she can learn from both."

"Sure."

Andy looks over at Maureen who waves at him with a wide toothy smile. She winks at him. He smiles back. "Where was I?" Hagen asks.

"I believe you finished," Samuel offers.

22. Thursday Night

A man sits in a chair next to the bed, his young daughter on his lap, but she quickly jumps down at the sight of the stranger entering the room, as if she were caught doing something wrong. Stretched out, slouching in the far corner is yet one more person whom Samuel cannot make out at all. "Mr. Samuel! It's you." Perry leaps from the chair ready to embrace Samuel, yet he stops short, sensing his friend flinch from this sudden intimacy, so instead he claps him on the shoulder and grabs his hand.

"Perry?"

"Ah. Mr. Samuel. I can't believe it. I feel God has sent you to comfort us."

"…What?"

"I did not know that you work here with my wife. There are many hospitals."

"Yes. Yes. Well," and he turns and nods at Lorena.

"Come. Come and meet my family. You have met my wife, Lorena, of course. That is my brother-in-law, Paco." Perry says hastily, waving in the direction of the man in the corner. Samuel squints but still cannot make out the man's features, for the corner is poorly lit. "This is my daughter, Emma," he says, pulling the arm of the little girl, still clinging and hanging from his leg. "Stand up straight, please, Emma." She is a pretty though awkward looking girl of about five, dark like her father, dark eyes, ragged teeth. "And now please, meet my son, Mr. Samuel. This is Guillaume." The little boy, who had previously been on his back, rolling and staring through his upraised fingers, suddenly springs upright at the sight of Samuel. The little boy stands on the bed now, swaying slightly, slowly waving his hands.

"Guillaume, baby. Sit down. Please," Perry says, gently. Guillaume, wide eyes, locks sight with Samuel. He starts jumping up and down. Perry puts his arm around the boy's shoulder and whispers in Spanish.

"I'm going out for a smoke," the man in the corner says. Samuel turns and stares at Paco, who smirks, looking him briefly up and down, before brushing past him.

The boy sits down and smiles, still staring and pointing. His smile fades and he puts his thumb in his mouth. "Guillaume," Samuel rouses himself. "Good prince," he exclaims, and at once the boy begins to smile again. "Wonderful and most honored to be in your presence, young Master." Guillaume giggles and speaks to him in Spanish, but Perry asks him to speak in English.

"Hi," is all he says.

"Hi. Yes, hi, indeed." Samuel wonders that the child isn't appalled at his rumpled buffoonery. "What can you tell me?" he says to Perry. "And how are you both doing?" he adds, turning to Lorena.

"He's fine. He's going home tomorrow morning, maybe," Lorena says. She snuggles her son.

"He had a seizure," Perry says. "My boy. I thought he was hit by a car. My brother-in-law was watching him. But not very well." Lorena looks at Perry.

"Was that… was that your brother in law who just walked out?"

"Yes," Perry answers. "He lives with us. At least until he goes and gets a job. He was supposed to be watching Guillaume when a car came out, our neighbor."

"I left him with you, Perry, not with Paco."

"Was the boy actually struck by a car?" Samuel asks, seeing Guillaume apparently unharmed.

"No," Perry said.

"But almost," Lorena adds. "Almost. And that's what caused that seizure. He was so scared, he had a seizure."

"The doctor didn't say what caused it," Perry adds. Lorena goes to her son, who has stood up once more, and she quietly lulls him into lying back down again, which he does, staring straight up, pointing lazily to the ceiling.

"I'm tired, Mr. Samuel," Perry confides. "So is Lorena."

"You don't have to tell a stranger that I'm tired," Lorena calls, her back to them, stroking her son's hair.

"Mr. Samuel is not a stranger."

"Well I don't know him, Perry."

"That's all right," Samuel says. "I should go finish my rounds. All the very best to you and all your family." He says this to Lorena's back who still leans over the boy.

The two men walk out and drift together meekly down the corridor. Donna calls out. "Your boy's OK and he's going to be just fine Mr. Ramirez. We'll see you tomorrow before eight o'clock."

"Thank you so much."

"You're welcome. Thank you, Samuel," Donna calls out.

"Donna, it turns out this is a good friend of mine," Samuel announces, recognizing with a shock the perfectly heartfelt sentiment behind his candid statement. She raises her head from her charting and nods, though he's quite sure that she hasn't understood him.

"My wife is very upset."

"Of course she is. You've already heard though that Guillaume will be OK." Samuel wonders if the boy might be an epileptic. "But of course this is a traumatic event. It's to be expected that you're both very upset."

"I mean she blames me. She blames me for what happened. That's why she is so rude to you."

"Your wife was most certainly not at all rude to me, Perry."

"She blames me. The car nearly hit him. So close, it was a miracle it did not happen." Perry chews the words beneath his breath, eyes red. "Our neighbor, who doesn't respect himself or others, who lets his house go to hell, who races out of his drive way without even looking. But I blame myself. I blame myself for letting Paco watch after him. Only for a moment. We were already outside. I went back into the house to check everything was turned off; the lights, the burners on the stove we used for lunch. We even unplug the toaster. Everything burns, Mr. Samuel. We were going to go to the park. But he cannot be trusted for anything."

"Perry." Samuel puts a hand on his shoulder. "I remind you that your boy is uninjured. A beautiful, healthy boy. Second, whatever Guillaume is going through is treatable and I believe it would have happened regardless. Do not blame yourself."

"How do you know this?"

"It's just not the way it works."

"No? It could have made things worse."

"Please. You'll talk to the doctor in the morning."

"But I have to be at work at eight o'clock. What do I do?."

"You need to be here. Call Mikros or even Hagen directly. You need to be here to take your boy home tomorrow."

"Lorena has to work, too."

"All the more reason why you shall be here first thing tomorrow morning."

"Yes, Mr. Samuel."

"Do you have any other family members that can also help?"

"Not in this part of town."

"Call them. And call Mr. Hagen. He will surely understand."

"Mr. Hagen? I don't know. All he talks about is the clients. The new client. How they all start tomorrow. He wants us all there. That's all he wants. Zzzzapping here and zzzzapping there!"

Samuel laughs, "And you shall be there. In plenty of time for the all the afternoon madness. After you take your boy home."

"But Lorena has to work, too. All day. He can't go to school. I don't know what to do."

"Well I don't know either Perry. But call Mr. Hagen first thing tomorrow. Take the whole day off. Right now, you need to do what you think is best for your family."

"It does my family no good if I lose my job."

"You won't lose your job."

"You don't know that." Lorena steps out of the room and looks at Perry. A thin wail begins to rise from behind the door. She crosses her arms, then signals Perry to come to her.

"It will be all right. I shall see you good sir at the lumpy couch. Not tomorrow, but Monday" Samuel rejoins, aware of being overly sanguine.

23.

With a heavy pit in his thrashing colon, Samuel walks off, sudden soreness in his throbbing heels, menacing at his knobby knees. He imagines Carter, indifferent, scanning the neglected back pages of the sports section, the want ads, the stock quotes, the want ads yet again. With an unsteady finger, Samuel presses for the service elevator and rides its stark, blanketed hull to the bottom level. He imagines he is riding in the bottom of a giant cargo chest. The door rumbles open. Slowly he edges his way to his ancient Camry. He opens the door and stiffly settles in, listening to the settling floats and ticks and creaks in his car.

The silence always surprises him. Soon it will be shift change and the walls will shake with new comings and goings, the groaning and screeching of cars and exhaust. He closes his eyes. And then he hears the foot falls and the feet that scrape to a stop; the soft rap on the passenger window. Samuel starts. He rouses himself and glances at the empty, grayly familiar face in the window.

"The door's unlocked," Samuel says.

The young man opens the door and slumps down, one foot propped up against the glove compartment. He leaves the door open for a moment before shutting it. "Roll down the window, will you? It's tight in here."

"Do you mean airless? I agree."

"So. Roll it down."

"Roll it yourself. It's a manual. Remember?"

The young man finds the handle and rolls down the squeaking window. Samuel rolls his down as well, part way. "Didn't you also have a nicer car? Besides this piece a shit."

"This is all that's left. I had a feeling you'd come." Paco takes out a small plastic fuel lighter and attempts to light his cigarette. "You will not smoke in my car, Paco."

Paco smiles and bows his head in silent glee. "What is this man? What the fuck are you wearing?" He waves the unlit cigarette. "Is this a fucking joke?"

Samuel looks down at his scrubs as if noticing them for the first time. "No joke, I'm afraid. This is my uniform."

"Yeah? Is that what genius pussy college professors wear to work?"

"This is my uniform when I'm delivering bed pans, thermometers, that sort of ware."

"'Ware'? Did you say 'ware'? Shit….. You moonlighting, bro? You teach your bullshit classes during the day and help out here at night like the saint you are? Help the sick, the poor? Like Jesus?"

"You know perfectly well I no longer work at the university. During the day, I work as a delivery driver. Since you ask."

"Ah yeah. Silly me. So you're a messenger. Just like my brother-in-law. You two work together?"

"You're a rare genius aren't you? Yes. He's a good man."

"You drop off papers and shit for other people?"

"Correct."

"You like that?"

"Sometimes. I'm not particularly good at it. Driving gives me anxiety, so it's difficult. What do you want, Paco?"

"When's the last time you shaved? You look like some fuckin' cave man."

"I asked you, what do you want?" Paco brushes his downy mustache with the edge of his soft finger. He flicks his lighter and poises the cringing flame to the cigarette drooping now from his lips. It crackles orange. Smoke pours from the tip and from his awkward mouth. "Please put out your cigarette." Samuel wonders what he ever saw in the young man's vacant face. Paco takes another drag of his cigarette and lazily stares back at Samuel. "Paco, you are in my car. Kindly, put the cigarette out." Paco merely squints through the smoke, as if curious what he might be looking at. "Put out the goddamn cigarette, Paco! Right now!"

Paco winks. He chuckles as he stubs out the cigarette on the outside of the passenger door. After inspecting the stub, blowing and flicking at it, he pockets it for later use. "Take it easy, man. You'll get a stroke or something."

Samuel feels his face burn crimson; his voice is dry and hoarse from its sudden exertion. He had intended to sound forceful, but instead his voice sounded cracked, high and weak. "State your business, or leave."

"What did you used to teach, man?"

"What?"

"You heard me. Tell me what really, really important thing you used to teach."

Samuel's tongue feels heavy, remote in his mouth. "European literature. Mostly."

Paco smiles and scratches his ear, shaking his head. "Euro what?"

"European literature," Samuel repeats, aware that Paco has made him feel unjustly embarrassed, as if he had just admitted to wearing women's underpants.

"What the fuck is that?"

"What is that? It is literature. Written by Europeans. To be precise."

"Oh man. For real. Who gives a fuck about that? Seriously. Who are you helping at all with that bullshit?"

"Just go," Samuel replies weakly.

"What a waste, man."

"Why are you so *proud* of your ignorance?

Paco shrugs and puts his foot higher up on the dash. He lets his seat adjust down backward. "I'm not proud of nothing.'"

"Appropriately so. Except your ignorance. You're like some....some Visigoth...jester, or something."

"What the fuck is that? Is that supposed to be an insult? V..visigoth....Visigoth jester? Seriously?" Paco starts to laugh. "Hey man, that's below the belt," he clowns and laughs some more.

"What on earth do you want from me, Paco?"

Paco is still chuckling but manages to say, "Fifty bucks. That's all, man. I need fifty."

"Well now it's my turn to laugh," Samuel retorts, though he clearly isn't laughing. "Do you really imagine I even have fifty dollars to my name?"

"We'll make it like old times." And Paco winks and puckers his lips at Samuel.

57

"I have no money. You are related to a friend of mine. And I am not even slightly interested. "

"I could care less what you're interested in. OK? I just want the fifty dollars."

"That is not going to happen."

"You can give it to me tomorrow. I know you still got money somewhere."

"I won't and I don't."

"Fifty bucks and we can keep all this good stuff just between us," and he vaguely points to his crotch and winks again.

"You disgust me."

"I disgust *you*? Have you looked in the mirror lately?" And he reaches over for the rearview mirror as if to force Samuel to contemplate his reflection but Samuel grabs it back and manages to push him away.

Paco laughs. "Come on, man. No one has to know. Right?"

"For God's sake, who on earth would you even tell?"

"My sister and brother-in-law, to start. And I know where you work, too."

"Go right ahead and disgrace yourself in front of your sister."

Paco stares at him, annoyed at having to think about this. "I just might."

"I doubt it, but it doesn't matter."

"Are you daring me?"

Samuel chuckles. "Yes! As a matter of fact I am. I *dare* you."

"I can take you down without them knowing about me."

"I *double* dare you! I'm six years old and I double dare you. What rot. You are a spectacular specimen of cretinism."

"You ain't just a little bit ashamed of yourself?"

"Of course I am. But not before you. Maybe that's why we get along so well. And by the way; the next time you engage in some petty shakedown, I would recommend that you time your extortion before your mark - that is to say, your intended victim - before such person loses his career, his reputation, his family, and his money. Before! Not after. Because you see, that way, your mark is far more likely to feel that he has something to lose and therefore something to fear by not complying with your precious demands. Does that make sense?"

Paco nods and smiles. "Sure. But I still want the fifty, man."

"There are many things that I want as well. Besides, I've already paid you that fifty many times before."

"How about giving it to me tomorrow?"

"Lovely catching up with you, Paco. I am going to go now." For a moment, both are silent.

"So go. We'll talk when you get back."

"Am I to understand that you are going to wait in my car until I go home?"

"I got nothing to do."

"I don't doubt it. Won't your brother-in-law be looking for you?" Paco shrugs. For a fraction of a second, Samuel feels sorry for him.

"Maybe." Paco pulls out his lighter and begins to flick it to flame. Samuel reaches over and slaps the lighter out of Paco's hands, surprising himself in the process. Paco laughs. "Come on, man. Where'd it go? Take it easy," he says, looking at his feet, holding out his hands as if he were still holding the lighter. "Here it is," Paco picks the lighter up. "It's cheap, but I still need it. This job must really be stressing you out."

"You are stressing me out."

"Maybe I just want to talk. Maybe you do, too. How come you're not teaching about the Euro people and their books and everything? Did you decide you needed to do something else? A change? Did you get tired of getting blow jobs from your students? Or maybe you got caught?"

"I never actually had dalliances with any of my students."

"Had what?"

"Dalliances."

"You never dilly-dallied with your students? You mean you never *fucked* your students," Paco said. "Is that what you mean?"

"That is what I mean."

"Then say *that*." Samuel says nothing. "So what happened to you, homes? Why'd you get thrown out? Why'd your family leave you? Because obviously you fucked up."

Samuel closes his eyes, determined to pick and choose what he says and does not say. "Yes. Yes I did. I *fucked* up very much so."

"What did you do?"

"You know very well."

"Say it."

"I was caught consorting illicitly with lower companions."

"Consorting? You were consorting?"

"Indeed."

"Consorting? You mean you got busted for getting' nasty with whores and hustlers on the boulevard? Is that what that bullshit word 'consorting' means?"

"That is what it means."

"You don't like to say things straight out, do you?"

"I say things the way I say them."

"You like to make it all sound fancy, like you're still teaching your little classes. You like to make it sound all proper when it's just plain nasty, don't you?" Paco has not yet guessed the truth. Doubtless, he would have laughed like a hyena before a kill had he known, but he does not know. Samuel only admits

59

what Paco already knows. "Don't feel too bad about it," Paco says, pretending to be of comfort. "OK? No one really gives a shit about whatever it was you taught anyway. It was all a big bag a bullshit and no one misses you there. Right? And your wife – your ex-wife I'm guessing. She's so much better off. I'm sure she loves fucking whoever she's fucking much, much more than she had to put up with you. Right? It's about time she actually enjoyed herself, instead of all her disappointment about your limp, weak little pecker. She probably screams hallelujah and comes real good and she and her new man probably laugh and laugh at you all the time, and people like to laugh. You know? You should be happy for her and that big dick she's getting' now." Samuel bursts out laughing. Paco laughs as well and for a moment, they resemble good if unlikely friends. He flicks his lighter again, this time lighting up his stub. He takes a drag, then exhales a cauldron of smoke from his mouth and nostrils. Samuel's eyes begin to water and he immediately stops laughing. "And your kids. Come on now, of course they are so much better off without you. How many kids have you got?" Are they grown?" Samuel stares, his lip curling back, marveling leadenly at Paco's penchant for cruelty. "Do you have any daughters? Are they hot? Are they? Are they hot? Are your daughters hot?" Paco smiles, noticing Samuel's teeth clench. "Yes. They're hot. Ooh yeah. I'd like to get with your daughters, man." And Paco makes an obscene gesture but Samuel bursts out laughing again. Again Paco laughs and once more they impossibly resemble good friends, until Paco says, "Forget me, man. How about you? Have you ever gotten nasty with your girls? Ever peeped at them in the shower.....Hmm? Ever felt them out while they were sitting on your lap?" Paco winks at him and casually continues to ask questions about Samuel's supposed pederasty against his own daughters. Samuel's throat begins to swell from the irritation of cheap tobacco. He figures he has maybe five minutes at most before he has to exit the car or he may have trouble breathing.

"Are you not worried about your nephew?" he manages to ask.

"My nephew? He'll be fine."

"I was thinking of him before you appeared."

"Isn't Guillaume a little young, man? Even for a sicko like you?"

"I was thinking how lucky he was to have not been hit by that car. Guillaume and both his parents are truly blessed."

Paco shrugs. "The kid'll be fine. They're making a big deal. Let's talk more about you getting it on with your girls."

"How did little Guillaume end up in the street, anyway?"

"He's a little boy. They run around--"

"Yes, little boys can run very quickly into the street if you don't watch them, if you don't pay careful attention."

"Whatever. Do you really care about that little boy? Is that what you want to talk about, professor, instead of the truth I just dropped on you?"

"Do you care about that little boy, Paco?"

"He's my nephew. And like I said, he's way, way too young for you, pendejo. You know what I'm saying?"

"Yes. Yes, of course. Your point is always obvious yet artfully inane, Paco. Brilliant. But yes, I do in fact actually know what it is you are saying. My question is, why did you let your three year old nephew run out into the street in the first place?"

Paco smiles. "That's a weak play homes. You tell me; how often did you get a boner for your own girls, man?"

"Your brother-in-law - who clearly, by the way, neither likes nor respects you - and who puts up with your freeloading, nevertheless trusted you for an instant - unwisely, of course - to watch his son for a brief moment. And you failed to do even that properly. But why?"

"I've watched that little shit many times and everything was fine. OK? You ever try and watch a three year old?"

"Have you already forgotten? I raised three sons and two daughters, all of whom are healthy and whole today, with or without me."

"Do any of them ever have to turn away stinky old farts who put money in their face so they can get their rocks off?"

"My turn. You're not employed. You're mooching off your family. And you failed to be trustworthy in even the simplest, most fundamental way. *Why*, Paco?"

"I'll bet you get hard with your own bitches because you can't get it up anymore any other way."

"Maybe you did it intentionally, Paco? I mean, you knew your neighbor was getting into his car, you know the street is dangerous, you know Guillaume likes to run out when he's excited. True, you're lazy and useless enough, I agree, but you are also devious. Not in an intelligent sort of way, mind you, but devious in intent, for sure."

Paco was smiling, but Samuel sees the color deepening on his face. "You're a pathetic little man. I would never do that to a little boy. OK? I don't know about *you*, though."

"But you *did* do that to a little boy. Or perhaps you were really doing it to your brother-in-law. I mean, you clearly resent him for always getting on your case to find work."

"So you and my brother-in-law talk about me? You got nothin' else better to do?"

"Perry has never spoken one word to me of you. But it is so obvious, isn't it? So painfully obvious. Everything about you, Paco is mind numbingly *obvious*. But actually, you don't care too much what your brother in law thinks. You're really much, much more angry and resentful towards your sister. Aren't you?" Samuel watches Paco's gaze narrow. "Counterintuitive, I grant you, because after all, she's the one who loves you, whereas Perry cannot stand the sight of you."

"You can stop talking about my sister now," Paco says, giving a courteous looking shrug.

"You dare to talk about my children you wretched piece of filth. But whereas your own taunts are utterly ludicrous, I tell you I am certain, quite certain, Paco, that every time you see your sister, you are reminded that you need her, that you are dependent, that you are helpless and weak. That you're a *burden*, Paco." Paco just gazes sleepily at the gear shift with a slight smile curling at his lip, nodding ever so slightly. "But your sister remains most dutiful. Does she not? She is a good woman, a strong woman, it's true. She is ready to take on the *burden* of taking care of you because after all, isn't that what your mother asked her to do? Wasn't your mother so very disappointed in you? To say nothing of your father who probably cannot or could not stand the sight of you. But your mother had a big heart, did she not. Your mother decided that she would always be your mother, that even if you were profoundly worthless and good for *nothing*, she felt obligated to see that you were OK, that you were still taken care of, that your needs were met by others, and so she asked your sister, she asked your sister to please, please, please, always take care of –

"Shut up!!" Paco explodes. "Shut your fucking mouth! You don't say shit like that!" He pounds the passenger car door, his face distorted by rage. As if on cue, Samuel's pager goes off. Paco claps him on the head and pulls at his hair, screaming. Samuel freezes for a moment while Paco beats on him, before flinging his fingers into Paco's eyes. "Shit!" Samuel escapes his grasp, flings opens the door and feeling a twinge in his back, he lurches from the car, erupting into urgent fits of coughing before slamming the door shut. Paco, curiously remains in the car, still cursing, his voice sourly ricocheting off the concrete walls. "You don't talk about someone's mother. And you don't poke people in the eye! You're out a line you weak, hairy motherfucker."

Samuel circles around, facing Paco. "I won't be lectured by you of all people as to how to fight fair. When I return I expect to see no trace of either you nor damage to my car. Otherwise I shall have you arrested. Good evening," and he turns as sharply and as briskly as he can and walks away, ignoring Paco's curses and his own empty threats, managing never to look back.

24. That same Thursday morning

He opens the passenger door for her. "Sorry about the mess". The upholstery is ripped and stale smelling but the cabin is nearly free of clutter - a Thomas Guide, a few scattered cassettes at her feet.

"Oh my God. Your car is immaculate." She gets in. Andy blushes, taking in the length of her legs, blue jeans tight, a round declarative ass. He gets in. "I'm very disappointed," she says. "You let me think there was a mess in here."

"Next time I'll spill some trash in here before inviting you in."

"Or you can ride with me," and she turns to him. "I'll show you a mess." And she smiles flaring her teeth and broad gums, lipstick lightly smeared across them.

"I'll show you all the local pick-ups we have," he clears his throat. "We have to be at all these places before nine. Stuff that goes out every day." Andy shrugs and heads out of the parking lot. "First, we pick up at this corporate travel agency up the street."

Maureen laughs. "So what do you think? Are you really gonna train me on how to pick up pieces of paper and drive them somewhere?"

"Yeah. It's a really easy job, I know."

"Isn't it like the easiest job in the world?"

"Of course it is."

"I love to drive around. Listen to music. Be in control."

"I know, me too. I like it. Too much. I feel like I could do it forever and end up like some of these other guys. Believe it or not, though, there's some things you can do to get things done a lot faster. The faster you pick up and deliver, the more jobs you get, the more mileage you can get paid for."

"What are these cassettes on your floor? Is this music? Do you rock out?"

"Those are mine."

"Yeah, I figured they're yours. What are they? They look funky," she says, rifling through them. "Are they all the same?"

"I recorded them. They're my music."

"Get out! Seriously. You're a musician?"

Andy pulls into the lot on Buckingham Parkway and parks in front of Express Travel Agency. "I moved to L.A just a few weeks ago. I'm hoping to start playing soon, somewhere."

"Cool!"

"Maybe. Sometimes I think it's pretty stupid. Let's go up. I'll introduce you to Corinne."

"Where are we?"

"Express Travel."

"Already?"

"Yeah. We got a bunch of pick-ups around the business park."

"How'd we get here?"

"Are you lost already?"

25. The previous Sunday

The face that looks askance back at him from within the mirror appears as jowly as a deflated rubber ball; clean shaven, washed, freshly cologned, yet a mash of infinitesimal insults, abrasions and purple capillary crashes. He rubs his hand over his face as if to blot away at least a little bit of slack, a modicum of decay. By contrast, the lopsided belvedere of his bald head appears clean and tight, yet somehow obscene, as if it had rudely outgrown its intended purpose. Tim puts on his ochre colored corduroy jacket over his argyle sweater and he inspects himself one last time, pulling at his sleeves and putting on his watch. "Let's went," he quietly says. He grabs his keys, glancing briefly at the framed photo of the little girl who sits by herself on the grass. "Alright, sweetheart. I'll see you later."

∞

"Right on time. Like always."

"I'm not too early?"

"Nah. Come on in and visit. Alice is not out yet. Just you and me. What you got there?"

"A little grape."

Jack inspects the label. He squints. "I can't read it, but it looks very serious." He wears a green print Hawaiian style button down, more than long enough to cover his ample gut. The color TV chatters on about toilet cleaner.

"I'm a serious man and I wanted to get some serious wine. You watchin' the ball game?"

"Huh? Nah, I couldn't find nothin'. " And he picks up the remote and flicks it off. Tim looks at the set, rather wanting to just sit and get lost in front of it, but he says nothing. "Sit down, Tim. You look good. What is this?" Jack asks, fingering the material in Tim's jacket.

"Corduroy."

"Yeah, of course. Nice. Sit down." Tim lowers himself gingerly onto the extreme corner of the couch. "You afraid you gonna fall off?" Tim offers a chuckle. Jack sits in his armchair recliner. "My friend, I got not one, but two gorgeous lovelies coming over here tonight. Brenda and Becky. How you like that? Friends of Alice."

"You mean you didn't just pick them up off the street for me?"

"Both are un-en-cum-bered," he pronounces, as if proud of a new word in his vocabulary. "Brenda and Becky. That's fun to say."

Tim smiles shyly at the floor, tapping his foot. "You mean I'm gonna have to choose?"

"Listen to you. I also invited another friend of mine, who's visiting from out a town. Palm Springs. Jerry Pawlenty. Business acquaintance. Owns a string of auto parts shops that I work with. He's married, so he won't even be any competition for you."

"Who's competing?"

Jack sits back and Tim sees that one of Jack's lower shirt buttons is undone, but at least he's wearing a t-shirt. He decides to say nothing. "Can I get you a drink?"

"Sure."

∞

"Jack, stop fussing and start selling some Japanese cars," Jerry implores. He's an energetic little man who looks a bit like Joey Bishop, Tim decides. "They're gettin' to be super reliable, they sell, they keep their value, and they're easy to get parts for. And guess what. They're startin' to make em right here in the USA."

"Thank you for that advertisement for the Japanese."

"Guys," Alice speaks up. "Do we really need to talk about business at the dinner table?" She sits to Jack's left but Jack seems to ignore her, so it would have made more sense for her to sit next to Tim. And she isn't as big as a house. She is as big as a big, salubrious lady. She talks with her mouth full of food because she seems to have trouble breathing through her nose. It is still Alice, still the same woman and Tim can see her clearly. Still the same brass. "How interesting really can this be for our ladies and for our resident poet?" She means Tim, with no apparent irony.

"Poet," Jack pipes up. "You can read one of his poems and still not even know it."

"Now *that* sounds like poetry," Jerry agrees.

"Why? Because it rhymes?" Tim hears himself say.

"Are you really a poet?" Brenda asks. Her shortness has a truncated, stumpy quality.

"No, I'm really not," Tim says, grateful to deny something somewhat interesting about himself. "I wrote a few poems about my kid," he mumbles this

65

last part...."and also to get me through the war way back, because it could get really long and boring at times."

"I'll bet you seen enough potatoes to last you a life time, Timmy," Jerry offers with a wink and a nudge on the elbow.

"Tim. Everyone calls me Tim."

"He'd sit way atop a big pile of potatoes and write while he's supposed to be peeling or cooking. The CO would come looking for him and would never find him because he'd hide inside a big pile of spuds." Even Alice laughs at this one, revealing a mash of pre-digested food gleaming in her mouth.

"How'd you get inside of there?" Brenda asked, wide eyed.

"Every single word he just said is pure and absolute BS," Tim winks at her. Brenda smiles and laughs herself. "You're a funny man, Jack Roehmer," Tim affirms. "A funny man, everyone."

"Don't take it to heart there, Tim." And Jerry claps him good naturedly on the shoulder.

"I didn't think I was, Jerry," and he lifts his own hand to clop Jerry back but thinks better of it, holding his hand there, wondering if his own hand is bigger.

"Hey Jack," Jerry calls out, mischief in his eyes. "How'd they get so many potatoes across the Pacific?"

"Aw bullshit, Jerry. Tim and I never left Travis air base." And everyone laughs. They eat steak and green beans. And potatoes. Hard to ruin a steak. Tim wonders wryly if the cow he eats knows how good it tastes. But many animals eat other animals. It is always the way, even in the most beautiful, serene of all forests and glades. Big things eat smaller things and are eaten by bigger things. Most living things die by being eaten by something else. But nothing eats us. Right? Except cancer. Except a million forms of bacteria, virus, fungi, and an endless litany of more complex parasites.

"Recite me one of your poems," Brenda smiles.

"Tim - look out for Brenda - she said, recite 'me' one of your poems. Not recite 'us'. We don't even exist."

"Oh you exist alright. You exist." Everyone laughs at this for some reason and it puts Tim in a better mood.

"Have you ever been published?" Brenda continues.

"Oh, God. No. I never even thought about that."

"You should try getting published."

"I should?"

"Sure. Share your work."

"I don't know. It isn't very good."

"Are you being modest with me?"

"No! No Brenda, he's not!" Jack calls out.

"Ah, leave my fellow alone," Alice calls. Leave *my* fellow.

"Well what do you like to read? Which poets?"

66

"Oh…. Well…maybe Tennyson. Robert Frost. Geez. So many." And he smirks at himself, feeling pretentious, when in fact, he is only answering a question. Geez. So many'? Am I such a big poetry scholar? I haven't even picked up a book, much less a pen, in years.

"How about John Wadsworth Spudsfellow?" Jerry offers. Jack suppresses a laugh, nearly loses his food, turning red.

"Can you believe these are grown men?" Alice says to the women. But even she starts to laugh. A little raspy, but still full and solid. Something about her laugh, Tim realizes, reminds him of a woman's full and firm breasts. Her breasts. He blushes.

"Who is John…Spudsfellow?" Becky asks. Jack pounds the table.

"Only the greatest poet who ever lived," Jerry says gravely.

"Oh…You guys. I get it," Becky says, rolling her eyes. She has a long, equine face. Combined with her short, feathered hair, this leaves her with an unpleasantly masculine appearance. "Real funny."

"Go on. Let's hear a poem," Jerry says.

"What?"

"Tell us a poem. You remember one of your own poems?"

"I'd rather not."

"But Brenda asked you to recite a poem. Plus I think we'd all like to hear. Are you gonna turn a lady down like that?"

Tim clears his throat. "You know. It's…it's not the kind of thing that you can just…or that I can just rattle off at the dinner table. Anyway, it's been a long time. Really Alice, why'd you tell everyone I'm a poet?" He tries to throw a good natured wink at her, but he guesses it likely looks like he has a facial tick.

"I know. Let's hear, Ode to a Spud," Jerry declares. Jack busts out laughing. Jerry pulls himself up very straight and proper. To Tim's astonishment, Jerry begins to recite, full throated "Oh, how I love a spud when mashed. Yes, I love them when they're hashed. And….spuds have such great appeal…that I love to sit ….and peel!"

Everyone bursts out laughing, if only to be in on the something that others find funny. "Funny guys. Jack, a real comedian this one here."

"Wait, wait," Alice says, her eyes squinted shut from laughter. She continues to laugh out loud at her own private joke. But with Alice, Tim thinks, she's never showing off. Even when she's the center of attention, she never shows off. She's just, well, being Alice, having a good time, laughing because she's laughing. Never because she's trying to impress anyone. "Wait! There's another line. What was that about liking spuds when they're mashed or hashed? OK," and she descends into laughter again, happy with herself. "OK and the last line is. 'But most of all, I love to eat them raw when I am…*smashed*!" And although everyone laughs in polite sympathy - for the moment has already peaked - Alice is completely overwrought, caught up with the poignancy of her own private hilarity, sometimes quaking silent, often bursting out loud with it.

"Oh....that's just so ridiculous." After a few more moments she begins to slow and to catch her breath. "Of course that is so stupid. But I can't help thinking of poor Tim, all serious, with a book by Shakespeare at his side, sitting......ahahaha... sitting on top of a great pile of potatoes, like he's The Thinker, or whoever that statue is..... and this is his Masterpiece, and he's so proud," and she descends again into great waves of hysterical peels of raucous laughter. Tim looks at her and smiles and relaxes and moderately enjoys the rest of the evening.

26. Thursday night

At the end of his shift, reluctant to walk back to his car and deal with whatever he might find in there, Samuel walks instead back to pediatrics, to room 2055. The music plays now quite loudly deep inside his head; Vaughan Williams' Third symphony, this time the final movement, which he always hears when he feels especially sad and futile. The room is ajar. He turns to wave at Donna, but there's no one there. He listens to Perry's soothing, soft voice, to the hopeful sound of his son yawning, followed by a giggle. Reluctantly, Samuel taps on the door. "Come in," Perry calls quietly.

"Come in," follows Guillaume in his high little reed voice.

"Ah. It's you!" Perry welcomes in his stage whisper. "I hoped you might come back." And he gets up to greet him, taking him by the elbow to lead him outside.

"You did?"

"Are you OK?"

"I'm fine."

"Well, you look a little stressed."

From inside, the boy insists. "Papa. Come back."

"I can't tell you how tired I am. It's not been good." Guillaume calls out again, more insistent. "I'll be right in, baby," he calls.

"Papa. I want you to come now!"

"I'll be right there." Guillaume continues to call out for Perry, rapidly becoming increasingly distressed.

"Well let's go in, of course," Samuel says.

"No, Mr. Samuel, only for a moment." Suddenly Guillaume appears at the door. "Baby. Did you pull your monitor out?" And he speaks with gentle urgency in Spanish. He picks up his son and holds him and rocks him the while he speaks to Samuel. The boy looks too large to be held like that. To his chagrin, Samuel finds he is vaguely envious of the boy. "Have you seen my brother-in-law, anywhere? I don't know if you remember, he was in the room and left after you came in."

"I believe I saw that same young man smoking in the downstairs garage, while I was on my break."

"I'm surprised he didn't go back with Lorena. He likes you."

"I beg your pardon."

"My son. He seems to really like you. He's very calm now." Indeed, Guillaume stares and smiles at Samuel, extending his hand, then putting it in his mouth. On the whole, he seems emotionally younger than three.

Samuel smiles. "Hello there young man. You've had quite the ordeal today."

"He seems to understand you."

Guillaume lights up. "He's a bear, papa. A funny bear."

Perry and Samuel both laugh. "Baby, is that a nice thing to say to my friend, Mr. Samuel?"

"Yes," the boy impishly giggles.

"Yes, indeed. I agree to all of that," Samuel affirms.

"Do you want to see my dinosaur?"

"Dinosaur? You have a dinosaur? How extraordinary. And that's quite a word, too, you know."

The boy giggles. "You talk silly."

"Guillaume. That's not very nice," Perry gently chides. "He loves and knows all about his dinosaurs."

"But it's very true. I do talk very silly, indeed."

"I like how you talk," Guillaume says

"Do I speak in a manner that's easy enough to understand? Some people think I speak in complete gibberish." In response, Guillaume extends out to him a small plastic dinosaur, glistening with sputum.

"I'm putting you down, big boy," Perry says.

Samuel squints at the toy, leaning towards Guillaume. "Ah, let me see what you have there." The boy holds out the toy, a squat, two inch, plate backed monster with a great hood crowning its savage face. "Indeed. That, young man that you have right there is none other than a Triceratops."

"Oh," Perry responds. "Can you say triceratops, Guillaume?"

"Tritheratopth." Samuel smiles and puts his hand out to further inspect the toy. Gravely, he assesses and nods his approval, squinting and viewing the object from several angles. Then he returns it to the boy, who patiently waits for it.

"Fascinating."

"Mr Samuel."

"Yessir," Samuel wipes his hands on his scrub pants.

"Are you working tomorrow?"

"Not until ten now. He cut my hours. A curious response to the expected deluge of new clients who will be calling us frantically for many urgent, important deliveries to far flung realms of their empires. Two more hours to brood in my cave, cringing from the morning sun like some wounded bat." He notices Perry's quizzical look and hopes his friend does not take his ramblings amiss.

"I'm supposed to start at eight. But I have to be right here tomorrow at the same time."

"I shall gladly cover for you. If he'll let me. And he will."

"Thank you. *Guillaume.* Please play inside the room for just a few more minutes."

Guillaume bites lightly and approvingly into his little dinosaur. "Will you tell me a story?"

"We shall see."

"No, I meant the bear man. Will you tell me a story?"

"I should be so honored," Samuel responds, to his own surprise.

Guillaume laughs and goes inside but sticks his head out, smiling, his mangle tooth smile. "You talk funny."

"Guillaume. That's enough," Perry said. "Mr. Samuel doesn't like to be told he talks funny."

To Samuel's delight, the boy just giggles and repeats, "He talks funny." And he disappears, still giggling.

"Perry, you have to agree that your son has certainly earned the right to have something to smile and laugh about with all he's been through today."

"Yes of course. But I don't want him to get into bad habits around others who might not understand. You know, when a puppy first begs for dinner scraps, everyone thinks it's very funny. But after awhile, no one wants that at all."

"Well. I suppose."

"Besides, I'm beginning to lose my patience with him. I feel like I'm a bad person for saying this….. He's a wonderful little boy, but….."

"He's a little needy right now. Wouldn't you say that's more than to be expected for a three year old who's had a very strange day in a strange place. And what you're feeling too is also perfectly normal as well, I assure you."

"Mr. Samuel, I need another favor from you. A really big one, I'm sorry."

"Tell me, please."

"I feel like I'm a bad father for even asking you this…"

"Say no more. Shall I stay with your son for a bit while you get some sleep? In your car."

"You will! I will be back in just a few hours. I trust you, Mr. Samuel."

"I worry though that the effect I seem to have on your son will not be sufficient for him to notice that neither you nor his mother are here."

Perry thinks about this a moment. "I know. Maybe it won't even work."

"I shall stay and tell your son a story. It wouldn't be the first time I've put someone to sleep with a story. And while I am doing that, you shall sleep on a cot. We'll get you a cot!"

"A cot?"

"A bed. A small bed that folds out."

"Mr. Samuel, I tried already to get such a thing and they told me they didn't have any."

"I assure you. We do."

"Well why did they tell me they don't?"

"Not everyone knows where all of them are. Or bothers to look."

"You know where it is?"

"I know where everything is."

27. That same Thursday - the work day

Maureen strides into the client's office, jeans tight, hair loose. She asks to speak to the executive named on the package, insisting against all necessity that she hand the package directly to such person. Andy is mortified then astonished when the receptionist calls the executive, more so when the partner comes to receive his package and dumbfounded when Maureen introduces herself, insisting that it is her pleasure to make sure that he is completely satisfied with her service.

"That was impressive."

"I was just being nice. And enjoying myself."

"You act like you own ZZZZAP!"

"Isn't that what we're supposed to do?"

"It's taking longer you know this way. We just need to drop off and pick up and smile. You're making it much harder than it has to be."

"It's not hard at all."

"Yes it is," Andy says, contemplating his growing desire for her. They visit warehouses, laboratories, and government offices as well as high rise corporate suites. If the clerk or receptionist refuses to call the executive, Maureen never insists, yet consistently charms "That's a beautiful necklace you're wearing today'" Andy repeats, as they get into the car and drive to the next client.

She smile. "*Shut* up. Do I sound like that?"

"No. You sound much better than I just did.....Thank you so much for your business Mrs. Schicklegruber. May I say, that's a spectacular pimple you have on your nose. You should be very proud.'"

"Shut *up*!" And she leans back in the seat, at apparent ease with herself and the world.

"You should sell real estate."

"I'm gonna be a nurse."

"Really? That's cool."

"I'm studying to get my EMT first. Like in an ambulance. Then I'll work in an ER." She snaps her fingers.

"Makes perfect sense."

"Doesn't it?" Andy grins at her. "What?" She laughs. "Oh what is it now?"

He thrusts his chest out, bellowing, "Hello ma'am. Just relax and we'll take outstanding care of you. And may I say, that's a glorious abscess you have oozing from your neck. You should be very proud."

28.   Thursday night

"Guillaume. The nurse already told you not to do that. Please lie down. Aren't you tired?"

"Where's mama? Is mama coming back?"

"Mama is with you all day tomorrow," Perry affirms in his stage whisper. Lorena had arranged to take the day off. "She's sleeping now. You should be sleeping now."

"I don't like it here. I wanna go home," he says, unhappy again, his face beginning to crumple at the renewed awareness of his dismal and unfamiliar surroundings.

Samuel steps towards Guillaume and offers in stentorian tones, "Indeed. I am not so inclined towards this repository myself. But together we shall light a fire of enchantment to illuminate and transform the gloom."

Guillaume at once brightens and giggles. But he also begins jumping on the bed again. "Funny bear! Funny bear!" he chants with delight. "Silly, funny bear!"

"Baby, settle down." And Perry rubs his shoulder and gives him another toy from a little canvas bag. "Mr. Samuel. What did you just say? Just now?"

"I barely know myself. But whatever it was, your son seems to understand."

"Listen to your Tio Samuel. He's going to tell you a story."

Guillaume remembers that he wants nothing more, not even mama. The Teddy Bear man. "Are you ready good sir, Guillaume?" the bear speaks to him.

"Yeth!"

"This is quite a tale. Are you sure you are quite prepared?"

"Yeth!" And the boy bounces his head up and down.

"Do you have to go pee pee?" Perry asks from his cot.

"No!" Guillaume insists.

"You remember now," and Samuel puts a didactic finger in the air. "You must lie back now. You musn't stand up. You can stretch if you need to. You may yawn, of course. You may even sleep."

"I don't wanna sleep. I wanna story!"

Clever boy. "Of course. And a story you shall have, a tale that shall dwarf the epic of Scheherazade." Samuel rubs his chin, aware that he has no earthly idea of what he is going to say.

"Listen to Mr. Samuel," Perry calls needlessly from his cot, his voice already weakening as his own limbs go heavy.

Once upon a time - for all great tales begin in this way - there lived a young prince; a most brilliant, brave, and happy prince.

"Did he have a dinothaur?"

"Yes. Indeed he did? You're very perceptive, young man."

"What kind?"

"Well. It was that most faithful and stalwart of breeds, the noble triceratops." At this, Guillaume looks at the plastic toys on his bed, but the triceratops is nowhere to be found. Samuel, sensing an impending crisis, looks down at his feet and is fantastically relieved to see the little toy lying on its side. "One moment please. I shall return presently with this very thing. I promise."

"Tritheratopth!" the boy cries out. Samuel washes the plastic creature in the sink before Guillaume can insert it back into his mouth. "Tritheratopth!"

"Shhhhh!" comes his father's voice, having been awakened.

"Here we are, Master Guillaume. Your triceratops. The very thing. Now please, let us continue."

Our prince rode out every day on his trusted steed, the loyal triceratops.

"What color was it?"

"Please, Master Guillaume, there is so much to tell that I fear I shall barely get through it. I assure you, the color is faithfully created already in your fecund imagination."

"What color was it?"

"Green and blue," he says, remembering the color of the toy.

"Yeth!"

They rode out far and wide every morning, surveying the magical, primeval forest.

"What was his name?"

"His name?"

"What was *his* name?" says Guillaume, holding up the triceratops.

"Well.....I believe his name was....*Guillaume*, in fact. Yes, it's true."

"That's my name."

"Of course it is. Now listen closely. Please," Samuel advises, praying that the story will reveal itself to him.

And might I add, the Prince himself, his name was William. And so Prince William and his best friend, Guillaume - yes, they were best friends - lived in the enchanted forest, which was trillions of years old, and shrouded in mists, which were far older still. I shall tell you just about just one of their many adventures. It was a glorious spring day and the two rode out into a lonely part of the forest, with thick hanging vines and a good many hollowed out and fallen trees, each one larger than the tallest buildings on earth. Most often, William was able to climb under these obstacles, but when he could not, his friend Guillaume took him upon his back and easily climbed over them, for Guillaume was nearly thirty feet long and was very mighty indeed. And so they came along together until they saw a faint light glowing from inside one of the ancient hollows. And it was William who called out, "Who dwells yonder in this humble hollow?" But no one answered. But there was a light, dim yet unmistakable. And William sensed there might be someone in need of assistance, for he was a good and kindly prince. "I say. Who dwells within? Will you answer me? You have nothing to fear and I will let you go in peace if only you will assure me that all is well with you. You have nothing to fear from Guillaume. He is here to protect us both."

Guillaume giggles and pulls the blanket up over his head, giggling and thrashing his feet with contentment. "I'm a tritheratopth!" he shouts.

"Shhhhh!" says Samuel. Guillaume frowns and shushes Samuel back. "I'm so sorry to shush you, Guillaume, but your father is sleeping. Do you understand? Shall I continue?" The boy nods and settles down.

"You need not show yourself, nor even speak aloud. But so that Guillaume and I might know that you are neither sick nor injured or hungry or lost, perhaps you might signal me whether you are well, by blinking your lantern for me. If you are distressed in any way, blink once. If you are well, blink twice." They waited. Just as they began to believe that no one was really there, the light went briefly dark, but immediately reappeared. "I see your light blinked once. You need help. Shall we approach you then? Blink once for Yes and two for No." This time there were two blinks. "Well how can we help you then? Oh blast!" William said to Guillaume. "I can only ask Yes or No questions. But what shall I ask?" Now Guillaume the triceratops could not speak per se, but there was still a strong communication between the two and after a moment of looking into the eyes of his friend, William said, "Thank you, friend. I believe I know how I shall proceed." And so he turns back to the hollow and says, "Would you feel more at ease if I were to play for you a little music?" Without waiting for a response, Prince William picked up his recorder and began to play. At first, only a few stray notes would emerge, but then, there it was. It was a melody strange and wonderful. As William found his way and Guillaume purred his assent, the melody emerged stronger; yearning, rising and falling until it finally resolves itself into a moment deeper than joy - a sad satisfaction, a completeness. Even Guillaume seemed stunned.

Suddenly a voice hailed them from the hollow of the tree, the voice of a very old man. "Wait. Please wait. It is only I, an old man; your humble servant. I was watching you. I am sorry that I was still afraid. Did this music truly come from you, young man?"

William laughed, "Indeed it did. Do you live here? Or are you lost?"

"Both, my prince," said the old man, for he certainly recognized him for the prince that he was. "I am profoundly lost indeed and have lived here inside this hollow for so long now that I can barely remember my life before."

"Let us take you away from here, straight away." And the prince took a few steps towards the old man.

"Ah, I wish it were all as simple as that. Let me explain. You see, I have been living under a spell, my lord."

Guillaume yawns curling his fingers and smacking his tongue and lips in soporific contentment, eyes closed. Samuel silently mouths the words, 'and so they lived happily ever after'. Guillaume's eyes open wide again. "More story," he insists, although in a whisper. "What happens?"

"My goodness. I was just taking a breath. Yes, Master Guillaume, we shall continue."

"More story," he says again.

"Do you understand it?"

"Guillaume is helping an old man."

"Yes. Exactly right. Guillaume and Prince William."

"And there's a magic bear."

"A magic bear?"

"Like you."

"OK," Samuel smiles. "Yes, we shall meet him soon as well. Very soon."

"Story."

"Very well, my friend. Very well."

29. Thursday Night

"Relax, Maxie. I'll get you a beer."

"OK," Max warily agrees, stepping back from the apparent tangle and mass of loud, meaty homo-sapiens crowding around the bar. The room reverberates with nonsensical cankers of human speech, spiked with menacing laughter, tattoos and facial rings, trench coats, hairy knuckles and beard stubble.

"Maxie! Here," and Rolfe hands him a green bottle. "Bottoms up," and he clinks his bottle against Max's and winks at him. "Just try a little bit. It won't hurt you."

For the first time that he can recall, Max feels safer with Rolfe than he does with anyone or anything else in the room. As long as I just look at Rolfe, I'll be OK, he thinks, pushing away the apparent possibility that someone or something might smash a chair over his head for no reason at all. "Alright," Max agrees. He takes a sip and it assaults him with its alien, bitter taste.

"You like it?"

"Maybe. I don't know."

"Max, have you ever been in a bar fight?"

"What?"

"Ever been in a bar fight?"

"No."

"Have you ever thrown anybody through a window?"

"No!"

"Ever been thrown through a window!"

"No, Rolfe. What are you talking about?"

"You don't know what you're missing."

"What?"

"I'm just kidding, Max. You'll be fine."

"I will?"

"Yes, Max, you will. You're safe. You're with me. Alright?"

"That's right."

"Keep drinking, though. You'll find out what everybody else knows." Curious, Max takes another sip. He finds it slightly more tolerable. Then another. Maybe it would go well with a chunk of cheese. "I'm taking you, my new best friend to dinner tonight. You'll see that beer goes well with steak. We'll eat well and then we'll meet some women."

"What?"

"I'll meet them but you can take them all home."

"What do you mean?"

"You're lucky I'm already married to a beautiful woman. Or I would have them all."

"Thanks. But I don't like this place. I'd like to go now."

"We just got here."

"This place is angry, Rolfe. It's angry and I want to go."

Rolfe looks at Max and nods. "Alright, Max. Let me just finish this one drink."

"Am I your new best friend?"

"Well, I guess you are tonight."

30. The same Thursday - during the day

"So what do we do now?" she asks

"We wait."

"For what?"

"For Mikros to page me with another pick up."

"You wait right here?"

"Almost every day."

"Let's get outside!"

Andy opens his door. "Yes, ma'am....." They both get out and stretch. They are parked in a narrow strip of cement lot overlooking a great stretch of grass.

"This is nice. What is this place?"

"Rancho Park."

"I have no idea where we are."

"I know. Maureen, you realize that in order to charm the clients, you actually have to find them."

"I'll find them. I promise!" she laughs.

"Tim is going to be very serious compared to me. Good luck with him this afternoon."

"Which one was he? Is he the old man?"

"Which one? There's two of them."

"Is he the bald one? The one who looks like a troll? Or is he the one who looks like a mummy of Sasquatch."

Andy laughs. "That's Samuel. Little Big Foot, if you like. Tim is the elf." He wants to grab Maureen and kiss her big fat juicy lips.

"OK. That's how I'll keep them straight!"

"They're both mythical creatures."

"They're not real?"

"Tim is real. He's very real." He catches up to her as she ambles through an empty ball field towards the trees.

"Will he like me?"

"Only if you call him an elf to his face." She laughs. "He loves that. *Loves* it!"

"I'll be sure to do that. So why are we here at the park?"

"Century City is across the street. We get lots of pick-ups from there in the afternoon. This is my favorite part of the day, hanging out here."

"Are you here very long?"

"Not long enough."

"Don't you want to make money?"

"Yes. But I also like sitting on my ass playing my guitar in the park. Staring into space. Once, I was here nearly all afternoon. I still got paid. So I'm a professional guitar player."

"Let's turn around. You are going to play for me right now."

"Sure." They turn back to the truck.

"He seems lonely."

"Tim?"

"There's like some great sadness in his life."

"I think that's true for a lot of these guys. I think they're all just a little grateful that they're not mining coal or pressing garments or working in a rendering factory."

"What's that?"

"A rendering factory? I used to work in one. For almost two weeks. You process all day long the parts of butchered animals that go to make sausage or even non-edible uses, like fertilizer. You're covered in blood and stench all day long. Covered in shit really."

"I'm so glad I don't eat meat. Why did you work there?"

"I needed a job. And I knew I wouldn't be there long."

"So tell me about the guitar. Is it just a hobby? Or something more."

"It's why I'm here in L.A., along with thousands of other losers."

"Well. Are you good?"

"It takes more than being good." He smiles and shrugs.

"Sure. But are you *good*?"

"I'm all right."

"Do you love it?"

"Playing and making music? It's my life. It's what I have to do. I'm probably unfit for anything else."

"Then you have to do it."

"I'm having difficulty getting started. Playing in clubs I mean."

"Play for me." He reaches for the guitar and they sit on the edge of the bed of his truck. Instead of one of his own compositions, he plays a simple piece by Mississippi John Hurt, fingering every note in its happy rhythm as the melody and counterpoint thump along. He increases the time, whirling the melody. Hearing his pager going off, Andy changes key to match the page and twirls on a thumping waltz before crash landing on its final strum. Maureen looks at him, her head cocked slightly to the side. "I knew it," she says in a low voice. "I just knew it."

"Tell me," he says, a little anxious. Is she disappointed? Or worse yet, mildly pleased?

"You're a fucking genius. Aren't you?"

31. Wednesday night (2 days before…)

Tim finds the remote and flips on the television set, scanning the channels for a baseball game or a boxing match. A commercial comes on; happy, enthusiastic young people at work, at play, at school, all together, sharing the common purpose of extolling their favorite beverage, uniting their voices which ring out as at a white revival meeting. 'Join the celebration…feeling free…feeling freeeeee…" He gets up and finds himself a can of beer.

"Feeling free, eh?" He puts the beer on his ring stained end table and promptly forgets about it. The news cuts away to coverage of growing famine in Ethiopia, including the now familiar tragic sight of emaciated naked children, crater eyed, on the verge of crushing death. The phone rings. "Hello," he answers, "Are you my secret admirer?"

After a moment of silence, during which Tim dares to hope that his daughter is on the line, a familiar voice calls out to him. "Tim! How did you know it was me?"

"Alice?"

"Who were you expecting?"

"I've been getting these hang ups on my machine every once in a while. Did you call and not leave a message?"

"You know, I might have called once and got interrupted, but it sounds like you've gotten a few."

"You called once before?"

"Only once. Do you think you might have a stalker? A jilted honey maybe?"

"Yeah, I'm a regular Casanova, for sure. Is everything OK?"

"It was good to see you over for dinner last Friday."

"Are you kidding? It was a hoot and a half seeing you, my dear."

She laughs. "You're a hoot and a half."

"I don't know. I'm half a hoot, and half coot."

"Ha, ha. You are not."

"And a dollar short and a day early, or something like that, whatever the hell that even means."

"So I was gonna ask how things were going with Brenda. But I hear you haven't even called her yet."

"Brenda. I don't know. She's OK, but…You know, we hardly even said a word to each other."

"She gave you her number, what do you want?"

"I don't know why."

"She probably wants to hear you recite her a poem."

"She's better off going to the library. What are you doing? Checking upon on me?"

"Maybe. Just a little."

"Are you OK? Is Jack OK?"

"Everyone's OK, Tim. Especially Jack."

"Especially?"

There's a breathless pause at the end of the line before she asks him, "Tim, how long have you and Jack been friends?"

"How long? Ah, since we met during the war. Nineteen forty four I think it was. That's forty one years."

"That's a long time. Years before I even knew him."

"It sure is. A whole life time it is."

"Jack's your best friend, isn't he?"

"Jack's my only friend. But I guess even that's not saying much," he adds, hoping he sounds good humored. "I mean, I know some guys I'm friendly with at the deli, I see 'em there all the time after work and all…."

"What was he like when you met him, Jack?"

"What was he like? He was exactly how he is right now. That's what he was like. I never saw a man change so little."

"Wasn't he a real player, Tim? With all the ladies. You know what I mean."

"Was he a player? Sure he was. So what? That's ancient history." Silence as he simmers in the lie that's couched in technical fact. "Come on girl, where'd you go?" Then he hears it, the wet sniffling and her breathless exhale that tells him this is going to be a long and very messy conversation.

32. Thursday night

The house is dark and empty downstairs. A lone blue light glows on the top floor, no doubt a television playing. They enter the pantry near his bathroom.

"This is nice," she says.

"How do you know? It's dark," he says in a stage whisper.

"So? It's a big house."

"Shhhh. Keep your voice down."

"Why are you telling me that?"

"I mean, *please*, keep your voice down."

"Are you breaking into your own house?" But she too speaks in a whisper.

"I don't like my roommates. And I don't like them knowing my business. There might even be people sleeping downstairs. They bring people all the time."

"Where's your room?"

"I'll show you. Wait; let me show you the bathroom. It's right here. Let me just check." And he finds the little door, turns on the light and peeks inside. Apart from a little sand on the floor and a dirty bar of soap it looks better than usual. God *Damnit!* There's a black pubic hair etched inside the soap. Eugene scans beneath the sink, hoping to find an extra bar. He fusses with what to do, the while vividly envisioning himself puking upon each of his roommates one by one, wrenching them each from their sleep with his righteous wrath, their piteous, agonized cries of contrition falling upon deaf and merciless ears as he wretches out every last acidic drop of outrage upon them. Indeed, the pubic hair had nauseated him and the fact that he would have to remove the hair himself flushes him red with fury. "I'll be right there, Caroline," he calls out. In his mind's eye the entire house is burning with his roommates and all their little friends trapped in flames, while he and Caroline eat Cheetos and shrug. "Talk as much as you want. You don't have to whisper. I don't give a shit who hears us."

33. Thursday night

"I feel kind of light, like my head is not really attached to my body. Something like that."

"Good. I'll tell you when to stop. So you're head doesn't fall off."

"Oh, that's funny," Max says, and smiles.

"You know, I've never actually seen you laugh, Maxie."

Max shrugs. "Sometimes I laugh."

"Are you happy now?"

"Mmmh. I'm a little scared. I'm kind of excited."

"There's nothing to be scared of."

"This place is very pretty and nice. I like it so much better than that other one."

"This hotel is where a lot of high end business people come to play and make deals. You never know who you might meet here."

Max nods and smiles. "I like this bread a lot."

Rolfe scans the elegant mirror riveted bar; men in sport coats and turtlenecks, women in short black dresses. "Would you like to meet one of those women at the bar, Max?"

Max shakes his head. "No thanks. I don't think so."

Rolfe beams at him. "There must be some women you like here."

"I like women," is all Max says. It occurs to Rolfe that Max might be gay. The waiter arrives, black shirt, white tie.

"Have you gentlemen decided what you want to order?"

"We're ready. Max, go ahead."

"Ok. I'd like…. A potato."

"A potato?

"Yes, please."

"A baked potato?"

"Sure."

"Sour cream, butter, chives."

"On the side."

"Very well. Anything else for you sir? Anything at all?"

"And a side of French fries, please?" Rolfe marvels at the waiter's stoic professionalism.

"And what about for you, sir?" The waiter is done with Max.

"I'll have the prime rib, medium rare, baked potato with everything, Caesar salad to start. Two house merlots."

"Very good. So that's one baked potato, everything on the side, with a side of French fries, and for you...." And the waiter completes his recitation and leaves.

"I've never heard of having a baked potato with a side of French fries before."

"It's good. You can have some if you want."

"Do you only eat potatoes?"

He shrugs. "I don't know. Sometimes. I like them. What shall we talk about?"

"Where are you from, Max?"

"Idaho."

"Of course."

"It's beautiful there. We lived in the farming part."

"And you grew potatoes?"

"Sometimes. I grew up with different families."

"You grew up with different families?"

"Well, my mom and dad couldn't take care of me. Sometimes I lived with my grandmother. Sometimes my uncle. Sometimes with other people."

"I didn't know that. That sounds kind of sad. Was that rough?"

"Sometimes. Not always. People left me alone."

"What about in school. Did you have friends?"

"Maybe. I kept to myself a lot. Can we talk about something else?"

"What makes you happy, Max?"

"That's easy. Animals. I'd like to have a pet, but they don't allow any in my building. Sometimes I leave food for some stray kitty cats. I like to go to the zoo when I can. I like to go to petting zoos. They have goats. They're so sweet. I like to think about anteaters."

"I have a cat."

"You do! What's his name?"

"Taxi."

"His name is Taxi?"

"Yeah. My wife's idea. Tanya thought it would be cute to call out, 'Taxi! Taxi!' like she's calling for a cab in New York City."

"Are you from New York?"

"I was born in Stuttgart, a city in West Germany. I lived there until I was twenty two."

"Oh. That's far away, huh. So you speak German?"

"Yes, Max….I speak German." Rolfe smiled. "Really, Maxie. Did you think I was a dumb mute or something until I came to America?"

"You speak English very well."

"Thank you. We all learn English in school."

"I don't know any German."

"I'll teach you some maybe."

"OK. Is it hard to learn?"

"I wouldn't know." Rolfe tears into a piece of bread.

"Tell me more about Taxi?"

"There's nothing to tell. He's a cat." Rolfe smiles to himself with a new thought. "Tell me, Max. Just out of curiosity….. Do you believe in God?"

"God?"

"I'm just…you know. Curious," Rolfe gives him a half smile. "You just seem like someone who would believe in God."

"I don't know. Should I? Do you believe in God?"

"No, I think it's ridiculous."

"That sounds kind of sad."

"Does it? What about you?"

"I don't know. I don't know what I believe."

"Really. You don't know. I thought you would know."

"I haven't thought about it in a while."

"That surprises me. You don't have power or ambition to distract you. Or sex. You might make a great priest."

"You think so?"

"It sounded like I just said priests aren't distracted by ambition or sex. But I don't know about that."

"You think I should become a priest?"

"You should think about it. Me. I can't believe in any of that stuff. It's all nonsense to me. But it comforts a lot of people."

The waiter arrives with the food. "Prime rib, medium rare. And…baked potato, everything on the side, with a side of fries. I'll bring some ketchup."

Rolfe indeed seems to enjoy talking while eating, wagging his fork around to make his point. "So Maxie, do you like the wine?"

"Yes, much better than the beer."

"Are you feeling it, Maxie?"

"I kind of like it now when you call me Maxie."

"I do, too," he says, pouring himself another glass. "So you should give it some more thought."

"Give what some more thought?"

"I think you should think a great deal about Jesus Christ and ask yourself if you could believe in him."

"I heard a lot about Jesus when I was a kid. I didn't know much, but I was scared of him."

"Scared! How could anyone be scared of Jesus? How could you be scared of sweet little baby Jesus?" Rolfe insists, talking about the Christ as if he were a puppy. "He looks after people just like you."

"But he also sends people to Hell. Doesn't he? I don't know. I kind of blocked all that stuff out."

"Hell...that's all nonsense. All of it."

"That's what I heard people talking about. Going to Hell. Especially in my family and in some of the families I stayed with. That we were all going to Hell."

"Well, we all quite possibly are. But not if your good friend Jesus has anything to say about it."

"Well then who is it who sends people to Hell?"

"No one does. We send ourselves there. We send each other there. Jesus has nothing to do with all of that."

"You sound very sure about that."

"Quite sure. Have you read the bible?"

"A little. I like the Noah's ark story. Have you read it?"

"Parts of it. Hell's just something the church put in there to keep us all in line."

Max thinks for a moment. "Well why don't you believe in Jesus?"

"Jesus, Buddha, Allah, Jehovah, it's all a fairy tale I think. Something to give us a noble, impersonal reason to kill and conquer each other. "

"Wow. But you think that *I* should believe in Jesus?"

"Think about it. Do a little research."

"But why?"

"Because...I'll tell you" and here Rolfe descends once more into confusing Jesus with an excitable new born puppy. "Because he's so sweet, so sweet, the little baby Jesus. The little bitty, cuddly, itty bitty, teeny weeny, teeny tiny sweet baby Jesus in his little teeny tiny manger." To his surprise, Max laughs out loud, a more forceful trumpeting sound than Rolfe would have imagined.

"You look so funny talking about baby Jesus like that."

Rolfe laughs, too. "Seriously, someone had to wipe clean the baby Jesus, all his poop and crap and everything." Max laughs again. "Right? Are you enjoying your potato?" Rolfe cuts another large bite of bloody meat.

"Yes, I am," Max affirms. "But are you serious though?"

"About Jesus? And you?"

"Yes. About Jesus and me."

Rolfe thinks about it. "Yes. I am. Just because I don't believe in it, don't be discouraged my little Maxie. Maybe you'll find something there that I can't see."

"You really think so?"

Rolfe holds the glass to his lips and gives Max a careful look. "Yes...I really, really think so. It won't change anything for me, but it might help you. Just don't try to preach to me once you've found him."

"Okay."

"Promise?"

"I promise."

"Just go and make friends with Jesus and see how you like it."

"That sounds nice. Maybe I will. How would I do that?"

"You'll figure it out, Maxie. You're probably very smart when it comes to things like that." Max seems to beam at this unexpected compliment. "Go to church. Talk to a priest. Read the bible. Or...here's a much better idea; screw all that other stuff and just start talking to him. I hear anyone can do that."

"Just start talking to him?"

"Wouldn't that be nice? Find a picture or something, or just in your head. There's lots of pictures of Jesus, too. He usually looks very nice and sweet."

"I appreciate that Rolfe."

"Sure. Shall we order some more wine, Max?"

"Call me Maxie."

34. Thursday Night

"You can sleep on the couch if you want. Or you could sleep in my room. Whatever you want?"

"I don't want to sleep alone in this strange house."

Of course this is what he hopes she would say. "You can sleep in my room. I don't know if it's very comfortable. I only have, you know, the one mattress. It's not even a bed really."

"You don't even have a bed?"

Eugene had not expected to be challenged thusly by a homeless girl. "No. I sleep OK though. I can find extra blankets. Extra pillows. I know where they keep that stuff for everyone that comes in and out."

"Extra pillows," she says, as if he had offered her doughnuts, he thinks.

"I'll go look." And he rushes off to find what larder his roommates have stored in the downstairs closet. Moonlight pours in through the un-curtained window. Somehow the contents look more dreary in the bare bulb light. He finds some bath towels and takes several of these, unclear as to how he might use them. After all these months of suffering his roommates and their whores fouling up his bathroom, he had at least as much right as any stranger on the street with a warm pussy and a propensity to smoke weed, to help himself to a communal towel or two. And then he sees it. Hanging there on the side rail, next to some

85

foul black sweatshirt, he sees a terry-cloth white robe, no doubt stolen from some hotel, Eugene imagines. There on the floor to his amazement are soft, puffy slippers, clearly a woman's. "Caroline," he calls to her. "I have some things for you to wear. For after your shower."

"Ah good. Where did you get them?"

"Who cares? Here. I'll show you where you can shower and then after, I have a robe and some slippers for you."

"Really? That's great." And they make their way back to the pantry. He places everything on the washer.

"You have a washer and dryer?"

"Yes. But I never get to use it. It's always being used."

"Can we use it tonight?"

"Tonight? Sure. You wanna wash your things while you're in the shower?"

"I'll take care of it. Yes, I'll take my shower now. Is it hot?"

"Yes. You want me to show you?"

"I can figure it out. You go make up the bed."

"OK. Yes, I'll go do that."

"Eugene. Come here."

"OK." And he approaches Caroline who leans in and kisses him on the mouth. "In a few minutes, I'll be all nice and clean for you."

"OK. OK."

"Where's your room?"

"Well. It's down there."

"In the basement?"

"It's not much. Do you need anything else?"

"No darling."

35. Thursday afternoon

They had spent the last uncounted minutes trading stories about bad dreams and creepy diners. "What are you doing tonight?" she suddenly asks.

"Is it possible that I might be hanging out with you?"

"It *is* possible. I know a place. It's a weird little club in Hollywood."

"Of course you do. I've been to a few of those."

"You're probably going about this all wrong."

"You're probably right. I've seen you in action. I want you as my agent."

"Are you going to let me listen to those cassettes?"

"We have all afternoon." The wind picks up and the trees begin to hiss. "Or maybe not," he adds. He recognizes Tim's dun colored hatch back, an odd and indecisively designed car. "Quick, it's Tim! He's coming!" Andy says with mock apprehension. "When and where do we meet up with each other?"

"Eight o'clock. I think I know how to find you."

Tim pulls up alongside the driver side of Andy's pick up, murmurs of gravel flecking at his tires. He cuts the engine and leans out across the passenger seat, "Hey Toben. Don't you answer your pager no more?"

"Hey Tim. I'm sorry about that. Did the office send you all the way out here just to see if I was OK?"

Tim gets out of the car, putting a hand on his lower back, "You think this is all a joke? Well. Maybe it is, but it's still my livelihood. Anyway, they were only gonna tell you to wait here for me. But then they had to call me back and tell me to hurry, the geniuses."

"Maybe one day we'll all have phones in our pockets."

"Yeah, well maybe one day you'll return your pages on time."

"So what are we doing?"

"I'm headed downtown. Lucky me. Give me everything you got goin' that way. And while you're at it, hand over your girlfriend there as well. Looks like I get to baby sit her this afternoon."

Maureen scrambles down from the truck. She wipes her hands and then sticks her right arm out, fingers splayed, "Hi Tim. I'm Maureen. Andy has really been saying how great and knowledgeable you are. So I'll look forward to learning a lot from you today." And she flashes her inordinate sized teeth at him. Andy avoids eye contact so as not to double over laughing.

Tim looks at the hand, then shakes it once. He scratches his ear. "Just don't learn your way out of my job," he says, as if to himself. Andy puts the undelivered packets on the hood of Tim's car, who quickly sorts them out. "Alright, boys and girls," he says, sighing.

"Let's went?" Andy offers.

"Let's went," Tim agrees. Maureen raises her eyebrows at Andy before getting into the car. "Remember, that gray thing that goes on your hip. Keep it with you and return your pages."

"And also," Maureen pipes up. "Remember to return all your messages you get at work. OK? Return *all* your messages." And she waves at him as Tim pulls away.

Andy thinks he hears Tim ask Maureen, "What messages?" He smiles and checks his pager. And turns it on.

36. Thursday Night

"So….what makes you happy, Rolfe?"

"We're still talking about that? Well. What makes me happy..." Rolfe surveys the bar again. "Good food. My wife. My cat. Winning. Driving really fast. Being the best."

"It's hard to be the best."

"This…this makes me very happy, right here."

"What's that?"

"This woman in white, the one who just walked in, by herself. That makes me very happy, Maxie. For you."

"What do you mean?"

"Because you are about to meet her?"

"I am?"

"It's decided. She's just your type. She's beautiful but I think you can handle her."

"What do you mean?"

"I'll make this happen." And he gets up, wiping his hands on the napkin.

"What do I do?"

"Sit here. Talk to your new friend, Jesus."

"OK."

Rolfe straightens himself, downs his third glass of wine, and strides over to the bar. The woman is older, Filipina, with dark polished skin and shiny straight black hair, dressed in white. He flashes a smile, deep set twinkling out of robust unblemished features. "Hi, how are you?"

"Hello," she says and she smiles back.

"Can I tell you something?"

"Maybe," she says cautiously.

He puts his hands up as if to assure her that what he is about to say is completely true, strange as it is about to sound. "I'm having dinner just over there with my friend. And I'm trying to have a conversation with him. And I keep saying to him, 'Max…Max'…his name you know. 'Max, I'm trying to talk to you. Why do you keep looking over here?'"

The woman smiles in recognition of where this is probably going. She begins to play with her hair a little. "Really? That's rather rude of him."

"Isn't it? You know," and he puts his hands down out palms up in front of him as if to agree. "I think so, too. I say to him, 'Max, that's so rude'. Your exact words. And you know what he says to me?"

"You'd better tell me."

"He says, 'Rolfie'. My name is Rolfe, by the way," and he puts his hand out.

"Pauline," she says leaning over crossed legs to shake his hand as well. "What kind of name is Rolfe?"

"I'm from Germany."

"Are you American or German?"

"I'm both."

"I'm from the Philippines. I want to be American so bad."

"Really."

"I love my country, but it's very poor where I come from."

"Yes." And he thinks of saying that his wife is from Israel. What a small world. But he doesn't say this at all. "How far away our two countries are and the odds that we should meet."

"What are the odds?"

"I would toast to that, but I don't have my drink with me. Maybe we'll have a drink together."

"So tell me about your friend."

"Yes. Max. I call him Maxie."

"Can I call him Maxie?"

"He loves it when people call him Maxie. You must call him Maxie."

"So what about him?"

"So...he's telling me. 'Rolfie, I'm so sorry. Thank you for taking me out to dinner and buying me this lovely dinner in this beautiful place, but I have to tell you, Rolfie, I have to tell you. 'What Maxie, what?' I say. 'Rolfie' he says", and Rolfe leans in, looking as if he was about to impart a secret that no one else can ever suspect. Pauline leans in as well. "'Rolfie. I've just seen the most beautiful woman I have ever seen in my entire life.'" That's what he said. That...is what he said." He nods.

"Really?"

"The absolute truth."

"Yes. But who, Rolfie?" she asks playfully. "Who was your friend talking about?"

"Pauline. Of course you already know. He pointed... right...at...you. I told him, 'that's not very polite you know, Maxie'. And he said, 'I know, I know Rolfie, but I can't help it. I have to tell you, how else shall I tell you? Yes, the woman in white over there. The most beautiful woman in white with the black hair and the beautiful skin.'"

She holds her chin in her hand, staring at Rolfe, and squirms a little. "That is so sweet."

"Isn't it? He's a very sweet man."

"Yes. And shy, too."

"Very shy, I'm afraid. But very sweet."

"He's shy but he has a good friend like you who looks after him."

"Maxie," he shrugs. "I'd do anything for my buddy, Maxie."

"So how long have you two been friends?"

"Ah...I see him every day. For as long as I can remember."

"So where is he? Do I get to meet him?"

"He's right over there, the single man at that table just over there."

They both look at Max, but strangely enough, Max is paying them no attention whatsoever. He seems instead to be talking intently to whatever remains of his potato.

37. Thursday Night

"I'm ready," she calls to him.

"I'm coming." He walks up the stairs past the massive heating unit, and he finds her in the pantry, the robe pulled tightly around her, for it barely fits. She wears the fluffy slippers. Her hair is wet and tousled. The washing machine gurgles. "You look great," he tells her. Her face and nose still hues a rough red from outdoor exposure, her lips still chapped. Bits of filth still cling tenaciously to her cuticles. But Eugene finds her utterly lovely.

"I'm all nice and clean now."

"How do you feel?"

"I feel wonderful."

"That's good."

"Why don't you take one now? And I'll be waiting for you."

When he takes off his clothes he wonders when was the last time that that he had ever stood naked before a mirror without shame. In his own eyes he is nothing but a doughy thing, an unbaked dinner roll, child's curls up top, effeminately hairless flaccid chest, stubby pink toes and fingers. His penis, he can barely bring himself to look, belongs to a weak little child, shy and useless. Into the shower he enters. It takes a long time for the water to warm, then to become blistering hot. He stands there, feeling the hot water mildly revive in him something closer to the border of reconciliation with his own creaturely body. When he finally emerges, he feels as if he has been away for a long while. He dries himself, taking his time, sleepy yet anxious at what awaits him. He dresses, fumbling with his things. Socks on his feet. Like a man in a dream, he opens the door slowly. And just as in a dream, the landscape has subtly and at first, unaccountably changed. He finds a clean pair of sweat pants and a sweater, both gifts from his aunt, neither of which he has ever worn that he can recall. They fit snugly. The washing machine gently hums, the lace of her own sweat pants ticking against the inside walls; a comforting sound, banal and safe. Candlelight illuminates a small corner of the darkness. She had evidently found candles forgotten on table tops and hidden away in the bottoms of drawers and cabinets. More light emerges from the chamber below. She has entered his appalling little lair to which he banishes himself every night, a misanthropic cave dweller, a gothic little gnome, gnarled and pasty, a shrewd and dyspeptic pest scurrying unmated in its shuttered darkness. She has found this place and lit the candles within, sending gentle throbbing tongues of pale light upon its barren walls. The furnace roars its peace, a sound cloud hovering over their world.

38. Thursday Night

The old man suddenly fell to his knees and hid his face in terror. Prince William smiled at his bestial friend. "I told you, old man. This is Guillaume, the brave, my greatest friend and protector of us both."

"Oh Prince, my eyes may be weak and rheumy, but tis not the good triceratops that vexes me, but it is what I can smell behind those trees. I fear it is the very ravenous and terrible beast himself." Guillaume scratched at the earth and prepared himself for battle, for to be sure, the old and feeble man indeed detected the approach of the dreaded Tyrannosaurus Rex.

"No, Guillaume! We must leave at once. For it is nobler to flee than to fight when the enemy is more deadly but not as swift or nimble. Come old man, come away with us. Come now! Guillaume will bear us safely away. We have no time to lose!"

"I cannot!"

"You must or I regret we will leave you here to your fate."

"Leave me, valiant sirs!"

"Very well, good foolish one! We shall leave at once." But instead of mounting Guillaume, Prince William grabbed the old man who was as light as gossamer and forcibly hauled him upon the triceratops along with himself, straddling his back plates. "Now Guillaume, bear us away!" And at just that moment a terrible cry like the shock of a thousand beasts being slaughtered shook the forest and the head of the beast emerged from the tops of the trees. Suddenly Guillaume lurched in a direction that neither human could have predicted and galloped into the forest with a blazing ferocity, tromping through streams and leaping over gorges. When the T-Rex called out once more, his scream was clearly waning in their ears. Further and further our threesome galloped away from danger. When they were safe and Guillaume had slowed to a walk, Prince William patted his friend. "Guillaume, the brave and mighty triceratops saves the day for his friends and lives himself to fight another day." Guillaume lets out a rumble and curtsies downward to let his charges safely dismount. "You risked endangering us all with your foolish reluctance to be saved. You must come with us now to the city gates, for night will soon be falling and my mother and father shall soon worry about what has become of us. Therefore; your choice - come with us and be our honored guest tonight at the castle of the king, or you may stay here in this unfamiliar wilderness. Choose now for we must surely make haste. Guillaume will know the way."

The old man sighed. "Very well. Seeing as I have not even my own humble hollow to call home, I shall gratefully come with you."

"Excellent choice." And so off they rode. And a good thing too it was for the sun had already set below the hills. There was still light and the city walls would still be open, but they would have to move quickly. Guillaume set off at a gentle canter.

"What a remarkable beast you have there," the old man says.

"More than a beast. Guillaume is as fine a comrade as one could hope for. Indeed he is like my brother." And at this Guillaume - the triceratops – let out another yawn of satisfaction as if to fully concur with the prince.

"Extraordinary. My prince, you may recall that I claimed to you that I am living under a spell. A curse really."

"Do tell. Was it an evil witch who did curse you?"

"No, good sir. That is the tragic part. For I have no one to blame but myself for my current state. I was once a man not unlike yourself, though that might be hard to believe. I was born a nobleman and rather than join the knighthood, I applied myself to become a scholar. I was successful at the university and I rose up into the ranks in many fine houses of learning. I was ever so blessed to have married the most beautiful young princess imaginable from a far off magical land, and together we raised five healthy, glorious children, all of whom….."

At this point, Samuel has to stop. He simply cannot help telling his own story for it is the only one he has to tell. He looks and sees that Guillaume is indeed at last asleep. Along with his father. Their steady, breathing fills the room and he sits in the dark and listens to them both. Meanwhile, outside the door an entire world whirls on, a world of alarms, chatty and plaintiff nurses, of rolling carts, rumbling down the corridor. He smiles to himself, realizing that he is quite relieved, but also a little saddened that his tale has seemingly come to an end.

39. Thursday - End of the workday

At the end of the day, Andy brings several packages back to the office, items due first thing the following morning. He looks at Mikros' tightly wound face and hails him good naturedly. Mikros responds without looking up. "Did you drive safe today?"

"Thanks! I certainly did."

"That's good. Very good. One thing I would ask of you though."

"Of course."

Mikros looks up, "If it is not too much trouble and if you could make just a little bit of time out of your incredibly busy day, would you please answer your fucking pages for me please."

"Sorry."

"It is fundamental." Mikros says, returning his attention to his papers.

"Oh, by the way, I left this number here for someone to call me. It might be business related….. I hope you don't mind. I don't have a phone right now."

"Ah yes. Look at me closely, Andy."

"Fine."

"What do you see?"

"What do I see?"

"What do you fucking see?"

"Come on, man. I see you. I see the dispatcher. I see my boss."

"Close enough. Do you see a *fucking* receptionist?!" Mikros takes a piece of paper, folds it and holds it out. "Here! This is what you want. No?"

"Thank you," Andy says, attempting to read it.

"You're most welcome."

"Club M? Got it. Is this….sorry…is that a nine or a four."

"That is a nine. Anything else?"

∞

"Thank you for calling Club M. How can I make your day incredibly fabulous?"

"Yes, thank you for taking my call. Is this a club by chance where the owner has naturally fuchsia hair?"

"That would be correct, sir."

"And would this also be the same person who is a charmer of bald little elves and trolls?"

Maureen laughs. "That would be incorrect, sir."

"Did you call him an elf?"

"I believe you told me to call him a troll. But that didn't work either."

"That's too bad. I want to hear all about it."

"And so you shall. Listen you, I've been waiting for your call for over an hour. It's nearly seven and you're supposed to be picking me up at eight o'clock. Remember?"

"I've been thinking of nothing else," Andy blurts. He blushes. "Anyway, I'm sorry I couldn't call before. Mikros didn't like being a 'fucking receptionist' as he puts it. Anyway, Club M? Nice."

"Mikros is a little tiny jerk."

"That's the first negative thing I've ever heard you say about anyone."

"It won't be the last. You piss me off; I'll burn you to the ground. Listen, bring your guitar tonight. And whatever else you use to play with yourself. Guess who's playing tonight at the Raja Club at ten o'clock?"

"What's the Raja Club?"

"Will you just fucking guess?"

"Who?"

She laughs. "You! You stupid idiot. What did you think I meant when I told you to bring all your gear?"

"What? You're fucking kidding me!"

"You know I'm not fucking kidding you. And you'd better be really, really good tonight."

"No problem. That's covered."

93

"Take my address down, will you. And get your ass over here. Now."

∞

He strums his guitar, standing against his truck in his sport coat and black t-shirt, his only going out clothes. Maureen bustles out, clopping stiffly. "Please don't hate me!" she says. "I had a fight with one of my roommates."

Andy looks up. "Damn. You *are* spectacular!"

She wears a black leather midi-skirt and ripped nylons, a black cardigan over a bright green blouse and sabre tooth high heels. Her hair is a rumpled bee-hive exposing her long, agile white neck. Black lipstick. Sharply horned rimmed glasses with green trim. She holds a little black purse demurely in front of her. "Spectacular's good with you, right?"

"Oh yeah. You're like....."

"Yeah, what am I like?" She floats closer to him.

"You're like a super hero! You're cool and you're hot!" He reddens again. "How about that?""

She smiles, squinty eyes beaming nearly shut behind her thick lenses. "Let's go fight some crime together," and she inches closer. For an instant it feels certain that they will kiss, but the instant passes and she walks past him to the passenger side of the truck. Andy races over to let her in.

40. Thursday Night

Max appears to be whispering to the remains of his plate. "Max. Max!" He looks up and stares as if he has no idea who either one of them are. "Maxie! Are you all right? I brought you a present."

"Hi Rolfe."

"Look who's here? This is Pauline."

Max does not even appear to notice her. "What?"

"Max! Say hello to Pauline."

"Oh. Hello. Pleasant to meet you" Max says, smiling in his cheerful way.

"Hello, Maxie," Pauline says to him. "You're shy, aren't you?"

"Yes. I suppose I am."

"But you have a wonderful friend here, don't you. Rolfie, you didn't tell me that your friend is so cute." They sit down. Rolfe beams at both of them. He pushes away the brick of thought; just what exactly am I trying to do here? For now, he is entertained and Max looks happy. "I like shy men," she says. "But not too shy. OK? Your friend told me what you said about me, sweetie. A woman loves to hear that."

"She does?" Max seems to ask.

"I'll order us more drinks," Rolfe says. He stands up to flag a waiter. As he does so, his eyes fall upon another woman, vaguely familiar at first. Suddenly, he becomes certain he knows who she is. The waiter arrives.

"Anything else for you at all? Another potato, perhaps?"

"We'll have another round. Whatever the lady is having. I'll have a scotch on ice. Max?"

"What?"

"How about another drink?"

"I don't know."

Rolfe turns to the waiter. "What do you have that's blue?"

"Blue?"

"I want you to bring me a strong drink that's blue. For my friend."

"I think we can do that for you, a liqueur or we have a gin that's –"

"The gin is fine. And put lots of umbrellas and funny little things and plastic swords and bullshit like that in there. Lots of colors. OK?"

"Right away."

Rolfe remains on his feet. He recognizes her - Mayra Granger - a skinny woman, short dark hair and glasses. Dressed in black.

"Rolfie. Yoo-hoo?"

He turns to Pauline and Max. "Forgive me. I need just a moment to go talk to an old friend of mine."

"Are you going to leave me alone with Maxie?" she asks, partly to be coy, yet perhaps somewhat in genuine alarm. "Will I be safe?"

"I'll only be a minute. You two get to know each other," he suggests. "Drink up."

41. Wednesday Night
(Two days before the storm)

"You know Tim, you talk a lot but you're really not telling me anything."

"Alice, come on. What am I supposed to tell you?"

"It's not like you to be all hedgy. It's why I always felt safe with you. You tell the truth."

"What is it you want to hear?"

"Would you tell me, Timmy, if you knew that Jack was foolin' around?"

"Alice….You think that? Why do you think Jack is having an affair?"

"Has he told you about anyone named Alma?"

"Alma?" The name he knows is Sophia. And before that was Lupe. And before that was Rita. And years before that it was Gaby. "I never heard about no one named Alma."

"No? She works at this steak house he likes to go to. They make eyes at each other, Timmy. They flirt right in front of me."

"Alice, that's your proof right there that nothing's going on."

"Oh really….How you figure? Oh I get it. If there was something going on, it wouldn't be with someone he flirts with right in front of his wife. Like he's not stupid."

"Bingo, Alice."

"Is that how you make me feel better, Tim? You make me think that I'm really in trouble only with the two billion women that Jack hasn't made eyes with yet?"

"I'm just telling you there's nothing going on with nobody named Alma."

"Then what's her name, Tim?"

"Huh?"

"OK. So it's not Alma. So who is it?"

"I'm not gonna…..I don't know what to say to you."

"That's not what you were about to say."

"What are you talkin' about?"

"That's not what you were about to say. You were gonna say something else. You were about to say, 'I'm not gonna tell you her name.' That's what you were gonna say, Timmy. 'I'm not gonna tell you her name.'"

"You're a real Columbo now, ain't ya."

"I know what I know."

"I was not gonna say, 'I'm not gonna tell you her name.' If I was gonna say that, then that's what I would have said."

"Men stick together even when one of them doesn't know right from wrong. You stick up for each other. Like you're still in the war or something."

"Yeah. Some war. Jack and I single handedly kept the Japs and the Nazis out of California."

She sighs "But you knew people that went over. And didn't come back."

"Oh yeah….We all did. We all knew good people who are never coming back. You did too."

"I'm glad you didn't go over there."

"Yeah….I'm glad, too."

"You're a strange man, Tim, but I still love you."

"I love you too, Alice."

There is silence on the other end of the line.

"I don't know what to do about Jack."

"You're worrying yourself sick, Alice. And probably for nothin'"

"Yeah?"

"Sure."

"Probably? Well what the hell does that mean? *'Probably'*"

"Well what do you think it means?"

"Tim, I can't get a straight answer outta you when it comes to Jack. What does 'probably' mean? 'Probably'."

"Probably. Probably means probably. He ain't cheatin' on you."

"Probably don't mean he's not. It means he might. It means it's still possible and you think that too."

"Alice, I don't know what I think."

"About Jack."

"About nothin'. About everything."

"That's…that's so convenient ain't it."

"What's convenient?"

"To know nothin'. About nothin'."

"I guess I know what you mean."

"Tim, if you know anything you have to tell me so I'm not just sittin' here like a fool."

"What do you need me to tell you for? You already made up your mind."

"You know what I mean."

"So why do you think he's cheatin'?"

"For starters, Tim, he doesn't pay hardly any attention to me at all. We hardly ever talk."

"Come on, Alice. No one talks. Especially not after thirty three years of marriage."

"Thirty three years. You remember. But I don't know what you're talking about with your nobody talks to each other anymore kind of a line."

"There's not that much to talk about."

"After what happened to Lois, I don't blame you for staying single."

"I'm over all that. It's just too much work," he tries to laugh.

"Really? So if we were married, you wouldn't talk to me either, Tim? You wouldn't pay any attention to me at all."

"I think, young lady, you would be pretty difficult to ignore. I'll give you that."

"Eh. I'll take that as a compliment."

"It's nice to do things together sometimes, just to be together, without a lot of noise, a lot of chit chat. Men don't like to talk."

"Not like us women."

"Not like women, right. But we like to be with our women. Watch TV. Share the paper. Have a cup of coffee. And we like to laugh. You always had the greatest laugh, Alice. Ever."

"Well. Not so much to laugh about now."

"I wouldn't a thought there was much to laugh about with me peeling a million potatoes on KP. But I was dead wrong about that."

"Oh I laughed so hard. I must have looked the fool, too."

"Nah. You looked great."

"I just didn't care. And what a sport you are. I hope you didn't mind, too much. It was all in good fun."

"That's exactly what I thought it was. I'll tell you something else. When that blow hard, Jerry Pimento or whoever he was started mouthin' off, I'll tell you the truth, I really wanted to pop him one. That was different. But when you had fun with me, it was just that. It was all fun. That's you. Full of life. You're fun, Alice. That's a big deal in this world. Not enough of it to go around. Fun. The good kind I mean. Not the mean kind. That's you, Alice. And I loved it."

"Ah...Tim, you are a sweet man."

"And you're still the same exact girl you always were."

"I'm just...uneasy because the whole time we've been talking you never actually denied anything. You never said that Jack wasn't having an affair."

"That's a fact. I wish I could say that he wasn't. But maybe I don't know that either. The man doesn't tell me everything."

"Now you're lying to me, Tim. Before, you were just bullshitting but now you're actually lying to me."

"Alice, you're getting' a little cracked there. Slow down. Maybe we don't talk so much as you think... it's not like you might talk with a girlfriend or something. You should hear the crap we talk about."

"He's your best friend. Your only friend."

"I know," he softly agrees. "But honestly, I don't know if that's sayin' a whole lot."

"That was real nice what you said to me just a few minutes ago."

"What'd I say? Maybe I should write it down so I can be nicer to people."

"About how I'm...the same girl you always knew. That's real nice, Tim."

"It's true."

"You really see me now as you saw me then."

"You're exactly the same. Maybe a little crazier."

She laughs. "But I'm not crazy right now."

"I hope you are."

"You already know whether I am or not. But anyway, I'm glad you said what you did. I needed to hear something nice for a change."

"Well... it's just the way it is."

"I'm just disappointed in Jack." A final space of silence. "Just call me if you know anything. Would you?"

"Maybe I will."

"Or….just call me if you ever just wanna talk to a friend. I'm usually here in the morning when Jack's at work. Maybe call me on one of your breaks. Just to say hello. That'd be nice."

"OK….….OK, Alice. Sure. That's nice of you."

"I'm usually here at night, too, when he's out with his girlfriend."

"You take care of yourself, Alice."

"You, too. Goodnight, Tim."

"Goodnight, Alice."

42. Thursday Night

"Do you like it?" The room is lit with warm, quivering, candlelight.

"Where did you find all these candles?"

"They're everywhere. Candles and incense. On the tables, behind the couch, in the drawers."

"You're kidding."

"What do you mean?" she laughs. "See for yourself."

"How did you light them all so fast?"

"I'll bet you never even spend any time in your own living room. Or your own kitchen."

"I don't feel like any of it is mine anyway. Or that they want me to be any part of it."

"You live here, right? You pay rent. You don't have to hole yourself up in here all the time."

"Well I'm not here very much anyway."

"Maybe not. I think I know exactly where you go."

"You do?"

"Of course I do. You go to all the seven elevens, looking for Cheetos and chicks! Ha!"

"Ha. I usually find the Cheetos."

"Anyway, Eugene, this is your house, too."

"It's not that simple."

"Well it's not that complicated either. But come. Let's not think about it anymore right now. Come sit here next to me. Across from me."

"OK." He looks around at the soft throbbing light.

"Come. You look so uptight. Sit down. Next to me"

Eugene leans over, putting out his hands. He breathes heavily. "You know you're not nearly as fat as I am and you're making a big production out of sitting down," and she starts to laugh. She's so pretty that Eugene laughs as well.

"You're not fat," he says.

99

"Of course I am."

"You're beautiful."

"So are you." She sits cross-legged on the mattress, her borrowed robe tightly corded around her. The roaring furnace protects them with its foggy leaven of sound. "You're right," she says softly. "It is warm and toasty in here. I like it. I like the furnace. Everything."

"I'm glad…. You don't find it….Really ugly and creepy."

"Hah. Maybe. Maybe I wouldn't like it if I were alone." She leans towards him. "But all I see right now is that this place is warm and it's dry and its safe and I'm with you."

"Yeah. Me too."

She smiles at him. "You're like a little boy, Eugene." He shrugs. "We can be innocent together."

Eugene smiles back at her, a loopy, lopsided grin. "OK….What do you want to do?"

"I want us to go back to our favorite places. Only let's go there together."

"OK," he says, uncertainly. "How do we do that?"

"With our imaginations…..We have to blow the candles out."

"What do you mean?"

"I mean we have to blow them out. We can only do this thing in the dark. We have to forget where we are completely."

"OK. But what are we going to do exactly?"

"How dark will it get in here once we put the candles out?"

"Completely. You won't be able to see your hand in front of your face."

"Good. Let's leave one candle burning. We'll leave it right next to us. Actually bring all the candles here next to us." He gathers all the lights, two or three at a time. "Good," she says. "Now we're going to blow the candles out, except for the last one. This one over here. Move them away just a bit from the mattress so you don't get wax over everything. Good." Quickly, one by one, the candle light turns to smoke, until there is but a single small light probing a sea of darkness. "Trust me. We can do this."

"I trust you."

"I do this all the time by myself. It works. We can hold hands. You'll still be able to find me when the light goes out." And she winks at him. "You'll be my first that I take with me."

"Alright; you'll…you'll be my very first, too."

43. Thursday Night

Samuel opens his eyes. Guillaume stands on the bed, gently bouncing, silhouetted against the shadowy city light peering through the window. "Silly bear!" the boy whispers. "Silly bear!"

Samuel feels his ire rise. He considers simply walking out of the room, but that would surely disturb Perry still snoring on the cot. "Guillaume. What am I to do with you?"

"More story."

"More story!"

"Tell me the part with the bear."

"Tell you what part with what blazing bear, Guillaume?"

"Tell me the part where Guillaume becomes friends with the bear."

Samuel takes this as a sign of affection but he is still irritated and tired. "I tell you what, my little despot; I shall continue, but *only* if you can tell me one thing about what this story is about."

"Silly bear!"

"No. No it's not about a silly bear. There's no bear at all. Or there isn't one *yet*. Good God!"

"Tritheratopth!"

"You'll have to do better than that, Guillaume, even if you are a grubby little invalid. What is this story about?"

Guillaume stops bouncing. "Guillaume helps the old man."

"True enough. But you said that before. And what else?"

"You said 'one thing'. You said…"

"Please. Tell me something you haven't already told me from long before. It's only fair. Come on, Guillaume."

"No. You said one thing."

"One *new* thing. Remember? They're in the forest and they want to help the old man, and then….and then…

"A monster. They run away from the monster."

"A T-Rex. True. Fair enough."

"And the old man; he's very, very……very sad." Samuel settles back into his chair. "Because he lost all his family."

"Ah…..Well done, Guillaume," Samuel admits. "Well done."

"More story?"

"Yes, Guillaume. More story. You shall have the rest of your story. You've earned it."

"With the bear."

"Indeed. We shall soon meet the bear. I won't forget about the blasted bear. But….you must lie down." Guillaume does so at once. Samuel pulls the blanket up and leans over the bed rail. "So. Where were we then?"

"The old man was sad."

"Yes, of course."

"Good prince, all of my children have grown to be fair and stout and red of cheek and fine contributors to their communities. This of course fills me with great joy. But you see, it also fills me with sweet sadness. For I....for I fear I shall never see any of them or my lovely princess ever again. It is because of my affliction, which I admit I have foolishly wrought upon myself. And instead I am doomed to endless exile and the best I can hope for is my humble little hovel."

The prince told the old man, "Tell us exactly what has befallen you and how these things came to pass."

"Before you could know such a thing, I feel I should tell you--" But once more the old man interrupted himself and looked about in alarm. "I dread very much to tell you this, your highness, but I sense the presence of yet another malevolent force bearing down upon us. Only this time, I am frightfully sorry to tell you that I have unwittingly brought this evil here myself. It is indeed part of my affliction."

"I neither see nor hear nor sense anything amiss.. Neither does Guillaume who is yet much more sensitive than I am."

"Most probably I am *not* of sound mind, my liege. No matter, I tell you we must overcome another danger, and very soon."

"Well...well what is it? And what shall we do?"

"As to what we shall do, in this instance, permit me to assist. I may be old and feeble, but when it comes to my own demons, I have been endowed with the means to assail them. Or at any rate to hasten them away for a period of time, which I admit grows shorter and shorter with every episode. But leave that to me, my lord. As to your first question of what it is that awaits us, you shall know soon enough." Indeed, just at that very moment a terrible, ghostly howling began to rise in the air, along with a yellow mist that rose with it. Guillaume gave out a low groan of displeasure. The howling increased, along with a sharp hissing sound.

"What manner of menace is this?" said the prince.

"Unfortunately, the worst is yet to come. Here now, they shall fully manifest, presently."

And indeed, out of the mist slithered three creatures terrible to look upon, mangled monsters, distantly human, with giant mouths and preposterous tongues, eyes scattered in unlikely places, their heads twisted at impossible angles, their legs twisted, and their arms like tiny disfigured stumps. Blood pours from all their orifices, wherever these might be.

"No!" Guillaume shouts. At this his father snorts and falls back to sleep. "No more monsters."

"I'm sorry. I realize this is insanely over stimulating and unseemly. But the best part is just about to happen. Your favorite character is about to make his noble appearance."

"No!"

"But the bear is coming. The bear! Right away. Fear not."

"Ah...the bear." And Guillaume settles down again. "But no more scary."

"Well, just a little scary."

"No. No more scary."

"Si. Just a little tiny bit scary."

"No more scary!" Guillaume insists, yet still containing himself to a ferocious whisper.

"Just a teency weency eentsy bit more scary," Samuel rejoins, measuring out the amount of scary for Guillaume in the tiny space between his thumb and forefinger.

Guillaume sits up, points to Samuel, and sternly says, "I don't.. like... these... monsters." And he folds his arms over his chest to make his point that much clearer.

"Well I don't like them either," Samuel sneers, "But they're part of this infernal story which you have duly extorted me to...to....to *explicate*!"

Guillaume frowns, then bursts out giggling. "Silly bear. Hahaha."

Samuel smiles too, but still pretending to be indignant, persists, "So you think it's funny, do you mein kampf."

"Yes," Guillaume laughs aloud. "Yes."

"Shhhh! Remember your papa."

"Yes!" Guillaume whispers.

"You'll just have to endure the scary a tiny bit more before you meet the bear. That's my final offer."

"OK. OK. OK," Guillaume giggles, lolling on the bed. "Teeny teeny tiny tiny bit more scary, but then the bear."

"Yes."

"Teeny teeny tiny tiny tiny tiny teeny tiny teeny tiny..."

"Guillaume. You are of course procrastinating. Please cease and allow the story.....to continue."

Instead, Guillaume continues to chant, only now, indeed, in the quietest whisper possible, "teeny tiny teeny tiny...." Recognizing this as Guillaume's way of self-soothing, Samuel tolerates this ritual and carries on.

The three monsters stagger forward. The prince exclaims in disgust. "What in heaven's gate are those...things"

"First of all, you and Guillaume must remain calm, my lord. The calmer you are, the slower they move, if at all. As to what these things are, they are in fact the all too common demons born of some of man's worst traits; arrogance, self-righteous anger, and solipsism. Everyone of course has them to a degree. I'm afraid I am laid low to tell you sire that I possess all three in exceptional abundance."

"I cannot just sit here while - What was that you say? Solip - what?"

"Solipsism, my good prince. That's the ugly one in the middle.... It is the most extreme and paranoid form of self-centeredness, whereby the afflicted act as if they were the only authentic being on the entire earth and all the rest of us were nothing but projections. You can only imagine what endless horrors this can lead one to."

"I have no time to imagine. Guillaume and I shall fight them."

"And how shall you do that, my lord? They are phantoms and they will feed off your reactions and only grow stronger."

"Shall we run away then?"

103

"How shall we hide from a demon? They can materialize anywhere, at anytime."

Guillaume, though trembling, prepared to do battle with them, raising himself up and roaring his threat and power. But the demons only approached faster. When *suddenly!*

"The bear!" Guillaume shouted, at which point, a moan of alarm rises from the cot. Samuel and Guillaume both freeze, waiting until Perry falls back into silence. Samuel and Guillaume look at each other. "The bear," Guillaume whispers.

"Yes, Guillaume."

There was a tremendous roar that indeed came from a bear, a fantastic beast, as large as Guillaume, with great teeth and claws. William and Guillaume were in great distress, for it seemed they were set upon by yet another enemy. "What in heaven is this now and where did it come from!" But their increased predicament was extremely short lived, for the bear stood facing down the demons, setting himself now between them and our two heroes. "This creature is our friend, Guillaume! In any case, he certainly cares as little for these demons as we do." Guillaume growled his assent. "But where is that loquacious old man?" Perhaps he had run and hidden behind a tree, ignoring his own advice to the prince. The demons continued their slow and dreadful approach, their howls and taunts becoming ever more foul, the shrieks of so much unfulfilled desire, squashed and undigested spawns of lust and avarice throbbing in their wake - but the bear! The bear roared again and galloped forth opening his mouth wide so that incredibly, all three demons and their shroud of foul mists were quickly and impossibly consumed whole! Gone, that is. They all disappeared down the throat of our new hero, the bear.

"Yes! Yes. The bear. No more monsters!"
"Let's stay focused Guillaume."

"Great heavens, Guillaume," said the prince. "That beast, whatever it was, has saved us all. But where did it go?" Guillaume gave out an inquisitive groan and snuffled and snorted, drawing William's attention to a body lying in front of them. It was the old man who lay in the very same spot where the great bear had swallowed the terrible demons. "Are you alright?"

"Do I look alright to you, good prince?"

"I should say not, my aged friend, but are you wounded? What has happened to you?"

The old man chuckled and dusted himself off. "If you would be kind enough to help me up, it will add to my indebtedness to you, sir."

"Of course, of course," and so William helped lift him up. "Come. Sit upon this log over here." The old man sat down. "Now tell us? What happened to you? A great creature came to our invaluable aid, but the whole time you were not to be found. And now I find you lying in the very spot where the battle was raged. Do you recall anything?" Suddenly a new thought dawned upon the Prince. "Great cyclones and hailstorms; could it be?"

The old man winked and smiled more contentedly than he had since they had first met. "Would you care to state your theory, my liege?"

"You and the bear are one and the same. You are he and he is you!"

"Correct! Correct! We are one and the same. I am the bear. And the bear, is me!"

"Ah. The old man is the bear," said Guillaume.

"That's right, my good lad. The old man is the bear! Exactly right. But wait, there's more."

"Extraordinary," exclaimed the prince. "Well perhaps I should say, Guillaume and I do owe you our lives." To this, Guillaume gave a great surging groan. William rather sheepishly cleared his throat, for his bestial brother was actually protesting rather than agreeing, apparently a little sore at being shown up by.... A hairy mammal.

The old man sighed. "I should like nothing better in this world than to have a prince...and a princely beast, to have you all in my debt. But alas, that would be a bit of trickery. Far from being grateful to me, you must realize that it was I, my friends, who endangered you both to begin with. As I was saying to you, those hideous demons - well they are *my* demons. I spawned and nurtured them myself through my own decisions. Therefore I brought them upon you as well.   Had you and Guillaume never found me, I would have battled them anyway, and in exactly the same manner."

"I see. Well....you are honest at least."

"Not at first. But yes, you see now, my lord, why I was so reluctant to answer your kindhearted call. I bring danger upon all whom I meet."

"This is a terrible affliction indeed," said the prince.

"Those demons will return. The bear provides only a temporary solution. He is borne from my power of will. But the demons I'm afraid are not gone.   And you have not heard all, my lord. Leave me please and be well."

"Are you not worthy of help? Do you not suffer and regret the cause of your suffering? I say we should carry on to see if we might restore you back into the community of men....and noble beasts," William hastened to add.

"I must say that I am filled with some hope that you two can actually help me. I only hope that you never have cause to regret it."

Guillaume lets out a soft and slightly drunken squeal of satisfaction, followed by a wide gaped yawn. "Silly bear."

"I wouldn't say he was exactly silly. He was rather ferocious, too. Wouldn't you say?"

"You. You're the silly bear," Guillaume said, pointing at Samuel and giggling in a stupor. And the boy reaches out and touches Samuel's beard, then his face and nose as well. "The old man is the bear."

"Yes, the old man is the bear."

"He's a nice man."

"I suppose. A bit troubled, I'd say."

"You're nice."

"Thank you, my boy."

"And a bear," and he giggles again, loopy and half dreaming already.

"And a bear, yes. A silly bear. Indeed."

"A silly bear. Ha ha." The boy yawns again. "No more story."

"What was that I heard you say?"

"Tomorrow. More story tomorrow."

"But there is so much more to tell," Samuel mischievously suggests. "Let's stay up all night, Guillaume. Shall we? Shall we resume our story now?" But Guillaume is already asleep. Perhaps he will sleep through all the excitement of his discharge and wake up safe and sound in his own bed. As if it were all just a dream. Samuel settles back into his chair. Reasonably comfortable and padded it is. Knowing his back will scold and reprove him all day tomorrow, he remains seated.

"Silly bear!" he whispers aloud and smiles. But he knows, the story is not yet really over.

44. Thursday Night

The last candle flame disappears and the room is plunged in darkness. First the silence, and for a chilling moment, Eugene wonders whether he is suddenly alone as if he had imagined the entire evening.

"Caroline?"

"Shhhh," she tells him. He squeezes her hands, forgetting that he is still holding them. Caroline, he still calls in his head. Caroline!

As if hearing him, she speaks in a whisper, "I'm right here."

"Yes," he says, relieved.

"It's perfect." He inches his way towards her until their knees are touching. She smells of soap. "Let's go to your place first."

"You mean the place I told you about?"

"Of course. The place that you think about every night when you're eating your dinner. Only you're going to take me there."

"OK." He realizes he is embarrassed to do so, even though he doesn't know what this means. The furnace continues to roar. "What do I do?"

"You just take me there."

"How?"

"Just see the place. See it. And when you see it, you just tell me. Wait. Wait until you see it." She squeezes his hands even harder. Her nails dig into his palms.

"OK," he squirms a little, suddenly feeling quite sleepy. "OK. I still don't know what to do."

"Just wait. And when you're ready, tell me where we are and what we're doing."

"All right. Fine. Just wait a bit."

"I'll wait."

It's hard to see just now. Sometimes it's very foggy. I can hear the furnace. It sounds like fog to me. It's gray and it's cold. I know you don't like to be cold. You're wearing a thick trench coat like me. Mine is gray. And yours is white. You're the only one with a white coat. It looks beautiful on you."

"That's nice. What are we doing?"

"Right now, we're just standing there. No one can see us and we can't see them. It's gray and foggy."

"And what else?"

"We're in an alleyway between two very tall, very gray buildings. Papers are blowing all over. Old papers. Receipts. Pages of documents. We walk through. The doors are all boarded up. We walk out of the alley. There's a huge square. All the streets and bridges seem to lead to this place. There are other people, but they are all far away and walking or standing on the bridges or on the streets."

"Have you ever been to this square before?"

"Yes. Lots of times. I think there once was a statue here, some great tribute, something that was the whole reason for this square. But now it's gone and there's nothing here. Except a hole. There's a great ditch, a big hole now where there was once this giant monument."

"I see it. Ah, what a strange place. Is there anything inside the hole? Is there anything hidden down there?"

"No!"

They walk around the hole, marveling at how large it truly is when they finally reach the center of the square. What had seemed to be a mere ditch of thirty or forty feet was in fact large enough to fit an entire city block inside or perhaps more. The hole seems to grow exponentially as they approach. "Let's keep walking, please," Eugene says.

"OK, darling. That's fine with me."

"Maybe," Eugene says, "We should get out of here and go to your secret place instead. It looks as if there's nothing more here."

"Are you sure?"

"I just think it would be a good idea."

"There must be something else out here that you can show me."

"We're leaving the city now."

"What's outside the city?"

"Nothing. I never thought about that."

"Are you sure?"

"I don't know."

"Well what on earth is that up ahead?"

"How can you see anything if I can't?"

"Well just look, Eugene. Look. Up ahead. Through the fog."

"Wow….That might be the tower."

"The tower! I knew it. What about this tower?" Out of the mists, emerges a tangle of iron works stacking like a gargantuan gargoyle into the sky, its top obscured in the mist. It was not unlike the Eiffel Tower, but mangled and bent and wrapped around itself, and many, many times bigger. Much further still in the distance is the first evidence of an actual landscape, a series of jutting yet hazy distant mountains. "Nothing is known of these mountains. We can't go in them or even approach them. I wouldn't want to."

"Well let's go see this tower and what else might be out there."

"There's nothing else."

"Are you sure?"

"I don't know."

"How can you not know?"

"I've never been here before. You're making me go places I've never gone. I was always imagining papers and buildings and a big, huge cafeteria, and sometimes a bridge or an alleyway. I was never out here."

"I want to see."

As they approach, they begin to see that the great tower is completely surrounded by an even larger land fill that extends for many miles, a gray, endless mass of trash which raises a mist of lingering gray dust. As they come still closer, the trash appears to be mostly paper, gray and yellow triplicate forms. "How did it all get here?" Caroline asks.

"I don't know," Eugene says.

"Do you recognize any of the papers you signed, any of your own forms in that dump?"

"How could I tell?"

"Some of it must have come from you."

"I guess."

The entire behemoth hunches over from its stratospheric top, lurching and leaning as if it might all come tumbling like some meteoric cataclysm. "It's amazing! Isn't it?" Caroline said. "Who built it?"

"I don't know."

"How did they build it?"

"Well *why* did they build it?"

"You know so little about your own world, Eugene. Take me up the tower, so we can see."

"You can't go up the tower."

"I bet there's a stairwell, or better yet, an elevator around here."

"There's no elevator."

"Let's take a look." And they walk beneath the great tower. Eugene fears he will get queasy, but Caroline seems to move easily through his world. It is a long walk from one side to the other, the massive trunk of the tower emerging and disappearing behind the gloom. "I see an elevator," she says.

"How can you tell?"

"I see it. Come on." And she leads him around the corner of a great iron pillar. There, they see it; a rickety elevator cart, resembling a chipped and dented metal filing cabinet.. No doors, only thin aluminum rods and cross bars hold the apparatus together. Up above, a lonely strand of rope disappears into dark shadowy chambers of iron lattice work. "Let's get in."

"Get into that? We'll be killed."

"Of course we won't be killed. We'll see everything we came to see. From a distance."

"I don't want to."

"Please, Eugene. You must."

"Why must I? This is my world, isn't it?"

"That's why you must see. You've only seen a little part before. Now you must see the rest."

"Alright. I don't want to. But I trust you."

"Press the button."

"Where?"

"I'll press it." He sees three brass looking button sticking out from a cheap wood pulp panel. Caroline presses the top one. Nothing happens at first. She presses again. Suddenly, a great hollow grind of metal groans around them. Eugene grabs onto Caroline. A high metal screech rings out and the little car jolts them so that they nearly tumble out, yet they keep their footing somehow. "I got you," she says, winking at him, beneath her hat, looking younger and brighter than he remembers her. Such soft blue eyes. He looks at her, but even in his periphery, he sees the landscape expand, overwhelming him with its endless gloom and menace. "That's right," she says. "Look at me. We'll wait until we reach the top. And then we'll look together."

"I don't want to see."

"After we look, we'll be done here, and I promise you, we'll find our way quickly back to my world and we'll have all that we can eat."

"I'm not hungry."

"And we'll be safe and warm."

"OK."

"You have nothing to fear." And he sees and feels that she is still holding his hands. The car continues to rise and rise and rise. He steals a furtive glance but looks away, feeling sick, the expansive dead landscape growing and blackening.

"I don't want to see," Eugene repeats.

45. Thursday Night

"That's just awful. Oh my god, don't make me even think about that." She laughs. They sit in a narrow, crowded restaurant, waiting for their main course while munching on deep fried pita chips. "How can you even talk about it with such a straight face?"

"I do believe you grilled me for all the various details."

"I know. What's the matter with me?"

"What *is* the matter with you?"

"So how long did you work *there*?"

"In the slaughterhouse? Maybe a month. In the rendering factory – two weeks."

"How did you stand it?"

"Beats coal mining or telemarketing"

"So I'm trying to keep track of all your jobs now. You worked at the landfill – that's great fun - swept floors at the construction yard, washed dishes, worked at the candy factory. I think that's my favorite. I need to start writing it down."

"I think you should."

"I'm repelled. And strangely envious."

"They're all experiences. Maybe that's it."

"I'll be right back."

"Are you gonna be sick?"

"No!" she stands, awkwardly at first, in her high heels.

"I'm picturing you now, working in the slaughterhouse, wearing those high heels."

"We're changing the subject when I get back." He daydreams about her until she herself interrupts his reverie with her return. "What?" she says.

"You look spectacular in those high heels. I could never do it."

"They can come in handy, the heels."

"My ankles feel like they're about to snap just looking at you."

"For example; like if I'm ever grabbed from behind by some serial killer, I know exactly what I would do."

"Really?

"I would *stomp* his foot," and she acts it out, in slow motion, a vicious aim at the murderers toes. "And then, once he lowers his head, because he will when I fucking stomp him, I do this. I crouch, and bam! I sling my right elbow up to catch him below his chin. And then," and she acts out turning whilst her right elbow is still jammed against the underside of her assailant's jaw, "I'd spin around" and slowly she twists her agile torso, "and smash the palm of my hand into his nose and *crush* it into his brain. Oh yeah. *That* I would." And she points to the business part of her palm.

110

"How did you come up with that?"

"Doesn't it make sense?"

"Yeah. You've given this some thought."

"I took three weeks of self-defense a couple of years ago."

"Three weeks?"

"I'm no victim," She smiles, showing her teeth. "You can count on that. I'm choosing how I go. How do you want to go?"

"How do I want to die?"

"Yes. That's right. We all die. Choose your death. Now."

"In my sleep. At 107."

"That's so boring."

"I like living."

"I want to hear something interesting."

"Interesting. An interesting death. Alright." Massive stroke while having boisterous, tangled sex with Swedish triplet teenagers. Dying in my sleep at age 107. Asphyxiation while falling from thirty thousand feet. Massive stroke while having uninhibited sex with giggling Chinese flight attendants. Triplets. Or with you, Maureen. "Maybe....being massively electrocuted while having a freak out jam on my guitar, playing in front of hundreds of thousands of screaming people."

"Not bad," and she shakes her head and adds, "That's one way I'm sure I'll never have the chance to try."

46. Thursday Night

"Hello, Mayra"

She sits wagging a pen, cross-legged in her little black dress eyeing a document; short black hair, glasses, light green eyes, wan complexion. He notices her drink and another one beside it. She looks up. "Excuse me? Do I know you?"

"My name is Rolfe Gunther. I've most definitely heard of you," he says instead.

She pushes her glasses slightly up the bridge of her nose. "OK."

"Mayra Granger. You're the Vice President of Marketing and Development at Latham, Trumbull, and McCurdy contractors, the fastest growing developer of commercial properties in the western United States."

"Associate Vice President." She smiles at him.

"The youngest vice president throughout the firm; destined to become the youngest and the first woman CEO before you're thirty five."

"I see you know how to flatter, Mr. Gunner."

"Gunther. And please call me Rolfe. May I buy you a drink?"

"Might you state your business, Mr. Gunther?"

"Latham, Trumbull, and McCurdy. I intend to work for you."

"I see. As what, may I ask?"

"Project Manager," Rolfe asserts, redoubling his smile.

"Mayra," Rolfe looks up at the familiar voice. Frank Giambi. Double breasted, olive suit. "I'm so sorry it took me so long....Rolfe?"

"Frank. Did you fall in?"

"Almost.... Rolfe? Rolfe Gunther? Is that you? Where's Tanya?"

"She's not here."

"How do you know Mr. Gunther?"

"Please call me Rolfe."

"He's married to Tanya," Frank explains. "Tanya Gunther. She's an assistant in leasing."

"I don't think I know her." She looks at Rolfe with a wan smile. "I guess you get around then."

"Oh yeah," Frank agrees. "Rolfe here gets around all over town, every day. That's what he does. Don't you?"

"It seems he is very determined to work for our firm."

"Rolfe, is that true? I could get you into a construction crew tomorrow or the day after. Seriously. I've actually been hoping you would come to see me."

"Frank," Mayra begins, "I don't think you know Mr. Gunther all that well. He has indeed set his sights on becoming my project manager. Right away."

"Project Manager?" Frank repeats, rocking on his heels, hands in pockets. "Very ambitious, Rolfe. Mayra only has one project manager at the moment, actually."

"I didn't know that."

"Got a short memory there. But for future reference, how many commercial buildings have you built, Rolfe?" Rolfe smiles and shakes his head, as if to reprove Frank for being naughty. "I didn't hear you Rolfe."

"Please," Mayra breaks in, amused. "That's not necessary."

"I respectfully suggest that it is, Mayra. He wants to be a high grade project manager, reporting to senior leadership. How many, Rolfe?"

"Zero."

"How many?"

"Zero. Nada. None."

"Fine. How many have you assisted on, served as foreman for, you know, helped to manage, helped to develop."

"Zero."

"Zero, you say."

"Zero."

"How many crews have you managed? How many buildings have you bought or sold or leased? How many have you designed? Let me guess. Zero."

"That is correct."

"Do you even have a real estate license here? A contractor's license?"

"Not yet."

"You're talking about moving up from a messenger driver to a six figure management position. What exactly have you done?"

47.

"Has your friend forgotten about us?"

"I don't know."

"I wish he would hurry up."

"Me, too." It was something they seemed to have in common.

"I may have to go before he gets back."

"Oh. OK. I'm sorry."

Pauline looks at Max, puzzled, nostrils flared, as if there were a large unknown species of beetle crawling on top of his head. "Maxie. Do you really think I'm beautiful?"

"Sure."

"Do you really think I'm the most beautiful woman you've *ever* seen?"

Max thinks about this. "Yes. I think you most probably are."

She smiles; then gives him a narrow look. "Did you say that to Rolfe?"

"Did I say what to Rolfe?"

"Ay! Did you tell him I was the most beautiful woman you'd ever seen?"

Max frowns. "No. I think he said he wanted me to meet you."

Pauline shakes her head. "Your friend Rolfe is quite a liar."

"I'm sorry. I don't always understand Rolfe myself."

"He told me that you are his best friend."

"Really?" Max seems to brighten at this. "Wow. I didn't know that. Well maybe I am. This is only our first time doing something together. He came to me because something was bothering him. We know each other from work."

"He's a strange man. Why would he say you two are best friends?"

"Maybe we are."

"You don't get to be best friends in one time going out. Maybe he's lying about that, too! Who knows? And why would he tell me that you said I was the most beautiful woman ever when you didn't even notice me."

"Well you are."

"But you didn't *say* that to him."

"But he knew."

113

"Maxie, you're strange, too. You're cute. But strange. I think I'm going to leave." She grabs her purse, but she doesn't actually get up.

"It was nice meeting you, Pauline."

"He really wasted my time."

"Well that's not nice. I don't think he meant to."

"Maxie," she leans in. "OK. I have to ask. Why were you talking to your potato? Are you a crazy person?"

He straightens up. "No. I don't think so. Well, I wasn't actually talking to my potato."

"Well what were you doing?"

"Well….I was praying. I think."

"Ah, you were praying?"

"Yes."

"What were you praying for?"

"I wasn't praying for anything."

"You what? You pray for nothing?"

"No. I didn't pray for nothing. I just didn't pray for anything."

"What are you talking about, Maxie?"

"I was just praying. To Jesus."

"Ah. Are you Catholic? I was raised Catholic."

"No."

"But you are Christian."

"I don't know."

"Then why were you praying to Jesus?"

"I just wanted to talk to him."

"What were you saying to him?"

"I was just telling him that I was here."

"That doesn't make any sense."

Max shrugs and smiles. "It felt nice. I liked it."

"But that's not the way you do it."

"But…that's how I did it."

"But you're not supposed to."

"Really? Well, why not?"

She thinks for a moment. "That's not the way they teach you."

"I didn't know someone had to teach you."

"Do you want me to tell you how you are supposed to pray?"

"That's very nice of you. But no, that's OK. I have a feeling I wouldn't understand. I just like talking to Jesus."

She smiles. "How long have you been talking to him?"

"That was my first time."

48. Thursday Night

"I was wondering when I'd hear from you."

"Yeah. Well, here I is," he says, settling further into his arm chair.

"Have you called Brenda yet? I think she likes you."

"No. Not yet. And not ever."

"Don't pretend your dance card is full."

"Jack, I wanna talk to you about something. I mean I don't really want to, but I'm gonna.'"

"I hope you're not sore about Jerry. He just likes to joke with people."

"Huh? Nah, don't worry about that. I'm not calling you about that asshole."

"Asshole?"

"Listen, Jack. I want to tell you somethin'. As a friend."

"Are you OK?"

"Yeah. I'm OK."

"Cause I don't think you take too good care of yourself."

"Jack. I'm OK. I'm not great. But I'm OK. OK? Look, Alice called me."

"She called you? When?"

"Yesterday. She asked me if you're having an affair."

There was silence at first on the other end of the line. "Alice called *you* to ask if I'm having an affair."

"That's right."

"Well, what'd you tell her?"

"I told her you're not."

"Good. Why is she calling *you* to ask about me?"

"I guess she figured I wouldn't lie to her."

"But you did lie to her, my friend."

"That's why we need to talk." He rubs his face.

"I can't believe she called you. How could she do that?"

"How could *she* do *that*? What's the matter with you, Jack? You're screwin' everything that moves except for Alice. Anyway, listen to me. I discouraged her from thinking you were foolin' around. But I still have to live with myself."

"What else did she say?"

"She thinks you're foolin' around with someone named Alma."

"Alma? Jesus."

"Jack? *Are* you foolin' around with someone named Alma?"

"Tim. It's complicated."

"No, it's not. It's simple. Is you or is you ain't messin' around with Alma?"

"There is someone named Alma."

"Really Jack, why don't you just divorce Alice?"

"Because it would break her heart!"

"Too late. Look; you've been my friend for a real long time, Jack. And as a friend, I want you to do somethin' for me."

"I'm not givin' up these women. I know it's dead wrong, goddamn it but I can't do that."

"You ain't givin' them up for your wife, so I ain't dreamin' you're givin' them up for me. I just don't want to be put in the position of lyin' for you; or lyin' to Alice. Whether you mean to or not, you're involvin' me in your mess, Jack."

"I guess I am. By tellin' you. I guess I won't tell you anymore."

"But you can't un-tell me, can you. No. I need a break from all this."

"What? What do you mean? A break."

"Oh God," he sighs. "Jack, I need a break my friend from *you*."

Another silence. "Tim…..She's not gonna call you again."

Tim's turn to be silent. "I feel like I'm gettin' in the middle of this thing. And I want nothin' to do with it."

"You're not in the middle. Look, I didn't ask you to talk to my wife."

"But she called me! No matter what I do, I'm taking sides."

"Stop whining. It's gonna be fine. Just relax."

"I don't want either one of you to call me. That's what I'm saying."

"That's just stupid. Do you even have anybody else to talk to?"

"I'm not sayin' we ain't friends. I'm not sayin' that."

"Well Tim, that's exactly what it sounds like you're sayin.'"

"I just can't have you calling me. Just not for now. Neither one of you. Not until you come clean with her or quit it."

"That sounds like we ain't friends."

"I don't know what to do, Jack. It ain't right."

"Tim, if Alice figures you don't want neither one of us callin' you, she's gonna guess why. It'll be as if you told her everything."

"Well. I'm sorry. I don't know what to do about that. I didn't force you to cheat on Alice and I didn't force Alice to call me. I'm not tryin' to get righteous or anything. I'm no saint. I've said nothing for years. I don't know what else to do."

"Just go on saying nothing! That's what you do."

"It's different now Jack. It's different."

"Tim….Just…. change your mind and come meet me at the diner tonight."

"It's different now, Jack. It just is."

49.

"We thought you had left us!"

"I'm sorry. But I'm back," Rolfe tells Pauline, "Isn't Maxie entertaining you?" He looks flushed and holds a new drink in his hand.

"Entertaining? Your friend is very different, Rolfe."

Max speaks. "Pauline gave me a postcard."

Rolfe peers at it and sees a beatific image of Jesus, blond and blue eyed, sad and beautiful. "Very nice, Maxie. Did you like your drink?"

"Hmm? Oh. Yes. It's blue. I like the umbrella, too."

"That's right! Blue. It's curacao."

"Rolfe," Pauline speaks, "Are you going to still ignore me? I almost left before you got here. Why am I still even here?"

"Now how could I possibly know that, Pauline?" he tells her, red-faced, his smile larger and tighter. "Already our relationship is so complex. Many facets and angles. Anyway! We musn't forget that I brought you here to meet Maxie."

"Rolfe, are you OK?" Max asks. "You don't look well."

"Of course I'm all right. I'm amazing."

"Well you don't look as amazing as usual. You look strange."

"Strange? Straaaange!"

"I'm sorry. You look angry, Rolfe."

Rolfe slams his drink now, spilling an ice cube on his coat. "Max! Enough with that bullshit, OK my friend. Not now. Really, not now," he says, holding up a finger. His pager goes off. "Ah! What is it now! Stupid thing. Why is it going off now?" He scowls as if he intends to smash the device, but instead he looks at the number and his face goes slack. "Shit. Sorry. I'm sorry. I'm sorry for everything. I'm sorry for life. All right? I have to make a phone call."

She tells him, "I won't be here when you get back."

"Well I have to call my wife."

"Your *what*?"

"Why don't you take Maxie home?"

"What? Why don't I what?"

"Please! Take Maxie home. He has a wonderful book to show you." And he leaves to find a pay phone.

"Your simple little friend will still be here. I will not." Pauline turns to Max. "What is with your friend?"

Max just shrugs. "He seems angry. I don't like it that much either."

"He's drunk." She gathers her purse. "This is insulting."

"I'm so sorry."

"Where do you live, anyway?"

"Hmm?"

"Will you stop talking to Jesus and tell me where you live? That *is* insulting."

Max puts down the postcard. "Sorry"

"Maxie," she puts her hot hand on his arm. "Forget I even asked. You are a child. You are not even a man. So I have to be going. Good luck to you, Maxie….. And God bless you."

50.

He feels lightheaded from the one beer and the buoyancy of his lust and their strange conversation. They make their way unsteadily through the back entrance down a narrow, empty, dim corridor, approaching the rush of exotic yet familiar jazz. They pass through what was once a tiny kitchen until they emerge at the back seating, red glow light. He recognizes the band, the same beautiful band from the Blue Aztec Lounge. Inwardly, Andy lights up. He loses himself in the music, forgetting even Maureen and his upcoming set. The lights come on over the tepid yet lingering applause squeezed out by ragged and rumpled youths wearing sharp faces and spiked hair. Sitar music suddenly blasts from the speakers. Andy looks about. A tiny waif figure approaches in his dirty white shirt. Andy recognizes Henry from the Obsidian.

"Hello, Maureen, my favorite wench."

"Hello, darling Henry," she affects in a rude impression of some cartoon high society lady.

"Hello, Henry. Shall I set up?" Andy says, guessing that Henry does not even recognize him. Since he gets no response, Andy brings his guitar and his equipment on stage. Only one young man from the band remains, threadbare beard, black t-shirt, putting away his percussion and drums. Andy speaks. "You don't have to clear that off now for me. I mean, if you're staying anyway, you're welcome to leave it there, if you want to until afterwards."

The man looks up. "Are you the last band?"

"I think so. It's just me."

"Please," Henry calls out. "Go ahead and do your set up. You start at ten and we like to keep the trains running on time."

"Am I the last act tonight?"

"Are you what? Yes! Ms. Maureen says you're wonderful so I'm throwing you in. Our former ten o'clock left town in a hurry this morning."

"Fine." Andy addresses the black t-shirt man while setting about his gear. "You were fantastic."

"Thanks. Have a good set."

"I saw you play before. I've wanted to meet you. Will you stay? I wanted to talk to you all afterwards."

"Sure. What do you do?"

"Guitar. And some effects."

"Right on," T-Shirt man says with a shrug as if saying, 'I guess.'

"I'm Andy."

"Jared." They shake. "Well. Have a great set."

"Thank you."

And so at last the lights seem to dim of their own accord. It seems to Andy that Henry must have just introduced him, yet it sounded like drunken gibberish in some half remembered dream. Someone coughs. Somnolent drifters loiter in pajama like garb, draping themselves a-flop their chairs. Three very straight young men, including a dim replica of Jared, quietly take their seats near the back. The lights dim a little more. Near the front sits a wax statuette of Maureen. Andy's left hand hovers, grazing above the strings, right hand loosely on the neck. He turns and looks at the settings on his equipment. With one hand still on his guitar, the other on his mixer, he begins.

After a while – after many mini adventures lost inside his guitar - Andy opens his eyes, looks again at the gargoyle replica of Maureen, greenish in the dim light, a lovely sea creature in her aquarium. He glances at the three straight statues in the back corner. The cut out figure of Jared opens his plastic eyes. Letting loose another long growling peel of yearning from his guitar, he takes his hand away, letting the note replicate in the marmalade, glowing and he looks at Jared and he nods, puts out his open hands, gestures to Jared, calls him to life, gestures to the drums, to the stage, back to Jared, back to the drums again. Nods. The percussionist points to himself, glances around, stands and waits. Andy nods again and Jared walks on stage.

51.

"Where's Pauline?"

"She left."

"I'm sorry. I thought maybe I could set you two up. But I guess I had to stick around for that, didn't I."

"Set us up?"

"Look, Max. I have to go home. My wife needs me."

"Sure."

"I'll take you home. She'll probably kill me though."

"Why do you say that?"

"Never mind. Let's go. We're already paid up. She'll kill me for that too."

"Is she OK?"

"Yes." They stand and make their way to the front door. "But she's very angry. And now that goddamn cat is sick so of course it's my fault."

"How is it your fault?"

"I was being sarcastic. But maybe it is my fault. And now it's going to take me an hour and a half to take you home and drive back."

"Where do you live?"

"Just up the hill. Like five minutes."

"Rolfe, go home. I can get back myself."

"What? Are you crazy?"

"I don't think so."

"It's after eleven. You'll wait forever for a bus."

"I can walk." They stand now near the hotel entrance.

"Max. Please. It'll take you all night."

"I'll be home in a couple of hours."

"No, Max. You'll be home by dawn if you can find your way home at all. I'll take you. Please," Rolfe concludes, heavy sigh.

"Go home, Rolfe. It'll be fun. I want to."

"You *want* to walk home? Do you have any idea where you are?"

"I know exactly where I am and how to get home. Go see your wife."

"I feel rather responsible for you."

"OK. But I'll be fine."

"Be careful. Stick to the main roads. It's not such a great neighborhood."

"Jesus will protect me," Max asserts.

"No he won't, Max."

"It's OK. Really. And thank you, Rolfe."

"Don't be an idiot. You have to work tomorrow."

Max shrugs. "I can't help being an idiot," and he puts out his hand.

Rolfe shakes his hand. "Alright, Max. But I'll be very angry with both of us if anything happens to you."

"You offered to take me home. That's enough."

"Yeah, but I whined about how long it would take me and that my wife would yell at her little, tiny husband. Please. I manipulated you. Come."

"Goodnight, Rolfe. Thanks again. For a magical evening. I'll see you tomorrow. Maybe we'll do this again," and he walks off.

Rolfe looks after him. "Max!" he calls. "Max! You're going the wrong way!" Max smiles, thumbs up, and turns around.

52.

"Why, Eugene?"

"Why what?" he mumbles, still hiding somewhere in her bosom.

"Please. Why don't you want to look?" He opens his eyes and he sees and hears the fog once more, feels the lifeless breeze of the cataract sky. He hears the fog - in the worlds above, the furnace - now it is the fog. But now it is something else still. He hears what sounds like a swarm. Whereas the fog was a single sound the swarm is an infinite combination of infinitesimal, nauseating, needful particles. He closes his eyes once more. "Eugene"

"What?"

"Talk to me."

"Are we still rising?"

She hesitates. "No," she says. "We're here."

"What do you see?"

"Eugene. It's beautiful."

"It is?"

"Yes."

"What do you see?"

"Waterfalls"

"Where?"

"Everywhere. All in front of me. They're so huge. Bigger, taller, than anything you've ever imagined."

"Really? Mountains too?"

"Mountains! Yes, I see them. Amazing, brutal mountains. Beautiful, clean mountains. Glaciers. Cold mountain tops. Great forests below. Come on, Eugene. Open your eyes and see."

He opens his eyes. "Wow….It really is beautiful. And scary."

"Scary? How is it scary, Eugene?"

"It's overwhelming."

"Yes. Yes it is. But have you ever looked up in the world out there and looked up at night and seen the sky? Even in the city, you can see the stars. Did you look and see while we were on the beach?"

"This is different."

"I guess it is. But think for a minute. How overwhelming is the sky? How huge is the universe? It's much, much bigger than these mountains and these falls. And it's real. How we often lose sight of what is really beautiful and overwhelming, Eugene."

"I guess." He looks down. The fog is thinning. "Oh no," he says softly.

"What is it?"

"The fog is starting to break up. We'll be able to see below."

"That's good."

"I don't want to see."

"You must or you will carry it around inside you, anyway." The swarm of noise begins to differentiate, to atomize. "Your hand feels cold, Eugene."

"Do you hear it?"

She slowly looks about. "Yes, I hear it."

"What do you hear?"

"It's like a great crowd. A great crowd of people roaring and cheering."

"Cheering? I don't think it's cheering."

"Well what is it? What do *you* hear? What do *you* see?" The clouds below thin to a skimpy gruel. Little black tears begin to lacerate the vapors; little black holes begin to blaze and expand. A yawning black maw, toothless jaws pierce the fog below. Eugene stares into the gathering blackness and for a scalding moment it seems that Caroline is gone and he is lost in this ugly world.

"Caroline!"

"I'm right here, baby." The blackness itself begins to resolve into a gargantuan gray, endless pit, a deep jagged valley, saw toothed, stretching out towards both horizons. The jagged teeth marks in the pit are great man-made mountains of dung, swarmed by trillions and trillions of frenzied flies.

"The longer we look, the worse it gets."

"What are they?" Caroline asks.

"I told you; I've never been here before, you know. I was just in some building with dirty linoleum. Checkerboard. Lots of papers. I've never been to this shit place. I'll never hear the furnace again the same way. Now it will sound like swarms of shit flies. Thanks for that."

"It's your world. What does it mean?"

"Those are…… mines, I think. People are mining below. We can't see them."

"What mines?"

"There are all these mines I think, down below. And people working in those mines."

"Mines? What kinds of mines?"

"I don't know…"

"It all looks the same."

"I know. It all looks the same. Nothing but mountains of shit."

"You sad little man!"

"I never saw this place before! You understand? This is *not* my world!" He stops short, trembling. "Why didn't you take me to your nice place?"

"I wanted to know you."

"Really? Well then. What do you think!" he sniggers

"If there's more, we should see it."

"Please…"

"You must show me, Eugene. If it's the worst thing, you must see it. Now. Once you show me, we can leave this place. And you will be rid of it. Forever."

53. Thursday Night

The night is raw and electric and home is far, far away, and this precarious fact seems to invigorate him. Max takes long, purposeful strides down Hollywood Boulevard. He had heard it was a strange and haunted place, full of sick and isolated people. Touching the postcard in his pocket he tells himself, nearly aloud, "Well, here I am. Here I am," and he shyly adds under his breath, "Here I am, Jesus. Here I am. I'm taking a walk. See? I hear you are everywhere, looking down at everything. Or if you are everywhere, then maybe you don't have to look down. If you are everywhere, then you must be with me now, and must always be with me. Other people can talk to you right now, too. How is that? Are you like the ocean or the moon? You can be everywhere at once. But did you create these? Are you bigger than them? What does that mean? I'm a little scared right now, but kind of excited. This place is somehow ugly and beautiful at the same time. Is that how I am supposed to see it? Would you protect me if something bad happened to me right now? I wouldn't be able to protect myself. But I don't think anything bad will happen. But you wouldn't do anything, would you? Bad things happen every day. Why do people ask for your protection? Do bad things happen only to people who don't know you, or do they happen to everyone? Do you love everyone or no one? What if I just talk to you? That would be good. Am I just talking to myself? Or maybe I'd never be alone. And when bad things happen, you would be sad. Would you do anything or just be sad for me? Are you busy enough since you created everything? Did you create everything? Why do people look to you? I like to think about you. As a baby. As a comfort. I'd like to be a baby. I feel like a baby. If I were a baby, I would be taken care of. But then again, I'd be completely helpless wouldn't I. If you are so comforting and you love everyone why do you get so mad if people don't believe in you and do as you say? And why am I talking to you now? Are you real? I like talking to you. I don't know why. I don't care. I'm just talking. If I talk to you then maybe I'm never alone. But then, neither are you. What do you think of that? It's dark right here. I'm a little scared; there's something mean and unlovable about this space right here. Are you here as well? Is this place beautiful, too? Just keep me company, Jesus. If I talk to you, you are with me. Unless I am just talking to myself. I don't know. Maybe. I like talking to you." He walks past shuttered buildings and he nearly stumbles over an inert homeless man in a sleeping bag. The toothless gray green buildings look over their noses at him. He passes a brightly lit liquor store with an electric sign housed in a yellow plastic covering with big black letters. Gower Liquor. He stops right next to the sign such that his face is nearly absorbed in a sea of canary yellow. He can hear the buzz and crackle from the power. He feels peaceful and lost for a moment. The street has utterly disappeared and the sign feels clean and safe. Slowly he turns and continues, a little dazed, thinking now about the homeless man and wondering if he, Max, could ever end up like that. What would the man do the next day? And every day? But what do I do? Suddenly, Max misses his quiet, clean little room and his sweet little book. Two young men, Mexicans, nervous energy, nasty laughter, reel past him. Without thinking he stares after them. The shorter one looks back and their eyes lock, the other man's eyes bloodshot beneath the street lamp.

"Do you know me?" Max opens his mouth but nothing escapes. "Hey, do you know me, asshole?" The expletive does not sound violent on the man's lips; it is merely a mode of address between strangers on the street. Max feels as if he must have replied to the man. But he has not. The man's face goes slack. "You gonna just stare at me? Do I look that pretty to you?" And at this, the suggestion of violence creeps into this voice.

"I'm not staring," Max says, as if to apologize.

"You're staring at me right now!"

"I'm sorry. I don't mean to."

"But you gonna keep staring at me anyway?"

The taller man now turns to Max. "Just turn around and walk away, dumb shit, so we don't have to kick your ass." Max finds that helpful.

"OK. Thanks," and he promptly pivots and walks briskly towards a sudden, on-coming wave of dark, menacing people. The apparent leader of this gang is tower tall with a bone thin face and a long black trench coat, pale skin and a jagged blood red Mohawk spiked from his bald head. I'm staring right at him! But the wave of people passes through him. "Relax," it seems he hears the man mutter, the stale breath of his long coat slipping away.

54.

The apartment is dark, yet still exudes a waxy, bitter light, abandoned and still. "Tanya," he calls out, but he knows she must be gone. Forever? He walks to the refrigerator where he looks for and finds her note taped to the freezer door, her girlish scrawl.

I couldn't wait for you. I took Taxi to the Vet hospital on Gower.

She writes the address large and clear enough to suggest that she expects him to come. Why didn't she wait? Taxi must be very ill. He opens the fridge and finds a can of beer that had lurked ignored for many months. He tolerates the acid pissy taste, cold, cheap American beer left over from some forgotten party. He wants to stay still in this interim moment, a private drink that touches nothing else in his life.

55.

Max stares at it, a visage from a dream with its gothic green edifice, Asian pagodas, and its hot red tongue of carpet inviting the public into its surreal chambers. His favorite movie was Willie Wonka and the Chocolate Factory. Willie Wonka gave Charlie the chocolate factory. But Jesus gave us the whole world and more! Max stares at the Hollywood stars. Salmon colored brass rimmed pentagrams against a gritty, black empyrean; the copper coated names in the middle form a complete mystery to him. No Willie Wonka. Max's reverie is interrupted by staccato shouting. He turns to see a lanky black man, bald with eye make-up and a dirty flower print house dress draped over his soiled slacks; the man shouts at no one, looks at nobody, hands gesticulating wildly. Max looks away and down once more at the salmon stars. He recalls a place exactly like this place in his dreams, looking through a glass darkly, almond bright lights and shimmering cities beneath briny waters.

He turns left down Highland Avenue. Empty boarded recording studios, a long, merciless stucco wall. A wild sound pricks his ears. Max walks briskly closer to the sound. It's music; a restless yet comforting wrestling of rhythm and fairy tale music. Max stands still in the limbo of dream and waking, oblivious of his surroundings.

56.

The night receptionist in her colorless scrubs leads Rolfe down the hall and knocks on an unmarked exam room door. She opens it. "Go inside," she says. Rolfe catches himself staring at her buttocks. He enters the room and he immediately sees Tanya and the doctor, a younger woman with curly hair and thick glasses standing over Taxi who lies quietly, too quietly on the table. Neither woman seems to take any notice of him. The doctor holds open the cat's mouth to display its roof, its sour yellow teeth and black gums; she pulls the loose skin upon its skull back to keep him immobile and she carefully places a gloved finger up the creature's anus to which the cat emits a long, low indignant grumble.

"I'm surprised he didn't hiss at you," he hears himself say.

"Are you Mr. Gunther?" the doctor asks as if talking to the cat.

"Yes," Tanya answers.

"I got your note," Rolfe adds. Tanya looks at him as if amazed by his stupidity.

"We'll take some blood tests to rule out poisoning. When's the last time he was outside."

"My husband let him out around six or six thirty. He only came back an hour ago. The cat."

"When's the last time he vomited?" Rolfe is struck by the violence of these words.

"He threw up three times before I brought him over."

"In the last hour?"

"Yes," she says, choking on the word.

"Poor little guy," the doctor says, rubbing the cat's neck with one hand while feeling its gut with the other. "We'll have to sedate him to do the blood test. It won't take long. Less than an hour if you want to wait."

"How much will it cost?"

"I can't say. You can talk to Sonja up front."

"I might. But go ahead."

They sit together in the waiting area. Hard blue plastic chairs. Barren white walls. Where are the pictures or paintings of dogs and cats? Rolfe tries to take her hand. She removes it. "Don't."

He stiffens and after a moment he asks her. "What's the doctor's name?"

"Does it really matter?"

"No, I suppose not right now." They sit for a moment. "Does the doctor think Taxi is poisoned?"

"It's Goshen. Her name. And you heard her say she has to take his blood to find out. You were in the room when she said it. No?"

"OK. Fine. Maybe I missed that part when I saw our cat lying there like that."

"Oh you poor thing. You must be so traumatized," she says in a nasty voice.

"We always let him outside." They fall into a lumpy silence. "He's a tough cat. He's going to be OK."

"He's tough because he survives you treating him like a toy."

"It's true."

"Don't try to comfort me right now. You're just no good at it."

"Fine. Tell me what I can do."

She glances wearily at him. "You can tell me where you've been all night."

"I met a friend. From work. His name is Max."

"You just run out of the house like a little boy."

Rolfe begins to wag his foot rapidly, unaware it seems that he is even doing it. "What's wrong with Taxi?"

"You heard! He's vomiting and now he's not doing anything." She begins to weep.

"He'll be OK, Tanya."

"How the fuck do you know that?"

"I just think he will."

"Well who gives a shit what you think?" He sighs and he rises, hands in his pockets, jaw clenching. "There he goes," Tanya narrates. "He's standing up. He's standing and he's ready to run away. Right?"

"Who are you talking to?"

"Ready to run?"

"I'm not running away!"

"No? Walking away? Are you walking away?"

Rolfe sits down. "You act like you *want* me to walk away."

"Yeah…well part of me does want you to go, Rolfe."

"Well I can do that if all you're going to do now is throw shit at me."

"The other part of me needs to know you're not going to leave. No matter what."

He takes her hand again and she lets him. "I'm not leaving."

She squeezes his hand before suddenly withdrawing it. "I'm angry at you, Rolfe." He says nothing. "Do I get to be angry with you? Without being afraid that you'll leave?"

"You blame me because Taxi is sick. I don't think that's right. But I think I understand."

"You're so stupid, Rolfe," she says, almost gently. "Do you realize you're always acting like you're afraid that I'll leave you? Like it's your greatest fear. But it's always you. It's always you who's leaving me. Like tonight."

"I should have called you. But I didn't know the cat was going to get sick."

"That has nothing to do with it. You leave me alone all evening. What does that have to do with the fucking cat? You walk out like you want to punish me. Why are you so jealous of other men? What have I ever done? It's not just Frank. It's all men. Do I just go and stay out for hours in a bar or something? Spending money we don't even have. Running up bills, big man, because you have a credit card. You do that. I hate that."

He hates even the mention of her lover's name. Ex-lover. Especially now. "I've done it before?"

"Are you fucking kidding me? Two or three a times a week you leave and I don't know where you are."

"That's not true."

"Sometimes until nine or ten. But last month you stayed out until past midnight. Yes, I keep track. You're my husband."

"But I'm not doing anything. There's no other woman, for sure. I can guarantee you that." He can see Pauline and feel her hot bony hand on his wrist. She was for Max. Nothing happened anyway.

"You know what, Rolfe. I never accused you of cheating on me. OK? You think it's OK to just be gone all the time as long as you're not with another woman? Is that it? So what are you doing?"

"I drive around. OK. That's all. I just drive around. That's all I do. Sometimes I get a beer, like tonight. But not usually."

"Why?"

"Why?" He turns away and kicks the air in the shins. "I hate it when you ask why," he mutters. She just looks at him. Hands in pockets, he answers, looking away. "Sometimes, I just need to relax. I just need to clear my head. Is that so hard to understand?"

"You drive around all day long. Then you go and drive, and spend money on gas or go to a bar to go 'relax'. And...and you can't relax at home. Yes. Yes, that is *hard* to understand." She shrugs and he looks at her and he sees a face suggesting that he is a foolish, exasperating person. He stands again. "Ah! He's standing. Ready to leave."

"That's enough, Tanya......I'm just standing here," he adds. "That's all I'm doing. Standing here, looking at you." He sits down again and sighs heavily, "Let's argue some more in the cat hospital."

"It's not a cat hospital."

He lowers his voice, "Tanya, I've never been with another woman, never would be with another woman. I know you think I'm defensive about that, but I have nothing to hide and you're still wondering what I do and....so I feel like I do keep having to tell you."

"You don't even listen to me. I never thought you were cheating on me. Did you even hear me at all?"

"You're still angry with me."

"For God's sake, I'm really just worried about Taxi right now. Not you. Can't you understand that?" He looks at her. "Yes, I'm mad at you because when I need you, you're out wasting gas and money in some hotel bar clearing your head. I don't know and I don't even care right now. I just want my cat - our cat – to be OK. What's so difficult about that?"

Rolfe stares at the dull gray baseboards. They seem to cling rather than merge with the wall. Soon they will curl up and after a heavy rain they will separate. Shoddy workmanship. A tall florid man with an empty pet cage walks in the room, a white bandage covering his left eye. He sits down heavily across from them, barely fitting on the little bench. Joining them is a skinny black woman with a little boy about three years old, his finger stuck it seems in his right nostril, casting a worried look at the blank walls. The woman, who appears to have a broad dent in the left side of her head calls out loud, "What kind a pet place is this? Ain't no animals in here, far as I can tell. Come on Damian, sit

128

with mamma." She pulls a coloring book out of her purse. "Come on over, baby." The boy remains rooted to where he stands, finger wedged deeper up his nose, staring wide eyed at Rolfe.

Rolfe turns to Tanya and takes her hand again. "OK, baby. I understand." He turns away from the little boy. "I want to.....I do."

57.

Magically the audience has somehow doubled and tripled, everyone standing and cheering, everyone but Maureen. Then Maureen. All of them cheering until Maureen alone is the last one standing. The cheering and shouts and applause continue until exhausted, everyone settles again, the lights come up, cleared throats, scraping chairs. Ecstatic incoherent congratulations from irascible Henry. The exchange of information with the band on little misshapen strips of paper. Motes of future plans. After everyone packs and loads their equipment, after all that, there is only Andy and Maureen. They sit in the truck and she smiles at him, lipstick melted on her teeth. "You're a fucking genius," she whispers. "I told you."

"You like that?"

Her smile fades for a moment. "Yes. And you are. It's a fact."

"That was fun."

"Let's go for a ride."

"Sure!" he agrees, exhausted and exhilarated, never wanting this night to end. "Where?"

"I know a place."

Down the boulevard they float, yellow light, palm trees, raggedy hotels, diners, the odd studio leering out from Sunset boulevard. "Look!" she shouts. "It's Max. I see him."

"Where?"

"On the right. See him bouncing along? Max!!" she calls out. Andy had never noticed how Max bounces up and down as he walks, as if there were springs on his feet. It looked like a lovely way to move through life. He looks as if he might be talking to himself.

"Max, it's us. It's Andy."

"Maureen," she shouts, pointing at herself. "Max! It's Maureen and Andy!"

Max looks over at the car. "Hi! Hi!"

"What are you doing?"

"I'm walking."

"Do you need a ride?"

"A ride? No, thanks. I like walking."

"Where are you going?" Andy asks

"I'm going home."

"Where do you live?"

"Palms."

"Max, get in the car," Andy instructs. "I'll give you a lift."

"No thanks."

"You're gonna walk all the way to Palms?"

"Yeah."

"Max, you're a madman," Maureen shouts with admiration. "You're mad Max."

"I am?"

"He's an idiot," Andy mutters, smiling. Max starts to walk again, still waving. Andy creeps along beside him. "Max. Last chance. You're twenty miles from home."

"No, no. It's no more than ten or eleven."

"Get in the car, Max."

"No thank you Andy."

"Get in the car, Max!" Maureen screams. Andy looks at her.

"Thank you Maureen. But I'm having an adventure. I feel great."

"You're on an adventure?"

"I feel like Jesus is guiding me, telling me that he's looking after me. You know? It's like I'm walking with him now."

"What?"

"Hey, Max," Maureen calls out again. "You are so cute. You sure you don't want to come and sit with me in the back. We'll make out."

Max's eyes go wide and he slowly shakes his head. "No thanks. That's very nice of you."

"You're scaring him, Maureen. He thinks you're serious."

"Maybe I am," she says, still looking out the window.

A small clique of ragged teenagers strides past shouting, "Get in the fuckin' car, Max! Get in the car. Get in Max! Max!"

"Don't curse at my friend," she calls out.

"Shut up you ugly bitch," one of the youths calls out. "Horse faced bitch"

"Fuck you!" she lashes out, "I'll grind your balls in my heels, you worthless bag a shit!!"

Andy gasps, "That's enough, Maureen!"

"You'll shrink my balls with your nasty face, Mr. Ed." The kids laugh.

"I'll rip your face off!" she screeches and she continues to curse at them, shrieking like an angry witch. Something hard bounces off the truck and Andy turns to catch one of the youths slamming his hands against it. A second youth grabs the back of the cab, looking as if he also plans to jump in.

"Fuck, we're getting out of here," he begins to accelerate.

"Careful. You'll drop him in the street."

"What do you care? You were gonna rip his face off." And Andy begins to pump the brake. The kid jerks and jumps down and thrusts out his middle finger. An unseen car sounds his horn and they hear the sound of brakes slamming as they pull away.

"Are you OK?" Andy asks. They sit in silence. "Am I going the right way?" No response. "I'm gonna guess we're going the right way." They pass La Brea. Andy glances at Maureen, her eyes glassy, far away.

58.

"What is the one thing you don't want to see that we haven't yet seen?"

"Isn't this bad enough? What for, Caroline?" he mutters.

"Just look at it. See it and we can go."

"Let's go now."

"Accept it. And you'll never see it again." Could she be mocking him? "You already know what it is. Turn away now and you'll never be rid of it."

"We need to leave. Can't you see? The hills are rising. So are the flies. Let's get the fuck out of here. Now."

"You can leave at any time. With or without me. You're not even really here. Remember?"

"Yeah. I know. But let's go."

"You're sweating baby. Are you that scared?" She squeezes his hand. He remembers she has been holding his hands the entire time.

"Of course I'm scared. I'd rather look at you." She smiles at him. "You look really beautiful."

"Let's see if you tell me that again, in the morning. Back in the world."

"I will. I promise."

"You can't know that. Trust me. You don't even see me as I really am."

"I told you before. Didn't I?"

"You weren't seeing me then as I really was. As I really am."

"Let's leave right now. We'll turn on the light and I'll tell you again."

"No!" She says in alarm. "Look. Leave now and this place will never leave you. It's only in the world up there that this place can harm you. Not here." Eugene nods, uncomprehending. He turns, his stomach lurching as the mountains have indeed breached the pits. "Keep looking." Out of the tallest of the hills, a strange misshapen thing begins to form. His gut begins to clench.

"Do you see, Caroline?"

"I'm looking."

"Can we go now?"

She squints and studies the strange cancerous growth from out of the dung hills. All is silent now. Suddenly she gasps – but in laughter instead of horror. "My God, Eugene."

"It's not funny. How is that funny?"

"I know. It's horrible. But it's so ridiculous."

"That's a fucked up thing to say," and he feels himself on the verge of turning on her, since it surely is all her fault.

"Don't be mad at me, baby. This is your world."

He thinks he can forgive her, for she called him baby. He turns to look back towards the city from which they came, but there is nothing out there, only a chalky gray sky and a featureless, formless white plain below spreading out forever. "Is it still growing?"

"Maybe. But it's not a monster."

"It's disgusting."

"It's *you*!"

"No it's not!"

"No it's not. But you made it." Rising now above the pits is a dung sculpted statue bearing Eugene's unmistakable likeness; naked, bulbous stomach, wobbly looking legs, curly hair - shaped by horrible curls of writhing excrement - all set in a mock absurd pose of DaVinci's David, a look of utter, helpless foolishness on its agonized features, bug eyed and slack jawed. Insignificant, retreating genitals. Eugene. Flies begin to swarm the statue, multiplying in a fury. The statue appears ready to cave in on itself at any minute. Yet it continues to grow. Soon the latent stench of shit and defeat will burst in upon their overstimulated imaginations.

He turns to Caroline, "Goddammit, we have to go now!" But her face, still serene, is swarming with flies. "No!!" and the flies pour into his mouth. Sudden silence as he feels himself choking. They fall and land instantly upon their blankets in the pitch black warmth, in each other's arms, furnace blasting, Caroline's hair in his mouth. Eugene coughs, wheezes, catching his breath, unsure for an instant whether he has landed in his own basement or at the bottom forever of the dung pit itself. "No! Goddamn it! No!"

"Eugene. We're back."

"I wanna go home!"

"You are home."

"I wanna go home," he repeats weakly.

"You are home. You're safe now."

Moments pass.

The darkness feels as if it's inside his skull, as if he had no eyes. But he hears. The furnace still flows along the hush like a river and closer, much closer is the tiny wheeze of Caroline's gentle snore. He realizes he is safe, wrapped up and nestled against her. Her warmth is close to his, but where is her spirit? Has she found her pre-dawn feast without him? He wants to go there and stay there forever in a place without a place, without a time, forever before the dawn.

59.

Andy winds his way up a stunningly steep dark road. Instantly, the boulevard is gone. Maureen sits impassively, glassy eyed beside him. A cross road appears on the right. "Turn here," she says. Andy turns sharply and they pass several homes, perched against the hill above them, and more of them clinging to the tops of hills below them. Houses disappear, and Andy slowly glides through the dark lane which turns and suddenly ends in a cul de sac. "Pull over," she says and he does so. There are two large homes set apart next to an empty lot facing the glow of the great metropolis radiating below them.

"Did you want to get out and look?" Andy asks, feeling stupid. She gets out and pulls off her shoes, tossing them on the hood of the truck where they crash in Andy's ears and she continues walking awkwardly across the dirt. He follows her. The city glow resolves into the panoply of red and white points of light spread endlessly in every direction. "Are you OK?" he asks.

"I'm sorry. For losing it. For screaming like a freak. I'm embarrassed."

"We all let stupid people get to us sometimes."

"Would you believe me if I told you that I've never done that before?"

"Probably not."

She smiles. "Did it bother you?"

"A little. I just hope you don't get that mad at me."

"You just need to act right." He folds her arms and winks at him.

"I guess I will."

"You probably think I'm a crazy woman, don't you."

"No."

"Don't you think I'm just a little crazy?"

"I think you're crazy beautiful." It just came out.

She seems to think about this. "That's not what I asked you."

"You might be a little angry." And yes, you might be crazy.

133

"You're never really alone, are you? And you're never without your purpose." She looks out at the city again. "Do you think that all those people out there have a purpose, have a passion?"

"There's a lot of artists that feel lonely."

"Not you though.......You think I'm beautiful?"

"Yes."

"Really?" she probes, casually.

"Hell yeah."

She looks away. "Do you think Tim has a passion or a purpose? Or Samuel? Or Max?"

"Who can know that?"

"Will you get me free tickets to your concerts when you're a big, cock raging rock star?"

"I'll leave them at the will call window."

"Shut up," she says playfully. "You're giving me a back stage pass." And she softly hits him but then she folds her arms and walks to the edge of the little field overlooking the city. Conveniently, she finds a saddle shaped stone which she sits upon. "Come here" she suggests. Andy sits beside her, tingling at her warmth through the fabric of her dress. They sit in silence.

"You came from Indiana?"

"Yeah."

"It sounds nice to be from somewhere else. You wandered around in the desert for a while?"

"A little something like that."

"Have you ever seen those guys before?"

"Which guys?" He thinks of the teenagers on the boulevard.

"The band that was up there with you tonight." As if reading his mind, she playfully hits him again with her purse.

"Once. I saw them play last week. I wanted to play with them even then. But I never got to meet them."

"It was like you always knew each other."

"I want to play in a band. I want to have that conversation, if you will, with other people. It's a powerful thing. I don't want to always just play with myself."

She giggles, "Stop saying that."

"Not as long as you keep smiling when I do."

"That is so Henry, to say something like that."

"How do you know that guy?"

"I talk to people. Remember? Especially weird people."

"I've seen how you talk to strangers." He regrets saying this, thinking once more of the teenagers on the street.

"So you never played in a band before?"

"I have. Many times. But nothing really stuck. The only time that was really memorable was..... just before I got here."

"In Indiana?"

"New Mexico. I was on my way out here, to L.A. Just a few weeks ago. I made a long kind of pit stop in the desert."

"Just like that, you formed a band in New Mexico?"

"For a day. Two days."

"Really? Tell me about that."

"You want to hear about that?"

"I do. It's a story. Right? Tell me all about it. Right now."

60.

It settles soft yet darkly upon his being like a fine chalky silt, the kind that sticks to the inside of a lung, that vague unease, his disrupted reverie, the comically violent verbal outburst from that girl, unhinged like a crazed puppet doll whose wires catch fire. What was her name? Those heaping ragged youths that pounded the car; why were they so angry? He accepts the reality of violence, of chaos, but it mystifies him. All he knows is that it seems an ever present under current, something never outside ones peripheral vision, an ugly form of communication that remains an option, an ancient way of establishing order through chaos. He touches his own face and feels its softness, its smoothness. Max marvels and shudders that he's never been beaten - at least not as an adult - he doubts very much if he could do anything to stop it now any more than he could stop it as a child. Jesus, what do you think?

"Hey. You," Max turns. He blushes at the rude sensation that he has been caught in the act of doing something wrong or foolish. A young man nods at him, slight of build with a wispy, thin mustache. Max considers he should just keep walking, but he stops and nods his head.

The young man speaks again. "You lookin' for something?"

"I'm sorry?" Max says.

"You're sorry? What are you sorry about, man?"

"I don't know."

"You don't know? Let me ask you something. No come on, man," he laughs, "I don't bite. Seriously." Max stands still. "Are you looking for something?"

"Am I what? Am I looking for something?"

"Yeah! Maybe you're just goofy. But I thought you were looking for something."

"I'm trying to find where I live."

The man nods, takes another drag of his cigarette. "Well, I can't help you with none of that. But I think I know how you feel."

"That's OK. I mean I know where it is but it's just far and I have to walk the whole way."

"You got any cigarettes?"

"I don't smoke."

The man exhales smoke from his nostrils. "Damn. My last one. You're lucky you don't smoke. These things will kill you."

"Really? Why do you smoke them?"

"I don't know. It's just something to do. Smoke to pass the time," he says, "Until you die."

"Sometimes I've wanted to smoke."

"So....smoke!"

"It's not good for you. But it seems to keep people company. Like you're not alone. Is that why you smoke?"

"What are you doin' out here? Nobody like *you* just *walks* around not looking for anything?"

"I told you, I'm just going home."

"Where do you live?"

"I live in Palms. Near Culver City."

"So why the hell are you way out here? That's messed up."

"Yes. Well, my friend Rolfe, we were in this big hotel. This bar. I just wanted to....walk home. He had some kind of emergency or something."

The man takes another drag. Looks thoughtful. "It's OK. I can like, relate to this. You know? My own brother-in-law; I go with him to the hospital even though I don't really need to be there, and we're all there because his kid's in the hospital. This dude stays up there. Never comes down. Forever. I mean I get it, the man is worried about his kid. But I can't wait forever while he sleeps it off. Right?"

"No, I don't suppose anyone can wait forever."

"What am I supposed to do?"

"I don't know."

"I start walking! Just like you. That's a fact."

"I see what you mean. Do you live far?"

Paco tosses his hand up. "I'm just staying up the hill tonight. I'm not going back up to my sister's now. That's far. And bogus."

"What's wrong with your brother's child? Your nephew."

"My brother-in-law. Not my brother. And there's nothing wrong with the kid. He's fine."

"Well...why is he in the hospital?"

"There's nothing wrong with him, I said. He just got scared or something by a car. What are you asking me for about that, anyway?"

136

"I was just…you know. I was just listening to you. And you said…well anyway, I was just curious. That's all."

"Yeah, well, if you were listening you woulda heard me say that there is nothing wrong with him. That makes three times now I tell you that."

"You seem angry. Maybe I should wish you a good night."

"No, no, no, come on man."

"You seem angry."

"I just told you, homie. I'm not angry. I'm never angry. Come on, you wanna be my shrink now?" and Paco winks at him.

"I don't know what that is. But I'm glad you're not angry."

"You don't like it when people get angry. Does that piss you off?" And Paco laughs at his own irony. "Get it? So you're just like me, man."

"I am?"

"You don't get angry, right? Hey, did you know you were talking to yourself?"

"What?"

"I said, did you know that you were fuckin' talkin' to yourself?"

"You mean, before you first started talking to me?"

Paco raises his brows and spreads his arms out as if to fully embrace the obvious. "Uh. Yeah!"

"I guess it looked like that."

"It looked a lot like that. I shoulda just figured you for crazy, like everyone else around here."

"But I wasn't talking to myself."

"Were you talkin' to aliens. Spirits? The CIA? Shit."

"I was talking to God."

"Alright then. There's nothing crazier than that, you know."

"Really?"

"Are you like retarded or something?"

"People keep telling me that, but I don't believe so."

Paco laughs. "You talk all the time to God. You and he are buddies from way back?"

"Actually, I just started tonight."

"What? For real?"

"Yeah, I just started talking to him this evening."

"Get out."

"Excuse me?"

"You're for real?"

"Um….I guess. I mean. I exist,"

Paco laughs. "Oh man. I like you. So you were just talkin' to God? Did he talk to you back?"

"No."

"That's good."

"It is?"

"Jesu Christo?"

"Who?

"You were talking to Jesus? Or some other God."

"Jesus. Yes! How did you know?"

"Come on. Nearly everyone talks to Jesus if they talk to God at all. Unless you a Jew or something. Or a Buddhist."

"Who do they talk to?"

"Shit, I don't know."

Max brightens. "Do you talk to Jesus?"

"Hell, no. Ah! That's funny. I said, 'Hell no' about Jesus. Get it?"

"Never?"

"No more."

"You used to?"

"Maybe"

"Why don't you talk to him anymore?"

"Nah. I don't believe in that stuff no more. I hardly did before."

"Before what?"

"Before...." Paco begins, impatiently. "Before I stopped believing altogether."

"Well what happened?"

"Did anything happen? Nothing happened. That's just it. I quit praying. Nothing ever happened. Maybe it's good for you, praying and all. Not for me, though."

"That's pretty much what Rolfe said."

"Rolfe?"

"My friend. The one I saw tonight."

"Oh, your friend. I guess I'm not keeping up, man. Yeah, your friend, the one who left you out here."

"He did not leave me out here. I chose to walk."

"I chose to walk away from my brother in law. Maybe it wasn't too smart. But I'm not as bored out here. And maybe something could happen."

"Something?"

"Yeah. Something. Anyway, maybe you need to get back to your praying and stuff. "

"I'm not really good at it. I don't know any prayers is probably the problem. This woman I met tried to teach me, but..... I don't know."

"You just said you were talking to Jesus."

"Trying to. Yes, all evening."

"You like it?"

Max smiles. "Yes. I think."

"Well relax. Talking to God. Prayer. Same thing."

"I think Rolfe said that, too."

"Maybe he's a smart guy. Anyway.." and Paco restlessly looks around. "Look man, let me ask you." Paco gestures him towards a locked storefront with an awning. "You got any money?"

Max looks at Paco, wide eyed. "Not really."

"Not really?"

"I have two dollars."

"Ah," Paco sighs. "Keep it. I figured....but check this out." And he puts his hand in his pants pocket and pulls out a small plastic bag, half filled with little blue pills. "You see that? You know what those are?"

"Yes. Pills. Those are pills."

"You know what kind?"

"Blue. They're blue pills."

Paco laughs. "Yeah. They're blue, alright."

"What are they for?"

"These two here," he says, pinching the bag, "They're for you."

"Do I want them?" Max asks, wide eyed.

"You wanna see God, right?"

Max thinks about this. "That might be overwhelming."

"I thought Jesus was your friend and all?"

"I want to believe that."

"Well, homes; you just take two of these, and you will see your friend, Jesus." Paco puts the bag back in his pocket. "No money. No God. Maybe that's best."

Max shrugs. "I don't really know what you're talking about."

"I just told you. You take these blue ones, you feel right. You see right."

"I don't understand."

"You like to say that. You like to say, 'I don't understand'. You take...these pills...you understand."

Max ponders this. "God.....God is not in a pill."

"Sure he is. God's in here," Paco says, pointing to his temple. "You want to open up your mind." And he winks and cocks his thumb as if shooting himself in the head. Paco pats the pocket with the pills and winks again and says, "I'm looking to meet a good few people who want to open up their minds."

Max shrugs, "God's in here," and he points to chest.

"Hey man, if you're pointing to your heart, it's on the left side of your chest, not smack in the middle."

Max moves his hand over. "I think we're supposed to open our hearts to see God."

"Open our hearts. Open our wallets. How about that?" Paco grins "That's what I'm hoping for."

"Well, you can't sell God."

"You sure? You can sell anything. Especially God. It happens every day. Wake up."

"I thought you didn't believe in God."

"I don't."

"I don't understand."

"Stop *saying* that. Are you a retard?"

Max bites his lip and squints at Paco. "You know, that's not a very nice thing to say."

"You want nice? Sure. We can do nice. OK…Tell you what. I'll give you a taste for free. See? That's me, see opening up my heart. To you," and he takes out the plastic bag once more.

"Why are doing this?"

"I'm a nice guy….I'm a really nice guy. And you are too. So you'll be back for more." He puts the pills into Max's hand.

61. Last October

Andy recounts to her everything about those few still moments in the airless little gas station, and about his unlikely yet inevitable meeting with Louie. It was almost like the little man was famous, as if Andy had seen him on television, the little drunken man who was chased from the bar. Without even looking behind, the man shoots out his thumb, carrying his saxophone case with his other hand, rumpled back pack slagging off his shoulders. Andy pulls over.

"Where you headed?"

"Seriously?"

"Yeah, of course. You want a ride?"

"Yes sir!" The blonde man tosses his hair back, throws his gear in the bed of the truck, and jumps in the seat.

Andy starts driving. "I'm going to L.A. Where are you going?"

"Anywhere but here."

"What are you doing out here?"

"Not a whole heck of a lot. Getting thrown out of bars," the man turns to him, the skin still purple around his right eye. "As you will clearly recall."

"Sorry I couldn't help you."

"I wasn't helping myself much, was I?" His clothes look slick and yellowed with wear, his flower patterned silk shirt pasted against him. Yet somehow he doesn't smell.

"How'd you get that shiner?"

The man turns to him again. "By asking too many questions."

"Sorry."

"Don't be. I'm Louie."

"Andy."

"Pleased to meet you. So you're going to L.A? I was headed there once. I got a little side tracked."

"How's that?"

"The last couple of weeks it's just been me and my saxophone. Is that a guitar I see behind the seat?"

∞

He plays the cassette of Mahler's Tenth symphony for him. "Does it put you in your place, Louie?"

"It most decidedly does not put me in my place."

"Really?"

"I can't help but see old folks in their diapers cringing from the smell of shit and death."

"That sounds like being put in your place to me."

"Black Flag. Dead Kennedys. That puts me in my place alright."

"Loud and fast. You disappoint me, Louie. I thought you had more imagination than that."

"You realize you haven't stopped talking about this little crippled girl or her cassette for the last I don't know how long."

"Sorry, maybe I'll stop."

"I doubt it. I'm not asking you too, either. You said she's a musician?"

"I think so."

"She sounds odd."

Andy sighs. "Thanks. I'm sure she is."

"So? Am I complaining about odd? I like odd. Look at me. Am I even? No. I'm odd. I myself am definitely odd. It's not a bad thing. Except it is inconvenient."

Andy nods and they drive on in silence for a moment. "Louie, are you in a hurry?"

Louie smiles. "You wanna go back? You want to play music with this chick? This odd little crippled girl. Just don't leave me alone back there. Let's go play some music."

∞

141

The sky has thinned as they arrive back at the gas station. A rakishly thin man with a John Deere cap appears behind the counter. "Hi. Is that woman still here, the one who works here?"

"There's just me. Can I help you?"

"Show the man the cassette," Louie suggests. "We wanted to tell her how much we liked it. We're musicians," Louie explains as if this explained everything. Andy shows the cassette to the man.

"I don't know anything about that."

"All right. I'm sorry to bother you."

"No bother. I can tell you though if you like where you can probably find her right now."

Louie speaks. "Please do!" and he claps Andy on the shoulder.

∞

The commercial district consists of a single broad and mostly empty thoroughfare of stucco boxes for buildings. Andy pulls his truck into the gravel lot in back of El Gaucho, the sunset exploding blood orange to the west. Just beyond the road, the plain spreads away towards the mountains. Their feet crunch along the ground. As they pass the air conditioning unit fixed to the wall near the kitchen, Andy stops for a moment to listen to it. Louie sniffs, "It smells good," he whisper. "You're buying, right?'

"I guess." There is a single room, surprisingly large and spare, white walls with velveteen style paintings of the desert and the mountains, large booths and a long counter. Aside from a large disheveled man in short sleeves, sitting at the counter, the restaurant looks empty.

Louie spots the back of someone's head at the far booth. "Is that her?"

"Maybe."

"Well let's go find out. Come on."

Andy is convinced it is Maggie but suddenly he feels like a creep. "Sit anywhere you like," the waitress calls out. They stand before Maggie who is lost in a thick, well-worn paperback, a plate of what might have been beans and rice sits before her.

"Hi Maggie. I listened to your tape. It's amazing."

She looks up at the two of them frowning to recognize them. "My tape?"

"Mahler's Tenth. It put me in my place."

"Wow. You decided to stick around this shithole?"

"Maybe. For just a little bit."

"There's two of you now?"

"This is Louie, my new friend."

"You find each other at the side of the road?"

"We certainly did," Louie affirms. "I'm a musician too. And you play piano. Right?" Maggie just stares, her mouth falling open. "May we sit down?"

"Sure." She gestures towards the empty section of the booth. "Did someone hit you in the eye?"

"*He* did. In the mouth, too."

"Can I help you?" The waitress has returned. She's a blonde who looks to Andy like she might have once been beautiful; her face appears prematurely ravaged by cigarettes, sun, and stress.

"Sit down already. You're making Candy nervous," Maggie says. "Did Caleb tell you I was here?"

"The guy at the gas station? I hope that's OK. Are you busy?"

"I don't think so. You wanted to talk about Mahler?"

"What are you reading?" Louie asks.

"'Breakfast of Champions.'"

"Right on. Long live Kilgore Trout!"

"That's right."

"Kurt Vonnegut," Louie explains. "Trippy book."

"It's a good book."

"What's good *here*?" Louie asks.

"Nothing's great. Everything's OK."

Candy arrives. "Sorry to keep you waiting. Can I get you anything? Some menus?"

"Do you still serve breakfast?"

"What did you need, hon?"

"Huevos rancheros. Corn tortillas."

"I'll see what I can do. Hon, that's a nasty shiner you got there."

"You should have seen the other guy."

"Good for you. He looks worse?"

"I didn't hit him. He was just ugly is all." To Andy's surprise, Maggie bursts out laughing.

"OK. Well you got pretty hair at least, don't you?" Candy says.

"Thank you very much."

"Are the girls jealous?"

"Everyone is jealous. Many people hate me because I am so freaking beautiful." Maggie laughs again, a girlish giggle that surprises Andy.

Candy smiles. "They probably don't hate you because of *that*."

"Oh, I just *love* her for that!" Louie says, pointing to Candy.

"And for *you*?"

"Just a diet coke," Andy answers.

She finishes writing, promising salsa and place settings. Louie leans in and speaks. "Get it? I'm not beautiful and people hate me for much more heinous reasons. Well done."

143

"We get it, Mr. Obvious. You flatter yourself," Maggie offers.

"Nice!" Louie seems pleased. "Clearly I am a hideous gnome and any estimation of myself is way too high. Yes."

"I would never say you're a gnome," Maggie says.

"Awesome," Louie whispers excitedly. "Hideous, but not a gnome. Marry me." She puts her hand over her mouth and laughs again, then purses her lips to stop herself. Louie shrugs. "I'm a hideous leprechaun, perhaps."

"Yes. You're a leprechaun. A gay, hideous leprechaun."

"That's the worst kind, right? How did you know?"

"Oh pleeze! You're as queer as a three dollar bill!"

"Will you marry me?"

"Of course."

"So what is your name, dear?"

"Maggie," she answers. "Maybe I'll hit you in your other eye."

"Make it even. At least it's some kind of attention. You want to get out of here and eat ice cream and complain all night how terrible things are."

"Sounds good. Can we watch TV?"

"Anything."

Andy breaks in. "We're here….. because we want to play music with you…..are you busy tonight?"

Maggie looks at him and laughs. "It's not my baby sitting night. I live with this family. You want to have a jam session?"

"Yeah. Can you come out and play tonight?"

"Alright. Hell yeah."

Candy brings Louie's food. "Thank you, love….You too, Andy. Where?" he says turning to Maggie, digging his fork. "Can you fit us all in your place? Andy's got a lot of gear."

"I know a place."

∞

As the sun disappears, Andy parks behind a sickly sea green door in the midst of a stucco powder blue wall. Louie rubs his hands over the stucco bumps. "Don't worry," she says. "No one cares. Walt's cool with it. As long as we clean up. And we're out of here before dawn."

"Who's Walt?"

"The security officer. He's hardly ever here anyway, and there's no cameras or anything. There's no nothing." She takes out a set of keys and begins to try and fit similar looking ones through the back door. "Ah, here it is." She opens the door with a grind and a clatter of keys and they are in. The light is dim. Their eyes adjust. The hallway is narrow and stuffy, checkerboard scuffed floor.

"Isn't there a light in this hallway?"

"Somewhere." She opens an unlocked door and flicks on the light. The room comfortably seats about thirty chairs with folding desks attached.

Louie comments "Power outlets?"

"Yeah. In front and over there," she points to the wall on the left.

"We must be a good hundred yards from the next building."

"And look at these," Andy says.

"Yeah. Look at those."

"They're in crappy condition," Maggie says. "Broken keys, outta tune."

Pushed against opposite corners are three small and elderly wooden pianos. Andy smiles. "Just like you told me. How did they get all these?"

"We had one and it needed repair and the principal or her secretary found another one super cheap, maybe a friend or relative, who sold or donated it. It was cheaper to buy it than to repair the other one. Same thing with the third one."

"How do you even manage to have a school at all?"

"The town used to be bigger. There's about a hundred kids here. K through sixth."

"And you come out here and play all night?"

"Often."

"You're not worried?"

"About what?"

"Monsters? Rapists? Aliens?" Louie suggests.

"Something like that," Andy says

She smiles. "No more than when I'm in my own bed. Maybe in L.A. Or Albuquerque. Not here in Gary. Are you scared right now?"

They all stand for a moment staring. "I'm a little bit scared," Louie says.

Andy says, "Let's get started."

∞

He looks at Maureen. "You sure you find this interesting?"

"Yes. Continue."

"It was slow at first. Setting up. Snack food. Water. Beer. In a school building. Smart. Louie had to bang on every piano to 'break it in', to see how different they sounded from each other. One of them had so many busted keys that Louie figured it was fit for percussion only, which it was, very cool. We took our turns warming up on everything, playing each other's instruments, and badly, but…. We sounded like a bunch of toys breaking. Everything sounded like we were pissed off or insane. Finally things got really quiet." Andy looks at Maggie who stares at the keys, her hands resting, fingers twitching it seems. Louie turns the room lights out but moonlight still pours in from the windows.

145

Red and green lights glow from Andy's amp and mixer. Maggie's piano is illumined from a street lamp, but she herself is in the dark. She begins to slowly play in the stressed, highest octave, a seven note suggestion of a strange melody, anchored by a sudden chord at the gravelly bottom. Andy releases a mournful lament and after that there was no clear distinction between players and no precise moment when Louie finally merges with them both.

"It wasn't until I woke up, that I realized I'd been sleeping. This happened more than once. As long as it was still dark, we'd rouse each other, eat potato chips, drink a little beer, play more music, and there was always something more to play, even though…. we were almost afraid, I think, of what else there was. We played from maybe eight o'clock until dawn, stopping to rest and sleep for five or ten minutes at a time. Until someone - any one of us - began to play again. Except this one time. It was very late or very early, three or four in the morning. We stopped to talk. Me and Maggie. Louie was passed out. I brought her a beer and sat down beside her. We sat on the floor against the wall."

"No thanks," she says. Andy shrugs, thinking he'll drink it himself. "Bringing beer and drinking in a school building. I should have told you not to do it."

"We'll clean it all up. All of it. Louie and I."

"You may have to help me get up later."

"Of course. Are you comfortable now?"

"I'm OK."

They sit in silence for a moment. There is the very occasional car passing outside, so infrequent as to sound almost wistful. Louie's intermittent snoring. The mild wind rouses the sun flavored dust from outside. "I'm having a great time," Andy says.

"Me too."

"This is the best band I've ever played in. By far."

A long pause. "Me too."

"You're amazing."

"You're the one who's amazing. Louie's pretty wild as well."

"Can I ask you something?"

"Yeah. I guess."

"Why do you walk with a cane?"

"I have MS."

"MS?"

"Multiple sclerosis. You've heard of that, haven't you?"

"Of course…I'm sorry to hear that."

"No. Don't be sorry. Come on."

"Sorry. I mean…..How long have you had it?"

"A few years. But I don't really want to talk about it. Is that OK?"

"Sure."

146

"I mean, I don't like to talk about being sick and all. It's boring. Right?"

"Well…no. It's not."

"It gets worse. It doesn't get better."

"That must be really difficult. At least you have your music."

"That could go, too, Andy. I could lose some of my feeling in my hands. One day I won't be able to play. I don't know when." Without even thinking, Andy puts his arm around her. Her neck is warm. "Feeling sorry for the little crippled girl?"

"Do you want me to take my arm away?"

"No. It feels good."

"Thanks for bringing us here."

"This is where I come."

"You come every night."

"Just about. I come here and I play with myself. Or I stay at home….and play with myself. You and Louie are both a couple of mad men….I get so bored here."

"Well that's what I wanted to know. What are you doing here?"

She nestles a little more snugly in Andy's arms. "I like it here. I know, I just said I get bored. But I like it."

"Tell me why you like it?"

"It's peaceful. It's slow. I feel protected and safe. People put up with me. It's like this big empty space of just existing. I love feeling like I'm on an island when I look out into that weird desert. It reminds me of what it really means to walk on the earth, this wild rock floating out in endless space forever and ever. There's room. There's room to be completely ordinary, to be a nobody. There's freedom in that. You can't be a nobody in the city, especially in L.A, even if almost everybody really is, especially in L.A. You can't be a freak in L.A unless you're a fashionable sort of freak."

"Wow," he says softly "…..Did you grow up here?"

"God, no. I grew up in Queens. Until I was ten. Then we moved to L.A."

"So you used to live in L.A?"

"Yes. I don't recommend it. Are you going there to be somebody?"

"I already am somebody."

He can feel her turn to him. "Of course you are. When I say I'm a 'nobody', I don't mean it in a bad way."

"I believe you. I think I get it. You can just kind of live simply, almost outside of time, I guess."

"I won't be here forever, though. I'm not stupid and I know there is such a thing as time."

"Maggie. Are you hiding from anything? Can I ask you that?"

"Well yeah…. But not forever."

147

"From what?"

"From me. And I just don't want to have anything to do with my father right now."

"Is he a bad guy?"

She seems to think about this. "No. He's not. He's not. He's just a shut-down loser. He gave me up for adoption after my mother drank herself to death."

"Oh God."

"It was a nice family, my adopted family, but I never felt like I fit in. I was never close with anyone there except one of the girls. Everything looked great on the outside. They had money. But the mom and dad were so far away, they just had to have some deep seated secrets." They sit in silence and she puts her head on his shoulder. "I've been here two years now. I say I like it here, but I also say I'm bored and I talk like I feel sorry for myself."

"Except when you come out at night and you play your music."

"I'm bored because I don't have anyone like you I can play with." He looks at her and he can see her looking at him. He kisses her once and her lips are full. "You know what...you can ask me anything you want." Through the limited light he can gaze at her eyes and her mouth and he can reconstruct her as completely beautiful and whole and waiting outside of time. Just for him. He kisses her again and this time they converse in this way effortlessly, hungrily, and without pause for a long, long time.

∞

He loses track of whether he is sleeping or awake, when suddenly she whispers his name. "Was I asleep?" he whispers back. He has held her the whole time.

"Yes, of course."

"Am I awake now?"

"It's breaking dawn now. We need to go soon."

"Oh....I was hoping we'd have more time."

"I need to be at the gas station by seven. Will you take me?"

"Of course."

"Maybe you and Louie can stay one more night."

"Maybe. I'll have to ask Louie."

She blinks. "Yeah. Of course. Go ask Louie."

He pulls into the gas station with her. She is too quiet. "Too bad we don't have time to have breakfast," Andy offers.

Maggie nods as if to herself. "Thanks for the ride and for stopping by my place," she says and struggles to get out of the car.

148

Andy gets out. "Let me help you." To his surprise, she lets him, and they slowly walk towards the little shack.

"O – Kay," she says as she fits the key into the door. The door opens and they stand there, helpless.

"So what do we do?" is all he can say.

"Are you gonna stay tonight or not?"

"Or maybe you could come with me, Maggie."

"Seriously?"

"Why not? What are you staying out here for? Someone else can look after this....place. As though that mattered."

She brushes a lock of hair from her face, "I don't know what you're proposing. Are we living together? I don't know. Anyway, I hate L.A. I told you that."

"I want to form a band with you. And record fantastic records. I just don't know what you have to lose."

Maggie seems to think about this. She leans upon her cane and then she sighs and looks at him, her eyes red and heavy laden. "Andy. You're the best thing to come along my way in a long, long time. And I know I have nothing here. But... even the fact that I barely know you doesn't seem important in this. It's what I do think I know that's holding me back."

"What do you think you know?"

"That you can't be serious. That you don't know what you're talking about."

"Maybe I *don't* know what I'm talking about. We don't know each other. I know that. Why not take a chance and do something?"

"I don't think you mean it. I think you know I won't go." She trembles, eyes watery. "That I can't...that I can't go with you. You just don't want to stay here one more night. With me."

"That's not true."

"What you ask is so big and what I ask is so small. Stay." A pick-up truck, new and larger than Andy's pulls in to the pump. "I gotta go open now. You got all day to let me know." And she walks inside.

62. Very Early Friday Morning (the day of the storm)

Had it all just been a dream? Is she a witch? And as he contemplates this, he is dreaming once more, walking through a strange and empty land and the sky is huge and bloody and he remembers the shared dreamtime with Caroline whereas now he is awake and wandering alone and the desert flings out forever away from him and he is weary and lonely and it seems he has always staggered alone through this land. He bolts up right as she speaks to him.

"What time is it?" Eugene grabs for his flashlight and points it straight into Caroline's face. She flinches and puts her hand up and he drops his arm.

"Sorry," Eugene whispers and he feels angry and ashamed, for he sees a homeless street person, her eyes puffy, her face a rough network of lines and splotches, her lips chapped and dry. "Sorry," he repeats.

"What time it is, Eugene?"

"Five seventeen. You need to be somewhere?"

"You said….you would buy me some shoes and socks today."

"So nothing's open right now. I get up at seven."

"The markets are open now. Downtown. It's all cheap down there."

"You wanna go *now*?"

"Please? I want shoes and socks. And you told me you have to work later. What if you don't come later? Or I don't see you."

"You wanna go now?" he repeats. "Fine," he snaps. He realizes she's right. "I woulda found you later, though."

"Please, I really want to have them now."

"I said alright just now. Didn't you hear me say that? Don't worry."

"I'm sorry. I didn't even know how much I missed them until you offered them." Eugene struggles up and using his flashlight he finds the cord for the overhead light bulb. "I wonder if it's like that."

"Like what," he asks irritably, looking for his pants. "And would you turn away, please," he says, even though he is still wearing his underwear.

She turns, "That…that you get used to not having something. Or not having anything at all. You might let go of it. Until one day you think you can have it. And then…you have to have it."

"Are you getting dressed?"

She rolls up clutching the sheet. "Can I ask *you* not to look?"

"No problem," Eugene answers truthfully. He finds his own shoes and socks. "Why don't you just go to your own special place? You know, with the nice bed and all the food. Maybe your shoes are there." She doesn't answer. "Fine," he continues, still not looking at her. "We're going. Let me know which street, if you've seen it already, so I don't have to go wandering around. I got…." he counts his money. "Shit. I got sixteen dollars…and change."

150

"I've seen shoes for only six dollars a pair. Socks are like three for a dollar," her voice humble.

"Do I still need to keep looking away?"

"Wait," and he hears her struggle for a moment. "OK. You can turn around now." She is dressed in her newly washed old clothes. Somehow they look even worse than before. "Thanks again for letting me take a shower. "

"Yeah, sure."

"I cleaned up real good. It's the first time I've gotten this black off in awhile. It'll be perfect when I get my new socks and shoes."

"Yeah, yeah. I get it." Eugene grabs his pager. "I'll be right back."

∞

He shits and lingers, trying to conjure up an image of desire around Caroline, soft and pink, young and blonde. He gives up and washes, inspecting the bathroom approvingly. The pantry. Both are cleaner and more orderly than usual. He glances into the living room and starts. Standing straight ahead is Thomas, or at least his outline jagged in the feeble dawn light. Naked.

"Eugene?"

"Yeah?" the light from outside is too weak to illumine his face yet bright enough to highlight his dangling protuberance, like a rubber glove, a gnarl of seaweed, a rooster waddle; his disgusting penis! Eugene realizes he is staring at it, a surge of raw hatred blowing through him. "What is it?" he snaps.

Thomas pauses, taken aback perhaps by this uncommon ferocity. He says, "There was a bathrobe in here, in the living room closet. And some slippers. Now they're both gone. You know anything about that, by chance?"

"Really......What the hell are you asking me for? Ask one of your stoner friends."

"What?"

"I didn't touch your bathrobe, Tommy."

"The name is Thomas and I did not say that you did anything. But no one else is in the house tonight except for me and Marcy. So I'm asking you."

"I resent you accusing me. You know I never even go into the rest of my house. I stay downstairs like a good little rat, don't I?"

"That's up to you, isn't it? I told you I'm not accusing you, but you are acting awfully defensive."

"Could you please step over to the wall please? Out of the light. Do I really have to look at your ugly junk?"

"What is your fucking problem? You have a complex, don't you," Thomas barks, yet still in a whisper. But he still steps aside just as Eugene has asked.

151

"I will tell you my fucking problem. All of you and your asshole friends and stoner strangers make a fucking mess out of my bathroom and the pantry."

"It's not your bathroom, Eugene. It belongs to everyone."

"How about some common courtesy. How about that? Everyone uses it. No one cleans it but me. Ever. Ever! Why is that?"

"Calm down. We can have a meeting of all of us and discuss this."

"And I never use the other bathrooms. Just this one. And everyone is always using it, but no one cleans up."

"I just said we'll discuss it. We will. As a house."

"What's to discuss! Just clean up after yourselves and your guests, too. I see your shit and your shavings and your fucking *cum* all over everywhere. *Cum!*"

"Calm down."

"It's rude and disgusting. You're like animals." They are shouting now.

"Eugene. *Please* calm down. You gotta lot of complaints for ninety bucks a month."

"What I got is a hole in the ground for ninety bucks and I gotta clean up a bathroom that looks like a train station whore house."

"You're exaggerating, Eugene. It could be a lot worse."

"What does that mean?"

"I'm just saying. I've seen a lot worse in some places where I've lived. I've been around."

"You know what, Thomas. I don't give a shit what you've seen. What *I* have seen is unacceptable. "

"You've never said anything before, so it's not my fault if you're losing it now. We have to have some communication. Yes? But fine, we should talk about it later. Set some rules if we have to. That's twice I've told you."

"Good. Just clean up after yourself and use your own goddamn soap."

"I said we'll talk about it later. There, that's three times. How many times do I have to tell you?" And he turns to head back up.

"And no leaving your panties and socks and bikinis all over the place."

Thomas turns, half way up the staircase. "Eugene?"

"What!"

"Have you seen Sherry's bikini?"

"Who the hell is Sherry?"

"Have you seen it or not? A bright, orange bikini?"

Eugene remembers. Throwing it away in a rage. "Yes. I have. It was hanging in my shower. So I threw it onto the living room floor, a room where I almost never go and which I never use."

"Well we haven't seen it. No one ever said, by the way, that you can't use the living room. Or the kitchen. Or anything else."

"Can I throw my underwear on your kitchen floor?"

"The bikini is missing. You should be a little more respectful with other people's things."

"*Fuck* you, Thomas!"

"You're about two inches from being evicted."

"No I'm not."

"That bikini is missing. And now the robe and the slippers and your attitude. It'll be better for you if they turn up." He turns to go back upstairs.

"I'll tell you what's *not* missing. You wanna know what's *not* missing?" Eugene calls out. "There's plenty of pubic hairs in my goddamn soap. *My* soap. No one else's. You understand. You want to talk about respect? How much respect is there for me in a pubic hair in my *fucking* soap?"

Thomas stops almost near the top, turns around and stands silently and Eugene can feel but not quite see him. Then he turns – Thomas - and continues up the stairs while Eugene watches and waits until he is gone.

63.

Sunset Boulevard rolls upwards and down again. Painted ambiguous beings loiter in heels and wink at him, chatting behind bus stops, leaning against walls, smoking. The lights get thicker, the crowds get bigger, the clubs get faster and louder, and suddenly the prostitutes are long gone. Max crests the boulevard and looks out across Doheny and down into another world, floating like a mossy aquarium it seems, a green, dark, lantern filled boulevard of marquis homes, lawns and trees. He had known what it was like to feel oppressed by his sense of invisibility, but tonight he feels liberated by it, forgetting his sense of impossible distance from the world and feeling safe instead in the midst of the street. Now he crosses over the velvet divide at Doheny and he turns left, then right again at a street called Elevado. The avenue stretches ahead for miles. Max has the street to himself, beautiful, blameless clean homes, each one as large as his apartment building, block after block, rarely encountering a car or a light. The sprinklers turn on, one after another, up the street and down the other side. Max is happy. Thank you, Jesus, he says to himself. He suddenly skips in and out amongst the sprinklers, holding his arms out, letting his pants get wet. He turns and flinches at the blast of light upon his back and all around him. A disembodied voice, instructs him, "Step across the street and onto the sidewalk. Now."

Max notices a cobweb illumined by the cop car, spun from a low hanging branch. The torch light dances furiously upon the window. Could a child inside see the branch lingering there? Could that child reach out and take hold of it? Of course he could. Max knows, for he is that child, if only in his imagination. Would the shadow of that branch be scary or comforting? That he does not know. Can never know. "Over here," the voice commands. Max turns and squints. He sees the outline of a large officer looming in front of him.

"I'm sorry," Max says, putting his hand up. The radio crackles. The flashlight trains on Max's face again and the cop holds up a finger.

"Identification." The cops face is nothing but shadow.

Max pats his pockets but of course there is nothing there but the key to his apartment. And the two pills that the stranger had given him. "I'm so sorry," Max blurts again. "Really. I have no ID on me right now." He feels the cold glaze of regret and perspiration at his temples. "I'm sorry."

"You have no ID? Where's your ID?"

"I left it at home. A friend of mine took me out tonight. He was driving."

"Where do you live?"

"I live in Palms."

"Your exact address." He gives it. "So you don't live anywhere near this street."

"I was walking home, officer."

"That's a long walk. At two o'clock in the morning. What are you doing out here?"

"It's a nice street. It's just a nice safe street and I've been walking for hours from Hollywood."

"Did you have a fight with your friend tonight?" The cop does not seem to be making small talk

"No! I just felt like walking."

"From Hollywood?"

"Yes sir."

"Where in Hollywood?"

"Somewhere on Hollywood Boulevard. This nice hotel."

"What is your friend's name?"

"I'm sorry?"

"Your friend. What is his name?"

"Rolfe. His name is Rolfe."

"Rolfe?"

"Yes sir."

"I'm not familiar with that name. What's his last name?"

"I don't know his last name. We work together is all."

"Sounds like he's not a very close friend. Where do you work?"

"ZZZZAP Messenger!"

"What?"

"Zap messenger? It's a messenger service. "

"I gathered as much. What kinds of things do you deliver?"

Max frowns. Why does the cop care about any of this information? "I deliver mostly envelopes….small boxes, cardboard tubes…maybe chilled specimens, pharmaceutical samples."

"Pharmaceutical samples? Like pills? You carry pills?"

"I don't know what they are. Everything is all packaged and goes from one lab to another or someplace else."

"What's your name?"

"Max," he says, the name dry and appropriately small in his throat.

"Max? Do you know your last name?"

"Yes of course. Max Plum."

"Plum?"

"Yes."

"Spell that."

"P L U M"

"All right. Max. You say you were dancing? Have you had anything to drink tonight?"

"Yes."

The cop radio crackles and squawks. "I want you to tell me exactly what you've had to drink and how much."

"I had a glass of wine with dinner. I had a few sips of beer at a bar. That was before we went to the restaurant." The light goes on in the window behind the branch behind Max. He turns for a moment, hoping to see the child, himself, reaching out.

"You were at a bar tonight? You had a few sips of beer."

"I also had some sips from a blue drink. Something blue. Is that OK, officer? I'm not drunk, sir."

The cop continues writing on his pad, shaking his head. "Why were you dancing through the sprinklers at two in the morning?"

"I was happy. I was praying. I was talking to Jesus…."

"…..Did he talk back to you?"

"No, sir."

"You can do that in Hollywood all you want, I'm not gonna bother you. But that's not acceptable here. I need you to leave this area now. Take this street right here all the way south to Pico."

"I'd feel safer walking on this street."

"It's not a request. You'll be fine on Pico. Take this street all the way down. End of discussion."

"Yes, officer."

"Better yet, get in the car with me. Personal escort."

"You want me to get in the car?"

"You're not under arrest. I just want you out of this area now. I know you're not gonna give me any trouble, right?"

"God no, officer. No trouble."

"Let me see your hands. Hold them up for me." Max does so. "Anything in your pockets?" Max shakes his head. The cop flashes his light on Max's crotch. "Turn around." Max does so. "Empty your pockets. I have to check if you're going to ride with me." Max flashes upon the blue pills burning in his pocket. The radio squawks and a small gust of wind rises. "Wait here. Do not move." The cop turns his back and paces as he talks to the dispatcher. Max grabs the pills and for a brief moment cannot get his hand out of his pocket; the pills feel greasy and half melted in his hand and he feels like a five year old who's been caught by his dad, only he would never have dared to trick his own father, and he flings the unknown pills towards the very branch, the very window where his five year old self is still there contemplating the night. The pills tap against the window.

64.

She rolls down the window, leans her head out and seems content to let the air blow recklessly through her hair. The tree tops bend and dance in a steady wind. At last he pulls into her rutted narrow street. They glance at each other and she gathers her purse and reaches for the door. There were a dozen moments throughout the night when he might have leaned in and kissed her, or simply taken her hand. Yet he never did. He walks her to the lobby glass door. She fumbles for a long time for the key. When she finally finds it she drops it and she curses. Her eyes fail to meet his.

"Well. I guess I'll see you tomorrow," she says.

"If both of us can manage to make it up out of bed," he says, feeling forced.

"Oh come on," she says brightly. "We're young and sober. We can do it." She puts out her hand. Andy looks at it. "You're an amazing instrumentalist," she says. "Thank you for a great night."

Andy takes her hand and shakes it. And then he leans in to kiss her. She pulls back. Hard. Instrumentalist. She lets go of his hand which he had forgotten he was still holding. "So.... I had a great night. But...this is not what this night was about," she says. She is almost unrecognizable.

He tells her, "Sure. That was too fast I guess. It's OK."

"Well...Too much not what this night was about or what I'm...what I'm doing here."

"OK.... Well.... I really did have a great night. Thank you. Thank you for taking me to play. I owe you. Big time."

"You're quite welcome. Henry will love me for it."

"Well you gotta love that I guess. It was a great night."

"OK. Well, I'll see you tomorrow."

"Later today really."

"Certainly."

"OK. Get some sleep," he says, turning away, feeling red like a schmuck. Like a schmuck being smothered by a pillow, and like a pillow being stabbed by a moron. Feathers everywhere. But he also quietly knows for certain that he had not in fact acted like a schmuck. Back in his room, Andy replays the evening in his head. Does every girl have to want you, and on the very day you meet her, no less? There is no going to sleep. He sits restless and incomplete. Until he reaches for his guitar.

∞

"Strange, no doubt," Louie is saying. "But it happens and believe me I've seen it before, many times." They had both lingered in Gary the whole day after all - that second day - spending most of their listless time in the Mexican restaurant, staying cool, talking about music, waiting for Maggie's shift to end. And now it was over, their second session together. They had said their goodbyes. "I mean I've never played in a school hall in the middle of the night, in the middle of fucking nowhere. But I've certainly seen it happen where you hit upon something…something that's mind blowing, something that must be true, that must be real and then….just like that it's lost again. It's all fucked up. I've seen that before. And it's no one's fault." They are still sitting in the car at the side of an empty road. Louie gazes out the window at the stars.

"I just… I just wanted that first night to last forever. And tonight it was almost boring. We were like strangers."

"Being strangers is what made it magical. Tonight we played like one of us felt jilted. Right? She's fallen for you. Forget all that bullshit I said before. She's fallen for you and you're oblivious. So yeah, it actually is your fault."

"So why won't she come to L.A with us?"

Louie still looks at the stars. "Did you hear what I just said? I told you, she's fallen for you. But you got no feelings for her. Not really. And she knows it. I can see the Milky Way it's so clear."

"I'm going back."

"What on earth for?"

"I just didn't like where we left things."

"She lives in a house with small children. It's kind of late," but Louie is smiling at him. Andy grabs his guitar.

"I know which window is hers. There's no dog."

"That doesn't mean there's no trouble."

There's a flat patch of dirt between two little houses. He floats past the side of the house. Seven notes on his guitar, repeated several times after breaths of silence. He develops their theme from the night before in a familiar yet convoluted way, a simple yearning reprise. From the house behind him a dog begins to bark. Maggie's light goes on.

She raises the window. "Is that you?"

"Maggie." He approaches.

"Are you crazy?"

"Maybe."

"What do you want?" He stands right in front of her. "Are you here to sweep me off my feet now and take me with you to Los Angeles?"

"Would you come?"

"Thank you for staying one more day, Andy. But I'm not ready. And you're not serious, anyway."

"I don't know how you can know that." She says nothing. "Then I guess I've come to say goodbye. Or so long."

"I thought you already did."

"We didn't say anything. We just left each other. I wanted to see you. Alone."

She shakes her head. "Are you coming in?"

"Can I fit through this window?"

"Or I can let you in the front door. How about that? You just have to be quiet." She lets him in front and turns on the light. The room is full of comfortable, stuffed furniture. The floor is covered in plastic toys and dolls. He follows her to her room and they sit on the floor against her bed, moonlight pouring in. "Where's Louie?"

"He's in the car, probably asleep already. I'm glad you let me in."

"I don't know why you're so glad…. I'm sorry about tonight. It was my fault we were so weak tonight."

"It's no one's fault."

"I just couldn't be in the moment. Not like last night."

"Me too, I think. Louie says it's common."

"If I came out to L.A. with you, what would you do with me?"

"We'd each get a job. Maybe you could….I don't know, maybe you could stay…"

"Stay with you? Really? Is that really what you want? Anyway, I don't know if I could get a job out in L.A. Wouldn't I become really dependent on you? And then I'll hate you. And I'll become really difficult and surly and not at all nice to be around. Don't you think I'm a bit of a bitch as it is? Seriously. Of course I am. And then I wouldn't be able to come back here where it's nice and safe and quiet and easy."

"And lonely. Small."

"I could be a lot more lonely and a lot smaller in L.A."

"Well maybe when I get somewhat established, you can come out and we'll play together. In a band."

"However long it takes you to do that.... Anyway, Andy....you will meet someone else so quickly out there that....."

"Well, I guess I'll have to. But we share this music. I mean, I really like you, but I know the music is all we have for sure. But it's a lot. It's a special kind of friendship. Don't you think?"

"That's what I thought," she says. "I'm your music buddy." He takes her hand and squeezes it. "I know what that squeeze means."

"It means I like to feel your hand."

She squeezes back. They sit for a long time saying nothing. "Almost every night the moon passes by my window. When it doesn't come it breaks my heart a little bit. But usually it comes. It's not always at the same time or in the same place. But it doesn't vary too much from one night to another. I usually know when it's coming. And I sit right here like this and I welcome the moon. I welcome it. Like it's my friend. Did you know that sometimes it can be more wonderful to sit right here and look out and see the moon outside, that it can be more wonderful to do that than to actually be outside and to be dancing completely beneath it. I know. I've tried them both."

"It's like the moon is visiting you. Instead of simply existing for the whole world, it's here just to be with you, Maggie."

"Isn't that sad?"

"It could be. It's beautiful, too." They sit for quite a long time saying nothing. She leans her head against him. They imagine saying so much to each other, to have all the time in the world to ask each other banal things about their music and what they like and what they imagine and about other worlds and places and visitors. But there is no time. So they kiss instead.

She whispers, "You said Louie's asleep in the car."

"Probably."

"Good. Enough about him then. Get into bed with me, Andy."

∞

While tuning his guitar, Andy's pager shrieks. He grabs it, irritated, but he checks it anyway. Maureen.

65.

Heading south on Rexford, the tranquil homes now seem jaundiced and stale, the air coated in iodine. Everything seems so old to him as they turn on Santa Monica, even the tree branches and the seldom used rail line that divides the street. The car smells of metal, air freshener, and damp upholstery. "This is your lucky day," says the cop. Max doesn't feel lucky but he tries to take the cop at his word. "I'm heading out your way on a domestic dispute." They cross old Wilshire and continue southbound to Pico. The cop stops. "You know where you are?"

Max looks around. "Yes, officer."

"Go home. Understand? No dancing or skipping. Go on." He gets out and he wonders if he should thank the cop or shake his hand.

"Thank you."

"Go on," says the cop, not looking up. And so Max trudges up the hill towards Century City; silent towers, dream limbo shut and perfect, a dead city every night. Now comes Rancho Park, an abandoned land, waiting, waiting for him. He often sits here during the day waiting for his pager to call him. It seldom does because he is slow and he daydreams. He is happy to be forgotten here, to be invisible. He stares at the strange light cast across the grass by low lurking lamps. He wants so badly to run and dance across its great lawns and to disappear in this world which is forever night, forever safe and lonely, where the familiar world is just beyond his sights though never beyond his reach and where nothing can ever touch him except starlight. But he does not dare.

Suddenly the wind picks up again and a great scuttle of dried leaves hiss across the lot and up the sidewalks. Regretfully, he leaves the magic park, the forbidden forest and he walks through rolling avenues. He passes a city electrical box. He puts his ear to its vibrations, barely a whisper, yet it's an entire world inside a world. He descends finally into the very last, very short leg of his venture. He looks out into silent Palms when his knees feel cold. So close yet so far, Max anticipates that the real danger of this night lies just ahead on this frozen street, so close to the sanctuary of his little courtyard, his little room, his little book.

66.

"Maureen? Did you page me?"

"Yes."

"Are you OK?"

"I didn't like the way I said goodnight."

"I'm glad you paged. I'm still up."

"Do you want to come back over?"

"To your place? When?"

"Now."

".....Yes. I would."

"I'm unit 327."

$$\infty$$

He knocks softly and almost immediately the chain knocks back and the door opens. Her eyes look naked with no make-up and no glasses, tamed by her bony, apologetic nose. Her hair is down. Long white t-shirt, argyle cotton pants. Gently she shuts the door. She walks back to the middle of the room and turns to face him. He walks towards her and they kiss, still and slow. "You're delicious," he says. After a while she takes his hand and leads him to her room.

Afterwards they lie still, Andy's entire body throbbing with the adrenalin slowly ebbing from him. They do not speak and Andy descends into a dream where he and Maureen are watching dilapidated rock bands audition for them in this very bed room. He wakes up and her naked body softly quakes from silent tears. Instead of speaking, he rubs her belly and presses himself against her. She puts her hand over his. "Are you OK?" He kisses her neck. "Did you have a bad dream?"

She snuffles and then reaches over, pulls up a tissue and blows her nose. "Did I wake you?"

"No. I was kind of having a bad dream myself."

"What about?" she asks in an unsteady voice.

"You and I were auditioning rock bands in your room; while in bed."

"That was your dream? That sounds like fun."

"I know. But there was something menacing and boring about it."

"Andy, I'm a little messed up."

He holds her tighter. "Tell me."

She reaches for another tissue and blows her nose. "I was embarrassed about losing it tonight in front of you. Like you'd think I was a freak. So I shut down a little bit. But I didn't want you to think I didn't like you. That's why I called."

"Well...I'm glad you did," he says. She laughs. "This was very considerate and all." They whisper and continue laughing in the dark.

67. Last October

"I want you inside of me, Andy"

"What?" He squeezes Maggie's hand.

"Ow! That hurts."

"Sorry."

"Did you hear me?"

"Yes. Yes of course."

She looks at him in the dark, then leans over and kisses him. He kisses her back, replacing ardor with force, feeling her lips clamping impatiently upon his own. She pulls away. "What's the matter with you?"

"What do you mean?"

"Are you serious?"

Andy sighs. "I'm.... I'm sorry. I can't. I don't know what's wrong with me. I just wasn't expecting this."

"Expecting what?"

"You know."

"Of course I know. But you can't say it. You weren't expecting me to throw myself at you?"

"If you want to put it like that. I just...."

"You just didn't think of me quite like that?"

"Maggie, come on. You think any guy is just ready to go any time anywhere?"

"That's pretty much been my experience. But you're more noble than that. You kiss me because you want me for...for the music, or something. But you don't want *me*." Andy rises and looks at the moon out her window. He leans down and gives her his hand. "I'm fine."

"Let me help you up."

She curses in whisper, "God *damn* it," and she give him his hand and he grips hard and leans back while she struggles up and sit upon the bed.

"Do you want me to go?"

"Louie is waiting, isn't he?"

"He's asleep."

"Just leave us be. Me and the moon. There's no place for you here anymore. Just be on your way."

∞

Louie snores but promptly wakes up when Andy returns. "How did it go?"

"Not good."

"What'd you do? Break her heart some more? Rub it in?"

162

"Hey. Easy. I didn't mean to do anything."

"What did you mean to do?"

"Nothing….. Say goodbye."

"What happened?"

"Let's just go," and he turns the engine over.

"Wait."

"What."

"Just wait. Wait! Wait a minute. Please." Andy cuts the engine.

"What's goin' on?"

"Wait. I'm sorry.... I've been thinking. Thinking and dreaming. I've been going over this and...I'm not ready."

"What do you mean?"

"I'm sorry."

"What are you sorry about, Louie?"

"I'm not ready to go. I don't want to go to L.A."

"What? You serious?"

And Louie reaches in the back, pulls his duffle bag out and his saxophone case. "I'm staying here."

"Really?"

"I can't explain it...... I'm safer here for now."

"Didn't someone just smash you in the eye? How many bars have you gotten yourself thrown out of?"

"All of them. But I want to stay here..... I need to stay here with Maggie."

"What if she doesn't want you there? Or have any room?"

"She needs me. I need her. I'm staying here….." Louie hands him a note from his pocket. "It's Maggie's address. I don't need it anymore. Write to me when you get settled in L.A. I'll look you up."

"You sure about this?" Louie nods and gets out of the car. "…..Take care, Louie." And with that Louie turns once and salutes Bob before walking off towards Maggie's light, which is still on.

68. Early Friday Morning

They keep Taxi in bed with them all night long. Rolfe holds the cat on his chest, kissing him and talking to him. Tanya lies on her side and strokes it, gently calling to him. Rolfe looks at his wife and though he cannot see her clearly, he reaches for her and strokes her hair. She snuggles closer to him and Rolfe exhales.

∞

Tim awakens. He reaches over the half empty beer can, his first and only for the evening, and he takes a sip but it is flat and acrid. He pulls out a half empty pack of cigarettes and pads to the next room and lights up, sitting next to the window. Absently he turns on the television but turns it off again. "I'm right here, baby. I ain't goin' nowhere. I hope you're all right."

∞

Tom Hagen opens his eyes. He looks over. Just past three. Of all days to predict a freak shit storm. He stares at where his wife used to sleep. Now on top of everything he else, he gets the call earlier tonight that he has always dreaded yet longed for, the call from his virtuous cop asshole younger brother, the one still married, the one still taking care of dear old dad, the one who thinks he knows best in that shit hole of a town he still lives in, the one who buys into the glorious story and the lovely adage that blood is still thicker than water, still thicker than money. Suddenly the trees begin to sift and the wind begins to howl at the bottom of his window.

∞

Perry awakens, unsure of where he is. He rubs his neck and he looks around. He sees Samuel asleep in the chair, his head back and Guillaume sitting on his lap. "Papa!"

"Baby, are you OK?"

"The funny bear came," Guillaume responds in English.

"What are you doing, baby?"

As if it were the most obvious answer in the world, Guillaume responds, "Silly bear!"

∞

Max runs faster and faster, so close and yet so far from his destination. All he wants is to stay ahead of the mugger or the lunatic bully who will spring out suddenly and laugh as he or it bleeds him to death with its rubbery arms upon the unforgiving pavement. Lit up to his right is the all night gas station and though he is only one block from his own building, he detours and rushes inside. The little store is brightly lit and clean with no strangers out front and the cookies and the sodas seem festive and friendly yet orderly. He recognizes the man at the counter, the younger of the African men that run the store. Max hasn't seen the older one with the wall eye in several weeks, at least. He pulls out the two dollars from his pocket, feeling he should buy something, though this will leave him nothing at all for the muggers. He buys an orange creamsicle bar and approaches the counter. The man smiles.

"Quiet night?" Max asks, hopefully.

"Sure."

"Just this."

"Ninety-nine cents." Max pays him and pockets the other dollar.

"That's good, what you got there," the man says. His cadence is musical.

Max looks at the name tag. Jesus. "Your name is Jesus?"

"They pronounce it Hey Zeus. But you can call me Jesus if you want. Same thing. My family is Catholic."

"Oh. Is it weird to pray to someone with the same name as you?"

"Well, I don't get confused about who I'm praying to if that's what you mean."

"Yeah, sure. Well I never met anyone named Jesus before."

"It's not uncommon where I'm from."

"Where are you from?"

"We are from Belize."

"Where's that?"

"It's in South America. Very nice place. Very green. But poor. Rich in people. Rich in spirit. Poor in everything else."

"I never heard of it. I wonder why."

"You must travel and read perhaps. The world is quite large. Don't let anyone tell you otherwise," and the man proceeds to tell Max more about his country, most of which seems utterly mysterious, as though it exists in a wholly different dimension. He is certain that he would never actually visit such a place himself.

"Where's that other guy? I haven't seen him."

"The other guy?"

"The guy with the one eye. Older guy. He said his name is Smokie."

"Oh…" Jesus smiles. "Of course. My cousin. Well, you know he got very sick and he died."

"What? He died?"

"Cancer."

"But he seemed fine!"

"When did you last see him?"

"I don't know. A few weeks ago."

"It was rather sudden. He was ill for quite a while but no one knew. I don't know if even he knew. But he was in pain for a while. Back pain mostly. When he finally went to the hospital, it was already way too late. He never came home."

"Oh my God. That's awful." Max cannot understand why the man is smiling. "Isn't it?"

"Of course it is. These things in life happen. One day we will all be dead and have no more trouble."

Max wonders what to say. "Wow. That's terrible to think about."

"Not really. You just have to accept it. Death is perfectly safe."

"Really?" Max doesn't understand, but it seems like a wise thing to say. He wants to say something wise as well. "Well. I had an uncle once who died. I didn't know him that well. He wasn't really my uncle. He was sick too and then he died. Everyone kept saying he was in a better place."

"Is that so?"

"Yes. Do you think Smokie is in a better place?"

"I have no idea where Smokie is. The last I saw of him, he was in the ground."

∞

Max waits until the light changes, though the street is empty. He has a single block to go and he feels somehow calmed and unafraid after hearing the strange news. To his right are shuttered businesses in short order food, party rentals, junky antiques, and a nursing home. He passes the Laundromat where someone once warned him never to go into after nine o'clock at night. Max reaches for his key and opens the gate door to his apartment building. The door whines as he closes and rattles it shut. Safe. "Hey!" the voice rings out and a shadowy figure suddenly appears before him outside the gate. Max leaps back. "Hey man. It's you."

"No. You're mistaken!"

"What the hell, man," and the shadowy man starts to laugh and Max realizes there are two people, one much smaller. "You don't recognize your own neighbor, homes? You think I'm the bogey man." A man and a woman. "Hey baby, this dude thinks I'm the bogey man. You think he's right about that?" Max turns to leave, realizing they are both drunk. "Hey! Douchebag. I'm locked out." Max turns and recognizes his upstairs neighbor, Jeter. "I'm sorry, I'm sorry. I shouldn't of called you a douchebag. I'm a little funny right now. I don't mean nothin'," and he starts to laugh. "Seriously, can you just let me in so we go upstairs," his voice changes and the girl giggles, "so we can seriously bang the shit out of each other."

"Jeter!" the girl protests. "You fucking pig!" but she laughs again. "You really still think you're gonna get lucky that fucked up."

"You are so coming up. And I'm already lucky. Or I will be if this fine gentle man neighbor of mine - who is not, I repeat is not a 'douchbag', " Jeter says loudly, "if this guy decides to let me in… So let me in already or I'll wake up the whole building," Jeter promises, starting to laugh again. Max opens the gate and the two stagger in, arms around each other. "Thank you, neighbor!" he shouts. A sharp Shhhhshhh! erupts from upstairs. "Oh fuck off!"

"Quiet. Or I'm calling the police," an older woman calls out.

"Shhhhhhshhhhhh!!!" Jeter hisses. In a loud whisper he calls out. "Oh Kay!" The woman shushes him again and Jeter shushes right back but they quiet down. "Thanks man," Jeter whispers. "I'm sorry I called you a douchebag. Nighty night."

Once inside, Max closes the blinds, turns on the light, and pulls out his picture book. Rhinos. Elephants. Orangutans. Black bears. He flips the pages into the quiet. The magnificent Anteater. There he is. Such peace. Standing in his domain. Unique and humble. Frankly odd yet beautiful. The back of Max's neck begins to tingle. What were you thinking oh Jesus, the day you invented this creature here? Poor Smokie. Above him he hears some muffled laughter and some periodic bumping as if furniture was being moved. Max returns his attention to his book. More muffled laughter. He flips the pages. The noises continue and he realizes that the noises have become repetitive, a low rhythmic squeaking that continues and continues. He stares at the Anteater. Stares at its hairy face, its droopy proboscis, its blankness of expression. A kind of roar, also repetitive, muffled yet unmistakable begins to rise above him. Max continues to stare at the photo, unable to find a way inside the creature's world.

BOOK TWO – The Storm

69.   Friday Morning
(The Day of the Storm)

The morning is cloudless and uncomplicated blue. Andy sits in the back of his truck and plays his guitar. A gust of wind sprays leaf dust at his eyes. He rubs them and spits. There won't be any gardeners with their leaf blowers today. Tom Hagen is paying him to sit there and so he shall. If only he could get paid to sit here all day and if only the day would stay as still and cool as it is now. A car pulls into the lot, a small dented thing. Andy looks over, feeling annoyed until he recognizes the driver. "Hello" Samuel calls. He seems to limp forward. His shirt looks rumpled and his eyes are bloodshot. "I was going to close my eyes, but I felt compelled somehow to announce myself to you. And so....I announce myself to you."

"Good morning."

Samuel holds his sides and squints. "Lovely morning."

"They say there's gonna be a storm today. Big one."

"So I've heard."

"Is your back hurting you?"

"Yes. I'm quite stiff. I slept in a chair last night, at least briefly."

"Were you reading?"

"No."

"I didn't get much sleep either." Andy smiles.

"Pity. Mr. Hagen is counting on us. Today promises to be quite busy. I suppose that's why we're both positioned here."

"I think we can handle it. We're just driving around."

"I must confess, I am not very well suited for it. In fact, I find it quite stressful, actually. I love storms but I absolutely dread the idea of trying to drive in one, I must tell you. In fact, when I feel too riled up, I am prone to nose bleeds and I fear I shall succumb to one today."

"That'll be tough. But there's not a cloud in the sky."

"Maybe the wind is bringing it."

"Samuel. Come up and sit with me?"

"That's very nice of you, but I doubt I'd be able to get up there."

"I'll lower the haul door and we can sit on that." Samuel agrees and they do so. The wind rises again. Andy says, "Can I ask you a personal question?"

"Oh, I suppose."

"Why are you a messenger? Especially since you don't seem to like it very much. You seem much more like you're a professor, or a scientist."

"I was indeed a professor at one time, in the Humanities, literature and such. I went into teaching as soon as I finished my education. But I am a professor no more. Let's just say, I made some very bad choices. I put everything at risk over trifles and I lost it all."

"I'm…well I'm really sorry to hear that. I was hoping you'd say it was just something to do in retirement."

"Hah…" and Samuel chuckled. "I needed a job and this is what I could get. I was quite surprised when they hired me. I've nearly quit several times. I was hoping I could simply putter about in a golf cart on that course just there all day long picking up and delivering notes from love sick golfers in their checkered pants."

"Now that sounds like a good job."

"There really are some disturbingly ugly parts of this city. Shocking. Haunting. Compelling in a way. Like a dream and I confess, I somehow ……." Samuel stops himself, glassy eyed. "Any city, I suppose, has all that. Did you know, this is actually a second job for me?"

"What's your other job?"

"I work in a very old and very large hospital. I don't actually touch the patients. Nothing so intimate. But I see them. I collect the dirty linen, take it to the laundry, bring supplies all over the hospital, and sit in the most boring room imaginable during my breaks."

"You seem like a good guy, Samuel."

Samuel looks at Andy and after a moment continues, "I like it better than working here. At first it was shocking to me. Especially in the oncology ward. But it's strangely almost comforting the routine there. It's better than sitting in my room next to the freeway…. Anyway, it must be marvelous to be a musician, though. Yes?"

"I'm in love with it. But she can be a harsh mistress at times."

"Do you mean it's rigorous?"

"Yes. And lonely sometimes."

"I would not have guessed that. Does it help that you're young?"

"I don't feel young. I just turned thirty. But I don't mind most of the time. It's just that I've chosen music that most people don't listen to, as if it weren't hard enough to become a rock star."

"What sort of music do you play?" Andy takes up the guitar and plays a quick rondo of macabre chords in a kind of dance beat, interrupted by a long moment of the seven note melody. He redoubles the original theme, ending with a jolt. Samuel frowns thoughtfully. "So that's the sort of music you play."

"Well, that's one style."

"I like it, Andy. Very much. Quite bracing and exhilarating. You are surpassingly accomplished, no doubt about it. You're a musician who has not yet found his audience. But I think you shall."

"Thank you, Samuel."

"Last night – and I don't think he would mind my telling you this – our friend Perry and his family came to the hospital where I work. His wife already works there, but their little boy had a seizure following a narrow escape from a speeding car. Somehow, the child took a fancy to me and Perry thought it would be help the child to go to sleep if I told his son a story. He stayed awake for hours, indefatigable. Afterwards, I fell asleep in the chair. My entire body is so stiff and sore, I feel like I'm about ninety years old."

"That's terrible....How's Perry?"

"He's relieved that the boy is coming home today."

Andy strums and picks a little. He asks, "Samuel. You like classical music?"

"Of course. My first love. I have a piece playing in my head right now. All the time in fact. Why do you ask?"

"Do you know of a composer named Mahler?"

"Well, of course! He used to be my favorite."

"Used to be?"

"Well... I just can't listen to him anymore these days. What brings you to ask about him anyway?"

"Do you know his Tenth symphony?"

"Did you say his Tenth?"

"Yeah."

Samuel frowns. Slowly he say, "I heard rumors about such a thing."

"Well...I have a cassette of Mahler's Tenth. Just the first movement. They're not sure if he really wrote more than that."

"You possess this cassette?"

"We can have a listen right now."

Samuel opens his mouth. Then shakes his head. "No. There's no need for that. I believe you."

"It's disturbed. Beautiful but disturbed. More disturbed than anything I've ever played. It sounds like death and dying."

"Yes, yes. Well that sounds like Mahler.... Picking up where he left off from his Ninth. Now that you should hear. The story of a man's life, from brash and energetic youth to wise and surrendering old age. And all his bourgeois conceits and contrivances in between. Everything comes to naught in the end. Everything you want to know about life and death, it's all there in Mahler's Ninth. And believe me, that is difficult enough for me to listen to these days."

"What do you mean by conceits and...."

"Contrivances? Career, ambition, pursuit of prestige, money, power, achievement. Everything really."

"Love?"

"Mmmh. Especially love. Mahler died of a broken heart."

"He did? What happened?"

"Of course, medically he probably died from some infection or heart problem, but his soul had been laid to waste by the betrayal of his young wife. Forget about young lovers like Werther or Romeo. There's nothing so pitiful or forlorn as an old man in love. Mahler was….genius. Too painful, too much truth for me right now." And his voice trails off.

Andy looks at Samuel for a moment, realizing that the man was no longer talking about Mahler. "So…. what's this piece of music you keep listening to. Over and over in your head."

"It's Vaughan Williams. Do you know him?"

"Not personally."

"Most witty. He was English. Actually he died only a generation ago. He wrote marvelous symphonies and the most exquisite pastoral sounding music, inspired by the English countryside. His Third – is a deceptively heart breaking piece. It suggests to me a place of rest, a place of beauty."

"Somewhere you'd like to go?"

"I tried to take Guillaume there last night. With my story. That's Perry's young son - Guillaume - so bright and energetic and insufferable. The point of the story was to find this place, this place where all my burdens and shame would be forgotten. We were adventurers together. But in my efforts to spin a tale long enough to put him to sleep, I managed not to finish it at all…Andy, allow me to skip to the end and tell it to you right now, if that's all right."

"Sure."

"This is how I envisioned the ending. When we complete our odyssey, our journey home, all we shall find is a great waterfall. But what lies beyond - is not pleasant at all."

"That's the story you would have told to a little boy?"

Samuel laughs again. "No, of course I would have lied. But the truth - of my own imaginary story that plays out in my head - is that what lies beyond the waterfall of the enchanted forest is a great nothingness, a great desert. But even that's a lie. There's plenty there. I knew none of this of course before last night. It simply came to me. There was a great pit. A mighty pit of suffering. All the suffering the human world has ever known; slavery, violence, depredation, exploitation, sickness, despair. And in the middle of this pit is a great statue. Hundreds of feet tall. And do you know what this statue is?"

"Of course not."

"It's a reflection of whoever looks at it. So when I look at it…I see myself. An effigy if you will. All my faults, all my obsessions, all my pretenses, all my fears, and all my resentments. Now that's a statue that needs to fall."

Andy looks at Samuel. "This place you visit when you listen to Vaughan Williams - in your head - forget about the story - is this a real place or just imagined?"

Samuel sighs and checks his pager. "It is a real place. I know it well."

"Tell me about it."

"I was there many years ago, a few times with my family. Once with just my oldest son; we went hiking through there. And once on my own. There's a village or a town that overlooks Mount Rainier. Have you ever been to Mount Rainier?"

"No."

"A place that is forever cool and clean, facing ice from the mountain; lush forests and grasslands. I've been all over the world, but….when I was there, I felt a great peace, a kind of hope. I fancy that one day - hopefully very soon – and I've been planning for it - I will be able to pack up and move there."

"So what's keeping you here? Why not go there right now?"

"Just this week, my youngest daughter, Joanne, she just turned eighteen. I didn't want to leave before that."

"So you're close to your children?"

"I made a miserable deal with my ex-wife who wanted me out of their lives. The older children have moved on and I don't know where they are. We also adopted a young girl….. and she ran off years ago. Now that the children are grown…..Joanne still needs a college education, but I believe her mother can handle that. I…… Maybe I am more comfortable having this place as a dream."

"You've got to get out of here, Samuel."

"Yes."

"Find some beauty. While you can. Your children are grown. If you're meant to be with them, they can come to you. Drive on out of here tonight."

"….. I just might," Samuel looks down at his hands. The wind rises again suddenly. Samuel's pager sounds off. "My first call. This is not going to be fun." He turns around. "Curious that you have not yourself been paged. I would certainly have expected you to be called before me."

"Maybe he wants to send me somewhere else."

"If you don't hear from Mikros soon, it wouldn't hurt to check your pager."

"Thanks for the advice."

"Be safe out there."

"You too." He watches Samuel walk as fast as he can with his cane to the nearest payphone. Then he pulls his pager out and looks at it. It was never turned on.

70.

"There's nothing open on this street."

"Keep going. Maybe it's on San Pedro. I've seen it."

"You get around I guess."

"You don't stay forever in the same place when you live on the street, Eugene."

"How long have you lived on the street?"

"All of a sudden you're curious?"

"Maybe I was curious before. I just didn't want to ask you a whole bunch of questions."

"Can we talk about this later? Please?"

"What are you so uptight about? Relax."

"I'm scared I won't get any shoes or we'll miss the store or something and you'll leave."

"I told you, we'll get the shoes. Just relax." He tells her, his voice rising.

"What do you mean 'relax'? You're the one who is so stressed. And you have nice warm shoes and socks. Not me."

"All I said was 'relax'. What's so hard about that?"

"Exactly. Yes, that's what I want to know."

"Good. We both want the same thing!" He barks. Now shut the fuck up! He wants to say. But even in his agitation, he's not ready to risk pushing Caroline away altogether. It's better to keep her here for now and to simply loathe and resent her. They drive through the dawn lit streets, the brick and concrete paths, the shuttered venues, a grid of pathways that Eugene used to imagine was filled gangs of tattooed Cyclopes with Mohawks, shrieking with anticipation of mayhem, oiling their crimson penises, doing back flips from heaps of wrecked and shattered cars that lean from graffiti, blood spattered garages. Months of driving these streets revealed that these were simply blocks of low rent businesses like auto parts and pipe and plumbing pieces; safer by far than more residential streets further south featuring low rent motels, liquor stores, and improvised churches.

"Try Eighth Street. I know it's around here somewhere."

"Fine. Fine. But if I can't find it real soon, I'm going to have to get to work. I can't be driving you around or have you in my car all day long."

"What's real soon?"

"Real soon is real soon! It's soon. Not a whole lot of time."

"We have time. It's only six thirty. If it takes longer you just call in and tell them you're downtown. Maybe they'll need you downtown?"

"Don't tell me what to do!"

"I'm not telling you what to do. I'm just saying, just an idea."

173

"You get nothing when you're downtown! OK? You get shit. No miles. You just drive around in circles trading love notes between lawyers and you end up getting a ticket. No thank you. They send me on the long runs because I'm fast. I'm the fastest and I can't have you in the car with me then."

"Why not? It sounds fun! It's not like I have anywhere I have to be. You can drop me off later."

"No! That's insane."

"What's the matter? Why not?" Elliott puts his foot on the accelerator and the car lurches and roars and he passes a pick-up truck on the right, then cuts in front and passes through a light just turning red. "Whoa. God! That's how you drive? Oh! Wait!!! There...there it is. The mart on the right. Stop. Stop!"

"Ah Jeez!" And Eugene slams on his brakes and narrowly avoids bouncing off the curb.

Caroline lurches against the seat belt. "Ah! You're gonna break your car. Or me."

"My car is none of your business! And if there's one thing I can do, it's drive a car."

"What is your problem?"

"No problem. I don't have any problems. Got that? I have no problems. None. You're the one who seems to have a problem. You said stop! Remember. So I stopped. I even let *you* boss me around. Are you happy?"

"Happy?" She looks at him side long. "Not really. No, not right now, I'm not happy."

"No? You're not. Well I think maybe you will be happy, won't you? You'll be happy when you get your shoes and socks? Right? I know you'll be very happy then."

"Why are you being so mean to me?"

"Mean?"

"You're being mean!"

"I'm not being mean. I'm about to buy you your shoes and socks!"

"Lower your voice."

"Don't tell me to lower my voice in my own car-", but Caroline has already gotten out the door. She stands for a moment and begins to walk away.

"Where are you going?" Eugene gets out of the car. "The shoes are in the other direction. Did you forget? Come on. Don't forget your shoes and socks."

She stops and he looks at her long broad back. Her shiny thin clothes appear sun bleached and faded, in the morning light. She looks like a hulking brute. At least they're clean, he thinks. She turns to face him. He looks away.

"You're right."

"About what?"

She walks back towards him. "I will be happy when I have my shoes and socks."

174

"Of course you will." He looks at his own shoes.

"But I might still be unhappy, Eugene."

"Whatever that means," he mutters.

"Look at me."

"Let's go get it over with."

"Look at me."

Eugene looks at her through squinted eyes. It hurts to look at her. "What do you want?"

"I told you this would happen."

"What are you talking about?"

"When we were in the tower. I told you then."

He looks off. "I don't wanna talk about that."

"Why not?" Her lower lip trembles.

He blinks and turns away. "I don't wanna talk about that."

"We were together. We were together in the tower."

"So? Was it such a wonderful experience for you?! That hellhole."

She whispers. "Please lower your voice. I don't want you to yell at me."

He lowers his voice and his eyes. "It was awful. I hated it. I hated it. Why did you take me there?"

"I didn't take you anywhere, Eugene." He looks up at the mention of his name. Caroline herself is now looking down. "Eugene," she repeats. "You took us to a place deep inside of you. It was very sad, I know, but it was you, and we shared it."

He says nothing at first. "It was not me. That was not me."

"It wasn't all of you. There's a lot more, I'm sure. A lot more. Pleasant things. Much more pleasant things. And….we can go there together if you like."

A chill runs through him. "I don't know what you're talking about."

"You know exactly what I'm talking about."

"What are you? A hypnotist? What are you doing out here, you could be making money with your little tricks. Are you a witch? I know we were in my basement the whole time."

"Whatever you want to call it. We were there together. You didn't dream it alone, Eugene."

"Are you a witch?"

"We were looking at each other. And you told me I was beautiful. I remember. But I warned you, Eugene."

"You warned me?"

"I told you that you wouldn't see me the same way in the morning. I didn't want you to be disappointed."

"I don't remember."

"Yes you do."

"Maybe you should stop playing your little tricks."

"…..It's all I have."

"I don't know what to say here. Do you want your shoes and socks or not?"

"Yes. Yes, I do. Let's go." He turns and he watches her walk over to the mart. She smiles and gazes at open boxes of clean white shoes. The vendor, a young Mexican gives her a puzzled look and starts to wave her away. Caroline, undaunted, looks at Eugene. And smiles. She gestures for him to come towards her.

71.

"I'm at Triangle now."
"You're in Woodland Hills?"
"Yes little Mikros. Why are you so surprised? I told you. I'm the best."
"Eugene is the best. And do not call me little Mikros."
"I'm sorry baby Mikros." There is nothing funnier, Rolfe thinks, than imagining Mikros' face when he is irritated, so humorless, purple with apoplectic and futile rage. Funnier than seeing it live. But he resents the reference to Eugene.

"Just get to Triangle. Downtown. Now. I'm sending you to Riverside. Happy?"

"I love you, baby Mikros!"
"Go to hell!"
"How many miles to go to Hell?" But the line is already dead.

∞

"You wanted so badly to see my pretty face?"
"Look at all I have for you. Mr Hagen picked them up especially for you. He is a wonderful man. We are all most fortunate."

Tim exhales and shuffles through a slew of envelopes, some bound together with rubber bands. "O – K….. Different day. Same old…"

"Come back here as soon as you're done."

"Why not! I'll just be right around the corner anyway. As soon as I'm finished spinning around the block I'll come back here so you can get off by sending me around the block again. I get it."

"I send you exactly where you are most needed."

Tim tucks the packages beneath his arm. "Is that right? You mind telling me where you're sending your girlfriend."

"I have no girlfriends here. Thank you very much."

"Where's Rolfe?"

"That is not your concern."

176

"My pocket book is my concern. Where's Rolfe?"

"For the last time, Timothy, please just do your own job and let me do mine."

"I do my job, *Mike*. And the name is Tim. Where's Rolfe?"

Mikros meets his stare. "I sent him this morning to Woodland Hills. Soon he will be on his way to Riverside."

Tim turns and shakes his head. He mutters, "I really ought to call Hagen about you."

Mikros calls after him. "He may pick up something out there and take it to San Diego. And from there he will rush off to Santa Barbara. Or maybe Fresno.....The name is Mikros, Timothy, Mikros!! A very, very fine name it is."

72.

"Did you page me?"

"Yes Perry. Please, we have an urgent pick up Downtown on Figueroa. Where are you now?"

Perry looks down the hallway, as if that would tell him where he is. "I'm still at the hospital."

"Well how far are you from downtown? I mean, how is your son? Please I am sorry to ask, but I need to know when you can come and if you can come now?"

"Did Samuel tell you what happened?"

"Yes, he told me you are at the hospital. Terrible. And that you would be in later. So maybe now is later. Just tell me what is happening. Please."

"We are going home soon."

"That is wonderful news. He is OK?"

"Yes. He is OK, but I need to stay here a little bit more. I have to help my wife. Once we are home, I can come in. I can stay late."

"Yes, but how soon can you come? I've already had one call out this morning. That silly slut that Hagen hired has already called out sick. I can't get a hold of Max, and Andy had his pager off and so now he's behind. What a twit, eh. Can you believe it? Why can't they all be reliable and easy to work with like you?"

"I am sorry."

"Perry. I know I can count on you. Is there no way you can do a pick up for me now? Just a pick up. Just so the client doesn't wonder where we are."

"Let me talk to my wife. I need to see what she needs from me."

"Perry." Mikros shuts his eyes. He grits his teeth and slams the receiver as if it were Perry's head. "Ah! So sorry. I dropped the phone. Very well.

Yes, of course. Check with your wife. My prayers for your son and your family. Please call me right back. OK?"

73.

"Max....Max. What's wrong with you?" Max hears the question, but it doesn't make much sense to him.

"Mikros?"

"What are you, asleep? Were you fucking asleep? Today of all days. Get up Max. What is wrong with you?"

"I'm sorry Mikros. I'm so sorry. I don't know what happened."

"Max, I need you in North Hollywood right away. I mean now. At Gilroy Labs. Tell me how soon you can make it."

"Ah. I can leave right away. I can leave in five minutes."

"Be there within one hour. Sixty minutes. Tick tock, tick tock. Take Highland through Hollywood to the 101. Like I told you."

"Yes sir." He hangs up the phone and looks out the window, blinking. The only sound in the little concrete courtyard is a bird chirping. His head feels empty, nameless dreams rapidly draining. Time to get up. The enchantment and dread of last night is gone. But Smokie is still dead.

74.

The envelope flaps in the wind, pinned down beneath the windshield wiper. Not a flyer, not a take out menu, not an appeal to accept Jesus and now. A parking ticket. Twenty-two dollars. "Blast!" Samuel exclaims and he wrenches the ticket and crumples it but restrains himself from ripping it apart. Gone are what meager profits he expected from the day. As he stares glumly at the wrinkled ticket the first plump drops of rain land on its edges, on his hands, and everywhere. As he drives, his windshield wipers whine and protest. More than once, cars wheel around him, skidding ahead, blaring their horns. Samuel clenches the steering wheel, the music swelling inside his head.

∞

The outer office of London Graphics is cool and calm, blue fluffed carpets in the waiting room. The window slides back. "Well, hello Samuel," a slight and pretty young Filipino man greets him. The man has caramel colored highlights in his black hair.

"Good day, Malcolm."

"Don't be so formal. Have you got something for me?" Samuel hands him several envelopes marked, Do Not Bend. "Do not bend," Malcolm repeats.

Samuel looks at his shoes. He notices the front sole of his left foot beginning to curl back from the rest of his shoe. "I think you'll agree they are quite straight."

"I'm quite sure that they are." Malcolm stares at the envelope, holding them up to the light as if to try and view their contents.

"Where is Tamara today?"

"You mean Tammy? Taking her mother to a doctor's appointment. Again. So it's just me up front. "

"I hope everyone's all right. Please sign."

"Of course," and Malcolm does so, adding, "Samuel, can you wait for just a bit longer? I have something extremely urgent that I was just about to call in. They're just now getting it ready now and it has to go out right away. So please...have a seat."

Samuel looks at the sofa. "May I use your telephone, please."

"Come on back. You know where it is." Malcolm opens the door to the office.

"Where is this extremely urgent package going to?"

"Pomona."

"I see." A juicy run if Mikros will let him carry it, instead of handing it over to another driver.

"Do you know Claremont College?"

"Claremont? Claremont McKenna?"

"It must be the same one. So you know it."

"Yes. Yes I know of it."

"Well this piece of work needs to get there yesterday."

∞

"Samuel! Our friend Perry has decided to come to work after all."

"He has? How is his boy?"

"He's fine. Absolutely fine. That's not the good news. I mean it is....Listen, Perry is doing a pick up downtown and he has drops for two of the same clients as you have. I want you to meet him outside the loading dock of the

First Interstate building. Give him everything you have left and then high tail it out to Pomona."

"What? *I'm* going to Pomona?"

"Yes. A nice, straightforward run on the freeway with lots of miles. I may send you further east from there. Miles, Samuel. Miles! I take care of you. See?"

"Yes. Yes well I hear that and I thank you, but listen, are you sure that this is the wisest course? Perry will be much more effective on the freeway than I will be, especially in this weather." The roof comes alive with the sound of rain pounding above. "Do you hear that? That is quite a torrent out there now. I really believe Perry will get there much faster than I would. Much, much faster," he speaks rapidly. "I'm thinking of the client now."

"Nonsense, Samuel. No one moves faster than anyone else in this traffic. Listen to me. You're a driver. You can handle a little rain. It makes no sense for Perry to wait for you. Quite frankly, he will be much more effective at making all those little stops than you ever will."

"I suppose he will. I see what you mean by 'taking care of me.'"

"I *am* taking care of you, Samuel. Now please stop arguing with me and get over to First Interstate immediately."

"First of all," Samuel bites his words, suppressing his volume, "The package isn't ready yet. I should think you would expect me to wait for it. And second, this package is going to Claremont McKenna College. Claremont McKenna. Did you know that? Do you understand? Do you understand what that means?"

"Of course I know that. What's the matter with you?"

"Do you not recall, Mikros, that I used to be a professor at this very same university?"

"What? No, I do not recall that. And so what is your point?"

"Have some decency. I cannot show my face there. Not in this condition."

"And may I tell you that I now see what *you* mean by thinking of the customer first. Are you ashamed to be working as a messenger driver?"

"Precisely. Yes, I am ashamed. That's the word."

"You're a working man, Samuel. There's no shame in that."

"There is shame. There most definitely is a great deal of shame. There's shame for me and embarrassment for everyone else concerned."

There is silence. "Samuel. You cannot believe the number of headaches I already have today."

"Shall you then give me a far larger problem?"

"It was years ago, Samuel. Did you not tell me yourself you are almost unrecognizable now? And that you are ready to work."

"I am indeed unrecognizable as to who I have become. But they will still recognize me for who I used to be. I cannot bear it."

180

"Hold on, Samuel, there's another call coming in." Samuel clenches the phone and listens to himself breathing. He looks at his gnarled cuticles. Many years ago it seems his finger nails were perfect sliver moons. Clean hands posing out from a starched white shirt and a charcoal gray woolen suit of yesteryear. A scholar's hands. Now his hands make him think of a decrepit albino chimpanzee. Mikros returns to the line. "Samuel, is that package ready yet from London?"

He stands and looks about but Malcolm has not yet returned. "No."

"I may have to send Perry to meet you further west. He is the only one that can deliver all these packages. Not you, Samuel. You're already behind, aren't you?"

"Mikros…..How about if I leave the package at security."

"That will cause a delay, won't it, especially in this storm, and I won't be able to explain that to the client."

"Of course you can. Tell him your driver was too busy to come onto campus."

"That is not the service we provide."

"You're being quiet inflexible about this. Truly."

"A college is a big place. Right? You'll be fine. And you'll make money. Is there a warrant out for your arrest? Do they keep your photo posted on the walls and on milk cartons? Samuel, please. This is your job. If you won't go out there now where I need you, what good are you to me? I need you there and I need you to be a professional about this."

"I need you, Mikros, to be a human being about this, you unpleasant little man. Unless I'm delivering to their engineering plant or leaving it at security, I am almost certain to be recognized. That is unacceptable to me, Mikros. Unacceptable. How can you not understand that? I tell you I simply will not - I repeat – I will not do it."

75.

He spends the morning running from building to building in Century City. No miles whatsoever, he thinks. He channels Maureen. Good morning! How are you today? I will take good care to get this to your client right away. I'll be there in a flash. Good morning! Staying dry? Yes, it's wet out there. Windy, too. Don't go out unless you have to. That's what we're here for. It occurs to Andy that the weather is stimulating building to building exchanges that some might have simply handled themselves, but instead are willing to pay to stay bundled and dry in their glass towers. He runs, long loping strides smacking confidently through showers and puddles. Somehow not even tired. Mikros had scolded him. This is already your last warning. This is the third time in a week.

181

How difficult is it to keep your pager on? Obviously I cannot communicate with you unless you turn it on. Andy lets the dispatcher's words buzz about his head like an addled fly.

"You're done?"

"Yeah.."

"You sound out of breath. Did you run the whole way?"

"A little. Yeah."

"Don't trip and fall in the rain."

"Nah. I'm fine."

"I don't want packages spilling and soaking in this weather."

"Thanks for your concern."

"Impressive, Andy. But be careful."

"Thanks. What now?"

"Wait right there. I have a call coming in from Samuel. I will page you very soon. Be ready." Andy heads back to the park instead.

76.

Samuel smiles at his friend as he himself pulls into the narrow shelf reserved for deliveries inside the parking structure. Solemnly they exchange their packages, placing them carefully in their respective backseats. Then they embrace. "My son. He is home now."

"How is he?"

"He is OK. They say he is OK."

"That is marvelous. Wonderful. I am happy to hear it, friend."

"Thanks to you."

"Whatever are you talking about?"

"My son. You're all he talks about. He is in good spirits. He wants to see you so you must come and visit."

"My pleasure. I shall come soon. And meet your entire family."

"But they want to see him. In the clinic. "

"The doctor? That's good. Good follow up. Be thorough."

"Yes? Mr. Samuel. I am happy for my son. But.... I don't know how we are going to pay for all this."

"Do you have any insurance?"

"My wife. She has a little through the hospital she works at. But...there will be other expenses. There was this lady who talked to us about all this paperwork. I was so tired, I couldn't really understand. "

"It can be confusing to anyone." Samuel puts his hands on his hips and grimaces with a general stiffness located nowhere in particular in his body. "I suppose we should be off, Perry."

"Wait, Mr. Samuel. I need to talk to you for a little bit."

"Fine. I'm not too keen to race back out there."

"Do you remember I told you about this man I was working for? Only for a few days. He was training me."

"Something about air conditioning. You were keen to get into that."

"That's right. Well. He called me this morning."

"Yes?"

"He just got a huge job at this new hotel and he wants me to work for him."

"Well done. Congratulations."

"He says he likes me and there is work I can do right away helping others while he is still training me. He says he will pay me $12 an hour to start. I can make up to $20 an hour later on. And he has a special job where he will pay me $200 in cash. For just one day!"

"Wonderful. You will learn a valuable trade that will always be in demand and provide for your family. When will you start?"

Perry's mouth fidgets. He sucks his teeth. "Today."

77.

"You're having me do what?"

"Eugene, please. You heard me plain enough."

"You put your best driver on this piece a shit? Three days *in a row!*"

"That has nothing to do with it. You are right there. I need this done. Act like a professional."

"Three days in a row! Your best driver?"

"You'll be done in no time and then believe me, you will go plenty far. Plenty, plenty far. Now enough with the arguing already."

"You owe me."

"I told you already. You will go very far today. Call me when you're done."

"Duh!" And he hangs up the phone. He doesn't even hurry while walking back to his car in the rain, double parked, blinkers on, on San Pedro, near 9th street.

"Get in Eugene. You'll get soaked," Caroline pleads.

Eugene gets in, the interior exhaling rain breath and motor oil. "This is bullshit," he mutters.

"You're soaked."

"So what. I'm in no hurry. I'm not making any money."

"What happened?"

"I hate this stupid job." He turns the key and the engine sputters before exploding into life.

Caroline marvels, "I can't believe this old car handles so well."

"Yeah? That's because *I* handle it. That's why." The car squeaks and lurches into gear as he quickly pulls out and roars down the street.

"Oh is *that* why?" she teases.

"Damn straight."

"Got it." Eugene glances at the gas gauge. Less than a quarter full. And he just spent his last cash on Caroline's stupid shoes and socks. He'll have to find an ATM somehow before very long. And as it is, he'll have to pull cash he was going to use for his miserable little rent. He shakes his head and gives Caroline a hard side long glance. "Hold on." And he steps on the accelerator.

78.

"Today? Did you say 'today'?"

"Yes, Mr. Samuel. Right away."

"As in right now?"

"Two o'clock. In Long Beach. What am I to do?"

"But are you sure? What kind of day is this to be opening a hotel? This is the most hellacious day in the world."

"The storm will be over, but they need to keep moving. They open next month. We work inside, not outside. Mr. Murray, he wants me right away. Two o'clock today."

Samuel leans back against his car and strokes his beard. "Most extraordinary. What are you going to do?"

"That's what I am asking you. I don't know. This is a very good job, Mr. Samuel."

"Being a messenger?"

"Messenger? No. Not this. Mr. Murray. He says he pays me $200 a day. And then he will pay to get me trained to get my contractor's license."

"Perry. If I may. Is this not the same man who.... who let you go because...well because it was not working out?"

"Yes. He fired me once. But I'm not actually doing that kind of work today. He just needs help with, I don't know, other stuff, helping him, I guess. He likes me."

"And he needs *you* to do this?"

"Of course he could get someone else. But he knows how much I want this. I mean I know I can do this. I just need more time to learn everything. I can be a professional just like you."

184

Samuel laughs out loud, then coughs. "Dear Perry. You certainly don't want to end up like me."

"Whatever you did, I don't care. That's between you and God. You're a good man. You took care of your family. You were a professional man. That's what I want - a profession," They stand for a moment saying nothing. "I guess I should go now," Perry says.

"Yes, we should go. Look. Perry, for what it's worth….there are other messenger jobs out there. You need to go for your dream. But if you're worried, why don't you wait until you have nothing left to deliver and then tell Mikros you got into an accident. You're obligated to stay with your car to have it towed and maybe go to Emergency. They won't like it but you won't be blamed either, or not much. I realize that is not truthful, but perhaps the truth serves no one in this instance."

Perry thinks about this. "It's busy today. I may never be empty."

"Maybe not. But that's the best idea I have. Even if it is a lie."

"Are you OK, Mr. Samuel?"

"I'm alright, Perry. I'm tired. Very tired. Thank you for asking."

"I can see. I am sorry about last night. You are a very kind man."

"I've been thinking of leaving….finally leaving this horrible state I am in. Taking what little I possess and moving to some place smaller, quieter, and more lovely; to a place where I fancy that the grass indeed grows far greener, if you will." Samuel puts his hand on Perry's shoulder. "Wouldn't that be nice?"

"I would miss you. But you should do it."

"Someday, Perry. Someday very soon. I'm almost ready."

"Why not today?"

"Hah. That's what I've been told. Why not, indeed?"

"I'm serious. You and me. We could both quit our jobs. Right now. I need to leave to be on time at two o'clock. But you, Mr. Samuel. You should quit right now."

The sweet, remote music finally rises again in the mists in the back of Samuel's mind. "A most intriguing notion, I admit. Why not indeed?"

"It's something we are doing together, Mr. Samuel. Like brothers."

"Like brothers," Samuel agrees.

79.

Andy waits in the park and imagines his gig tonight, playing with his new musician friends. Meanwhile, the wind furiously stresses the trees and wet branches and the mulch floats in rivulets in the uneven pavement. Curb drains are torrents of brown water. From above, a large tree frond races across his sight before being buffeted and finally cracking to the pavement. He thinks about one day making a record. But then he ceases all thinking and he simply listens to the banshee and he keeps the wipers playing so he can keep watch on this beautiful, beautiful storm.

80.

"Hi Tony."

"Hey Max! Come on back."

"OK." Max slowly rolls his car inside the warehouse. The man waves him forward then puts his hand up for him to stop. Tony pats the hood and makes a note on his clipboard. Max admires the easy way that Tony has with everything he does. Dark with blue eyes; young, trim, muscular, and clean in his snow white t-shirt. How do you keep a t-shirt so bright and spotless in a place like this? Max wishes he could be more like that, but maybe he is just happier to have Tony smile at him. It would be too much trouble to actually be like him.

"Let's go Maxie."

"Maxie?"

"Yeah. Is that all right? Do people call you that?"

"My best friend calls me that. Sort of my best friend. You should call me that, too."

"Cool." They walk together through the warehouse towards the laboratory which is white and metallic. "You staying dry out there, today, buddy? Pretty crazy out there."

"Yeah. I guess it is a little bit crazy."

"You made pretty good time though. How's traffic?"

"Oh, it could be worse I guess."

Tony turns to him. "Oh it's gonna get worse. Count on it."

"OK. I will."

Tony smiles and turns back, walking. Max looks at his back. "I'm glad you're doin' it, not me man. I'm fine in here. You know what I mean?"

"Yeah, I know exactly what you mean." Max has no idea what Tony could possibly mean aside from the obvious. It's nice though, talking to Tony.

"Got anything nice planned for the weekend, Maxie?"

"Umm. Yeah. Well. No. Not really."

"Just hangin' out? That's cool."

"I might go to the zoo," Max offers.

"You likin' the animals."

"Yes, I really like animals. A lot. I have my favorites, too," Max adds, hoping Tony will ask him about his favorites.

"Do you have pets?"

"No."

"Why not?"

"I had a little turtle once." Tony says nothing but appears absorbed now with finding the delivery. "Do *you* have pets?"

"Used to have dogs when I lived with my lady. I let her have 'em when we split. We're still friends she and I - with benefits, I might add - so I still see my old buddies. Couple a Pitts."

"What?"

"Pitt bulls. You like Pitt Bulls?"

"I guess. Sure. You like animals then. You ever go to the zoo?"

"What was that?"

"The zoo. Do you ever go to the zoo?"

"Nah. That's kind of a couples thing I guess. I'm single now. I'm into a different kind of animal," and he smiles and winks. "It's right over here." And they walk down a narrow shelf of the room behind several work stations. Max recognizes the many trays containing little bottles of different colored lotions and creams, samples that were endlessly being tested at yet another off site lab. Tony lets him into a small office. Three small white Styrofoam coolers sit upon a bulky wood paneled desk. Tony grabs a grease-stained red dolly in the corner and loads the coolers onto it.

"I can roll that for you," Max says.

"I'm already doing it. Don't worry. Get the door."

Max follows Tony back through the lab. He wants to say something, but he can't think of anything. "How do you keep your shirt so white?"

Tony doesn't even look back, "Clean living I guess."

"Do you work out?"

Tony chuckles, "Yeah, a little. Plus I'm on my feet all day around here. Is that what you wanted to know?"

"How do I get to work in a place like this?"

Tony doesn't seem to hear him. "You want this in your back seat? Or in the trunk?"

"Back seat's fine." Max opens the door and Tony loads the three coolers inside in three easy movements.

"We need you to take this straight to the inspection center in Vernon. Do not pass Go or collect whatever the money and all. Right?"

"Sure."

Tony turns to him. "That's what we told your office. And that's what we expect. I know they like to combine all their different pick-ups and whatever, but we're paying your guys, paying you to go from A to B. Got it?"

"Yes. Yes, of course."

"You say 'of course' but I know that's not how it all works." He winks.

Max puts his hand to his chest. "Tony, please believe me. I'll go straight there. I don't even have any other deliveries or pickups yet."

"Even if you do. This one gets there first. Right?"

"Right. Directly there."

"No stops. No pickups."

"No stops. No pickups."

Tony smiles and winks again. "Good man."

"It must be important stuff."

"Oh…you know it's always important. We got to make sure it's the best. Right Maxie?"

"Right."

The noise from above the warehouse suddenly rises. Tony looks up. "That's the storm out there, Maxie. Be careful." Max smiles. He feels himself blush. "We don't want anything to happen to our goodies now."

"Oh.. of course not."

"Or to you, buddy."

81.

He presses the button to recline his leather seat and he places his sunglasses on to nap and so he waits, figuring he has a good twenty minutes before Samuel arrives. The wind races and lashes the rain hard against the driver door. Rolfe sips coffee purchased at the lobby of his Riverside pick up. He puts the cup down and settles back. Perfect. Let it come. Flood it all. Mr. Gunther. He pictures Mayra's boyish haircut, her elegant neck, her cunty stuck up way of talking. Mr. Gunther. He hovers over a tiny black cavity deep inside his gut and he peers inside and watches it expand, crowding him out. He watches his right fist clench, unclench. Mr. Gunther. She says it with a wry and patient amusement. Mr. Gunther. Who are you talking down to? Mr. Gunther. Clench. Unclench. Mr. Gunther. Do you happen to have any idea, just even the slightest idea of what you are talking about? Mr Gunther. My good Mr. Gunther. What is it exactly that you hope to accomplish by looking at me like that? Do you fancy you can make me want you? Hmmm? And even if I did, would I want to then do business with you? Do you think your pretty blue eyes can substitute for having the experience, the knowledge, or leverage to make your case? Mr. Gunther. She never said any of these things, not in so many words. She said them with her eyes and with her smirks that he thought he saw. You built your daddy's house. He would be so proud of you. Good for you. Should I then make you a junior executive and fire the one I have? Is that it? Clench. Unclench. Mr. Gunther. I know who you are. Clench. Unclench. I know what you are. He slams his palm into the car horn. Blaring at nothing. The wipers suddenly start tossing back and forth, revealing the dull leaden sky and shivering trees behind the university parking lot. He shuts them off again. Back to the blur. "C'mon, Samuel." He turns the engine back on, unable to relax, and he finds the Claremont college radio station on his dial, and he blasts a distorted clash of frenetic guitars and drums and caveman roars. The rain crashes down, burying him deep inside his own little capsule. He turns to the passenger side and starts at the hairy, desperate looking face in his window, poorly wrapped in a thin parka. He reaches over and opens the door, "Quick! Get in! Just get in!" Samuel seems to whimper in protest before falling into the passenger seat. Rolfe turns the radio off. The older man lets his head throw back and steam seems to escape from his mouth ajar. An unpleasant rotting smell seems to seep from him. An old man smell. And wet. Samuel blinks and takes off his glasses and wipes them with his Zzzzzap! T-shirt. "This is quite a nice car."

"Don't get too comfortable. I just didn't want the packages to get wet."

"Of course."

"What took you so long? I've been waiting almost half an hour."

"We've had just a bit of inclement weather today. A bit of rain. I wonder if you noticed."

"No, you're just slow. Give me the package." Samuel looks at Rolfe and produces three stiff, padded thick envelopes, bound together with a rubber band. Perfectly dry. "That's it? Nothing going to Santa Barbara? Palm Springs?" Rolfe gives him a half smirk. "I'm waiting on my ass just to go fifty fucking feet?"

"Your entire life revolves around the number of miles you get reimbursed for every day."

"I'm trying to support my family. Is that OK with you?"

"Perfectly." Samuel strokes his beard, a gesture that somehow Rolfe finds repulsive in this moment.

"You can go now."

"Do you know the two people who you most resemble?"

"Paul Newman? Jesus?"

"Not quite."

"Hitler? Goering?"

Samuel chuckles. "Mikros. And Tim. Except that you are far more desperate than either of them."

189

"I see. So now you want to take me on? Is that it? Listen you old faker. This package. This package right here? It's going to the next building. What's the matter with you? Why am I delivering it? Why aren't you?"

"That's none of your business."

"None of my business?" Rolfe burns him a look of clownish amazement. "Is that so? None of my business? Listen to how tough you sound, talking to me. Are you a tough guy? Are you a tough guy, Samuel? Is that it? Look how tough little Samuel is. None of my business. Isn't it obvious why you aren't delivering this package? You're ashamed, aren't you? You're completely ashamed of yourself. Aren't you? You think I don't know where we are? You think I don't get it? This used to be your place. Right here. This place, this stupid college. You used to rule this place, no? A fancy professor? Is that it?"

Samuel looks at his hands. "You're right."

"Get out of my car, Samuel. Deal with yourself."

"There's nothing more painful, is there Rolfe, then feeling like a fraud? Then feeling like a poser."

"Get out!"

82.

Tim's wipers smear weakly, whining back and forth. He looks down the hill at endless rows of red tail lights. Centinela. He sees a coffee shop on his right. The hell with it, he thinks. There is a single spot available in the corner of the lot and he barely fits in beside a large pick-up truck. The restaurant is surprisingly full of oversized men sitting at the counter. "Coffee. To go," he tells the server, a pretty blue eyed brunette with chewed fingernails, "You got a payphone, hon?" She points it out. He nods and rattles the change in his hands. Maybe he would just call Jack, after all. Was there any point to being so pure and principled? "Zzzzap! Messenger. How may I help you?" Mikros answers directly, his tight little voice higher than usual.

"Where's Sandy?"

"She is out. Who is this? Is this Tim?"

"You got her out on a run?"

"Everybody is out. Even Mr. Hagen. Are you at your drop now?"

"No. I ran into a little traffic in the rain. And when I say a little, I mean a helluva lot of it. I'm letting you know, Mikros."

"When will you be at your drop?"

"On Wilshire? If this pace continues, I'd say at least a half an hour."

"Ahh!....Very well. Call me from your drop."

"That's it?"

"Take Pico."

"It's full a lights. Venice is faster."

"Too much traffic." And he hangs up. Tim pinches his nose and sidles up to the register to pay for his coffee.

He crosses Venice headed north on La Brea. Turn right on Pico. And of course, Pico is a bum move, Tim thinks. Crawling. I do as I'm told but *I'm* the one who's difficult to deal with. Tim honks his horn at a pedestrian who runs across the street. I wish I could laugh like you, Alice. You need to laugh Tim when you got nothing to laugh about. Especially then. Crenshaw is just ahead but there is a giant line to make a left hand turn. Screw it. He sees a sudden opening on Victoria, one street in front. The light turns green and he realizes that if he slows down, the train of on-coming new traffic will block him in the middle of Pico without a left hand turn lane to sit in. He turns the wheel sharply, hissing out rain. Suddenly he sees the young couple stepping off the curb, a short young man with glasses and a heavy set girl with a cane. The girl turns and looks into the car with her large, indignant gray eyes. Tim lets out a cry and steps on the brake and his heart keeps sliding and so does the car and he realizes there is no way he can brake in time to avoid crashing into them, so all he can do is swerve again, water spraying and he glides past the couple and he no longer cares as much what happens next but he gets a sickening feeling that this is real, not just one more disaster dream of his, and so he simply smashes full on, unabashed, into the driver door of a parked car and he's OK with that and he jolts and bangs his head against the dashboard. He doesn't pass out. At least not right away. Of all things, he remembers the color of the car he has just hit. It was like a peach color. A peach colored car. Who the hell drives a car like that? It doesn't matter. Nothing matters. Whatever else happens now, however ugly, however painful, however expensive and irreversible, at the very least, and a blessing indeed it is, he did after all somehow manage not to smash into his own daughter.

83.

Samuel grips the wheel and he pokes along in the slow lane, pulling over beside a little donut shop. The rain has started to let up. His pager goes off, a long, long single cry like the death signal at the sour hospital bed of a dying patient. He orders a Danish and cup of coffee in a Styrofoam cup. He takes his time eating, wiping the crumbs. Then he calls on Mikros from a payphone outside. "Ah Samuel. Why did you not call me when you were done?"

"My apologies." He wipes some crumbs from his beard. "Truly. The weather is wreaking havoc with everything, especially getting on and off the freeway. Where to now?"

"How far are you from the school?"

"Why do you ask?"

"I need you to go right back."

"To meet Rolfe?"

"To make a pick up. Different department. Administration. They need to make some kind of legal filing immediately"

"You have a strange sense of humor."

"Samuel! I need you to make that pick up."

"Out of the question."

In a voice softer than he expected, Mikros explains. "Rolfe is already gone. And I can't hang up one of my best drivers more than I already have. I've already tried my best to cover for you. Have I not? Now you need to do your job. Assuming you still want it. Do you understand?......Samuel?"

"I will call you right back."

"Call me back?"

"Very shortly, I assure you. I need to think about your proposition. And all that it entails."

84.

The jet planes lumber like giant buildings falling in slow motion underwater. He might still be late for his brand new life, but he hopes that Murray will understand because of the storm and because of everything. He has no more packages, no assigned pickups. He is even relatively close to Long Beach. Perry cannot bear to stab his job in the throat. But how could he do otherwise? He picks up the payphone. "Murray, it's me. It's Perry."

"You still coming."

"Yes. Yes of course."

"You on your way? It's murder out there."

"I need to ask you something, real quick. Please." Perry feels himself turn red. "I want to know what you think of this." Murray listens. Then he offers Perry an even better idea, to smooth over his dilemma.

85.

Rolfe blasts his music. The rain lets up and the freeway at last begins to move a bit. His pager screams, a long drop dead pitch. Very nice. Rolfe begins to calculate for the fiftieth time the cost-benefit analysis for Zzzzap! to invest in a radio system. Each time he pulls off the freeway, finds a phone, and gets back on it takes a minimum of fifteen minutes, or twenty to thirty minutes for everyone else except himself and Eugene. Conservatively three such pages a day means forty five minutes, times five days a week, fifty two weeks a year (someone has to work while someone else is on vacation) that's forty five times 260, that's....forget minutes, it's something like almost 200 hours. There's the exit. Forget wages, how much average revenue can be earned in an hour? Maybe $50 of revenue per hour. Conservatively? Turn left, more commercial lights and buildings over that way. Fifty times 200, what is that? He spots a bank of payphones. I'll double park. Screw you, he says to no one. That's $10,000 of lost revenue per year per driver, some of which comes right out of *my* pocket. And that doesn't even include the impact on reputation and competitiveness. Nor does it account for the fact that most drivers are so much slower and so they lose even more time. But that's a whole other issue. Borrow the fuckin' money if you don't have cash, there's your business plan. He gets out and slams the door and strides towards the phones. His pager screams again. Shut the fuck up!

His pager screams again. The long, flat death scream. Max crawls along the 101, the items from Tony, that is to say, from Gilroy Labs, are secure in his back seat, sealed, and balanced. Do not pass Go, do not collect something something, some dollar amount. But when you hear the beep, you immediately pull off and you call. What will I do?

His pager screams again. But this time he is already at Maple Avenue, finished with the lame ass Cal Trans mail run in twenty nine minutes. In the rain. Eugene sneaks a peek at Tim's meticulous route and mileage logs. (He has good handwriting and attention to detail. He'd give him that.) Forty two minutes. In the California sunshine. What an amateur. "Is that your boss?" the clerk, Jeannine asks him. She's a large, pear shaped blonde with blue eyes. She's pretty, with a giant ass, only he had never noticed before.

"Yeah. My boss. Can I use your phone?"

"Anytime." And she nods her head while opening the mail bag.

He makes the call. "Mikros, it's me."

"I have so many 'Me s' today. Who is this?"

"It's Eugene! What do you want? You death paged me."

"I give you life my friend. Life. Just as I promised you. I shouldn't, because you are rude to me, but this is business and you are my fastest driver. I have a box that needs to go to..... El Centro. It needs to be there tonight. Top priority from the big boss."

Eugene looks up. "El Centro? Did you say, El Centro?"

"One hundred and thirteen miles east of San Diego. Yes, you will make big, big bucks, listening to your radio, cruising along. Some box of specialized machine parts needs to go out to a hotel, which is for something or other, I don't know. Something is shut down and needs these parts. The box is here in my office. Mr Hagen picked it up himself. Hurry back, so I don't give it to anyone else."

"Don't fuck with me, Mikros. I'll be right there." Jeannine looks at him and makes an apologetic gesture with her hand meaning he should lower his voice. Eugene shrugs.

86.

"Perry. I was just about to page you. But you called me first. Good man. I need you to go to Long Beach."

"Mikros. I am so, so sorry."

"What are you sorry about? You're right on time. As always. I need you to pick something up right *there* at the airport and take it to the Royal Hotel in Long Beach."

"Did you say the Royal Hotel?"

"Yes. It's a hotel that's about to open. Do you know it?"

"No," he hears his voice go higher. "No I don't. But listen, I need to tell you something. I am so sorry."

"Yes. What is it? Quick."

"My car. My car was towed!"

"What? What are you saying to me? Your car is gone?"

"It was towed. Yes. I parked where I should not have parked. I am sorry. But I was trying to be fast instead of finding a parking spot. Sometimes I have to look for a long time and it's raining and everything. So I parked it next to the curb to save time. I was sure I could get back in time. But they must have come right away. Now I have to get my car. And it will cost me money. Money I do not have. But it was not smart after all. I should have known better," and to Perry's surprise he suddenly begins to cry real tears. "I am so sorry Mr. Mikros."

There is silence while Perry weeps but it feels as though someone else is weeping for him. When the man on the other end speaks, he sounds almost unrecognizable. "Please. Calm down. Alright. There is nothing to do now but for you to go get your car and for me to figure something out. If you're able to work later, please call me." Mikros hangs up on him.

87.

"Thank you, dear. That's very kind."

She tells him, "You welcome. Enjoy." Though he had always had his morning coffee black, he comforts himself by pouring in generous amounts of cream and sugar. Samuel plays with the creamer lever and he studies the sheen of the cheap metal. A civilized country should really steam or warm its milk for coffee. The rain has abated and all he hears is water on the tarmac sizzling at the constant passing of cars. "Do you want something else?" she says, smiling once more.

"Yes, please. I wanted to ask you something." She looks at him and nods expectantly, but doesn't move. He gestures for her to come and she does.

"You want more coffee?"

"How long have you worked here?"

She begins to wipe the counter. "Mmm. About six months."

"Do you like it?"

"Do I like it?"

"Yes. Do you?"

"It's OK. It's nice most of the time. When most people are nice."

"Are people ever not so nice?"

"Most people are happy when they come to eat or have a coffee, because they not working or they with their friend. But sometime you know people are in a hurry or they don't like the food, it's not what they expect, but I don't know what they expect, it's pretty simple."

"Yes." Samuel smiles.

She puts the rag down but lingers. "Or sometimes people are sad and alone and when they like that they sometime get mad for no reason. Or for no reason that you *know*."

"Does that happen very often?"

"Not very often. Just once in a while. Maybe they don't like themselves. So they feel lonely."

"You never know what someone is going through."

"Yes," she agrees. "You never know. So I try to remember that and if I remember I ask God to please bless them."

"You ask God to bless them. To make them happier."

"Mmm. Maybe. But that's not up to me you know, whatever it is that they need."

"Indeed."

"Sometimes God wants the problem to go away, whatever it is. Sometimes he wants you to walk through it. Then you'll know you're done. Because it can't bother you no more."

"Because you walked through it?"

"Yeah. I think so."

"And....does God bless them because you ask Him to."

She smiles as if Samuel were sweet and smart in many ways, but quite silly in others. "God do what He gonna do....Ooh, Mister. You're bleeding. From your nose." He wipes his upper lip and looks at the blood and he begins to laugh, a raspy, wheezy chuckle. Could he really make himself walk through one more thing?

88.

Singing reigns inside his head. But soon it will start to hurt. Like hell. Tell Mikros I'll be a little late. He chuckles but it hurts. Some asshole is slamming his palm against his car horn. Well if it's me you want, go around ding-dong cause I ain't goin' nowhere. Drool rolling over the steering wheel. That's what this is. The steering wheel. That's what's so funny. He is his own Greek choir, the very same asshole with his head on the car horn. He lifts his head and the singing stops, but his neck cringes, a cutting soreness. He grips the wheel and pushes himself up, holding his neck still. There is a tapping at his window and he carefully turns to see a worried looking woman staring at him. With difficulty he rolls down the window. The wind and the light rain blow inside the car. It feels good. The woman's black hair is also blowing. She wears a long white rain coat. "Mister. Are you OK?"

Tim blinks. "I seem to be in one piece." His voice sounds to him like it comes from far away. "I can talk."

"You were passed out on the steering wheel. I thought you were dead."

He clears his throat. "Yeah? Well. Am I?"

"Did you have a heart attack? Is that why you passed out and smashed into my car?" Her face is brown and hard and lovely, from some place far away.

"Someone stepped out in front of my car. I was trying not to hit her. I hit your car?"

"You smashed into my car. I can't believe it. I wondered, 'who is this crazy man? I thought you were dead."

"Sorry to disappoint you."

"What?"

"I'm sorry I hit your car. I'm insured. I'll take care of everything. You won't have a problem."

"Yes. I don't want any problems. And I don't want to pay....Are you OK? You cut yourself on your forehead when you smashed my car. You need a doctor."

Tim blinks. His mouth is dry. "I do?" For the first time he notices a small crowd of on-lookers from across the narrow street. He squints and looks for her. For his daughter. Nowhere.

"Do you want me to call an ambulance? Call 911?"

"Ambulance? No. I don't think so."

"You need help. Lucky for you I wasn't in my car."

"I agree. Lucky for you, too."

"I need your information. Your license, insurance, and everything." And she starts digging through her purse.

"Can you make a call for me?"

"You want me to call someone?"

"My daughter."

"What's her number?"

"I don't know."

"You don't know?"

"I...I don't know. No. Sorry."

"So what do you want me to do? We cannot just sit here all day."

"Call my boss."

"You know the number?"

"Yeah yeah. It's toll free."

89.

"Rolfe. I'm so sorry to pull you off the road." It was highly unusual for Mikros to apologize for anything. "Before you stop downtown, I need you to go directly to meet Tim. He's still at the corner of Pico and Victoria. Just west of Crenshaw. He's been in an accident."

Rolfe snorts with laughter. "What did he do? Hit a parked car?"

"What is the matter with you? I just told you he was in an accident. How do you know he's not seriously hurt?"

"Is he hurt?"

"Yes he is. Probably not seriously. But he is done for the day, to say the least."

"What happened?"

"I do not have time to explain. Please just go get his packages."

90.

"I love my new shoes." She looks at him hopefully. "And my new socks. My feet thank you." She takes the canvas shoes off and smells it. "I like the pink lining. And it smells new."

"Probably made by some slave in Bangladesh." At Slauson, Eugene turns right and careens past graffiti stained industrial buildings.

"And my socks are white." She wriggles her toes. "And everything fits too. It's nice. You know?" Eugene slams his horns and passes a pick up truck on the right. "Wow," she says. "Are you running from the law or something, now?"

"What?"

"I said, I love my shoes and socks."

197

"Goddamn it, Caroline. Enough with the shoes and socks already. I heard you. And I'm a little busy here right now," and he puts his foot on the brake to avoid hitting a slow little hatchback. "Idiots."

"I was just trying to thank you for the shoes and socks. I can't wait to take a walk in them."

"You can take that walk right now if you want. Get it? Or you can please, please just shut up."

"Ahh.....fine." She frowns and Eugene out of some private malice begins to count. She says. "Aren't you going to run out of gas?"

"Seven seconds."

"What?"

"That's how long you managed to shut up after more than once I asked you to. Shit, I'm not gonna make this light. You're distracting me."

"You counted?"

"Yes. I did. To make a point."

"What kind of point?"

"The point that you can't keep your mouth shut."

She looks at her shoes. "Maybe you're not such a nice guy."

"I don't care."

"Maybe I won't ever take you to that nice place of mine."

"I don't care."

"You don't care? Do you care if you run out of gas? You're almost out of gas...... Don't you see?" She points at the gauge with an arm just below his nose.

"Yes, of course I *see*, all right? I see it. We'll be fine. But listen to me, I have to keep driving until we make this pick up at the office. That's all I care about right now. After I make the pick up, I can take all the time in the world to look for a bank, get some gas, and even enough time to listen to your bullshit. There will be plenty of time then!"

91.

"There he is!" Tom Hagen affably greets him, hands in pockets, standing next to the dispatch desk like a man at a bar. He looks to Andy a bit disheveled, tie loose and askew, hair not quite in place. Andy guesses he skipped shaving this morning.

"Hello, Mr. Hagen."

"Mr. Hagen, he calls me. Very respectful. Well. There it is. All ready for you." He points to a carefully sealed box, perched on the counter, large enough to package a toaster.

Mikros speaks, "I still think that Eugene could be here any minute, Mr. Hagen."

"Andy is here right now. You told me he's been running hard all morning."

"Yes sir."

"We can use Eugene's talents elsewhere. This is a straight shot."

"Well...not exactly. And I'm not sure there's any point in taking it right now anyway."

"Let's not keep them waiting," Hagen pats the box and strokes his chin. "They're paying a lot of money. I made sure of that. We gotta get this package there before someone dies!" he sings out. "Oh yes. Gotta run. Have fun with it!" Andy catches a fruity, rotten whiff mixed with Aqua Velva. "Mikros. Tell the hotel that I'm on my way."

"Yes, of course."

Hagen winks at Andy. "Possible new client. Concierge service from the owner," he pats the envelope. "I'll scope it out."

"Mr. Hagen, what we need are more drivers."

Hagen trots off, calling out as he heads away. "Too many drivers. Not enough drivers. Already working on it. Sandy, you're lookin' *awesome* today."

"Work fast. Please!"

"It kind of smells like Gin in here, somewhere," Andy offers.

Mikros looks at him, then at the box. "It's small but heavy. You can use the dolly to load it."

Andy lifts it and puts it down. "I can just take it down." He looks at the address. "Where is this? Orange County?"

"Ah. Orange County. Is that where you think you're going?"

"Yeah. No? That isn't it? Isn't this way down there, south of Irvine or something? Near Laguna Beach?...."

"Very good. That's El Toro of course that you're referring to. Nice try. Take another look at the address. Go on."

"El Centro."

"Correct. El Centro. Very different. Nothing is further away mind you from the center of things than this place called El Centro. Good luck." The phone rings, but Mikros doesn't pick up. "Tell me Andy, do you have even the slightest fucking idea where El Centro is?"

"Um. No. I do not have even the slightest fucking idea."

"Regardless, you are on your way" Mikros hands Andy a folded map along with a small envelope. The phone rings again and this time Mikros picks up. "Yes... ah good, it took you long enough.... Well that was like two seconds ago; I have other calls. Listen. Where are you now?...... No, no. That can wait. No, Max. I need you to make some pick-ups Downtown. Triangle. These are rush jobs going to Beverly Hills; then you can go to Vernon.......No, no, they're not paying for that.......I do not know anyone named Tony.....Yes, well whoever this Tony person is, neither he nor his boss are paying to get this delivered before five. You understand? …Max you will go to Triangle now, you're already right there, and you will make those deliveries. I cannot keep them waiting for over an hour. Call me when you are done." Mikros puts the phone down. "We're taking good care of you, Andy, so that you don't have to drive along shouting out for help from passers-by. Here's a map of California. How nice. And directions. Do yourself a favor and be gone before Eugene finally arrives. I wish I were not here myself. Believe me it was not my idea to have you both race here to come and get this. I do what I am told and it pleases Mr. Hagen to more than occasionally have us compete with each other, or else to simply contradict me. Just take it now and go. You generously have until eight o'clock before the client gets a very deep discount."

"Six hours? Where am I going? Mexico? Arizona?"

"Remarkably close my friend. Almost yes. To both your suggestions. Now go." Andy hesitates.

92.

"Come on! Come on! We're almost there!" he shouts. "Fuckin' idiots! *Now* you decide to put your blinkers on? " And he looks over his shoulder to see if the next lane is clear. "Caroline, move. You're in the way."

"Move? Where can I move to?"

"Just move your head down!"

She crouches down. "Eugene. You're scaring me. You're gonna kill us both." He lurches the car forward and he splashes through a deep puddle in the intersection. There's a loud clunk. The car lurches again, the engine sputtering and coughing. Someone rides their horn at them and speeds by, the horn's whine suddenly descending as it passes. Eugene grits his teeth and roars between his locked jaws, struggling with the wheel to pull the car, which is now adrift, over to the curb. He takes off his glasses and rubs his eyes, breathing heavily, muttering obscenities. Caroline wonders if he is crying.

Suddenly he begins beating his right fist against the steering wheel. "No! God damn it! God damn it!" Caroline bites her lip. He leans back and closes his eyes. Moments pass.

"What happened?" she asks. "Eugene, what happened?"

"What happened? I'm fucked!" he explodes. "That's what's happened." He hits the steering wheel again and honks the horn. "I've just lost the sweetest, best possible run. Ever! Ever! I've just lost two month's rent. Maybe three. I've just lost a hundred dinners. More! Twenty, thirty pairs of your dumbass shoes and socks. Everything that I've worked so hard to earn. It's like the ultimate. It was mine. It was mine! And now some loser, some *loser*! Some idiot is gonna get it." Eugene sweats profusely now. The rain resumes. They can hear it on the roof top and see it in the windshield and all around them. He opens the window.

"I'm sorry, Eugene."

"I'm out of gas. OK? I'm out of gas and I'm out of money and I'm screwed." Caroline stares away, then closes her eyes and puts her hand over her mouth. She begins to shake. Eugene looks at her. "What's the matter with you? Are you …..are you laughing?"

She shakes her head but she is laughing. "I'm really sorry. I know you're very upset, but there is something funny about it."

"No! No there's not. There's nothing fucking funny about it!"

Caroline bursts out laughing. "Please…..oh…come on Eugene. You have to laugh. I'm not laughing at you, you silly man. It's just…. I don't know. Just laugh at yourself."

Softly, he tells her, "It's because of you, Caroline. Yeah. It's because of you and your stupid ass shoes and socks." And he slumps back in his seat and looks out the window. He hears the passenger door open and she steps out and closes the door. Eugene looks over and she is gone. He scrambles out of the car and catches sight of her walking west down Slauson. "Hey!" he calls after her. She continues to walk. He runs after her. "Hey! Where are you going?"

"I've had enough, Eugene."

"Caroline. Come on back." She says nothing. "You're gonna leave me? Now that I actually need you?"

She turns to him. "You don't need me. You don't even like me."

"What do you mean? Because I said your shoes are stupid. OK. I'm sorry. They're not stupid. Your shoes are not stupid. I know they're important to you. But come on, I'm having a hard time over here."

"It's not just that, Eugene. You've been mean to me all morning. All morning you've been angry at me and you're rude. Last night you were sweet to me. But now I see how you are. How you really are."

"Caroline. Caroline. Please."

"Don't 'Caroline' me."

"I'm just trying to work here. Do my job. You know. It's nothing personal. I wanted to drop you off, back where I found you, but there was no time. It's nothing personal."

"Back where you found me? What kind of a thing is that to say? I wasn't lost. OK. I'm a homeless woman. But I knew exactly where I was when you came along."

"It's nothing personal."

"Well I don't even know what that means. Nothing personal…"

"It means…"

"Don't even try to explain. You're angry at me. You're angry at the world and you're just angry. Enough."

"You wouldn't be angry if all this happened to you?"

"Nothing happened *to you*, Eugene. You can never even imagine what my life is like, what it's like to be me, so I'm not so fucking impressed with your little problems, OK."

"I need you, Caroline."

"No you don't!" She responds sharply. "And I don't care. "

"You don't?" They stand in the rain.

"You don't need me. You're better off without me."

"That's not true, Caroline."

"Please. Please just let me go."

"You just get your shoes and socks. You get what you want and you leave?"

"Ahh! Do you want them back?"

"What?"

"Do you want me to give them back to you?" Eugene says nothing. He puts his hands back in his pockets. Caroline bends down and begins to untie her shoelaces. She pulls the one off, then sits down heavily to take the sock off.

"What are you doing?"

"I'm giving you back the shoes and socks."

"What?" She says nothing. "What are you doing?"

She struggles upwards. "Thanks for helping me up, by the way," she says.

"I'm sorry."

"Here. I'm giving these back."

"What do I do with these?"

"You do whatever you want with them." She holds them out.

"I don't want them, Caroline. They're yours. They're yours." She sits down again and begins with some difficulty to put her shoes and socks back on again. Eugene sits down with her and they both continue to get wet. Caroline stands up and Eugene attempts to assist her but she waves him off and he sits back down again. He looks up at her. "Will you stay with me?" he asks her.

"Thank you for the shoes, Eugene. And the socks. And for last night." He looks up at her and he tells himself that she is beautiful to him. But no words come out. "Goodbye, Eugene." And she walks away.

"Hey," he says softly. "I was supposed to take you back to the 7-11. Where we met. You made me promise. Caroline?" No answer. He rubs his nose and sits still and feels himself getting soaked. "It's not my fault, Caroline. It's not my fault that I ran out of gas. I would have taken you back, but I ran out of gas. It's not my fault." But of course it is, he thinks. "Caroline. Caroline." He remains sitting on the sidewalk in the rain, watching her recede. I have to call Mikros. I have to do that. And then after that, I have no idea. "Caroline!" He looks up as if waking from a dream and he stares down the street where she has already vanished as if she had never existed.

93.

They conclude exchanging phone numbers, insurance, and car information. "And again, I'm awful sorry about all of this. My insurance...and I will take care of all of this. I'm just thanking my lucky stars that neither you nor no one else was hurt. "

"You need to see a doctor, Timothy."

"You like calling me Timothy, huh?"

"Will you see a doctor?"

"Maybe. If you keep calling me Timothy."

"You're an odd man and you wrecked my car and you wrecked yourself. But I'll keep calling you Timothy if you like."

"I wish I had a cigarette."

"That's no good for you. You need to take care of yourself."

"Well, I guess I'm not doin' a very good job of that."

Two police cars arrive, lights flashing. "And now the circus comes to town." A police officer talks to the woman in the white coat with black hair.

"Tim," Rolfe calls out. "Tim!"

Tim looks up and squints at Rolfe without surprise. He leans back to pull something out of his back seat. "It's in the back seat. Door's open." Rolfe opens the back passenger door and collects several envelopes of different sizes off the floor. He also finds Tim's signature and mileage log and clipboard filled with his immaculate printing, but he puts it down.

"Are you OK? You're bruised up."

"I'll be fine."

"You need a doctor."

"Jeez. Everybody needs to let up with the doctor. Here! They're all marked with their deadlines. You know the drill. Drop this one first, will ya?" He taps envelope on top.

"I'll be right back." Rolfe says and he trots off.

"Back? You're outta here, aren't you?" But Rolfe is already out of earshot. "What is it with this guy?" The police officer talks with Pauline. Suddenly she laughs. He mutters towards the officer, "Come on. What are you doing?" Finally she turns back and walks towards him. She seems about to speak when Rolfe suddenly returns, holding an umbrella.

"Tim. Let's go."

"What are you talkin' about?"

"I'm taking you to the doctor. To the ER."

"You're not taking me anywhere. "

"You just destroyed a car, Tim. Two cars. Good job. Efficient and all, but you're hurt."

"She'll take me."

203

Pauline arrives. "Take you where, Timothy?"

"To the doctor."

"I have no car. Remember? You do remember that I have no car anymore because you destroyed it."

"Yeah, that rings a tiny little bell. We'll take a cab then."

"I have to wait for the tow truck."

"So do I."

"No you don't. Go to the doctor."

"Yeah," Rolfe speaks. "You're outvoted Timothy"

"Stay out. Don't you start calling me that."

"Are you his friend?"

"No, he's not. He's just another idiot driver. Why aren't you gone already?"

Rolfe and Pauline recognize each other. "It's you." she says. "I thought you were an architect." She looks at Rolfe's windbreaker jacket, seeing a glimpse of his ZZZZap!! t-shirt.

Tim looks up. "What? You two know each other?"

"Well. I'm a student," Rolfe explains to her. "I have to make a living in the meantime so I can go to school at night."

"I don't think so. You're nothing but a driver, aren't you?"

"Something wrong with that?" Tim asks.

"It is if you're a liar, Timothy."

"Is that right? Are you a liar, Rolfe?" Tim asks.

"I'm taking you to the doctor," Rolfe announces stiffly. "To the emergency room. That's what I'm doing. Unless you need an ambulance."

"I can't believe one hasn't come yet," says Pauline.

"Wait here. I'll pull my car around."

"You're gonna be late with those packages."

"He was passed out when I found him."

"Come on, Tim. Your brain might be hurt. Maybe it will work better now."

"Tim," Pauline says. "I'll be here when the tow truck comes. Where do you want your car taken?"

"You'll do that? Yeah, let me give you the info for this body shop. You should take your car there as well."

Rolfe interjects, "The cars are totaled, Tim."

"So you're a body mechanic and an architect? And a doctor? You're a regular whiz kid." Rolfe smiles and disappears again. "Pauline. It's not my business, but how do you know this guy?"

"He was trying to impress me at this restaurant, along with his little friend, Maxie."

"Who?"

"This cute little man named Maxie. Max.."

204

"Max? That's.... odd."

"What is odd?"

"Nothin'. I'll take a ride to the ER. And I'll call you. After I've spoken to my insurance company."

"Alright. Just go get well."

"Maybe we can go over the details sometime over a sandwich or cup a coffee."

She laughs. "Maybe. You think I like grouchy, bleeding old men who destroy my car?"

"I was kind of hoping you might."

"I don't think I'd let you drive me anywhere."

"Neither one of us has a car anyway."

94.

"I'm supposed to play a gig. In a band. Play music at a club."

"But you are working right now. It is two o'clock and you work until five, or until your last assignment. That's what we hired you for."

"I thought of this as a job where I would have my evenings for the rest of my sorry life."

"Fascinating." The phone rings again. "Ah. This might be the solution to your problem right here. Perhaps all will be well for everyone." Mikros answers. "Yes. Yes! Eugene. Yes! Where are you?.......What?" Mikros' face goes pale and he takes his glasses off. He wipes his brow and sighs. "I see. I see....Well what can I tell you. What am I supposed to say to you? I can do nothing for you......" Mikros sighs. "That is not something we can do for you right now. That was your job....I'm sorry. Eugene...you can call me back if you like in thirty minutes and I will see what I can do. But I cannot promise what will happen." He hangs up and says nothing at first but shakes his head. "You'll laugh, I'm sure. It's quite a good one." For the first time ever, Andy feels slightly sorry for the man. He seems much smaller to him than usual. "Let's talk about our drivers. One of them calls out sick. On her second day. One gets his car towed. One has an accident. Another is quite picky about his assignments and refuses to pick up a package when he is right there at the client. And one runs out of gas. Can you believe it? Can you believe this shit? He has the nerve to ask me to have someone bring him this package and forty dollars cash so he can drive it down to El Centro. No way. I'm tired of his shit, I don't care how good he is. I'm done with bending over backwards." He takes off his glasses again and rubs his eyes. "And if I do decide to get him the cash somehow, I am sure not to reward him by sending him off to Timbuktu." He sighs. "I'm about to lose you now, but you don't even want to work, do you?"

"I can work until five or six, maybe six thirty."

"I have no one else to take this package! Even Mr. Hagen is out on a drive and I suspect he won't be back either."

"What about Sandy?"

"Ah! She can barely drive and not at all at night. Besides we are supposed to keep our customers, not scare them away." Now, Andy thinks, he seems cruel and petty once more. As if reading his thoughts, Mikros adds, "Ah, there was no need to say that....I truly have no one else to go to El Centro. As it is, I will have to start turning to my competitors to do our runs for us if we get any more calls. I may need to do it anyway. They carry our packages and maybe our clients, too. And Mr. Hagen will have my ass if I call one of the big boys to give *this* package away to them. Please. Take this assignment. It will be worth your while. You need the money. I know you do. It will be an adventure."

"Mikros. I told you. I have a gig tonight. There was never any talk about having to work to eight o'clock or later."

"Ah, Andy." Mikros raps his knuckles on the counter. "Come on! Seriously!" He shouts. "Are you fucking kidding me? How much are they paying you at this club tonight?"

"That's not the point. I think it's OK for me to make plans after five PM. You never told me we would have to work until midnight."

"This is a one-time thing! How much are you making? Forty dollars? Fifty dollars?"

"It's a percentage of something. Maybe it's something like that." Twenty dollars. And a meal. "I can't flake out on them. I came to L.A to play music."

"You came to L.A to make money. How does two hundred and fifty dollars sound?"

"You really have no other choice?"

"Well. I guess I could go, but someone needs to mind the store. Right?"

"Four hundred dollars."

"What?"

"I'll do it for four hundred dollars."

Mikros looks at him quizzically. "What are you talking about?"

"I want four hundred dollars. And a motel room."

"What are you talking about?"

"You're asking me to give up something important to me. My guess is that you're being paid so much more to take this package that you're still making a killing."

"I really ought to *fire* you, Andy."

"You want to call the 'big boys' on this? Anyway, for ten hours and five hundred miles in this storm? What I'm asking is reasonable. You can fire me tomorrow. Four hundred dollars. Or I pass."

"Get out of here, Andy," Mikros says quietly. "Please. No one. I mean no one, not even Eugene or Rolfe has ever tried to shake me down. And I certainly didn't expect it from you. You are a great disappointment to me."

"Call me when my final paycheck is ready."

"I'll be sure to do that," Mikros adds. And Andy walks out of the room. He makes it as far as his truck when his pager goes off. The long bitter death page.

"What is it?" Andy asks, much louder than he had intended to ask.

"Take that package and get the fuck out of here."

"Excuse me?"

"You got your four hundred dollars."

"Really?"

"There's just one thing."

"What's that?"

"I will call the client and if they say you arrived even one minute past eight, you will get nothing."

"It doesn't work like that."

"That's the deal."

Andy thinks about it. "If I make it. When I make it. I want you to foot the bill for a motel. A cheap one. That's the deal."

"Fine. We have an agreement. Good luck," he slowly says.

"There's just one more thing."

"We have an agreement! No more one more thing!"

"I need to borrow some cash. Just borrow it. For gas! Take it out of the four hundred. "

"I wonder if you have heard of an ATM machine. Or cashing a check." Mikros starts to smile again.

"I don't have that. Don't you have any petty cash?"

Mikros slams his palm upon the counter. He begins to laugh. "What the fuck are you talking about?" He laughs again and slams his palm once more on the table. "Excellent. Excellent. Just excellent."

95.

A thunderclap explodes overhead. Samuel puts his blinkers on. Head down, he walks up the steps and into the hallway towards the administration office. Samuel tries to take a deep breath but everything is shallow. He trembles. He opens it and walks in, hunched over. It is like a dream. Being here again. And now to the desk for the pick-up. Instantly he recognizes the portly woman with beady brown eyes and pulled back hair. Dolores. What was her last name? She was never too friendly; she always took her proximity to leadership a bit too seriously. Perhaps she will instantly dismiss my presence as some anonymous errand boy, point to some packages or envelopes, sign the log in a crisp yet distracted fashion, and send me on my way. Instead, she holds up a finger, while she finishes her call. So he stands there, head down, thin black jacket, dripping water. She looks up. "Yes?"

He speaks in a low cracked voice. "I am here to pick up the package."

"For Dr. Stiles?"

"Yes. I am the messenger." And he holds up his clipboard, still looking downward. He clears his throat.

"I think he wanted to talk with you." Stiles is the Dean, he can't remember for what now. Business? Life Sciences? They had sat together during several endless banquets, had had a few drinks. A boring man, even when drunk, lacking imagination. Quite judgmental. "There was something he wanted to tell you for when you get there."

"Do you think we need to bother him directly? I'm eager to get back on the road. The storm is picking up again."

"Well you're here now and he said he wanted to speak with you."

"Ma'am, I really don't want to waste his time. Perhaps you could get him on the phone."

"Well that's exactly what I'm going to do. He's not walking across campus in the rain if that's what you're worried about," and she rolls her eyes and plucks her fingers across the dial pad.

"I can be paged at any time. Or you can call the main office. They know how to get a hold of me."

She holds up her finger again. "Dr. Stiles? The messenger is back. Different one. You wanted to speak to him? No? OK. I'll tell him." She hangs up. "Alright. Please just call us when you arrive."

"Of course."

"May I get your name?"

"My name?"

"Yes. Just in case."

"In case what?"

"In case we need it. You don't want to give your name?"

"Oh of course. Yes, I'll give it."

She holds a pen. Then looks up. "What is it?"

He smiles to himself. "Johnny."

"Last name?"

"Williams," popped into his head.

"Johnny Williams."

"Please sign this for me before I go."

"Sure." At last he is about to walk out. She stares at the log for a moment, and then looks up at him. "There's blood on this paper."

96.

"Nice car," Tim mutters. "You do all right with the driving, huh."

"Do you have a preference where you want to go?"

"Cadillac. You know it?"

"Yeah. I got it."

"Turn left on La Brea."

"I said I got it. And I'm taking Redondo. No wonder you're so slow."

"That didn't take long. You want me to leave you alone now?" And he shuts his eyes.

"........Hey.......Hey......Wake up. You can't go to sleep now." Rolfe looks over then shakes Tim's shoulder. "Wake up!"

"The *hell*...."

"You passed out back there. At the accident. What if you have a concussion or something? You're not dying in my car."

"I wouldn't be caught dead in your car."

Rolfe smiles but doesn't look over. "OK. So we agree on that, Timmy."

"Stop calling me, Timmy. You hear me? For the last time, goddamn it, the name is Tim. Tim! Have you no decency? And don't you fuckin smile or I swear I'll knock that smile off your face."

Rolfe levels him a look. "Please, Tim. OK? Tim. There."

"You want a parade? A medal?"

"I want you to calm down. I swear I wasn't trying to tweak you that time. It just came out. And we'll be rid of each other soon enough."

"Not soon enough"

"Fine. And you're welcome."

"Thank you then....for sticking your nose in my business. *Your* business is to deliver those packages on time. My name's on the client sign in sheet." Rolfe makes a face of mock concern. "And don't you ever fuckin' touch me again."

"Tell me, does decency include driving you to emergency?"

"Thanks for the ride. But can you please just leave me alone"
Rolfe gets into the left hand turn lane at La Brea. "Sure."

97.

"You're bleeding."

"Oh…I…I'm horribly sorry." He puts the envelope down.

She grabs a handful of facial tissues from a box on the corner of her desk. "Take these. Hold your head up."

"Yes, of course." He grabs them blindly and holds his head abnormally back, the while hoping to hide his face. His neck protests. He closes his eyes.

"Are you going to be OK?"

"Yes, yes," he nods in a weak voice. "I just need…some fresh air. I really should be going."

"Well hold on. I have to change out this envelope. Will you stop bleeding before you deliver this?"

"Of course. Of course." The question is marvelously impertinent, he thinks. But he understands. He staggers to the sofa and sits down heavily, the cracked leather groaning. He pinches his nose with a tissue, trying to staunch the traitorous flow of blood which seeks to escape him.

"Are you gonna be able to drive?"

Samuel tastes the ferrous leak of blood in the back of his throat. "Thank you kindly for your concern." Any moment now, Dr. Stiles or any one of a dozen former colleagues will walk into this room, instantly recognize him, and revile him as a besotted, worthless fool who fouls their institution with his presence.

"Should we call your office?"

"I just need to be on my way." There is a brown water stain on the ceiling the shape of Laike Baikal in Siberia, he fancies. Deepest fresh water lake in the world. Oh to be at the bottom of such waters right now, touching the sandy floor, somehow still seeing the reflected image of the Altais mountains and wild conifer forests from a thousand feet below the surface. "Are you replacing the envelope now?"

"Hold on.….I want to make sure you're OK. OK to take this package."

"One thing you might do," Samuel adds, "One thing that might give us both some assurance about my condition is if you simply put one envelope inside another envelope. A smaller inside a larger. Or you can give me extra envelopes. Quite simple." Will I ever leave this place again? Ever? Samuel closes his eyes. Immediately he is far away, not in Baikal or Rainier, but someplace indistinct and far away. The music begins to play again, but instead of Vaughan William's Third, it is Mahler's Tenth, its barren, merciless beginning, groaning in pain before blooming into its fungal burst of delusion and parodies of yearning. Of course he had lied to Andy, for no particular reason other than he did not like to summon this music, the music he had learned to forget even when looking at the wasted, ravaged bodies on the oncology ward. Now he is there again on his watch staring at an ancient woman. She opens one eye and stares at him. Samuel opens his eyes on a raw note. His head is down. Good God! Can he still be dreaming? He looks at his jacket and to his ZZZZap! shirt, soiled with rusted brown rivulets of blood. Slowly, Samuel raises his eyes, heart pounding sorely, ready to meet her eyes, or the eyes of all upon him wearing their clean, pressed laundry, or worst of all to see the compassionate, devastated face of Elizabeth. But he is alone.

98.

"Mr. Langham. Mr. Langham?" Tim opens his eyes. Two young men, stand over him. He thinks he must be in a hospital bed already, but he realizes he is still in Rolfe's car. Nice car. Not a scratch on it? That's because it was his own car that crashed, Tim reasons. You talkin' to me? Tim says, but nothing comes out. "Are you able to help us move you?" Sure. Why not. There is a jumble of movement and somehow he ends up on a bed, a gurney, under cover of a great awning outside the emergency entrance.

"Where's Rolfe?" he says out in a horse whisper. "Where'd he go?"

"Sir. Excuse me. The gentleman is asking for you."

Rolfe appears. "Tim." Tim looks as if he wants to say something but then frowns as if he's forgotten and waves it away with his fingers. "Tim. I'll see you later. We'll have a race when you're feeling better." Tim appears to crack half a smile and shake his head.

"Sir. Are you a relative?" A stout young man in scrubs, one he has never seen before, is talking to him.

"No. We're not related. At all."

"Are you a friend? A care taker?"

"We work together. That's all. You see this stupid t-shirt?"

The stout young man raises both his brows as he looks at this clipboard. "Does he have insurance?" Rolfe tells him that he does. "Will you or someone else be picking him up when he is discharged?"

"I don't know anything about that."

The stout young man looks up. "Who will be picking him up?"

"I told you. I don't know."

"Does he have any family or other friends?"

"I don't know."

"Do you know where he lives?"

"No. He should be able to tell you that."

"His work number?"

Rolfe gives it to him. "Is he going to be OK?"

"I don't know if they'll admit him or not. He's conscious. That's good. Was it a car accident?"

"He ran into a parked car. Totaled it." The man looks at him. "Yeah. You probably don't want us driving for you, right?"

"Is there a police report?"

"Yes."

"All right then. Well. Thank you for bringing him in."

"What'll happen if he doesn't have a ride home?"

"Oh…we'll get him home somehow. Cab, maybe. When the patient's a little confused, we always talk to the family member. Or, whoever is with him."

Rolfe sighs. "How long is he going to be here?"

"No idea. We may keep him overnight, or longer. Or he may go home tonight."

"If he needs a ride and there's absolutely no one else - and I mean if there's absolutely no one else in the whole wide world - I'll come pick him up."

"Got it. Let me just get your information."

99.

He looks about the room which is unnaturally still. Even the music is gone. Time to go. Now. He takes a breath and he lifts himself out of the sofa with surprising ease. But his head lightens, gold and black waves scatter in view and for a delirious moment he fears he will pass out. Instead he falls back upon the couch. One more time. He rises. Steady. Any moment now this moment will pass and the door will open and he will be trapped. Briskly he walks to the door, his hand trembles on the knob. Opens it. No one there. Out the front door and into the cooling rain. Soon he will be invisible in the storm. Down the steps. And here he forces himself to slow his pace, lest he slip and fall and break his back. He pulls his jacket up, lowers his head, grips the rail, counts the steps, watches his feet, wishing he could run, knowing that any misstep could be his last, broken brittle bones, bruised and feeble muscles. Two more steps to go. The rain comes down now in torrents again. "Mr. Driver!" he hears. "The package is here. It's ready." He stands for a moment, his heart feeling pressed in and cold. Samuel decides he will not turn around. Nor will she follow him in this downpour. "The package is ready! Dr. Stiles needed to add one more document. Where are you going?" The voice is higher, thinner. Samuel holds on to the bannister, grateful to be on his feet. Any moment now, the secretary will stand before him, wave before her a blood stained envelope (which makes no sense of course), make threats against him and his employer, none of which, he knows, will be much his concern. You'll never work as a messenger in this town again! He begins to laugh. Any moment now, he will hear her heels click upon the steps, her fingernails plunge into his dry, leathery neck, his blood a congealed oozing from the moment it weakly escapes its moorings. Or she will trip and fall backwards, supine, bitter, coccyx shattered. You bastard! You have slain me. Samuel walks on. "I'm calling your office right now!" she says, though her voice sounds faint. Samuel smiles, resists the temptation to wave. The rain lets up once more. Professor! A man in a long blue parka trots up to him. A black man, resembling a sea drenched postal worker.

"Professor!" The man repeats.

"Good God!" Samuel ejaculates. "Are you addressing me?"

The man stops short and smiles at him. No trace of irony in that smile. He puts out his hand. "It's George. George! One of the engineers here. You remember?"

"Are you sure you have the right man?"

"You're Professor Samuel. You always the professor."

Samuel takes his hand. "Hello George," he says. "To be honest, I was not inclined to be recognized."

"I understand. No one wants to stay out in this rain."

"Forgive me. I've been here on other business and no one has recognized me."

"If that's a disguise you wearin', so is a suit and tie. Just something you put on and take off. But I know you."

"But I was walking head down in the rain. How would you know?"

"Well I did. I just wanted to see you. I see you let your hair down. I heard you was here and I thought I'd come out. I've missed you. Lots a people miss you, professor."

"That's so very kind."

"You're very kind. You're a kind man. Did you retire and not tell any of us?"

"You might say. Yes. Yes, I'm sorry it was sudden. I....I'm sorry, did you say that you heard that I was here?"

"Yeah. This place is not so big. Word get out fast. Are you OK? Did you hurt yourself?"

"Good Lord. Please forgive me. I'm afraid I'm going to be horribly rude and leave directly." And he makes his way to his car, having taken on a new and unaccountable limp.

"Good to see you, prof. You need help with anything?"

"No!" He fiddles with the key. "Blast. I just need to leave." George frowns then raises his brows. Samuel catches sight of this. "I told you I was bound to be rude. I don't want to be. I'm just not well," he says fumbling with his key. "But you're a good man, George."

"If you don't mind, I'm just gonna watch to see that your car starts. Some cars get flooded out in this downpour and they won't pick up again."

"Fine. Fine." He opens the door and takes in its stale, forlorn smell. He casts a final courteous glance at George. "Thank you, George. Truly." Beyond the engineer, at the edge of the lot, even as a blur in the washed out ragged world, he instantly recognizes the tall, straight, elegantly dressed woman, holding her umbrella, standing still in the rain, facing him.

100.

The long afternoon is strangely quiet. No Hagen. No Sandy; he sent her out on several local runs, not expecting her back any time soon. No drivers. No phone calls. The worst of the winds are over. He makes himself a cup of coffee and gives himself permission to simply stand and watch the storm and the prematurely darkening sky, ink pools and now and then a flash of cracked bones haunting up above. He'll miss this place. It's a nice office. A ridiculous little business. He doesn't like the thought of not coming back. Too many missed deadlines, too many clients turned away, or turned to a competitor. The phone rings. Mikros turns to answer. At the very same moment that he reaches for the receiver, a wet sloshing stride disturbs the hallway and a shadowy being enters. Mikros puts the phone down, his hand weakening with surprise. Eugene stands and looks at Mikros blandly. "Are you gonna get that?" The phone rings again. "Sandy's not here. No one's here. Are you OK?" Eugene asks. Mikros observes his own hand trembling.

"Have a seat, Eugene."

"I think I will." And he plops down heavily on the couch.

Mikros grabs the phone, nearly fumbling it. "Zzzzap! messenger. Mikros speaking.......What? He what?" Mikros bunches his brows and twists his mouth as if he tasted something disagreeable. "He came but then he left without taking it?......I'll page him...of course....I can send another driver. Let me call you right back....I'm terribly sorry." Mikros hangs up the phone, his hand steadier than before "Eugene." Eugene lies on the couch staring up at the ceiling. "Eugene, did you walk or did you drive here?"

"I walked."

"I thought so."

"You got a water stain on the ceiling."

"What am I supposed to do Eugene if you cannot put gas in your car? It's not like we don't pay you."

214

"I know you have petty cash. I know you still have deliveries. You want me to go to Claremont? I could be there in an hour."

"Not even you could do that. And have you already forgotten that your car is not even here?"

Eugene struggles to sit up. "Give me the cash, Mikros. You need me."

"I *needed* you. I don't need anything anymore."

He changes his tone. "Please, Mikros. Just give me the money so I can put gas in my car."

"I have no money. I already gave the money away…to Andy."

"You what?"

"I said I gave the money to Andy. He needed it up front to get him to El Centro."

Eugene glowers at him. "I should really just kill you, Mikros."

"Perhaps you would be doing me a favor." Eugene lies back down again and closes his eyes. "What are you doing?"

No answer for a long moment. "What does it look like?"

"I thought you always hated this place. This room."

After a moment, Eugene tells him softly, eyes closed. "No. No, I like this room. Especially now. And I like this couch. What I don't like is not making money, not getting what I work for. I don't like idiots who are slow and who don't know what they're doing and who fail to take what they're doing seriously. But no, I don't mind this room."

"I'll pay you ten dollars out of my own pocket." No reaction. "If I give you some gas money, will you leave?"

"Eventually… Yes." Eugene's peaceful expression changes darkly behind his closed eyes. "Where am I going to go?"

101.

Rolfe gingerly peruses the envelopes that were in Tim's possession. Most are due at 5PM. Next day delivery by 8AM will almost always do unless it's a rush. One package is 3PM, almost always deliverable by five. It is now four twenty two. He looks at the address again. There it is. McCurdy Construction and Development, Wilshire Boulevard. As he unhooks the seatbelt the rains descend again. He places the envelope and his clipboard in the brief case he keeps on the ready. He looks at his papers neatly arranged, brief case in his lap, fake alligator black. He puts on his parka and reaches in his pockets to put a quarter in the meter. To his surprise, the lobby is locked and dark. He bangs on the door. Someone's flashlight. The black security officer, dark and wizened, looks Rolfe over. "Delivery!" Rolfe shouts, holding his brief case.

The man squints, only his eyes, disembodied souls, are clearly visible, his uniform and skin blending with the darkness. "For McCurdy."

"Round back!" The man points. "Come round."

"Are they still here?"

"McCurdy? They here. Come round the back." Rolfe rushes around the corner and turns into the small private surface lot. He steps into a hidden rut, a puddle, and as he crosses it, his foot refuses to move and down he goes. The brief case scatters but does not open, but Rolfe hits the pavement, hitting his wrist and toppling on his knee. He curses loudly, at McCurdy, at the security officer somehow. Mostly at himself. Instantly he gets up again, resentful at the interruption, willfully oblivious of the stinging on his palm and wrist and left knee. The back door opens and the security officer peers out. "You OK? You fall?"

"I'm OK!" He picks knots of gray and black tarmac gravel out of his knee. The entire curve of his knee is covered with a hovering glaze of crimson viscous and trickles of blood eel their way down his shin, burrowing their way inside his soaked and soiled socks.

"You don't look OK."

"I'm OK. Goddamn it!" Rolfe reaches for his brief case, the pattern of which is now slashed on one side.

"I'll help you if you ain't for cursin' at me now."

"Sorry." And he walks to where the security guard holds the door open. "You're a wonderful and amazing person."

"I may not talk correctly. But I know when someone's being disrespectful. There's no call for that. Now you want my help or not?" Rolfe nods that he does. "You gonna go up those stairs. That's six flights and it's dark in there. But it'll be light when you get on up there. Sorry I don't have another flashlight. You wanna clean ye self up first? They's a bathroom just over there."

"Yeah. Thank you."

And he follows the guard's light to the men's room. "I can light on ye while ye clean ye self." And he runs the waters and dabbles at his knee, but there is already a nimbus of swelling that he dares not disturb.

102.

"Tom, sorry to keep you waiting."

Hagen sits in a leather lounge chair near the bar, holding a glass of Glen Livet on a marble coaster. "I was thinking; take your time, Steve."

Steve Corbett, clean, tan, fit - slacks and a short sleeves khaki polo shirt, oblivious of the weather outside, "Danny, can I have a club soda?"

Hagen holds his glass by the tops, shakes it a little. "Clean living, Steve?"

Steve smiles. "I don't blame you for having one. Enjoy. Sitting in traffic?"

"That's what we're all doing today."

"How's the business?"

"It's incredible. Giant leaps. Growing real fast."

"Congratulations. Well you can spare your pitch for me. I'm on board. McCurdy says you've done all right by them." Hagen raises his eyebrows and smiles. "Yeah, I managed to make a call. That's only prudent. They like you real well…"

"Well, I love hearing that…."

The bartender brings over Corbett's drink. "Thanks… I'll be honest, though, Tom. After we open, I don't know how much regular business we'll be able to give you."

"Whatever it is, it's worth it. We figure you'll have clients in need of our services."

"Absolutely. We'll be glad to recommend you."

Hagen pulls out from behind the sofa two rolls of blue prints, sheaved in white cylindrical cartons. "You asked us to bring these by three o'clock. We tried calling you, but couldn't get you directly. I thought I'd bring these myself."

Steven makes a wry smile, crosses his legs, "Danny?"

"Mr. Corbett?"

"Tell Lance the updated electrical plans are here. Just tell him to come get them."

"Will do."

Steve turns to Hagen. "To be honest with you, I wasn't even expecting them until tomorrow morning. So relax. Those boys upstairs are pretty busy with the A/C and heating as we speak."

"I know that's how it is sometimes. But when someone pays for us to get here by three, that's what we do."

"You'd need a helicopter to make all your deadlines today."

"By the way, consider this visit on the house, Steve."

"Well… I expect my vendors to get paid. But…I guess I won't refuse a courtesy. Especially from an old friend, not to mention a first class scallywag like yourself."

Hagen lifts his glass again as if to toast Corbett. "Scallywags make excellent sales people."

"Do they?"

"Scallywags with integrity."

Steve laughs. "I haven't heard of that before."

"I play hard, but I work even harder."

"Not so much when we were in school from what I recall."

"I came through when it counted. And don't forget I was working two jobs the whole time."

"I remember. You know I just called you a scallywag for fun."

"Hell yeah. Like rascal."

"That, too."

"I'm both."

"A scallywag and a rascal. Just not a scholar or a gentleman."

"Hah!"

"It's all looking good, Tom. Was there anything else?"

"As a matter of fact, there is one little thing."

"OK, but you know you don't need to sell me any more on your business. What's it called again?"

"Zzzzap! Messenger."

Corbett shrugs. "Zzzzzap! Should be easy to remember."

"Right. And I do know how to take Yes for an answer, you know. Thank you. There's something else altogether I want to run past you."

103.

"Hey, Rolfie! You walk up in the dark to visit us?"

"Amber," he returns, limping. She's pretty, slender, skin the color of dishwater, vulnerable looking. He looks her over. "I have something for you."

"Great. We've been waiting on you so we can all go home." He hands her the package. "Are you limping? Jeez! What happened to your knee?"

"I slipped and fell is all. It's no big deal."

"No?" Her face reveals to Rolfe a horror of the truth of the human body, thousands of potential assaults upon our flesh and sooner or later one or more of them will rip into her as well. "I'll let Frank know you're here."

"I'll go see Tanya."

"She left already. Around two."

"She did?"

"She said your kitty's sick."

"She went to the hospital?"

"I don't know. She just said she had to go."

Amber raises Frank on the intercom. "Yeah." On speaker.

"Rolfe just brought that package.....Frank?"

"Rolfe's here? Send him in please. With the package."

"I have to leave," Rolfe whispers.

"He says he has to go, Frank. He's got other packages to drop."

"Hey Rolfe. Are you there? Rolfe?.... Come see me a moment. About that deal we were talking about."

"Alright. Fine."

Frank Giambi is already standing when Rolfe walks in. It is always a shock to Rolfe to see this man and his ugly rugged handsomeness, a violent face that echoes his violent, loud and sweaty, repeated violations of his delicate wife. Rolfe imagines spitting blood in his face. "You can sit down if you promise not to bleed on my couch." Rolfe remains standing. "What happened to you?"

"I slipped and fell in your back lot. It's full of cracks and holes. Someone could sue you."

"I meant why are you nearly two hours late?"

"The driver who had your package was in an accident. I took him to the hospital. Didn't they tell you?"

"Is he going to be OK?"

"He didn't look great. But he'll live. Anyway, the storm has fucked up everything in case you hadn't noticed and I've been covering where I can."

Frank nods. "No one else could take him to the hospital? It had to be you."

"I was there. He was injured. What do you expect?"

"I expected you before three," and he walks over to take the envelope and he holds out his hand and Rolfe just stands there and Frank puts his hand out again and this time Rolfe hands it to him. "Thank you." and with that, he walks slowly back to his desk, delicately holding the envelope, and he sits down comfortably in his leather swivel back chair, and he takes the envelope and he tears it cleanly in half, still in its packet; he puts the pieces together again and tears them once more into quarters. Then he straightens the pieces so that they line up with each other and he neatly deposits them into his waste paper basket. He points to the basket and leans back and smiles. "Are you going to ask me why I tore it up?"

"It's your package. You can do whatever you want with it."

"That was a request for a bid - a bid that was due downtown by five. Five o'clock or nada. "

"It's not even five yet."

Gently, Frank counters, "Don't be stupid, Rolfe. Not again."

"Sometimes they let you come after five. It's not our goal but they don't always close the doors right at-"

"You know you have to actually take a look at a bid request. You have to put something together. Something. I mean, as an aspiring project manager, I'm sure you can appreciate the value of deadlines as well as the concept of lead time. Sometimes you have weeks, sometimes days to respond. Today it was supposed to be two hours. We don't like that. But actually, it was a simple enough job this time out. The kind of thing we've done forever. A little remodeling, a few walls knocked out. We could have banged it out in an hour

219

because that's what we do. We didn't get an hour. We got nothing. So......thanks for that. And we're not paying for that either."

"You can take it up with our owner."

"You could take a little more responsibility."

"I'm sure he won't ask you to pay."

"That is the least of my concerns."

"Just because you lost business doesn't mean you get to blame us. I'm not going to cringe and go about on my knees just because I want to work for your boss. Isn't that what you really want to talk to me about?"

"*That's* your response?"

"That's where this is going so why not just say it."

"So I really don't care about losing out on a $200,000 contract? What *you* are saying is that what really tears me up..... is watching you flirt with my boss and making a pitch for my job."

"Yes.....Are we done here? Because I can't wait to walk down seven flights of stairs in the dark, twist my ankle on your busted lot, and drive some more through this fucking storm."

"I thought you wanted to work here, Rolfe. I thought you wanted to be a player," and he smiles like he's about to burst out laughing. "A project *man*ager. That's what you want. A project manager who can't even make a drop on time."

"Did you not hear the part about where I drove someone to the hospital?"

"That's unfortunate....but none of my concern." Frank rubs his neck. "....OK. So what *was* that all about last night?"

"Is it OK with you if I introduce myself to your boss, who happens to be in the same restaurant as I'm in? Is that a problem?"

"Not at all. Not a problem for me. How do you think it went?" Frank smiles. "I mean, you can't have thought it went well. Did you?"

"Believe me, I'm not trying to take your job."

"Well *that's* a big load off my mind."

"I want to work here...but I don't want to work with you or have anything to do with you."

"Well that just makes no sense. And what was all that talk about the building design of the hotel we were in and the homes you built with your dad?"

"Don't even think of talking about my father right now."

"You....you were the one who saw fit to bring it up last night."

"Why are we talking about this?"

"Don't you know that you've had a job waiting for you here for months and months? You knew that, didn't you? Working for me, yes. Working for McCurdy. Apparently it's beneath your dignity to apprentice on a crew and work your way up. You were *in*. You were in because I would have taken you in. All you had to do is ask. But not anymore. You were in but now you're out. And all because you're arrogant and insecure because of my history with Tanya."

"Leave her out of this."

Frank smiles and leans back against his desk, seeming to take Rolfe's measure. Now he stands straight drawing to his full height. He cracks his knuckles. "Thank you for making my point. By the way….You know all that is ancient history. Don't you? Your wife and I…..we had our time. Good times, Rolfe…..Really. But I moved on and so did she."

"Shut the fuck up!"

"Or what?" Rolfe says nothing. "Or what, Rolfe? Shut up or what?"

"Keep talking about my wife and you'll find out."

Slowly Frank replies. "This is my office you stupid idiot. And you can just leave."

104.

"I'm a salesman. Always have been. I wanted to grow my business and I did. Explosively. So much so that I realize I can make more money selling it then by growing it further. It's rich in accounts and low in debt. So let me tell you why else I had to see you." He looks at Corbett for signs of anticipation. Seeing none, he nevertheless continues, "I've made a few inquiries, and if I'm not mistaken, you're still looking for a director of sales. Well that's me, Steve. I started in hospitality long before I got into selling cars and longer still before I built my own organization. I love making the deal and I love the hotel business. I'd like to help - I *intend* to help you make the Royale the king of business travel, conventions, and tourism. This place and this location can have it all. So…what do you think? Can we talk about that?"

Steve sits back and crosses his legs and tries to appear thoughtful at Hagen's proposal. "Wow. You're full of surprises. I gotta tell you, I didn't see that coming."

"But it makes perfect sense, though. Right?"

"You're selling your business?"

"I proved my point already. Building your own business is more than just sales, isn't it? You have to do everything, 24-7. And that's what I did. But we all need a life outside of work. Anyway, sales is what I love and what I love to do all the time. As long as I can believe in it, or make myself believe in it. And this place here," he gestures, empty drink still in hand. "I believe, Steve. I believe in this place. It sells itself. In the hands of someone who believes in it."

"Well….I wish I had known a little earlier about this."

"I do, too. I've been thinking about it for a while now."

"Is the messenger business really that complicated?"

"Well….I mean…it has to be nurtured. Like anything else. You know that. There's insurance and payroll and taxes. Phone lines. Hiring and firing."

"There's some of that in this job, too."

"Sure. Sure. I'm OK with that."

"There's a whole staff, a team to lead."

"Absolutely. Can't do it all yourself. You need to develop, you need to inspire, move that team. Lead it."

"I mean…we've already made an offer to someone."

"Have you?" Hagen blanches and puts his drink down. "Is it a done deal?"

"Well…I mean we were probably going to get in touch with our candidate tomorrow. We think she'll accept."

"I see…. She. Very progressive, Steve. Hiring a woman executive. Well I appreciate you letting me talk you up about it."

"She's very qualified and comes highly recommended. Do you still want to do business with us as our carrier? I mean, are you still offering that service? Or have you already sold the business. I just want to be clear." Hagen glances out the window, sees the gray sky and the parking lot and everything looks little and cold to him. A group of workmen in white overalls, or jeans and t-shirts and windbreakers passes by. He sees Perry walking with them. "Tom?"

Hagen looks at him. "I'll be in touch with my buyer tomorrow. But I'm thinking that maybe a good move for me right now would be to accept a position with you on your sales and catering team. I mean, I wouldn't start of course until the company is duly sold and operational in my buyer's hands. These things can happen quite quickly you know. The big boys, they've been watchin' out for me and after today…..they'd be glad to get me out of their hair."

"Well, I have to make you an offer, first. If I do, Tom, are you going to be happy with something like that?"

"Sure. Great place like this? Or maybe I could be your food and beverage manager. What I'd like…what I think would be helpful for you is to look at what your needs are and how I can really help you and help you to get off the ground."

Steve cocks his head and seems to study Hagen. "I'm glad you stopped by, Tom. It's always good to see you. Really. And I tell you what. I'd love it if you'd call my office tomorrow… Ask for an appointment when we can both talk more about it. Will you do that?" He rises and Hagen rises too, discreetly tucking his shirt tails in.

"Unless you want to set something up right now."

"I really need Sherry, my assistant, for that. There's so much going on. You can imagine."

"Yes. I *can* imagine. Of course."

"So give her a call."

"I will. Thanks for the drink, friend." They shake hands and Hagen narrows his look and nods. He walks out of the room, into the cavernous, wood shine lobby, out the door. "I most definitely will." The rain has stopped and the air is ferrous and a salty breeze caresses him. He feels small, hands in pockets. Hagen remembers the group of workers, forgetting for the moment to feel angry and resentful at Perry, wanting instead to join the group for a sweet tasting beer.

105.

Today of all days there is no place to park, neither in the driveway nor on the street in front, until finally he finds a spot nearly three blocks away. Like a wet dog, he trudges up the street, cluttered with boxy, torn looking cars. Trembling with fatigue and rage, he turns on the light to his little dungeon, smelling the sour breath of unwashed sheets and underthings fetid in an airless, neglected subterranean chamber. His bathroom door is open now, steam exhaling. He hears the sound of pounding feet and he turns and sees an unfamiliar naked hominid shape retreating into the living room. The shower is full of the usual puddles, a khaki wet towel splayed and twisted across the shower door, sand caking the bathtub. On the whole slightly less infuriating than usual. He locks the door and washes his hands. The knob turns and sticks, then the knocking begins. Eugene pretends to ignore it. The knocking continues. Fuck you, he thinks. Fuck you to death.

∞

When Thomas enters the living room with a male companion, he finds Eugene sitting on the couch. "What are you doing here? Sitting in the dark. Lars, will you get the light?"

Eugene squints at the sudden glare. "I wanted the light off."

"Yes, but we're using it now. So we turned it on.....What are you doing here?"

"I live here. Remember?"

"Eugene, we need to talk." Eugene says nothing. "In private."

"What do you mean?"

"In the kitchen."

"I'm comfortable right here."

"Yes, but we should talk in private."

"I don't give a shit. Lars can go to into the kitchen. It's about time I got to sit on this couch. It's comfy, I'll give you that."

"We have friends coming soon and we're using the room."

"Well I'm using it now, god damn it. I live here, Thomas."

"Not for long." Thomas signals to Lars and both of them sit on the couch opposite Eugene. "We want you to leave."

"What?"

"We want you to leave, Eugene. You need to move out. Right away. We don't want you living here with us anymore."

He whines, "What the fuck are you talking about?"

"You're not really happy here anyway. So I don't see what the big loss is for you. But you need to go."

"I'm not really happy anywhere. But that's none of your fucking business!"

"We know you've been stealing from us. From those who live here and also from our guests. I know you think the bathroom in the pantry belongs to you, but it belongs to the house, just like this living room. It is not your bathroom alone. And even if you think it is it still doesn't give you the right to steal or discard other people's towels, or panties, or bikinis, or whatever it is that you do with them. I don't want to know. We don't go into your room down there. But *you* need to go. As soon as possible."

"I…" Eugene feels his breath backed up into a corner, an uncomprehending bunched wad of something viscous pulses beneath it, choking him. "I don't… What are you talking about?"

"Please don't deny it. Be a man and own up to it at least. We'll respect you that much." Eugene begins to mutter incoherent fragments of denial, the while Thomas calmly continues. "And of course," he adds, reasonably, hand held up for emphasis, "I should add that we will do the right thing and we will return your entire month's rent….the whole thing, even though you paid us nearly two weeks ago and we don't have to do it. And we'll return your deposit of course. We can't say that you actually damaged the room, though we will clearly have to do some cleaning, but you will still get your deposit, I think it was fifty dollars."

"But…..I'm not leaving," Eugene manages to say, catching his breath. "I'm not leaving and you can't just throw me out."

"We can and we are. We also found Marcy's robe in your room. I have no idea why it was there, but it was."

"Who is Marcy?"

"Does it matter? She is a friend of mine. She is one of our guests. And you appropriated her robe for your own…. purposes."

"You went into my room? My room?"

"Your room? Our house! A sad state of affairs it was down there. We had to inspect the condition of the room."

Eugene finds his breath. He had been bracing himself to sit up straighter, but finally he lets himself slump back down. A half smile wanders upon his face. "You lying sonovabitch, you just told me two seconds ago that you never go down there. Now you just admitted that you do. *Ass*hole."

"Enough!" Thomas collects himself and returns Eugene's sneering smile. "I've never gone in your room before, but it was necessary to inspect it regarding your deposit….. and to see if you had the robe, which you did. You can't expect to defend your theft by changing the subject."

"Here's a subject for you - I'm imagining you eating dog crap. And dying. *Fuck* you, Thomas. Fuck you so very, very much."

"We'll see who eats dog crap," Thomas spits, trembling slightly.

"Just go fuck yourself and drop stone dead. Will you?" Eugene senses that much as Thomas would prefer to completely dismiss Eugene's curses, that there is something in him that cannot withstand naked hostility no matter from whom.

"You're pathetic. Your anger is your anger, it doesn't impress me"

"And you're a piece of shit. A *piece* of shit." Lars snorts and smirks. Thomas casts him a sharp look, then turns back to Eugene.

"You have some insane rage that has nothing to do with me. Nothing! Go ahead and hate if you must. You obviously cannot control yourself. We however do not hate you. We have really tried to get along with you. So this is your problem. Not mine."

"Fuuuuuck you!"

"I expect you to be gone by tomorrow night. I will have a check waiting for you. I promise."

"Cash."

"What?"

"You heard me. Cash. You will give me cash."

"I told you I will give you a check. Tomorrow night. You can rely on that."

"Cash. I won't accept a check from you. You'll cheat me."

Thomas laughs. "Don't insult me."

"Haven't you been listening to me? Or are you just stupid. All I do is insult you, you stupid idiot. Right? So it's cash. Cash!

"I will not have time to get you cash."

"Make time. Or I'm not leaving."

"Yes you are."

"Cash."

"Look, I am not required by law to return your deposit in cash. And what if I withdraw my offer to return your rent?"

"You don't know shit about the law and you like it like that. I want cash, for this month, and for next month, my deposit; that's two hundred forty eight dollars, cash, or I'm not leaving."

"So now you want even more money than I generously offer you!"

"Two hundred and forty eight. That's what you *owe* me. If you want me out of here for no good reason."

"You will leave regardless. And if you don't, I will call the police on you because you are a thief!"

"So call them."

"I assure you I will."

"Call them now."

"You want me to call the police?"

"Sure. Have them come and arrest me for sitting on this couch in my residence for which I am fully paid up."

"Be reasonable, Eugene."

"I am. You're the one talking shit, Tommy. Two hundred and forty eight dollars, or you can get your friends to physically throw me out in the street and I'll call the police on *you, asshole!*"

Thomas looks at Eugene like he had just been made to chew on something utterly disgusting, "I do not call you names. I do not curse you. I call you by your proper name and you shall call me by mine. I show you respect. More than you possibly deserve. It's Thomas. My name is Thomas. Do you understand?"

"Yes, *asshole*, I understand. And I'm not leaving. And you can't throw me out. It's not even your house."

"I am managing it, yes."

"You manage shit. That's what you manage. I'm not leaving."

Thomas stands and looks stiffly down at Eugene, holding his arms hulking outward as if trying to make himself look larger. "Lars. Let's go....You! I want you packed and ready when I return. I will do one personal courtesy by not calling the police."

"I told you already – call them now! And would you do me a personal courtesy and drop dead right this second. Could you do that for me please?"

"Shut up!"

"I'm asking you nicely. Re*spect*fully. Pretty please golly gee. Just drop dead, will you.....this very second! Just clutch your hamburger helper of a heart and just die.....fuckin' die." Eugene lowers his forehead and raises his gaze. "*Fuck* you and everything little thing about you. Tommy!"

Thomas attempts to glower back at Eugene, but instead he breaks off and abruptly turns and walks out, his companion Lars wryly smiling, hands in coat pockets, following close behind. Eugene waits to hear the door close. He sits still in the silence and the gathering darkness.

106.

Perry walks as if in a dream in the comforting night mist, tired but happy, two hundred dollars in cash, counting it. Ten crisp twenties. More tomorrow. "Hello Perry." He drops the money but instantly he picks it back up, but two or three bills feather away in the teasing wind. He chases after them. One might still be missing. "That's a nice day's work. Can I help you there?" Mr. Hagen hands him a wet bill. Where had he come from? Perry puts the money and his hands in his pockets, lest his fingers turn white and cold, trembling, betraying him. He clutches his pay.

"Mr Hagen? Hello. What are you doing here?"

"Did you just ask me what I am doing here? Is that what you asked me?" Perry shrugs and says nothing. "Well, you know, I just had some dinner is all, and had a drink or two or something. Yeah. And then I thought I would come out and see if your car was OK. This is your car over here. Right?" He knocks on the trunk. His tie is loose and he looks unkempt, like a dresser with its drawers partly open. "I mean I guess you got here somehow."

Perry feels thirsty, a sore dry spot crackling at the back of his throat. "Mr. Hagen? How are you?"

"How am I? Did you ask just now, 'how am I'? Really?"

"Yes. I am sorry."

"You are? And why is that?"

"I don't know."

"You sure?"

Perry opens and closes his mouth, "I....I am sorry because I could not do the delivery to the hotel."

"To which hotel?"

"To...."

"To *this* hotel?"

"To this hotel. Yes sir."

Hagen looks at Perry's car. "When did you get here, because I've been here since about three thirty and I saw you then, you and your car. Glad to see you got it back from the tow company so quickly. It must have set you back some money. I mean you still have some money from what I just saw, so that's good, but..... even so," and he shuffles his feet and shrugs. "Do you think maybe we should....that I should reimburse you part of that money? What do you think? Seeing as how you lost it while trying to do your job for us."

"No, of course not."

"No? You sure......Because....you were in the tow away zone when you should have parked the car. I think that's what you told Mikros. That was you, right? Or am I incorrect."

"Yes, sir. You are correct."

227

"I see. You were trying to save time because we were so busy. That was why you parked in the tow away zone. Because of all the pressure."

"I am sorry, Mr. Hagen."

"But you made it here after all. You've been here longer than I have. I mean you're here. You're actually here, standing right in front of me....and yet..... you couldn't do the delivery. Even though it was right to this hotel right here, right where you and I are standing right now?"

"Yes sir."

"Well that's really kind of *odd*. Don't you think?"

"Yes sir."

"I don't get it."

"Did you...did you deliver the package yourself, sir?"

"That's right. I did. Earlier today I met with the general manager of this hotel to personally deliver his package, because it was late, because you," he points, "Got your car towed."

"Yes sir."

"Stop saying that!"

"I'm sorry."

"You probably tell yourself that you're being so respectful and all - calling me sir, yes sir, saying you're sorry - but you're not being respectful at all, are you."

"But I am sorry."

"But *why* are you sorry?!"

"Because I didn't deliver the package."

"Wrong! Try again."

"What?"

"Why are you sorry? You can't speak English anymore?" Hagen veers so close to Perry that the other must turn his neck up to look at his unshaven chin. "Be a man, Perry. Be a man and tell the truth."

"I don't...I don't understand," Perry says plaintively.

Hagen turns scarlet with rage. "You're sorry because you got *caught* lying to me? That's why you are sorry. Right?"

Perry shrugs, eyes glistening. "Right." He looks down at his shoes. "I meant no disrespect."

"Oh I see. You meant no disrespect when you lied to me? What are you? A little boy? Are you a little boy, Perry? Is that the problem?"

Perry takes another step back, the better to lessen the effect of Hagen's somehow unfair height. He hardens his look. "You are right. You are right, Mr. Hagen. I told Mr. Mikros that my car was towed. But you are right. It was a lie. The truth was I am working here now, for this hotel. I should have told him the truth but I did not know whether it would work out here or no. The money you saw, I made it working here today."

"No shit."

"None. There isn't any shit."

"Except that you lied to me."

"Yes, Mr. Hagen."

"How much did they pay you?"

"That is not important."

Hagen smiles and looks off. He rubs his nose. "Not important, huh. I'd say it was pretty goddamn important."

"This is what I want to do."

"Working in a hotel? Lying to me?"

"I'm learning how to be an engineer. Heating and cooling. I am sorry that I lied and if I hurt you. But I had to look out for myself. And my family. I only found out this morning. I was doing it on the side and I didn't think it was working out, but Mr. Murray, he calls me today and he says there is so much construction and he trusts me to work hard and to learn –"

"OK," Hagen holds his hand up. "Enough. I get it. I get it. I don't need to hear anymore."

"I wish you the best, Mr. Hagen."

"You do? What do you wish me the best at?"

"Your business. Your life."

"What business, Perry?"

"Mr. Hagen, I must leave now. I wish you all the best with-"

"There is no business, Perry. No more business. Understand?" Perry just looks at him, slack jawed. "That's right. There's no more business because you all *fucked* me today. All of you! Hard! So I'm selling it. Whatever's left of it. I told you to be ready. Right? I told everyone." He paces back and forth towards and away from Perry's car, as if considering whether to strike it. "Didn't I? I kept saying that today was the day. Max oversleeps. Eugene runs out of gas. That four eyed whore calls out sick. Tim wrecks his car and Rolfe decides to play paramedic and take him to the hospital. Andy decides to extort my dispatcher over a…. And Samuel is missing now. But *you*….you lied to me, Perry. Only *you* did *that*."

"Is Tim OK?"

"What? I don't know."

"Samuel is missing? What do you mean?"

"It means he left a client without the package and now he won't call us back. But let's get back to you, Perry. Let me ask you something."

"I need to go, Mr. Hagen."

"If you had to do it over again, would you still lie to me?"

Perry sighs. "Yes I would, Mr. Hagen."

Hagen leans in. Smiles. "Good. And that's the truth at least."

"Please! I am so sorry for all the other things that have happened to you, but it is not my fault these other things," and he reaches for his car door.

Hagen makes no attempt to stop him but he calls out. "What if everyone said that to me, Perry. Think about that! What if everyone had your attitude? Nothing would be anyone's fault. Ever!" Perry gets into his car, avoiding eye contact with Hagen. "Guess what, Perry. If you're working here, you're *still* working for me. You are. You know why? Because *I'm* working here now, too. Listen to me, Perry." Perry starts his engine. His door is still open. "You're still working for me."

"You're working for the hotel now?"

Hagen just looks at him and attempts a smile. "I just had a meeting with the GM, a good friend of mine."

"Who?"

"That money in your pocket. It belongs to me, Perry."

Perry closes the door. Hagen steps back. "I wish you well, Mr. Hagen. May God bless you." Hagen watches Perry carefully pull away and drive off the lot.

107.

Amber looks up from hearing her boss's door slam. Rolfe strides out then begins to stiffen and slow up in front of Amber. She throws him a weak smile. "Do you want to use the men's room? Looks like you're bleeding again."

"Are the lights on in there?"

"Yeah. The generator works in there I guess. I'm not looking forward to walking down the stairs in the dark, though."

He smiles. "Can I walk you out?"

"That's OK. Thanks. Frank'll be out soon and we'll go down."

Rolfe leans in. "Is he waiting for me to leave?"

She raises her eyebrows and shrugs. "Tell Tanya I hope she feels better."

"Sure. When did you say she left?"

"Right after they came back from lunch, I think. Frank told her she could go. She was lucky and left before the power went out."

"After they got back from lunch? Frank and Tanya?"

"Just the coffee shop downstairs." She looks at him wide eyed.

"….I forgot the address to the vet's. I'll bet it's on Tanya's desk."

"Sure. You know where it is. Do you want to call her?"

"She'll probably already be there. Thanks." The light in Tanya's cubicle is dim and indirect. He opens and closes drawers, unsure of what he's looking for. Some unlikely love letter or photo of the two of them embracing or having sex? A pack of condoms? Sponges? A hotel receipt? Ridiculous. It makes no sense what he's doing, he tells himself. Ridiculous prick. The only photo he finds is of Taxi, staring at him from their couch, his eyes a satanic red on camera.

He opens the upper right drawer a second time, a clinking sound arresting his attention. There beneath the little organizer tray holding thumbtacks and paperclips is a thick set of keys. Unfamiliar looking house keys, mail keys, other unexplained keys opening mystery doors and locks. He holds up his own set beside them. His are smaller, fewer and lighter, less substantial. There's leather casing that holds a car key. To a BMW. Impulsively he clenches the set as if to crush it, pressing it into his palm before stuffing the entire set in to his pocket.

108.

The storm mildly awakens him, flaring the soreness and chill of his stiffened limbs, the alien welling of despised and unwanted tears and the glaze of congealing blood that lacks even the will to flow. Red brake lights and on-coming headlamps, and he grips at the steering wheel and he sets his jaw. I shall go "straight home" he had pronounced to George; home to a stained and rancid closet, tattered carpets, wafer thin walls, compressed between transient and callous lives, his stiff and sour bed. The flash at the horizon sizzles at and cracks and rolls away and the sky smells of sulfur and he lets the word, "Yes" hiss in grim facsimile of some beseeched vindication. The rain pours down and the sky is dark.

109.

The door is locked. Max politely knocks as the rain begins to come alive once more. He stands on a small concrete ramp that leads to a little wooden door, modestly crouched at the base of a hulking warehouse. He clutches a Styrofoam container the size of a small toaster. Blue paint chips from the door frame. Max knocks again, feeling remorseful. Five forty five. The security lights flood down on the empty pavement. Is there another door? Is this the right address? Tony will be so disappointed. Max turns around and standing in front of his car, in front of his passenger door, standing there are two men, their faces shrouded in woolen ski masks. The two men are both small and slight, like they might be teenagers. They both stand straight, feet apart, staring at Max.

"Hi...Isn't this Gramm Chemical?" The two men say nothing. He holds out the package. "Is that what this place is?"

Slowly, the two masked men look at each other. The one on the left holds something small, dark, and heavy in his right hand that makes a clicking noise. He speaks. "We'll take the package."

"What?"

"I said come down here and give us that package. Now."

"Do you work here?" They say nothing. "I was supposed to be here a couple of hours ago. I'm so mad, you know, because I tried to get here, but they made me go to these other places first. It wasn't my fault."

The man on the left holds his arm out to his side and lifts it up so that Max can better see the gun without pointing it directly at him. "That's enough, dipshit. Step down here now and hand over that package."

Max squints in surprise, hugging the package closer to him. Huddled and slow moving, he progresses down the little ramp until he stands before them. "I'm sorry I'm late."

The man on the left shakes his head. He taps the gun on the box. "There had better be two more in the car just like this one."

"Do you know Tony?"

The man on the left cocks the gun, holds the barrel up. His companion, almost the same exact size speaks up for the first time. "Sure. We're good friends with Tony. He told us to meet you here." And he reaches out to take the package but suddenly Max snatches it back.

"Why are you so fucking stupid?" The first man asks, and he points the gun directly at Max. "Take the package...." He looks at his companion. "I said take it. Take it now. Even the retard finally gets it." The second man easily takes the package from Max who stares at the gun in rancid shock.

"Why are you wearing those masks?" Max asks.

"Because it's raining, you imbecile!" The second man laughs.

"You're not giving that package to Tony, are you?"

"Who the fuck is Tony!"

"You're stealing his package?" Max whispers, despite himself.

The second man speaks up, addressing his companion, the gun man. He sounds vaguely familiar, a soft, lazy way of speaking. "You don't know who Tony is?"

The first one turns sharply to his partner letting his arm fall. "Are you dumber than the retard?"

"I'm just saying."

"Maybe you really think we're wearing ski masks because it's raining."

"Hey.... You know I think I know this dude."

"What?"

"I think this is that fool I tried to sell to last night. That Jesus freak on Sunset."

Max speaks. "Are you the guy with the blue pills?" He hears the click, the safety chamber pulled back on the snub nose. He feels though he cannot see the barrel poke against his temple. Max blurts, "Ow! Why so hard?"

"This guy's gonna die now. And you just killed him, Paco."

"Bullshit," Paco turns away. "I'm not pullin' no trigger."

"Take a look."

"No fuckin' way. You're gonna make a big fuckin' mess and get us in trouble. Way over my head."

"He *made* you, you fool. You made yourself. Look now at what *you* did! Watch me waste him!"

"*Fuck* you! Let's just take the shit and get the fuck out." Max feels nothing, sees nothing anymore. He is bored with their antic cursing. His temple itches as the barrel lifts away and the gun man turns and aims his pistol at Paco. "Put that fuckin' thing down Wilson before you shoot your own self in the dick or somethin'."

The gun man screams. "I held this thing to his fucking head. Didn't you see none of that!" Max wonders if indeed he simply is a retard, after all, though that's not a nice expression, but only an idiot would do what he is doing now, he thinks, as he watches himself grab the package back from the second man. The look of amazement in the second man's face shows even through the narrow slits of the ski mask, but Max is at a loss of what to do next and the second man responds and they struggle now over possession of the Styrofoam package and Max notices that the ski mask is threadbare, with lint and loose threads peeping from it. He had thought it was black but it's really blue, a midnight blue, but with a little gray stowed in. The first man stands still, mutely as the struggle strips away his momentary authority. "Do something, Wilson!" Paco shouts. "*Now* you can fuckin' do something!" Something has happened but Max can barely register it, a shudder, an impact, a hot moist throbbing fills his ears, but still he only wrenches harder from Paco. The package as if deciding its own trajectory, rejecting both its suitors, leaps from their muffled grasps and smashes down on the pavement, the taped lid half torn already bursts off on impact and out pour not only the usual bottles and samples, the vials and plastic bags filled with its alien contents, but beneath all that in a plastic bag too poorly sealed, spills out a great family of shiny blue pills, splayed and glistening beneath the flood lights.

There is a brief moment of silence as the two assailants seem more awed than dismayed by their precious pills on the gritty pavement. Max lurches up and bolts away at a dead run, leaving his car, trying to keep his legs from getting tangled. He runs. He runs to be forgotten amidst the mean, dark scabby streets, amidst the generic, hard and concrete structures, doorless, windlowless, airless, running down the middle of the black top, past soot greased sidewalks, through empty, leaning alleyways. He runs.

233

110.

Andy exits the stalled freeway and back tracks, getting tangled in dead ends and residential streets, hoping to simply keep moving. Finally he reaches Imperial Highway. He passes the squat and faceless store fronts and liquor stores, stacked beside one bedroom churches and oily burger huts and single family houses next to pawn shops and shuttered buildings. There are stop signs now at every intersection and a bright red and yellow car wash on his left devoid of patrons, and iron gated thrift stores, and pay phones with their receivers ripped away, stumpy wires protruding from their severed metal arteries; there are mattress stores and discount furniture shops and a corner donut shop with a mounted eight foot donut, faded orange, and a drive through, run by local Chinese, steam escaping from the back. Andy locks his doors, feeling lost. He continues to move through the countless streets, passing the 110, then the 710, and he rolls through Downey and Paramount, cities that sound like foreign countries to west siders. He passes an unlikely water tower, larger, old buildings, streets that wander off at confusing angles. He passes the 605. One block after another, changing street sign colors, commercial districts giving way to seedy blocks of boarded store fronts, becoming sleek business parks, then phalanxes of apartment buildings from the sixties, with stucco fronts and faux stone in laid, and names like the Pelican and the Tropicana and the Hawaiian and the Palm and more commercial areas with brass colored Macy's, and the sidewalk itself is dark gray and on and on, the sky grows darker, distant thunder rumbling, street lamps alight, the fine rain falling on his elbow. Finally he reaches the rolling hills of Yorba Linda, closer to where he expects his journey to finally get interesting.

111.

The streets of Vernon curve away in distant angles and Max runs and he runs some more until finally he stops, embittered that as far as he runs he can find no end to these pointless alleyways and empty loading docks and comfortless warehouses with their great rotting inventories. Pacific, Alameda, 37th, Santa Fe, thoroughfares which seemingly lead to nowhere. He slows to a walk, hobbling along like a hunchback, sore and winded and strangely hot and cold. The intermittent storm and the distant thunder keep him raw and remote company. He staggers past a corner eatery. Menudo, it says, wisps of civilization. He passes a great hulking self-storage enterprise that rises like a great dinosaur exoskeleton or some gutted and ruined cathedral rectory, a concrete, engraved behemoth six stories high.

He reaches Long Beach boulevard, a thoroughfare like no other, he thinks, for it is a dark and dirty canal, a gritty train rail cutting it in half, the northbound car lane a single thread of traffic, trucks barreling towards downtown skyscrapers. Max walks the narrow sidewalk past a vacant dirt lot, vague machines, broken and bleeding poking out from the dark. He passes junkyards of scrap metal, and auto parts, used mufflers heaped high, scorch rusted locks and twists of barbed wire, and locked and corrugated warehouse doors with runes of graffiti holding something unnamed within, heaps of trash strewn before it, a urine stained mattress, a cheap maroon sofa with its cushions missing, and next to that a faceless gray white building, windows boarded and painted over, impenetrable graffiti. A young man listens to a pair of head phones, sitting by himself at a bus stop; he locks eyes with Max and he stares at him, not in a menacing way, but as if he were actually frightened of Max, who is completely unaware that his head is now bleeding, thinking only that he still sweats excessively down the back of his neck. Two middle aged Mexican women, dark skinned, heavy featured, huddle up in a door way, each with their heavy hand bags, speaking Spanish to one another. Neither catches sight of Max, though he takes a rude kind of comfort from seeing them there, bland and unconcerned. He sits at the next bus stop and goes through his pockets, but he has no money, no change. Should he ask for help? Quickly he dismisses the notion that he might go back and find his car, for he knows he could never retrace his steps and the masked men might even still be there. Max looks towards Downtown. Across 24th street. emerging from the mouth of a tiny liquor store, is a small band of young men crowing at the night, baying at the scattered street lights and the invisible moon, recalling to Max the conviction that nothing in this whole ashen world could delight them more than to commit irreversible mayhem against him. Though the light is red, he looks and he dashes across the narrow highway. "Hey!" he hears the shout. Any moment now his legs will betray him and he will fall and they will beat and sodomize him. "Come back here! We want to talk to you." The others laugh. He picks his way in the dark across four lanes of railroad. "Run faggot! Run!" More laughter. Any moment he will drop, twist an angle, entangle his shoe in a rail tie. "Don't get hit by a train!" If the gang were to pursue him, there would be no witnesses and no escape. But they have already forgotten him or else even they dare not tread upon this strange and twisted tunnel of a street, dark and narrow, industrial, channeling south without a sidewalk, heading towards greater more isolated ugliness, towards more lonely dangers still. But all he can do right now is escape the darkness, the cold and ghostly bones that reach for him and so he runs towards the jaundiced street lamp, regardless of his fears. He runs and he runs and to keep himself company he begins to call out the only name, the only being he can dare hope might be watching out for him, the name of the one who had almost nothing but enemies Himself towards the end.

112.

He hears a faint, shaky rattle over his own heavy breathing. Someone is here after all. It's a homeless man, swaddled in shiny, slick dregs, oily with wear, steeped in garbage. The man pushes a grocery cart and all his earthly possessions across the street. The man in Samuel's vision could have been Miles Davis come back from the dead with his ruthless feline stare, a survivor of a post diluvian disaster. He stops in the middle of the street. Then he continues, rattling away, and is gone, come from nowhere, heading towards nothing. Samuel unclenches his fingers and feels his heart ignite, his breathing accelerate, a quiver of strength that he could not muster before.

Here in the emptiness, in this nocturnal wasteland, darkness falls early every evening, and the sidewalk is alive with a fine dust that is rarely disturbed. There is nobody here in this frozen seabed. A pale of lightening, silent and vibrating, lights up the hollow concerns like great bleached sets of bones. He watches the wind whisk away the gun metal dust, the dead oxidized shavings of rotting fences, and the stray and stranded fragments of leaves across the street. He tastes the iron, thick in his mouth from his own blood and he reaches forth with a leathery hand like a creature that bays at the moon.

113.

The storm is over out here and the stars begin to boil up above and all around. He sits at the side of the road poring over his map in the overhead lamp, feeling quite certain he has missed after all the junction to board Highway 78 east. His fingers twitch and he knows he's screwed. What's in this stupid box, after all? Machine parts? Really? Who's waiting for it? Mexican drug lords? Soviet spies clandestinely stealing U.S nuclear technology? Someone's severed head? What the fuck is El Centro anyway? The sky lights up momentarily, a glimpse of distant rolling hills and sage. It was likely so very beautiful out here. Beautiful and peaceful and rare.

114.

Running and running. No one and no one. Blindly running so that he never sees the body until he nearly stumbles upon it. The talking in his head quickly ceases and he covers his mouth. No doubt here lies a homeless man, passed out on cheap wine and heartbreak. The silent square buildings sit curiously devoid of graffiti. This lonely world is simply forgotten, even by haunts, an empty, dusty basement. The body lies on its side upon the loveless sidewalk, naked except for his shoes. A single car, dimly familiar, sits twenty paces ahead, a boxy, dented sedan, both doors left oddly wide open. He gingerly approaches the car, whispering to Jesus. A familiar looking clipboard; the keys are on the driver floor board. Suddenly, Max remembers that he himself is cold and damp. He hears the body cough. Now he stands before the naked man. Trembling, he reaches and touches the hand. It is warm.

"Ah.....ahh!" He grasps Samuel's hand. "Samuel! *Samuel!* Wake up! Please wake up." Again, Samuel coughs inside his limbo slumber. His glasses are missing. His mustache and parts of his beard are thick with congealed blood. His shins and palms look raw and scraped. Max looks away from the dark and small hidden coils of Samuel's genitals. "Samuel! Please. Wake up." And he shakes him by the arm. Samuel sneezes and opens his eyes which weakly take in this new and uncertain dream. He squints at Max, at first uncomprehending. Then in amazement. "Samuel it's you. It's you. You're alive!". With trembling hand, Samuel touches Max's arm. Pokes it again as if to assure himself he neither dreams nor hallucinates.

"Are you...." and Samuel coughs again and lies on his back looking up at the pale city night sky. "It's stopped raining."

"Are you OK?" Max asks.

"Are you...real?"

"Yes....Yes, of course."

"Max? Is that you?"

"Yes, it's me. It's Max."

"Extraordinary," Samuel whispers. "Extraordinary." And he blinks and pushes himself in to a sitting position. Max tries to assist. His skin is chalky with dust from the unwalked pavement.

"Are you OK?"

Samuel coughs again. "Do I look OK to you, Max?"

"You look alive."

"Max, what on earth are you doing here?"

"What am *I* doing here? I found you naked lying on the sidewalk. Were you attacked?"

"Max, my clothes should be inside the car. Would you kindly bring them to me, please?"

Max does so, finding the clothes in the back seat. Slowly, Samuel dresses himself. The sounds of freeway traffic are faint but find their way in. Max turns away but asks, "Do you need any help?"

Samuel doesn't answer at first. "You may turn around now if you wish. It is safe for you to do so."

When Max turns, Samuel is fully dressed except for his shoes. "I could use a hand getting up, please." Samuel grimaces but manages to stand with Max's assistance. They look each other over for a moment, two ragged bleeding twins in their soiled ZZZZap! T-shirts, each of them like survivors at the bottom of the world.

"I'm taking you to the hospital," Max announces.

"You shall do no such thing."

"Are you sure you're OK? What happened to you?"

"It's nothing. I had some kind of seizure. Max. Are you aware that your head is bleeding? And your face and the back of your neck is covered in blood? You look most horrifying yourself. Perhaps I am still dreaming you."

"I'm bleeding?"

"Indeed. Does that surprise you?"

Max touches his neck and his head in alarm. "Oh God," he whispers. "Samuel! You're bleeding, too?"

"Quite a pair, aren't we? Mine's a nose bleed. Quite severe this afternoon. From stress. I must have...I must have been a bit delirious. What happened to you? Do you even know? Have you also blacked out tonight my friend?"

"What? No. No sir. I was robbed."

"You were robbed? Just now?"

"They took my delivery." And Max conveys the essential details of his adventure. "It was like they already knew what was inside. One of those guys must have hit me. With his gun."

"With his gun?"

"Yes. I can't believe I'm bleeding and I don't even know it."

"I believe there are millions of us poor souls out there."

"You do?"

"Max, in your case it must have been the adrenalin. You'll need some stitches though."

"I will?" He touches his head again and winces. "I guess."

"How on earth did you find me?"

"Well I had no idea you were anywhere nearby, Samuel. I was just...running away from these really mean and really weird people. And then those other mean people too, the ones by the liquor store. I was just running. I was running. And I got lost."

Samuel closes his eyes for a moment. "This place probably looks better without my glasses." He squeezes the bridge of his nose and he looks to Max as

238

though he might be dizzy. "Perhaps we should both get looked at after all. Will you drive?"

"Your car? Yes. Let's get out of here now."

"Max. Promise me you will say nothing to anyone about this. About me here. Especially not to the doctors. Do you understand?"

"What do you want me to say?"

"You found me in my car. We'll figure out something. But I was fully clothed. In my car. Do you understand me?" Max thinks for a moment and nods. "Max, I need to hear you say it."

"I found you in your car."

"With my clothes on."

"With your clothes on."

"Good. That's good. I can trust you on this."

"Yes. Yes, Samuel. You can."

"Thank you, Max." He looks around. "Ridiculous place this is."

"God has led me to you, Samuel."

"Really. Is that what you really believe Max?"

"That is what I know."

115.

She hears his feet scrape up the stairs and to their front door. A dog barks restlessly in a nearby yard. Tanya takes a drag off her cigarette caressing and kneading Taxi's neck. Rolfe walks in and she knows in an instant that tonight will not be a good night, and it makes her angry. "Hello," he says.

"Hello. Hey. You're bleeding."

"Still? Jesus. I thought I was done." He stomps to the kitchen and turns on the sink.

"Are you OK?"

"Yes, yes," he snaps.

"Well what happened?"

"Wait. Just wait a minute." He fusses in the kitchen and emerges with wet paper towels pressed to his knee.

"Rolfe, you're not gonna bleed in here on our furniture. Go to the bathroom and get some iodine, some bandages."

"I did that already, the disinfectant whatever. You shouldn't put a bandage on it. Let it scab."

"Well it's still bleeding."

"Look. Enough. It'll stop. OK? I'll wrap it with something in a minute. I promise I won't *bleed* on anything," and he sits on a hard plastic chair.

"What happened?"

"I slipped and fell in the rain. OK?"

"Fine. I won't ask you anymore. And thanks a lot for asking me how Taxi is. Or how I am."

"I was a little busy just now. Can't you see that? Right? I think I know anyway. Taxi looks fine. And you're smoking again. There. I know how you are."

"Great. Wonderful. So we don't even need to interact at all, because you're a genius. I'm a lucky woman. You know everything."

"I know that I hate it when you smoke in the apartment. That's a lot worse than bleeding." Tanya laughs out loud. "Is that funny what I said?" She puts out the cigarette in a coffee saucer sitting right next to her. "Remind me," Rolfe says, "Never to eat off that plate again."

"I'll be sure to shove it firmly up my own ass, just as soon as I am done, so you'll never see it again."

"Is that also supposed to be funny?"

Tanya laughs again, without joy. "It used to be funny, that sort of thing."

"What does it even mean?"

"It can mean whatever you want it to mean."

"I'm leaving the door open. Get some fresh air in here. And the back window too." He busies himself with these tasks.

She throws her head back and closes her eyes as if she might be somewhere else when she reopens them. "Well, it's nice to see you, too, honey." The window bangs open and she hears his heavy footsteps approaching. "Why do you slam that open so hard? You're going to break it?"

"Stop fussing with me! I'll break it if I want to break it."

"What the hell is wrong with you tonight?"

"Nothing! I went to the vet tonight by the way. I went there first before I came home. I thought you were there."

"I left there hours ago. And yes, Taxi is much better."

"Well thanks for telling me about your schedule. And how was your lunch? Your lunch with Frank?"

"What?"

"Your lunch with Frank. Did you have a wonderful time?"

She looks at him. "Sure. It was a blast." She reaches for her cigarettes and lights up another one. "He was very concerned about my pussy."

"That's disgusting." As if wanting nothing to do with their argument, Taxi jumps off the couch and disappears.

"I'm sorry you feel that way. And what has happened to your sense of humor. Or sense of reality. You remember we actually have a cat! Instead of being so concerned about me *fucking* Frank, you might try getting it up for me yourself once in a while." Rolfe stares at her. Tanya opens her eyes wider and stares back. Then she says, "He listened to me whine about Taxi because no one

240

else I know really gives a shit. How do you even know about that, anyway? That we had lunch together. Are you now actually spying on me?"

"I had a delivery over at McCurdy's. For Frank. That was fun."

"Did you two boys have a nice chat?"

"Not really."

"I'm guessing you still haven't asked him for a job."

"You would be correct. And I wouldn't count on that ever happening."

"No, I guess not. Silly me. But you just go ahead and enjoy your little messenger job, honey." Rolfe takes the keys that he found in Tanya's office desk drawer and drops them on the coffee table. "Jesus!" she snaps. "You're gonna scratch the table like that. What are you doing?"

"Fuck the table. It's a shit cheap table anyway. You recognize those keys?"

"What?"

"Something wrong with your hearing? Or your eyes, maybe? Have you been drinking, too?"

"You asshole," she sits up straight. "I had a glass of wine tonight when I got home. So fucking what?"

"Did you two have a drinkee-poo at lunch today?"

"Stop it, Rolfe. I don't even know you anymore."

"How about these keys?" he says, eyes blazing with mock jubilee over the marvelous keys. "Right here. Do you know these keys?" And he rattles them in front of her before letting them drop hard again on the coffee table again. "Oops!"

She looks at them and she picks them up and begins to laugh, "Oh my god! You went through my *drawer* at work?" She shakes them at him. "You fucking spied through my drawer, you psycho fuck!"

"Yes, you do remember them and you know exactly where they were *hidden.* Hidden! That's right."

"Not well enough, I guess. Asshole! They were there because that's where I keep them. So why did you take them, Rolfe? Why aren't they still in my desk?"

"Why were they in your desk to begin with?"

"Why were you poking around in my desk? To begin with."

"Whose keys are they? As if I didn't know," And he pinches the leather clasp of the BMW key, then wipes his hands on his pants.

She leans back on the couch and takes a cigarette drag, letting the smoke push out through her nostrils. Then she puts the cigarette down and she gets up, wiping the corner of her mouth slowly with a finger. She goes to the fridge, pulls out a half empty bottle of no name wine and pours herself a glass. She drinks about half, then pours herself more. "You caught me, Rolfe. Didn't you. Evidence. Big evidence," she says holding her glass up as if to toast him. "Big, *big* evidence, yes? I mean, it's possible I suppose that an employee might keep a set of spare keys for her boss, who travels frequently, in her drawer in case of some kind of emergency. But no. That couldn't be the reason. Obviously, I keep these keys so I can sneak out of our bed and visit Frank in the middle of the night and then sneak back again before you even know a thing. And *fuck* him! Yes. Congratulations. You're absolutely brilliant. You're the most brilliant psycho messenger the world has ever seen."

"And the lunches. In that cute little coffee shop. Downstairs. Is that your fucking idea of hardly ever running into your ex-lover, whose desk is down the hall and whose keys are in your drawer!"

"Rolfe. Tell me. Why, Rolfe? Why? Why are you so obsessed with Frank Giambi putting his key.... in my.... drawer." A melee explodes outside their front door, a ferocious, cutting roar, followed by a cat's wretched cry, quickly chasing higher and higher, an unrecognizable spasm of outrage, finally echoed by human shouting. Rolfe leaps up and disappears into the bedroom while Tanya runs outside. As she pushes through the open door, she screams in puny, helpless rage at the sight of the neighbor's boxer thrashing Taxi by the neck, it's jaws clenched, pummeling the cat with its claws. "No!!"

"Jack, get off! Get off! Down Jack, goddamnit!" Their neighbor, someone she recognizes by sight, but not by name, merely a buzz cut and a denim jacket, a young blond man, kicks his own dog in the ribs to get him to let go of Taxi.

"No!!!" Something pushes past her, leaping, a flash of her husband running with something in his hand. Rolfe lifts the baseball bat and smashes it into the back of the dog's neck. When this seems to have no effect, he crashes the bat down again, harder, this time directly on the dog's head and again until the dog squeals and finally lets go.

"Enough! Jesus Christ," the man in the denim jacket yells. "You're gonna kill my dog!"

Rolfe turns and brandishes the bat, his knees still bleeding, stomping hard again on the dog's neck, causing it to cry out and whimper. "You got something to say! You killed our cat you sonovabitch. Back off! Right now!" The man stumbles away, red faced and raw. Tanya's scream electrifies them both and they look upon the still and stiffening body of Taxi, throat torn away, it's eyes rolled completely in its head, it's jaw broken loose. The dog lifts its head and seems to blink at Rolfe, and as they make eye contact, the dog growls and feebly bares its teeth. Rolfe hurls the bat down on the dog again and again while the stunned owner falls to his knees, crying and cursing incoherently. Tanya throws herself on top of Rolfe but he shakes her off. She screams at him and flings herself at his legs and he knees her in the ribs and she lets go and she falls away and he steps over the dog and advances on his distraught neighbor. "You got something to say!" Rolfe says shaking the bat.

The dog owner falls and rolls and gets up, cursing. "You crazy sonovabitch. I'm calling the police."

"Call them. Call them now! Your dog deserves to die. You hear me. What if my cat had been a baby or a child you irresponsible asshole."

The man backs away looking for the gate. He begins to sob. "Jack was an animal! What's your fucking excuse you fucking murderer!"

"I thought you were calling the police," Rolfe shouts into the dark. Lights go on and off in other buildings and other dogs bark in fury and there's a tumble of pots and pans and shouting.

"You'll fucking pay!" the man whimpers and Rolfe shines a terrible smile and raises the bat with one hand and the man stumbles again.

"No! Rolfe!" and this time she tackles him to the ground. The man scurries off out of sight still shouting from the next level of apartments on the hill. "That's enough. That's enough, Rolfe! Please, please, that's enough," and she straddles him and she slaps his face and pulls his hair and scratches him and he doesn't fight back, but he covers his face and she flails her arms but she just can't hit him anymore, but still she tells him to stop, to stop, to please stop it, stop it, even though he is no longer doing anything at all and suddenly there's a loud and angry pitch tone, his pager. And Rolfe already knows that it must be the hospital calling, telling him to come, to come at once, to come for Tim, to take good care of Tim. Both of them lie frozen in their positions ignoring the sound, Rolfe with his hands over his face, Tanya sitting atop, her head bowed and sobbing. The pager sounds again as the first of the neighbors return, this time a small posse it seems of men and women, one with his own baseball bat, another with a hammer, and still a third holding a large skillet. They stand over the scene as Tanya sobs, still sitting atop her supine husband. The first man to arrive, someone bigger and older than the dog owner, the one with his own baseball bat says to Tanya, "Are you all right?" Tanya doesn't answer. "Ma'am? Are you OK?"

"No!"

"Well come on over here, ma'am. He is not going to hurt you anymore. If he moves, we're *all* comin' after him."

"Fuck off! All of you! Go away."

"It's OK. We're here to help you. The police are already on their way."

"Let them come! That bastard killed my cat!" She sees the dog owner cringing amongst his neighbors. "You killed Taxi!"

He shouts back. "Lady, please. I didn't want that to happen. That was an accident..... But your husband killed my dog! *Murdered* him!" he says, beginning to weep.

"Ray," says the first neighbor to the dog owner. "Let's just wait for the police."

"You poisoned him!" Tanya shrieks. "Didn't you! You were the one who fucking poisoned our cat."

"What? What the fuck are you talking about!"

"Ray. Let it go."

"Fuck you, lady. Now you're just talking crazy."

"Ray!" the first neighbor addresses everyone. "Lady. Whatever you all think happened, just keep your husband down for his own good until the police arrive. They'll be here any minute."

Rolfe stares out seeing nothing, nor does Tanya. Dead animals lay strewn behind them as the neighbors keep watch. As the colored lights begin to flash down the hill from the police cruiser, his pager sounds off for a third and final time.

116.

He passes small and frequent huddles of lights, anonymous hamlets swallowed in the dark. The great moonlit silver Salton Sea emerges to his left amidst silent ridges and flat lands. It startles him with its beauty exotic and he follows it through another town whose name he cannot remember and through street crossings that intersect at strange and maddening angles, past corner shuttered eateries, railroad tracks and freight yards and corrugated tin warehouses and then out into the wilderness once more and at last he reaches the 8 freeway and he heads east through the most desolate land imaginable, a flat blanket of chalky emptiness. Finally, El Centro itself, an inanely named town. Long empty commercial streets, mattress stores, Mexican restaurants, bail bondsmen, tiny clinics, used car lots. At what seems to be the end of E street, the road curves and becomes a frontage road paralleling the freeway. Up upon an elevated driveway is what turns out to be a Best Western motel. Ten thirty at night! A young man in a short sleeve maroon shirt comes out wearing a tight lipped facsimile of a smile. "Yes. Can I help you?"

"I hope I'm in the right place." Andy reads the address and the clerk confirms that this is the only place with that address in El Centro. "The name is Charles."

"Charles. Charles," the man finds a note on his desk. "Yes. This is it. They told us they were expecting something." He picks up the phone and dials. "…….Good evening, Mr. Charles. This is the Best Western….Yes. The messenger is here….Alright. I'll tell him. Thank you." He turns to Andy and explains. "Please have a seat. He's actually off site at the moment but will be here in about ten minutes." Andy gladly sits upon the couch.

Twenty minutes later a man in his forties, muscular, short dark hair and short sleeves, enters the lobby. "You're the one with my box?"

"Yes sir. I'm so sorry I am so late."

"You have the box?"

"Right outside. In my truck. I'll bring it in."

The man puts his hand up. "Yeah, show it to me. You don't need to bring it inside." They walk outside in the mild night air. Briefly, Andy wonders if he has driven eight hours just to have this man look at a box but not to actually take it. "Did you pick up the package yourself?"

"No sir. Our boss did. I brought it from the office."

The man doesn't respond. Andy opens the passenger door. "Open it for me please."

"Are you sure you want me to look inside?"

"It's fine. Just open it, please."

"Of course" Andy picks at the tape at the sides.

"May I?" And the man produces a pair of box cutters from his trousers and for an instant Andy expects that this man will cut his throat in a single, casual motion, somehow managing to avoid getting a single drop of blood spilled upon his watch. Instead the man quickly releases the flaps of the box, turns it and opens it, looking inside its contents. "All right," he finally says.

"Is it OK?"

"So far it looks OK."

"Would you like me to bring it to your room now?"

"Wait here. I want you to follow me."

"Follow you?"

"You'll give it to him yourself." Him. The man. Satan. Whomever. "My father."

"How far are we going?"

"Not far. Wait here." Soon the man pulls up in a black Lexus. Andy follows him to a narrow side road that seems to lead nowhere. His anxiety increases until they reach an open gate and drive to a modest ranch style house. They park. "Bring the box and follow me." Andy carries it awkwardly up to the porch stairs, mindful lest he appear weak or worse yet, even drop the thing. "Watch your step."

Andy stands now in the hallway repositioning the box in his arms. "Where do you want it?" he manages to say.

"Just put it down for now on the coffee table. Right there." Andy enters a dimly lit living room. He puts it down. "Wait here, please." He sits upon a large flower patterned sofa. To his amazement, he notices for the first time, two elderly people; a man and a woman, both likely in their eighties or older, sitting quietly, one in an arm chair, the man, wearing a plaid shirt and a John Deere hat, while the woman with thin white hair, jowly with glasses, sits on the far end of the couch. Andy discreetly scoots to the opposite end of the sofa but neither person seems to take any notice of him. The man who met him at the hotel returns pushing an elderly man, his father, in a wheel chair, oxygen tubing hooked beneath his nose, a small green canister of oxygen affixed to his left. The old man silently points to the box. "That's it, dad," the younger man affirms. "I checked it, too." The father feebly leans forward, trembling, as if to get out of his chair, but his son speaks again. "I'll bring everything to you, pop. Remember?" and he opens the flaps of the box.

The father weakly opens his mouth, a sound of gas escaping every few seconds, the flow of oxygen. He asks, "Where's Tom?"

The younger man twists his mouth regretfully and squats down. "I'm sorry, dad. Tom's not coming." He shakes his head. "He sent this man instead. Remember what we talked about?"

Andy blurts out, "I'm sorry I'm so late, Mr. Charles."

Mr. Charles gives a slow side long glance, his mouth working uncomfortably. He nods. The son speaks. "Dad. Shall we open the box?" Item by item, he lays them out, sometimes leaving them on the table, sometimes putting them directly into his father's hands for inspection; a lifetime – photo albums and boxes of letters; diaries and manuscripts of various kinds; delicate and intimate items of a younger woman from a different age – atomizers, a tortoise shell hair brush, costume jewelry. A small teddy bear. Mr. Charles runs his fingers over these items, occasionally trying to smell them though he knows he cannot. The elderly couple, dull and insensate a moment ago, seems to watch intently now as their friend or their brother comes alive at the sight, touch, and smell of these objects. Mr. Charles seems content to settle upon the hair brush and a photo album tucked on his lap.

"Dad? Are you ready for this?"

The old man casts another sidelong glance at Andy, then turns back to face his son. He holds up his hand splaying all five fingers.

"OK, dad. Will do." The old man points to one of the diaries, to a box of letters, and to another yellowing manuscript. "I'll tell him now," he turns to Andy who looks at him wide eyed. "I didn't catch your name."

"Me? I'm Andy."

"Andy. I'm Gary Charles. Go ahead and call me Gary."

"Yes sir."

"Come with me, would you please? Dad, we'll just be a minute. I'll brief him now." He turns back to Andy. "You can call my dad, Mr. Charles."

"Certainly. Uh...could you sign my roster, please?"

"Sure. Where? Here?"

"Yes sir."

"Fine." Gary takes a pen and signs. "What time do you want me to put down anyway?"

"Well....I was expecting you would put down the correct time."

"What time do you want me to put down?"

"Since you ask, my dispatcher says he wouldn't pay me if I arrived past eight o'clock. I don't know how you feel about that."

Gary snickers. "I'm surprised you showed up tonight at all. I'll put seven thirty. How about that?"

"That's very kind. Again, I'm so sorry I'm late."

246

"I expected him to make it this far. And he was asleep until about twenty minutes ago. You're fine."

"Good. I'm glad."

"You should have called though. Or maybe you weren't near a phone."

"No sir. I had to take the back roads. But they didn't give me a phone number."

"It's a hotel."

"It didn't say so on the package."

"Jeez.......Can you read? I mean, are you a good reader?"

"Can I read? Sure. Did I miss something?"

"No, you're fine. Can you stay? At least tonight. We'll make it worth your while. Trust me. More money than my brother's paying you, I'm sure."

"Your brother?"

"Tom Hagen. That's who you're working for. Right?"

"He's your brother?"

"I know. We don't even have the last name any more. But we're brothers. Anyway. Andy. Sit down. Please." They both sit in a little office adjacent to the living room, separated by an archway with no door. Gary wears a look and he sighs. "Let me tell you what I need and what I'll pay you. If you can't or simply don't want to, then I'll lead you back to the hotel so you can be on your way. But...first," he searches around the desk, opens drawers and pushes his swivel chair back until he finds what he's looking for, a folded newspaper. He opens to the back page and turns to Andy, pointing. "There. Please read that. The first article." Andy scans the paper until he sees an article on the Soviet Union. "Out loud," Gary instructs. "I want you to read to me. Consider it an audition."

"For what?"

"To read to my father. I'll make it worth your while. If you're any good. Please read it."

"How do you want me to read it?"

"Just....clearly. Go on."

Andy clears his throat and begins to read, "The future of strategic arms talks is now more uncertain than ever as the health of the new Soviet leader is rumored to be on the decline.."

"The other article. Try the other one, I meant. Continued from page one. The one about the school girl. It's a horrible story. But read it."

Andy finds it. "Headline - Search expands in its third day for missing school girl....Imperial County police feel they are no closer to locating a missing ten year old girl who was last seen on Tuesday afternoon leaving Roosevelt High School in west El Centro...." Andy reads on about the frightened parents and shaken community as well as the determined but clueless detectives.

"Stop. You read just fine." Gary walks over to a small cabinet where there's a frosted decanter of Scotch. He pours a shot into each glass, returns and hands Andy one of the glasses. Andy starts to shake his head. "Do me a favor. Just take the glass. You don't even have to drink it." He sits down. "I just think I'll feel better about what I'm telling you if we're having a drink together."

"Sure," Andy says. And he takes a very cautious sip of a substance that burns in his mouth and down his throat.

"My father, Mr. Lane Charles has anywhere from a few hours to a few days to live."

"I'm sorry."

"He still has his wits about him. For now. He has end stage emphysema and when I tell you that he has hours, days, or weeks, I can assure you that his preference would be for hours. His legal affairs are in order, but he has made it quite clear to me how he wants to end his life. This is it. That box that you brought to us, which my brother grudgingly let his uncle collect from him and charged us a shit load to deliver tonight, that box, or rather its contents, were considered lost until - well, it's a long story that I needn't bore you with, but suffice it to say that those contents were recently, all too recently, discovered. My uncle packed them up. And here you are......We need a reader. You."

"What's in the box?"

"His life. Letters, diaries. Painfully personal from what I can guess. Our mother left him and his own mother died when he was a boy. There's a lot of regret in our family. And for the privilege of unloading that regret, we'll pay you $500 for you to stay until dawn. My father may or may not be able to stay alert that long. Or alive. If he does, we'll pay you $500 a day through the weekend. We'll put you up in the Best Western to sleep. Will you do it?"

"Of course I will. I just need to ask an obvious question."

"Why you?"

"Yes, of course. Why some stranger?"

"There are certain things that I think he doesn't even want me or even his friends in the room for. Nor would I want to read some of that stuff and Bill and Lois can't do it. It's because you're a stranger that you fit the bill. No one in this town is a stranger. Not really. My dad's got enough money and too little time to not pay for the privilege of having a stranger do this. And he clearly can't do it himself. It's what he wants."

"As I said, I'll do it. I don't mind telling you I could really use five hundred dollars."

"Good. Just do a good job. Pay attention. You'll have earned it. I'll be nearby the whole time, in the room or in here. We'll all be near in case he seems to be in trouble. You don't have to worry about that."

"You realize I'm not really a perfect stranger. I work for your brother. And he knows that I'm here."

Gary smiles. "My brother has no idea I'm asking you to do this. And I presume that for $500 I can trust you to not breathe a word of this to him. Nor to anyone else. Ever. You understand."

"Absolutely. But what if Mr. Hagen should ask me about how things went tonight with this delivery."

"You tell him you met someone named Gary Charles who met you at a hotel - not here - and this Charles guy accepted and signed for the box. He left. You left. End of story."

"That works."

"I don't mind you holding a secret from Tom, if you don't mind. He's an idiot, anyway."

"Does he know about your father's health?"

"Of course he knows. Believe me, he's had every opportunity in the world to be here tonight and to make things at least somewhat right. But you know….no one really wants him here all that much anyway."

Andy nods and looks down to hide a smile. "When did you think of all this? For me to do this?"

Gary shrugs. "After we arranged the delivery. We knew it was a long shot. If you could barely read or speak English then I guess I would have had to do it myself….and that would have been more difficult."

"Alright."

"He knows he's dying, and he wants to die surrounded by the truth. Not to wallow in it. But just to face it. Maybe he thinks that when he dies he won't be afraid of anything."

117.

After his encounter with Thomas, there is nothing to be done but to retreat into his lair and to stay there for as long as possible - forever perhaps. This is the only way he reasons he can avoid being evicted. Suddenly he realizes that he loathes everything about his little room, his dungeon, cut off from where the rest of the world laughs and cavorts without him. He is plagued by fitful and chaotically vivid dreams, dismal, and pathetic. Bands of ragged beings welcome him and express their own loathing for his treacherous hosts. Yet he wants no part of them, for they are filthy beings in rags, violent and untrustworthy. Hour after hour he dwells in a sickly limbo. He imagines he can hear his ersatz roommates laughing and sexing and playing their vile music, the pounding sound menacing and intrusive. At last he decides that he will pick up and leave of his own volition. Not because they want him to leave! No! But because he chooses to leave, because he cannot tolerate to be in this place, cannot stand to be here a moment longer. It is all his choice. They will come for him, surely. They will come for him in the morning and he won't be there to give them the satisfaction and they will even be disappointed and sorry that he is gone, instead of relieved. Yes. Eugene decides that this course is in fact the truly defiant course for this will show his tormentors just how little he truly thinks of them.

118.

"You want me to continue, Mr. Charles?" As it turns out, Lane Charles had been something of a secret, unpublished author of semi-autobiographical sketches of growing up, discovering nature, of falling in love in Connecticut to someone other than his future wife, joining the military at 17 years old to fight in the Great War, but the war ended before he could fight. Then came the so called Spanish influenza that took the life of the girl he thought he loved and his own candid devastation and feeling of abandonment. More is revealed in letters from his mother to herself, written when he was still unborn, letters of both hope and dread over the unknown, doubts about the family she had married into, doubts about her distant husband, and most of all, doubts about herself and her own worthiness of motherhood.

"Are you sure you want me to read this next part? This next entry?" No one dares to ask Andy aloud which part he means. Mr. Charles gestures to his son and to his friends to leave the room. Gary shakes his head, shrugs, and kisses his father on the cheek, nods to Andy, who waits, then continues. And as Eugene drives the streets one last night on his own before he turns himself in to live with his spinster aunt, and as he cruises the old streets with what little gas he has, stopping at every 7-11, every ARCO, every corner where he has the slightest hope of encountering Caroline, or failing that, some other lonely waif who doesn't care that he is broke with barely more than a quarter tank left of gas; as he cruises up and down Lincoln boulevard into the nether regions of morning, as he casts one more lonely glance at the vacant bus stop, so too Andy reads aloud to Mr. Charles, letter after letter in his mother's diary where she regrets her marriage and she regrets her life, and most of all her unborn child whom she feels has sentenced her to a life of despair and drudgery, culpable even inside her womb, tiny Lane Charles, and she knows that she should be happy and she should be proud, but she is not, she is frightened and revolted, though in the very next breath she challenges her heart to see that the baby and the baby alone gives her purpose, gives her a reason, the reason to keep on, to hope for a better life, if only through her unborn child and his as yet unclaimed and unwritten future - a future now at this moment depleted and long spent - and all of this is read clearly and indelibly as Eugene gazes up at one more street light, passes one more shuttered taco shop, one more cop car that will soon suspect he is seeking illicit, anonymous pleasure but all he is really looking for is to feel anything at all, and all the leathery, withered whores that fascinate him from a distance only and none of them are even in the slightest like Caroline, and not one is even remotely likely to take him to that warm bed with the garden window and the forever violet dawn and the golden quiet feast that never ends, and the hot, clean bubble bath, where her face is always soft and cherubic, and meanwhile the boulevard is

250

cold and quiet, empty and indifferent and Andy keeps reading on and on the words of regret, an elegiac for the dying.

By the time Eugene enters the 7-11, already knowing that Caroline won't be there, but stopping to buy gum and to steal matches and lighter fluid, at that same exact moment, Mr. Charles finally puts up his hand indicating he is ready to go to sleep, perhaps to die, and Andy apologizes and Mr. Charles weakly smiles and Gary offers Andy a room at the hotel and Andy offers to sleep on the couch in the office, just in case he is needed again. Eugene smiles at the clerk while stealing from him. He drives one last time towards the house, his heart beating and he is weirdly alive and aroused, and he thinks of the young long legged girls in the house. He imagines them, one minute perfect, the next moment perfectly immolated. Crispy and fragrant. He walks the uneven street, hands in the pockets of his parka, scattered pasted leaves, sidewalk pavement lifted by the roots of trees. He slowly walks the middle of the street to avoid the trip hazards. It's a pretty street at night, he thinks, leafy, lamplight through the branches. During the early evening, the street just seems crowded, humans lumped together, young insouciant beings gathered in cruel and messy conjugation. Now he has it to himself and it is his. The ground is soaked and the wood beams of the house are likely still dripping, so his task will not be easy. He stands before it now at the bottom of that steep driveway. The house is still. For all he knows, the beings within are silently sucking and giggling and moaning, whispered miasmas of gluttonous pleasure that forever seeped all the way into his wretched basement.

The front door has a small awning of green and white striped canvas so the door itself turns out to be relatively dry. He approaches the door with the attitude of someone who justifiably might still be living there. No one passes, not even a car. He digs into his pockets for the can of butane and a greasy two bit paper lifted from a battered newspaper dispenser, a paper for hapless Johns seeking whores and transsexuals, three copies for the same quarter. His throat starts to dry as his pulse races faster through his gut. He holds the butane. He holds the porno rag. From upstairs he imagines he hears a young woman's laughter, some nubile, naked creature, no doubt giving herself to those brutes. He moves away and slips around the back where there is another door along a grassy driveway. There, he finds a cord of wet logs for the fireplace but often neglected, the stupid idiots forever forgetting to bring them inside. The wood is soaked, good for green smoke only. It's heavier than he thought but he still manages to lift it, still bound by a yellow nylon tether and he drags it and he places it against the back door, resting it upon the concrete step. He walks back to the front door, puts the papers and the butane down and he separates the papers, crumpling each into little balls or else stuffing the edges underneath the door itself, one after another, and he takes the cap off the butane and he pours it over the papers and over the door itself and over the adjacent areas, all modes of wood and he takes out the matches, and he strikes them one by one. And he casts it onto the papers and it lights up quickly, then dies. Given the chance to change course, Eugene instead lights another match and casts it upon the papers then another, then a third, and finally the flames catch hold and gently lick up the doorway, and he stands back as the papers shrivel brown and blacken and are consumed in ashes and gives off smoke but it's not enough and Eugene pours more butane and the white flame advances further and smoke and sparks fan out as well and tiny flecks of porno ashes sparkle and lift upwards and a light goes on upstairs and now the sides of the doors also start to smolder and Eugene finally turns and walks away across the unkempt lawn, dropping the can, and he walks down the driveway and he turns a corner just as a window raises up and bewildered voices and shouts ensue and he casts a quick glance around a bush and the door is white with fire and he turns and he smiles, hands in pockets and his heart is also on fire and his bowels burn as well and he imagines that at any moment an outraged mob of hormonal youth will descend upon him and beat him senseless but he knows this will not happen. The revelers will be coping with survival and with escaping and they can think what they like.

Unhurried he walks to his car. A thin pillar of smoke is faintly visible now, illumined by the flickering glow of cresting light from below. He sits in his car and he turns the key and as he shifts into gear, he can already hear the first sirens making their way from the south. Eugene turns northbound onto the quiet avenue, then after a few uneventful blocks, save for a few solitary souls standing hands in pockets on the sidewalk gaping southward, he drives on towards Lincoln with his very last gas to his aunt's home in Westchester. There, he will try to sleep in his car until daybreak.

BOOK THREE – After the Storm

119. Saturday (the day after the storm)

"Knock, knock. Mr. Pavonine?"

Samuel glances up from the bed. In his thin blue hospital gown, he looks to Max so vulnerable, so insubstantial. "Yes. Please come in."

"Good morning, sir. My name is Philippe," says the blond attendant. "I was told that someone was requesting a shave and a haircut."

"Hello." And Samuel tries to hoist himself up.

"Let me help you, Mr. Pavonine," and Philippe puts his arm around him. "I got you," and soon enough Samuel is sitting up right on the bed. "Shall we do this over here? You'll be more comfortable I think and it'll be easier all around."

"I'll move," says Max.

"I'm Philippe," and he puts out his hand, "And you are?"

"I'm Max." And they shake.

"Very pleased to meet you, Max. Are you Mr. Pavonine's son?"

"Oh no. Just his friend."

"Quite a good friend as it turns out," Samuel says.

Philippe assists Samuel into Max's chair. "Dr. Greene says you're going home today. Nothing broken, no sprains, just a couple of minor scrapes. You were a little hypothermic, but you're OK. It's a miracle though that you don't have pneumonia."

"I should not have been admitted in the first place! Believe me, I am thrilled to be leaving, the sooner the better, as I have plans."

"You know, you look familiar. I feel like I have seen you before."

"I work here. Mystery solved."

"Oh really? Are you one of the administrators?"

"I am one of the materials transporters. I work the night shift."

"OK..... Well, let's get started."

∞

"You're quite a handsome man beneath all that hair we lopped off."
Piles of it crouch in the waste can, a sight that Samuel finds nauseating. "Maybe we should donate it to some chemo patient or maybe some alopecia patients."

"You can do with it as you like."

Philippe washes his hands and cleans the lather and shavings from the sink and hands Samuel a small towel. "I'm sorry I nicked you. On your left cheek. I'd dab it a bit."

"Everything you've done is a vast improvement though I fear I have aged and gone jowly and papery. The death's head stalks me, eager to emerge."

"Hush now. You're a movie star. Don't you think, Max? Your friend is nice looking, isn't he?"

"Sure."

Philippe smiles at Max. "How exactly did you say you two knew each other?"

"We work together."

"Really? You work in materials? I've never seen you before either."

"No, I'm a driver. So is Samuel. I didn't even know he had another job."

"Well I see. So is that how you treat your good friends, Mr. Pavonine? Keeping secrets then." Philippe turns to Max, "You got a bit of a nasty cut on your head there?"

"Yes. They took care of it."

"I'll check back on both of you later. I've got other people to see. Sick people! And I'm overdue. Nice meeting you, Max."

Max says, "He's nice."

"Yes. Indeed I can imagine you two getting along rather well together." Max shrugs and Samuel hardens his look. "Max…Remember what I told you."

"I remember, of course."

"Say it. Please."

"After the robbery, I wandered and went into the liquor store. I was looking for a payphone….. You saw me on the street corner and you pulled over. You picked me up but then you complained to me that you felt bad because you fell in the rain on an earlier delivery. So I drove. I was too scared to try and find my car and you needed help - that's very true, by the way - and in any case we both thought we should go to the emergency department."

"Excellent, Max. Look, I know it's a rather unlikely story, but the truth is even more outrageous, isn't it?"

He answers in a low voice, his head falling. "You can count on me, Samuel." Then he adds, "I still don't understand though what really happened. Were you attacked?"

"Max I told you. I had some….some sort of a seizure, if you will. A strange episode that's not going to happen again. But if anyone should find out, I might not get out of here. It was a mistake coming here at all last night, at least for me. I should have resisted more forcefully their decision to admit me."

"You were weak. I was worried about you."

"Well I'm fine now. Much better and I'm asking you to trust me."

"I told you. You can count on me, Samuel."

"Yes....thank you. They probably won't ask.....But they might. And you? Will you report what's happened to *you?*"

"Report it?"

"You were robbed. You should go to the police. Plus it supports our story."

"I don't know. I need to get my car back is all."

"Look, Max. I want to tell you something. You're a simple, decent sort. Your heart is pure. And for that, I shall miss you. I'm leaving today. As was my plan. And I nearly fucked it all up, too, pardon my expletives. But I am going and there are still some things I need to do."

"Where are you going?"

"A place in northwestern Washington state. A cabin by a stream."

"It sounds nice."

"It does. And it is."

"What will you do there?"

Samuel gives him a wistful look and adjusts his glasses. "Die."

"What?"

"I don't intend to die immediately. I'll live a little bit, safely, peacefully. Maybe lie in a hammock. Sit as often as possible by the stream, just watch it pass me by. I've saved enough money to last for quite a while with my small accumulated pension and a little bit from social security." He stares out at a space beyond Max. "All my life, I was either the best and deserved better than anyone. Or I was the worst and deserved....to die naked on the ugliest street imaginable. But....now. I'm done. Finally. I'm done with all that. I leave today." Samuel looks up at Max.

Max looks at Samuel. "Well then I'm happy for you."

"Thank you, Max. Whatever it takes to walk out of here today, I will walk out of here. Today. And never come back."

"Yes, but Samuel, you had this strange thing that happened to you last night. What if it happens again?"

"It won't happen again, Max. I cannot make that point more plainly to you."

Max shrugs. "I don't know how you can know that, Samuel. But like I said, you can count on me...Will you give me a lift to my car?"

"Will I? Ah.... Yes, of course." A knock on the door relieves Samuel from having to further disguise his irritation. "Come in! Please."

The door opens. "Mr. Samuel. We all came to wish you well!"

"Perry! And it's the whole family," Lorena and Guillaume enter as well. Lorena is on duty in uniform. "How did you know?"

"I saw you," Lorena speaks. "I hope you don't mind."

"Of course not!" but Samuel secretly minds, associating their visit with a delay in his discharge.

"Max!" Perry exclaims and he embraces him, which Max shyly endures. "Max, come and meet my family. My wife Lorena. And my son, Guillaume. Emma is on a play date." Everyone exchanges greetings. Samuel expresses his pleasure at seeing Guillaume who is at once the same little boy yet much different, quiet and withdrawn, cleaving close to his mother. He stares at Samuel but with no apparent pleasure or recognition at seeing him. Samuel is secretly disappointed yet also relieved. A portal into the world they shared is now forever sealed. "What happened to your head?" Perry asks Max.

"I was robbed. And someone hit me. But I ran away."

"You were robbed?"

"Yes."

"How terrible," Perry pronounces, suddenly indignant. "I am so sorry!" he says, as if his own lack of diligence had fostered this incident. "Where did this happen?"

"I was late with a delivery in Vernon. These two men with ski masks took my package. It was like they knew what I was carrying and they already planned to steal it."

Samuel speaks, "I believe our friend Max has been the victim of some kind of scam, besides being robbed. He refuses to see this because of his affections for the individual who set him up in the first place. Max, no matter what time you arrived you would have suffered the same reception. The robbers work for whoever gave you that package to begin with. He is the real robber."

"I still don't understand what you mean, Samuel."

"Your naiveté is simply astounding, Max. Of course they knew what was in the package. Think! This is Tony's way of stealing drugs without getting caught."

"He wouldn't do that."

"Would. And did."

Lorena comforts Guillaume who clings to her leg. She strokes his head and whispers to him in Spanish. Perry speaks, "We're going to the park. I thought he would like to see you, Samuel. But I guess he's shy today."

"How is he?"

"They think he has…epilepsy. But he can still be a happy boy. And healthy. I am sorry. All he would talk about was his 'funny bear' but now he is shy. Baby," he says to Guillaume. "Don't you remember the nice man who told you the story about the bear?"

"He doesn't recognize him," Lorena says. "He looks different."

"That's precisely so," Samuel says. "I am not the same person at all, as far as Guillaume can tell. But let's not be sad about it."

"What happened to you?"

"I'll be right as rain. No worries. I had a fall is all. And I'll be leaving in an hour or two. The doctors were just being overly cautious because I am prematurely an old man," and he attempts a wry smile.

Perry frowns but brightens again, "Oh, Mr. Samuel, I'm getting a new job. I'll be helping to open a big, beautiful hotel in Long Beach. This man I work for, he will help me to get my training and certificate to fix air conditioners. I'm already working for him. I will no more be a messenger, so I will be a little sad not to see either of you on Monday."

"You're getting a new job?" is all that Max says.

"Ah!" says Samuel, "That is simply fantastic. Just wonderful. I know that's what you've been working towards. And it makes it all the easier for me to tell you that I too have retired from the messenger business. Once I leave here I'll be leaving today for Washington state," and he briefly tells Perry and his wife about his plans. He leaves out the part about dying. Max puts his head in his hands.

"Ah, congratulations, Mr. Samuel! Yes, I remember. I will miss you!" And Perry continues to fuss over Samuel when someone new enters the room, unnoticed at first. Samuel notices him first. Lorena speaks to her brother in Spanish who responds in English.

"Yeah, I filled out all the paperwork. They don't have any openings. Not even doing what you do." he says, with a curled half lip.

Lorena looks at him and Guillaume buries his face deeper in his mother's thigh. Samuel speaks. "Excuse me young man. If I am correct and it is a job that you seek, an honest means of earning your way in the world and helping your family, if that is truly what you want.... I shall be retiring today and you are welcome to apply for my position. I mean I'm not doing the hiring obviously but I could certainly tell you all about it and give you an early start on bidding for it." And Samuel smiles at him.

Paco cocks his head and narrows his look at him and slowly shakes it, his own smile creeping back over his soft features. "Do I know you?"

"No. You do not know me. Perhaps you have seen me. But I'm quite sure you don't know me in the slightest. But I recognize you as the brother-in-law of my good friend, Perry. Lorena's brother. Yes?"

Lorena and Perry both endeavor to make the unnecessary introductions. Samuel puts his hand up, "This young man was in the room with you the night your son was here. By the way, Lorena, forgive me if I seem impertinent, but your boy seems to have become rather upset since your brother entered the room. A coincidence, I'm sure, but I wonder if he might not be happier to be free of this crowd for just a short while." Indeed, Guillaume is already pouting, looking like a boy who would be crying but for a want of tears.

"Hey, old man. You don't get to tell my sister what to do with her son." Max looks up. He stares at Paco. Lorena, unsure what to do, takes Guillaume and sits with him on her lap in a far corner of the room, as if this resolved the pressure to leave or stay.

"Paco!" Perry barks. "What kind of way is that to talk to this man?"

"I don't need your job."

"Not interested in a job? Shocking. Shocking that you're unemployed and still not interested in a job, working. Most strange."

Perry asks, "Do you two know each other?"

"Yeah, I seen this guy before. When I'm out with my friends, I seen this guy. Riding around. Looking for young men, young women, boys, just lookin' around offering chump change for people to get in his car and get nasty with his ugly self."

"You're a liar!" Perry shouts. Guillaume starts to cry and Lorena gets up to take him out of the room.

"No he's not," Samuel says quietly. "Not on this particular point."

"You're a liar!" Perry insists.

"You're a thief!" Max suddenly shouts.

"Wha…?" Paco turns and notices Max for the first time.

"You're the robber! The thief!" Max repeats, standing up. "You're the one. You're the one in the ski mask! You and this other guy. I recognized your voice. You recognized me. Remember?"

"What! Hey man. Shut that crazy up! Ski mask? Seriously? You're saying you never saw my face, but you know it was me?" Paco looks about the room at everyone, palms up, a look of appeal to recognize the utter absurdity of his accuser.

"You're saying *he* robbed you!" Samuel asks, a half smirk crouching in his features.

"His friend had a gun," Max continues. "And he hit me with it. That's how I got these stitches."

Perry wears a hideous smile and in a low voice he tells his brother-in-law. "I must tell you that this man right here," he points to Max, "This man is incapable of lying. You however are very capable." Max reflects inwardly that he has just committed to lie for Samuel.

"So he's not lying. He's just crazy. Look, I saw this dude out on the street the other night, fine. I recognize him. So what? But now he thinks I'm the guy in a ski mask? Don't you think that's wacked?"

"It was you," Max insists. "While you were wearing your ski mask you said you recognized me. From that time on the street. You two were going to shoot me," and here it looks as if Max might cry, but he swallows and breathes deeply. "Because you knew that I knew what you looked like beneath your mask."

"You're crazy," Paco growls.

Emboldened by Samuel and Perry's presence, Max continues, "You two wanted those pills. When the packages fell and those blue pills spilled everywhere, I remembered."

"You what?" Perry demands.

"This other guy put a gun to my head. This guy named Wilson. I never heard that name before. Wilson was the guy with the gun." And with that the room falls silent. Paco looks over at Perry who stares at him with a look of such fierceness as Samuel had never imagined before in his friend.

Paco says to his brother in law. "You got something to say?"

Perry begins in a low, taut voice. "Blue pills. I have seen these pills. Blue pills. Little blue pills. In my house. They're round. Yes? Not long and thin. They're round."

Paco shrugs it off as if Perry is stating the perfectly bland and obvious. "Vitamins, man. That's all."

"You give these pills to my wife? Maybe you give these pills to my son?"

"No way, man."

"You love these pills."

"Vitamins!"

Max breaks in. "He called you Paco! And you told me I would see God if I tried your pills."

"You *would* say that. You *love* these pills. You love to take them. You love to sell them, you sell them to my friend Max on the street?"

"I *gave* him a couple."

"You steal them, yes? You kill for them, maybe? Yes. You do anything for these pills."

"I didn't kill nobody."

"Of course not. But your friend, Wilson? That pendejo neighbor of ours, the one who nearly kills my son with his car, while you were supposed to be watching him. That low life piece of dirt!"

"Wilson didn't kill nobody. Nobody killed nobody! If anything, I saved this goof ball!"

"How did you 'save' this man?" Paco says nothing. "How does he know about Wilson? How does my friend know this name? How did you save, Max? You were there!"

"We didn't steal anything! It was all a set up. It was that dude over at that lab in North Hollywood. He was stealing from them. We just got in on it. Hey," he calls to Max.

"Don't even speak to him."

"Your little friend over at the lab? You don't need to worry about him, man. He got everything he wanted, that's for sure. He ripped us off, too."

"Shut up now, Paco! Don't even talk to him."

"It's true. Who the hell are you anyway to tell me who I can speak to?"

"I am the man who is kicking you out of my house. Today."

There's a knock at the door and Philippe and a security officer enter the room. "Is everything OK in here?" Philippe asks. Two tiny Asian nurses hover in the hallway, peering in, leaning over, tiny hands clasped to their mouths. Lorena appears behind the security officer, holding Guillaume who is still whimpering on her shoulder. Samuel realizes that it was probably Lorena who requested security presence.

"Call the police," Samuel says. "My friend here is overdue to report a crime and the perpetrator has just confessed."

Paco turns to him. "What did you say?"

"Are you OK?" Philippe says to Max. "You want me to call the police?"

"I'm outta here," Paco announces. "Don't even think of touching me," he says to the guard.

"Sir, please leave right now or you will be escorted out," Philippe instructs.

"Fool, I just said I was going. Did you not hear me," Paco says getting close to the attendant. "You just wanna look all tough or something. You trying to impress someone. You tell me with a guard and other people watching after I told you I was leaving? Does that make you tough?"

"Fine. Then go."

"I will. As soon as you stop telling me to leave and you shut the fuck up!" Paco says, wide eyed. Philippe crosses his arms and stares in silence. Paco also crosses his arms. The security officer, a pear shaped black man, steps in. "OK!" Paco announces. "Now I'm ready."

"Wait!" Perry says. But they are already escorting Paco out of the room and so he follows calling after him. "Call the police. Do not let this man leave." But the security officer and Philippe pretend not to hear him. "Whatever my wife, your sister does to contact you is her business. But you are never to come near our home, never to come near our children, nor me, ever again. Ever. You understand!"

"What are you gonna do if I come visit?" They are all slowly walking down the hallway, past the nurse's station, past the staring faces, towards the elevator.

"I will treat you like any intruder or rabid dog."

"Which means you'll do shit."

"I'll do much more than shit."

Paco sniggers, "I'd like to see that." The officer suddenly pulls Paco's arm behind his back and yanks him. "Get off me man." A small crowd has gathered, nurses and family members as Perry and Paco begin to trade insults while Philippe exhorts Perry to back away which at last he does. The onlookers are without stake in the drama, watching from an apparently safe distance, wanting to feel excited about something, wanting to talk about something, to experience a drama that blissfully isn't theirs. "Fuck you!"

"That's your whole philosophy!" Perry shouts. "That's all you have to say about your whole life. That's all you know."

"Lorena!" Paco shouts as he is placed in the elevator. "Tell this asshole that I'm still your brother!"

She tells him in Spanish, tears rolling silently, "Call me later if you can. I will bring you your things."

"Que?" The elevator doors begin to close

"I'll bring you your things. Call me!" Paco shouts something unintelligible as the cabin shuts and carries him away.

"I'm sorry about all that," Samuel says.

Perry sits where Max once sat. "What are you sorry about? He tried to humiliate you. He did far worse to Max. I despise this type of person." Max looks up, hearing an elderly patient moaning in the next room.

"Perhaps I contributed to causing a scene."

"Please," Perry whispers. "Enough of that. It has nothing to do with you." But Perry levels a strange look at him.

Samuel nods as if accepting this answer. "Where is your wife?"

"She's in the lobby with Guillaume. Waiting for me."

"Before you go...Max, please help me up. Perry. Just...just shake my hand. Paco won't trouble you again."

"How can you know that, Samuel?"

"Perry. Just be good to your wife and to your son and your daughter. Like you always are. Please just do that."

"Of course, of course," Perry mutters.

"I am so sad to see you like this. You're a good, decent man. Don't forget. Now Perry...Shake my hand and wish me well. Please."

Perry stares at him. He shakes Samuel's hand and touches Samuel's arm. "God bless you, Samuel." He starts to leave when he suddenly touches Max's face, embraces him and tells him. "I know you always speak the truth. You must call the police and tell them everything. They will believe you. You've never caused any trouble."

"That's all true, Max," Samuel adds.

Max blushes and says nothing as Perry continues. "I don't know when I shall see you again, either. Be well." And he walks out and Max and Samuel both stand in place.

Slowly, carefully, Samuel lets himself down in his chair. "What a scene....Where is that doctor, anyway? Max......Max, don't worry. That patient doesn't even know he's moaning. He's practically unconscious." Max nods. "Remember what I told you, Max," then suddenly, Samuel shouts, "Good God, Max! Go! Go now. Find Perry before he leaves. Try. Find Perry and ask him to take you to get your car and then go to the police. He will do it!...Max, now!

There's no time!" Max hesitates for one more second but then runs off as Samuel gestures him away. Samuel grips the sides of his chair, determined to regain his strength as much as he might need. He closes his eyes. "Goodbye, Max." He lowers his head. And silently he begins to laugh.

120.

Maureen regards him from the bed, propping her head up on one shoulder. While the sky was still pink and lemon, Andy shook hands with Gary Charles for the last time. Mr. Lane Charles was not yet dead, but their work seemed to have run its course and Andy was relieved to end his gig, especially in the pale light of morning, happy with five hundred dollars in his pocket and the satisfaction of having gotten paid for a gig for which he might have been screwed, after all. Going home, he takes the 8 to the 5 to the 405, grabs a quick diner breakfast, wallet bursting, $473 in his pocket after gas. Maureen pages him and asks to come over, ready to love him, but all Andy wants to do is sleep. "Andy, it's a quarter to one. If you're not gonna fuck me, the least you can do is feed me."

Andy looks up from the classified. "Maureen, I'm glad you're here," he isn't sure about the truth of this statement, "but I need to get my ass in gear. Even if it's on one hour's sleep."

"What are you doing, anyway?"

"I told you. Looking for apartments. I need a place fast. And I probably need a job, too. And I probably need a band. Both of which I screwed up for myself last night. I've got nothing right now and I'm feeling it."

"Nothing? You've got a naked woman in your bed."

"That's not even my bed."

"The naked woman part was supposed to be the headline on that statement."

"I'm sorry. I've gotta get out of this motel. Now I've finally got the deposit money in my pocket to get my own apartment, even a single, just a place to lock up my shit. Or make a demo record. I don't know."

"I'll bet no one ever gets fired from ZZZZap! They'll go under before they let go of anyone. What a stupid name and what a stupid company."

"So what happened to you? You were all gung ho the other day. Then you punk out. Now you're quitting. Were you even sick?"

"That slime ball, Hagen, propositioned me at the end of the day before yesterday."

"What?"

"Oh, he's a scumbag alright. He takes me into his private little office, tells me I'm doing a great job, said he was going to help me with my career, move up to sales."

"Maybe so. You're great at sales."

"Suggested we talk about it over dinner or drinks. Winks at me."

"Uh oh. So you're looking for another job."

She rolls on her back and stretches, exhibiting herself. She grunts with pleasure at moving her limbs. "I already have a job, waitressing at a seafood restaurant on La Cienega. I can do that while I'm going back to school. Screw that guy. No! Don't. Ugh! He's disgusting."

"You know, you women can be harsh. You wouldn't like me talking about a woman like that."

"'You women?' Really?"

Andy shrugs. "I like Hagen. He's a blustery buffoon but he's OK."

"Oh shut up. Do you not even notice me over here, Andy? Can you just shut up about Hagen already?"

"He was a little drunk though when I last saw him and he's not very close with his family. That's for sure."

"I'm taking a shower!" And she stands up, completely nude.

"Wow, he really upset you, huh."

"Who!"

"Who are we talking about? Hagen."

"I'm upset with you, you stupid idiot," and she takes a pillow and hits him with it. "You're unbelievable."

"I'm running on no sleep and I've got to do something here!"

"You slept. Go do something," and she pads off into the little bathroom, slamming the door.

He hears the squeak of the faucets as the water sizzles on. "Hey," he shouts through the door. "You wanna go with me while I look for apartments?" Finally she responds through the curtain.

"My plan A was fucking and pizza - I thought that dudes liked that agenda - but now I think I'll go study or something. So you can go fuck yourself or your pizza, whatever." He returns to his ads while her shower lingers on. Apartments everywhere, but nothing yet that he could actually afford. It would be nice to see mom again in Indiana. For two days. Go back to New Mexico? Hide in the open glare of Gary? No one wanted to see him there. Even alien El Centro feels more like home than right here. He picks up his guitar and he plays a tune by Fleetwood Mac. And he lets the time flow on as he strums, the water from the shower continuing on as if she had no intention of ever coming out. Someone knocks at the door.

Andy looks up, expecting no one that he cares to see, but the knocking persists. "Andy! Open up! I can see your truck, dude."

"Who is it?"

"It's Louie! And," and the voice begins to sing, "It's Maggie!"

Andy leaps up and throws open the door, embracing both of them, only half seeing them. "Come in! Come in!" Louie's hair is short, cut just below his ears. Maggie smiles awkwardly at him as she tosses her hair back from her face and leans more decidedly on her cane. She has a streak of premature gray to match her eyes. "Let me get you a seat," and he pulls the one arm chair in the room forward for Maggie to sit down. He looks at Louie and his haircut. Louie grins at him. "What the hell is this?"

"Maggie did it. She's talented. It was time."

"I barely recognize you."

"It'll grow back."

"My head's exploding. What are you doing here?" The water stops in the shower. "Before we continue, I have another guest. She was about to leave anyway so I'll just get rid of her."

"Andy," Maggie says, "What are you talking about? Don't throw out your girlfriend on our account. We can get together later."

"You just got here. Maggie, she's not exactly my girlfriend."

"Well whatever, so what if she is. I told Louie here we shouldn't just go playing surprise party."

"Well I'm glad you did and I don't want you to go. So…just hang on." Andy knocks on the bathroom door. "Maureen."

"I'll be just a minute."

"Listen. We have guests. I mean some friends of mine just came over."

"…..What?"

"There are people here."

"People? What kinds of people?"

"Two people. Friends of mine."

He hears her sigh. "Uh….can you get me my clothes then. Please!" He gathers them and she grabs them and slams the door.

Andy turns to his friends. "OK. She'll be right out."

"I don't blame her if she feels put out," Maggie says.

"Don't worry about it. And don't move."

"Well then, let me get right to the point," Louie says. "Have you found a place to live yet?"

"I was gonna look today, actually."

"So that's a no. You're hanging out here like you have no intention of staying in L.A."

"It's cheap. Kind of."

"How'd you like to live with us?"

"Live with you?"

"Live with us."

"With you?"

"With us. As in all of us. The three of us. You, me, and Maggie. Live together. You live with us."

"In New Mexico?"

"In Los Angeles, stupid. We have a place."

"You live here now?"

"We've been here for a little bit already. I know it's strange, but we wanted to get our bearings before just showing up."

"You live here now. How did you decide –"

Maggie speaks. "Maybe you're still looking for a band."

"I'm dreaming." Andy sits down on the bed.

"We found a dumpy little house to rent." Louie says, "In a place called Mount Washington. We looked at different areas and we like this the best. We think we can afford to rent it if we have one more person."

"Can we just slow this down a little? I just need to catch up with you here."

Louie smiles. "I know. I just wanted to get to the point....What are you thinking?"

Andy says nothing at first. "There's just so much I want to talk with you about.... What's with the short hair?"

"I have a job now. This is my, let's get a job look for the eighties"

"What happened...?"

"After you left? I was afraid to come out to L.A.," Louie grins. "And that's what Maggie and I have in common. We're both so scared all the time. You don't look like you're scared of anything, Andy. Even if you are. But Maggie and I. We're scared of everything. But together, we're not," he continues. "There was a chance that we would have killed each other, but instead we keep each other from killing ourselves. We're good together."

"You're together?"

"Well. I'm gay, in case you forgot. Although it hardly seems to matter in my case. We make a good odd couple. But we need a good guitarist, with his own equipment. You know anyone like that?"

Andy looks from one to the other. "I'm happy, you know. Still processing. But happy. "

"You want us to come back, Andy? Or you want to come see us?" Maggie says.

"I want you to stay. I want to run away with both of you. But... things were pretty not so great between us when I last saw each of you." He looks intently at them. Rag dolls, Teddy Bears, come to visit him in his doll house. Wounded friends who smile at him. The bathroom door opens and Maureen slowly comes out, her hair still wet. Maggie continues as if nothing were happening.

"Louie has a job. You have a job."

"Maybe not."

265

"You'll get another job. I'll give piano lessons. For a little bit until I can't no more.... I'll go on disability. That'll be fun. None of this is forever. It may only be for a short time. From the looks of it, you ain't got too much goin' on here. Do this because you want to, and for no other reason." Maggie looks up and sees Maureen just standing there, playing with her hair, waiting, waiting. "Hi! I'm sorry to barge in. I'm Maggie. This is Louie." Andy wheels around. Maureen nods. "Hi....I know who you are."

121.

At precisely eleven thirty, Samuel arrives at the house on Old Ranch Road in the Palisades, a sudden world apart of trees, leaves blown to the earth where they mulch in the shade of a stick figure canopy. The house has a long stone walkway and Samuel had forever loved the smell of the grounds. A long white marble tile entrance way quickly leads to a sunken living room, cloud white carpet, long white sectional couches, clean spare lines in the side and coffee tables, sleek wall lighting and hanging lamps. Gone are the rich leather and dark wood interiors and he calculates in his head the likely cost of these changes. He wears a long overcoat and scuffed shoes and he gazes out the windows behind the sectional. Elizabeth appears dressed in white linen and sandals. "Samuel." He struggles to rise. "Please dear, don't get up," but he already is, and she kisses him politely on the cheek. He takes her hand and they sit down together. She removes her hand. "You're looking a little peaked."

"I was in the hospital last night. You however look simply wonderful."

"My God! Why were you in the hospital?"

"I fell. I was feeling a bit faint. And a concerned friend suggested we go to emergency. From there they made the most foolish row and admitted me."

"Samuel, does this happen often? You fainting?"

"Not at all. Thank you for your concern. Nor do I believe I really fainted. I'm a little weak is all, but I'll be fine. I'll die of obstinacy before anything else."

Elizabeth chuckles a bit and smiles. "Alright then. Perhaps you're being obstinate about not really fainting, my dear.....Can I get you anything? Coffee or tea."

"No thank you. I won't be staying very long. I must say, the house looks more beautiful than ever. Quite airy."

"You like it? I didn't really think it was your style you know."

"I like it quite a bit. You're right, it's not my style. I like my cave. I am sure I would have resisted."

"You did."

"It's your house now. I make it eleven years now since we moved here?"

"Yes. I think so."

"And you still commute all the way out to Claremont?"

"I only have seminars on Wednesdays. And meetings once a month on Fridays. They're a pain, but it comes with the job."

"I am sure you are a splendid administrator. A long overdue congratulations, face to face."

They speak for a short while of academia and for even less time about the household and the storm. She says, "I don't even know what it is that you do. You've respected my wishes of course and I thank you for that."

Samuel nods. "I think of you every day. And the children."

She stiffens and sits up straighter. "I've moved on, Samuel. We've all moved on."

"I'm not being sentimental; I'm just stating a fact. You are my family. As for moving on, you can do what you like." He looks at her and slows his speech. "But these are still my children, too."

"Why are you here, Samuel?"

"To say goodbye. I'll be leaving town. Tonight."

He gives her a side long glance, enough to detect a look of relief catch upon her face. "Oh...." She says. "That sounds final. Where are you going?"

"I will send you my address when I get there. Somehow I don't care to go into it now."

"Well. I hope it's some place that suits you."

"Dark and stormy, quite frequently, I assure you."

"I wish you well, Samuel."

"How *are* the children?"

"Honestly, I don't hear from them much myself. None of them are married yet. Joanie just turned eighteen. But I suppose you already knew that," she says and a look of recognition clouds her face. "Also," she goes on, "There's still no word from Melanie since before you left."

"Yes, dear Melanie. I confess I feel so empty without them. As if they never existed and I simply dreamed them up."

"Samuel, you were always a rather distant father, you must admit. Kindly, but distant. And of course you were more involved with your students, wouldn't you say?"

"Well my dear, I hope you hear more often from the children yourself. No doubt they are stretching their wings. As for Joanie's eighteenth birthday, you are correct that I know exactly when this happened. Effective immediately, my child support payments are at an end."

"Of course, Samuel. Of course."

"Any additional funds needed for college, I can provide for her if I am able, directly to her, as she is now an adult. Furthermore, I have directed my bank to retain my pension, all of it, modest as it is."

"Yes of course, Samuel. You've always been exceedingly generous, Samuel. Extremely so. Perhaps to a fault."

"Perhaps. I'm sure it was no doubt useful to you as you set about refurbishing this gorgeous house, seeing as it must have been unbearable to you in its previous state."

"Given the nature…of your choices, I asked you to leave. These were your choices."

"And we have gone through this before. Thoroughly."

"Samuel, it was never my intention to put you in penury."

"You asked me to stay away from my children. That was the tough part."

"And you complied. Thank you."

"At pain of force majeure, my dear."

"Let's not argue. I didn't trust you, Samuel. You complied because you didn't trust yourself."

"I may not trust myself on many accounts, but not when it came to my own flesh and blood," he says hotly. "I went along." He settles back. "Perhaps at the time, I was ready to surrender everything."

"……Have you gotten any help? Are you still out there?"

"No. I am not….still out *there*."

"That's good. But I do hope you will get professional help."

"Thank you. Thank you. Your solicitude is most comforting."

"I hope you came to be civil. Please don't patronize me."

"Fair enough."

They sit still for a moment. "Thank you for the financial reminders. That was courteous, although you could have sent a letter. I'm sure you are quite busy with your preparations….Anything else?"

Samuel clears his throat. "That was me yesterday."

She blinks. "I know."

"Did you know right away?"

"It was like an hallucination. But you're unmistakable even when you're coiffed like a Neanderthal." And suddenly they both break out into laughter. "I was so relieved when you showed up just now looking handsome, like yourself. Is that what you have been doing with yourself? It makes no sense."

"For about six or seven months. I thought it would pass the time. My head was no friend to me. And I needed money. I thought it would be easy and so it is for my fellows, but I found it quite unpleasant. I also work part time as a kind of materials transporter for the county hospital."

"How extraordinary."

"I thought I was doing it to humiliate myself." He thinks of how Max found him last night. "But I rather liked it. You get to see a part of the world that you know exists but which you don't have to come into contact with as long as you are amongst the healthy."

"Samuel, I know you'll think me difficult, but I really don't know the world that you used to inhabit. Was it not more than one world? You lived in a world that I knew nothing about, all the nights you stole from us when you claimed to be working in the world that we thought we knew."

Samuel seems to think about this. "I was making a different point of course. About the world you see when working in a hospital, a world that hangs over us all but which we don't like to think about. But I take the point that you were making."

"And you're really done with all that. All that other life?"

"Honestly, I still have other problems. Let's just leave it at that. There's no need to go into it and that too is over and done with."

She looks away at a spot on the carpet. "Indeed, whatever it is, I don't need to know."

"Agreed."

"Is there anything else? I know you mentioned you could not stay long and I too have to be getting on with things."

Samuel looks about and stands quite easily, stiff as he feels in his back. "There is one more thing. Only one, I promise. I will be writing now to our children. To all of them. Alan, Linda, William, and Joanie. Obviously, neither of us can write to Melanie."

"I am aware of the names of our children."

"And you are also aware that I no longer have their current addresses. I would like you to give them to me. Now.....And if you don't then I expect you to at least forward my letters to them. Unopened. I expect that we can settle this now without recourse to third parties. I will of course provide all the proper postage. Have no doubts about that."

"Free postage you say. Well now at least I know why you are here. Do you really think that I should be a kind of mail courier for you?"

"I just told you I would prefer that you simply give me their addresses and phone numbers directly and I shall trouble you no further."

"Or, I could ask each of them whether they wish to be contacted."

"No. Those are the choices. Forward my mail to them or provide me with their information directly. Either choice will do. I will send the enclosed letters with a request for return receipt to avoid the need for you to confirm your part in this. As you know, I have waited a very long time for so little and I gave up more than I needed to."

"You were ashamed, Samuel! That's the truth, more so than any kind of duress from me or the law. You wanted the details of your adventures to be kept hidden from them."

"Nevertheless! I still expect you to do this for me."

"You don't ask me? You just tell me? And what if I won't?"

"Elizabeth. You won't refuse. Because I truly ask for so very little and you know that. Now just do it. Look, it will only be once or twice, anyway. If after two letters I never hear from any of them, well then there it is. I would admit there is no point in pressing on."

She looks at him. "Everyone thinks you are so affable. Agreeable and doddering. Charming and harmless."

"Elizabeth."

"For God's sake's Samuel. I will do it."

"Unopened."

"Yes!! Of course. Unopened."

"Thank you...... Goodbye, Elizabeth."

"Goodbye, Samuel." He turns and slowly he makes it back to the front door. He quietly lets himself out.

122.   The same Saturday (the last day)

The maroon vinyl booths are cracked but delicious to sit against, so Andy observes. "I like to bounce up against them. Yeah! Nice and comfy."

"Settle down," Louie admonishes and they both laugh.

Maggie sits down last next to Louie, Andy next to Maureen. In the car they had talked of nothing but music and clubs. "You are so cool," Maggie says to her. "Andy, you have to keep her. You have to be nice to your girlfriend. She knows every dog and dilettante in this town and we'll play for every one of them." Andy shakes his head, thinking, she is not my girlfriend, but he leans back and folds his arm around Maureen who settles in more closely next to him. He smiles.

∞

"Thank you," Tim says. "Can I get some extra napkins?"

The server walks off to get them. He dabs his perspiring forehead. "Geez. You can see that I'm not myself. Haven't been since the goddamn accident. Pardon my French."

"You and I are somewhat a pair," Samuel observes buoyantly, "Both with our distinctive canes and maladies."

"Distinctive? As in old? Weak?" Indeed, it appeared as if Tim has aged savagely since Samuel last saw him two days ago. His skin is pasty and his hair wispy and he has deep bruises, yellow, purple and blue and stitches on his forehead. He wears a neck brace and he has just been released from the hospital himself.

"Thanks again for coming out with me, today."

"My dance card is pretty empty and I'm grateful to get out. I...I don't get many callers. So you're really leaving today?"

"As soon as I see you home. That's it."

"And I'll ask you again, because I couldn't follow the first time....."

"I know we haven't exactly been chums these last few months. Honestly, I'm no one's chum. But I feel there is something we share. Maybe I just wanted to talk with someone my own age, with someone with whom I imagine I shared some common experience. And perhaps to ask you something."

"Where'd you say you was goin'?"

"About a mile north of a little hamlet called Emmet. Off a side road, off another side road. About 20 miles southwest of the great Mount Rainier. A cabin on two acres of property."

"Wow. You bought yourself some property?"

"A long time ago, yes. Something that I've kept tucked away somehow. The recent expense was having it kept up and such. It's the only thing that's really kept me going these last two years. For longer than that, really."

"Good for you. Does it snow up there?"

"In the mountains, yes of course, but not where I'll be. It rains though. Quite a lot."

"Hope you don't get flooded."

Samuel frowns. "Perhaps I will simply be washed away cabin and all to another dimension. Wouldn't that be nice?"

"I don't know that I'd like all the rain."

"I'll be inside when it does. It has a fireplace. And a generator, too."

"Whatever floats your boat?"

"Haven't you ever wanted to get out of here? Find some place better, safer, quieter?"

Tim smiles. "Sure. But thinking about a place like that and actually living there are two different things."

"That is self-evident, is it not?"

"I'm not discouraging you at all. What are you gonna do there anyway?"

"Be peaceful. If I live through next year, who knows? I've already lost all contact with my children. It's a long story."

"And I know it well. Got one of my own. She won't talk to me either, my daughter. I got only the girl. I can't blame her."

"Really?....What happened? If that's not too personal."

"We gave her up for foster care, then for adoption. It was hard times and my ex, her mother, was a piece of work. But I blame myself."

"Did you stay in touch with her? Or with her adopted family?"

"It was a closed adoption. That was the deal. But then she contacted me when she turned eighteen. I was happy. But then things didn't go so well. She was disappointed, I guess. Then she kind of disappeared."

"Extraordinary. And terrible, of course."

"Worst mistake I ever made in my life. Giving her up. Apart from marrying her mother in the first place," They sit in silence for a moment. "How's that for sharing and opening up."

"I'm terribly sorry."

"What good does that do? I mean dwelling on the past." Tim dabs himself with a corner of the napkin and a small piece sticks to his forehead.

"You've got a small piece on your right forehead, my friend." Impatiently, Tim wipes it away, and while still looking at the rumpled paper, he says to Samuel. "It's no good living in your head. I like the city. It drowns out this just a little," and he points stiffly to his temple. Samuel chuckles. "Why don't you talk to any of your children? If I can be so nosy."

"For many years.... I deceived my family. I sullied myself with hustlers and wayfarers and bathhouses. I sullied *them*. I was discovered at long last when in rapid succession I was first arrested followed by an unrelated complaint filed against me."

Tim nods. "Got it," he says softly. "You sad sonovabitch. I wouldn't have thought it."

"I can't tell if I hear judgment or compassion in your tone."

"You don't need to worry about what I think. That's for sure."

∞

"Did we tell you yet about our near brush with death yesterday?"

"You started to, but no."

"Some maniac in the storm yesterday nearly killed both of us."

"What!"

"He was making a sharp left turn through a puddle," Maggie explains. "We were in the middle of this narrow street. I guess he was going too fast and he hadn't seen us, so he cuts away and crashes into this other car. A parked car."

"He kills this car. No one was in it, thank God."

"That's insane," Maureen says.

"That's L.A," Louie responds. "No one seems to know how to drive in the rain. I've been here before."

"What happened to the driver?"

"Don't know," Maggie says. "We got the hell out."

"Excuse me. I see someone I know," Andy says, "Maureen. It's the Wolfman and Grumpy the Dwarf."

"Who?"

"Never mind. It's..... never mind, I'll be right back."

∞

"Have you heard about Perry? It's wonderful news."

"No, do tell."

"He has a new job. Actually an entire new career. He's some sort of an apprentice in the field of heating and air conditioning. A repair and installation professional."

"That so? Good for him. When does he start?"

"Immediately, I think. Rather sudden."

"No kidding. Where'd you hear that?"

"From Perry. His wife works at the same hospital which I recently escaped from....or actually was honorably discharged from this morning."

"Good man, that Perry. Best of the lot. Including you and me. Family man. Making something of himself."

"Yes, I'm rather fond of Perry myself. Lovely wife and a spirited little boy."

"Spirited," Tim snorts. "That means he's a pisser, eh?"

"He's a very good little boy. Fond of a good yarn. Smart as a whip, too. Knows his dinosaurs. Not even four years old."

"Samuel!"

He looks up, recognizes Andy and smiles. "I'm almost surprised you recognized me."

"You look great!"

Samuel extends his hand to shake Andy's. "What good fortune to see you today. But it seems you have not yet noticed I am dining with a mutual friend."

"Hola! Tim!" Andy says with forced enthusiasm. "Sorry, I didn't see you from our table. Both of you, together here! Cool!"

Tim raises a hand up in curt acknowledgment, his eyes wide open and distant looking. He clenches his lips in a minimal smile. "How do."

"Well anyway. I don't want to keep you. I'm just with some friends. And I don't think I'll be seeing you on Monday, cause I think Mikros is going to fire my ass after last night."

"What'd you do?" Tim asks weakly, sniggering. "Extort him for money?"

Andy looks at him for a long moment. "You got me, Tim! Bingo!" Samuel laughs. "Let's just say I missed a deadline and the client was of special importance to Mr. Hagen."

"'Let's just say…let's just say'" Tim repeats, "That's a popular expression these days."

"Well," Samuel says, "Let's just say that it's certain that you won't see me Monday for I am leaving this very day for good. Out of town. Greener pastures. And other such clichés." And Samuel quickly tells them about his cabin in the woods.

"You told me about that place when we were in the park."

"I remember that conversation very well and I enjoyed it. Enjoy your music, young man. You are a rare talent and I know you work hard at it. You will find your audience. You take care now."

"You too. You too," They shake hands and Andy feels touched by these kind words, yet also dismissed. He turns to Tim. "So long, Tim. Take care."

"Oh kee doh kee."

"Goodbye Samuel."

"Fare well."

∞

"I do a lot of their production stuff, editing promos late at night. Mostly I baby sit the board, press buttons, stuff like that."

"If you work at night, will you still be able to play any clubs?"

"I don't start my shift 'til midnight and I'm off on the weekend. So it's fine."

"Hey!" Maggie says, seeing Andy return.

Maureen smiles. "I just figured out who you were talking about."

"Wolfman and Grumpy, yeah."

"I think of them as little Sasquatch and Golem from Lord of the Rings."

"Sasquatch shaved! He's Mr. Chips now. It's these two old dudes who work at the messenger service," Andy says to Louie and Maggie. "Golem looks terrible by the way. Like he fell or was in an accident."

"What happened?"

"I didn't ask."

"Why not?"

"Because I don't care for him very much. I don't think he likes me either. But Samuel is leaving town today. Oh! Maggie. You need to meet this guy."

"I need to meet him? Which one? Golem or…who?"

"Samuel. He's into Mahler. *Mahler*. With the dead children and the putting of punks in their place? This guy is great buddies with Mahler, yet says he has never heard of Mahler's Tenth."

"So."

"So! *You* need to put him in his place. I know you have at least two or three of those cassettes in your purse. Right? Come on. Give him one of those cheap little cassettes you're always making."

"I don't see that happening. And you can give it to him yourself."

"That means you do have them. I'm telling you. You would so be putting this guy in his place. Isn't that what you live for? Isn't that what Mahler was all about, your buddy, your soul mate."

She smirks. "Get the hell outta here."

∞

"I don't have a huge problem with that guy. He's just not a favorite of mine like he seems to be of yours."

"I'm curious as to why."

"He doesn't seem to focus or take his stuff seriously."

"He takes his music very seriously I can assure you."

"Don't bother assuring me, I'm talking about when he's doing a job. He doesn't answer his pages and he's making time with his new girlfriend on the job. He's just a flake."

"Hmmm. Interesting."

"How the hell is that interesting? It's boring. You gonna tell me that he and I are really alike, too? Like you had the nerve to compare me with Rolfe already? Is that what you're trying to figure out?"

"Well," Samuel responds waggishly, "Are you?"

"Ah, save that stuff."

Samuel laughs, "It was the furthest thing from my mind until you yourself brought it up just now..... Ah! Look here. It seems we have one more chance to ask him ourselves. Yes, my friend!"

Andy comes up to the table. "You know it was such a great goodbye that I hate to spoil it, but I wanted you to meet a friend of mine who apparently is a bigger Mahler fan than even you."

"A what? What was that?"

"I wanted you to meet my friend who loves Mahler. She has something for you."

"Mahler? Ah yes, your friend who touts the controversial Tenth symphony."

"The same."

Samuel chuckles. "Very well. Does she have a cassette for me? I have a confession to make about that.... Well anyway, I might have to buy one of those little machines so that for the road I might be properly put in my..."
Samuel seems to break off in mid-sentence.

"Thanks for waiting for me, Andy," Maggie says, sharply, struggling with her cane between the tables. She stops abruptly, but it is Samuel's face he notices first, his earnest blue eyes swimming behind his glasses, hard furrows of alarm. Tim perspires, staring at nothing perhaps, in Maggie's general direction. Andy looks behind him, but there is no fire, no gunman, no mystic visage. There is only Maggie. He peers into her large gray eyes and he clearly sees that she herself is more shaken and frightened than anyone.

"Maggie?" Her eyes are wild, lower lip trembling, her skin translucent and damp. Slowly she turns from Tim to Samuel, from one to the other. "Maggie," Andy calls "Are you all right?"

Samuel whispers. "Melanie."

Tim grumbles, "Maggie. Her name…. is Maggie."

"Are you," she slowly says. "Are you kidding me?" The hand on her cane is shaking, the bottoms of her eyes turn red. "Are you *fucking* kidding me?"

"Baby," Tim says, his mouth working in strange ways. "Baby."

"Melanie," Samuel clears his throat. He looks like there are words stuck in his mouth.

She looks at Andy. "What the hell is this!" she insists.

"I have no idea!"

"You didn't know?"

"Know what? Know what?"

"It was meant to be," Samuel says. "Please, Melanie. Won't you sit down?"

"She goes by Maggie! You call her Melanie? Christ," and his mouth works hard, bubbles of foam pursed at his lips, breath rising, wide eyed and silently weeping. Andy looks on helplessly.

"A sick joke." She turns to Andy. "Why would you do this?"

"Do what? Do what! I didn't know. I just work with them and…." Words seem useless and confusing.

Samuel turns from Maggie to stare at Tim, gripped by a look of gaping amazement. He whispers. "I knew it. And yet it can't be."

"Either one of you," Maggie says, "Either one of you would be crazy, right here, right now. But both of you?" She glances from one to the other. "Both you losers? Here together. Both of you? What kind of sick fucking joke?"

"We didn't know, Melanie," Samuel says. "We had no idea, Tim and I. Neither did he," turning to Andy. "It's a fool's fate."

"You two idiots got together and got this so called friend of mine to bring me here so you could …." She doesn't finish the sentence.

"We didn't know. He didn't know," Samuel says.

She reels to Andy again. "Are you telling me you didn't know?"

"How could I know? And why would the thought even cross my mind?" he insists, forgetting for the moment that indeed the thought had crossed his mind

276

a while back, at least regarding Tim. Those obsidian gray eyes. As if too tired either to leave or remain standing, Maggie finally sits down in the booth on the side next to Tim, who seems harmless enough in his ailing state.

"Either one of you," she repeats as if to herself. "But *both* of you? At the same fucking time. Both you *idiots*. What the fuck!"

Louie walks up at last. Andy turns and whispers to him, "Please do not say anything. And don't even ask. You'll find out everything soon enough."

"You don't looks so good," Maggie says, looking at Tim. "Are you ill?"

Tim, who still stares where Maggie had stood turns and looks at her, resembling a man nearly a hundred years old, but his eyes come alive as he looks at her face, four gray eyes staring at each other. He looks down at her cane.

"You have a cane, too?" he says, pointing at it with his own.

"I have MS," she says, as if telling him the time.

"What was that?" She repeats herself and he frowns deeply. "That's what I thought you said. Geez. I'm so...I'm sorry, baby." Silently, he weeps.

"That part's not your fault."

"I'm sorry," he repeats. Samuel stares from a distance at father and daughter. Tim says to her, "How are you getting on?"

She looks at him. "I'm OK."

"Good. You look...you look so beautiful. You look really beautiful. First rate," and he starts coughing. Then he wipes his mouth.

"Thanks," she says. "What about you? Are you sick?"

Tim seems to labor, his eyes slightly bulging, "Well. I'm weak right now, is all. I got to get my strength back. I was in an accident the other day." He grows more animated. "Where you been? You get my cards? Does your mother pass them on? I miss you so much." He coughs again.

"Mom's dead."

"I know that. Sorry."

"Are you still smoking? That stuffs no good for you."

"It's not the cigarettes," he coughs again. "They don't help, I guess.... I was in a car accident yesterday. It was raining. Real hard. I was going too fast and I turned and lost control and I'm all shaken up. I hit a parked car. A parked car. So stupid. No one was hurt."

"Except you," Samuel says.

"Yeah. Except me. Always the way. But I'm glad."

"Was it on Pico, near Crenshaw?" Louie asks.

Tim looks up. "Who the hell are you?" Andy gives Louie a look.

"Sorry, I'm just a friend."

"You ain't my friend. I never seen you before."

"I'm with Maggie. Was it a peach colored car?"

"I don't remember what color the fuckin' car was."

"Don't worry about it." Maggie says. "You looked worked up."

Tim stares at nothing on the table. "I think she was Filipino." He looks at Maggie. "She's the kind of lady that would have a peach colored car. She was real nice. Real pretty. Maybe you'd like her." He looks down. "I'm so sorry. I can't believe it. That's why I crashed into that car. I had to do that. I'm so sorry."

Maggie's face crumples and she silently shakes. Then she bursts out laughing, tears streaming down her face.

BOOK FOUR 1987-1991

123.   1987

The street is shuttered, cramped with little salons, clinics, and tailors, and faceless buildings and everything is hued with rancid, copper light. Adams Boulevard near La Brea. A solitary young man, his mind and his body distorted by an alien substance fills the silence with his chants. He wears a black t-shirt and jeans and laceless sneakers that look like they were dredged from the ocean. His head is shaved at the sides but he wears a large floppy black Mohawk He argues with a stop sign. "Shut the fuck up! Just shut the fuck up, asswipe!" and he laughs shrilly for the moment as if had just said something quite clever. Then, "You don't tell me to stop! You don't tell me nothin'." A short, overweight woman in a leather skirt walks westbound a block away. They seem to take no notice of each other. Then he kicks the side of a postal box, denting it. "Mail tampering, yeah! Whooh!" and he pumps his fists in the air above his head. And he reels and kicks the box again pretending it's a piñata to pilfer. "Gimme some a that hot mail. I'm committing a federal crime!" He gives up on this and now the only sound is the electrical wires overhead and the click of the traffic lights. "Shut the fuck up!" he says, putting his hands to his ears as if the faint mechanical noises were crawling up his neck and into his head. "Shut the fuck up," he whimpers. "Man, I gotta piss," and he starts to laugh.

A large brown Chevy Nova pulls up at the red light, puttering comfortably. "Hey!" he calls out. "Hey!" And he runs over. "Open up, man." The car revs its engine but doesn't move. "Roll down your window, hombre. Roll down." The window rolls down. "Nice car. Chevy." He peers in but can't seem to make out the man's feature. "Are you a fatty? Are you a fat little fuck? Don't make no difference if you are. Check this out," and the Mohawk man removes his erect penis and presents it to the driver releasing a fierce expulsion of urine directly in the man's face. "Whoooo! Oopsy! Hahahaha! Yeah baby. Check that out. Check *that* out." The car roars into gear and away down the boneyard street. The man watches the car speed away, turn, and peel off towards unknown parts. "Hey!" the Mohawk calls after him, penis still exposed and dribbling. "What am I supposed to do now! Where am I supposed to piss now! In the goddamn street! Haha! Whoooo!" A dog barks from some unseen yard around the corner. "Shut the fuck up! Keep quiet, goddamn it, so I can hear myself think. People can't sleep because of your *fucking* dog!" And he cackles yet again, a high, strangled little laugh. This last little speech takes him out into the middle of the street, which feels like the safest place to him. He looks about, arms stretched open. "This is my street! This is my fucking street! I own it. All of you are mine. I am your king. Little chicos and chicas everywhere, you are all mine! I'll fucking rape you all. You can't stop me. You can't stop me. You can't do fuckin' nothin'. Cause this is my fuckin' street, homes." And he holds his arms up in a victory sign ignoring the distant sound of a car idling. The roar of the engine makes him turn around. The Chevy sits two blocks down, also in the middle of the street. "Hey! Is that you? Is that you, Chevy. You want more?" And the car, as if hearing him, revs its engine. "Wait. Wait. Wait. I got you something. And he digs into his pocket and there finds a soiled brown napkin which he straightens out, though it remains irreparably rumpled. He holds it out with both hands and waves it, posing like a drunken bullfighter. "OK! Fair fight. Let's go," and he begins to sing an hysterical version of a twisted bullfight anthem. He tries to wave the napkin again, but it blows away this time. "Ah, shit!" But the Chevy screeches into gear and rapidly picks up speed heading straight for him. "Wait a minute! Wait! I don't got my cape, pendejo! Wait!" And he holds his arm outstretched. "You stop!" And the car smashes through him at, rocketing his body several car lengths until it bounces and rolls inert on the pavement.   The car brakes after impact, tires screeching and spitting, then lurches forward again, veering towards the man, and the driver, a man who was once arrested for arson two years ago but never convicted for lack of conclusive physical evidence, this same man now uses Paco's chest and head as speed bumps, shocks bouncing, before the car rights itself into the correct lane, runs a red light, and barrels into the night, the unseen dog barking once again, the traffic light above the body clicking quietly from red to green.

124.   1988

Still youthful yet wizened, tousled blonde hair, wearing jeans and a fatigues replica army jacket, he walks his jowly trotting bulldog, ugly yet endearing, drooling and eager to please. Both of them enjoy the cool winter sunshine, the bright colors and the open grassy fields. The dog pulls to the left, growling and snuffling, and the man eagerly follows. "Whatcha got Benny?" Soon, they both hear the bark and see the perked ears and tentative tail of a long brown Dachshund.   The man shortens the leash on Benny, soothing him and they walk a safe arc away to get a better view of this new dog and its owner. "Hello," he calls out. A young and slender, beautiful black woman, white shorts, sits on a blanket, text book opened. She looks up and squints warily at first, but then she returns the man's smile. "He smells your dog," he says. "He's friendly though."

She raises her right eyebrow. "Oh, I'm not worried," she says. Yes. She is the same woman he has seen before. "He's beautiful," she adds, meaning his dog, but the man takes the compliment as if it had been intended for himself. The Dachshund barks and growls. "Hush, Shanie. No one's talking to you."

"You made his day. Most people think he's so ugly that he's cute," and he playfully massages Benny's jowls and neck, while the dog looks up at him with beseeching and grateful eyes, drooling and lolling his tongue. "How condescending. Aren't you beautiful, Benny?" and the dog licks him and whimpers. "I think he wants to meet your doggie. Her name's Shanie?"

"Shanie. Yeah. She'll be OK with that."

"Sometimes the little ones are the most rough and tough."

"Oh, she's a wimp. Believe me."

"You sure my Benny's safe? He's a bigger wimp."

"Yeah, I'm sure."

"I'm Rolfe."

"I'm Jade."

∞

Benny and Shanie sniff at each other, but Benny quickly loses interest. Shanie barks and starts to run as if wanting to be chased. Benny begins to lick himself. "She really thinks she can run. It's so ridiculous," both of them laugh. "She's such a puppy. But she's four already." The Dachshund begins to sniff again at Benny who stretches out in the sun, rolling over and over in the grass. Shanie barks and runs in circles, tail whipping furiously. "Ain't that like a typical male," she says. "Once he's got her all into him, he just rolls over and wants to hang out."

"They get along pretty good. He's a show off, it's true." Rolfe learns that Jade is a medical student at UCLA in her second year.

"What do you do when you're not chasing Benny?"

"Benny's my best buddy. Aren't you," he rubs the dog's belly and smiles. "I love this baby. You're my baby! .....I'm a painter."

"You're an artist? What do you paint?"

"Mostly houses. Sorry," he smiles, "I should have said I'm a house painter. Furniture too, like tables and dressers. I'm a contractor. I also custom build dog houses for rich people. It's good fun." This last part he unaccountably made up. Indeed, the painter had made a dog house for Benny and had once or twice seen such underused vanities in the larger yards of wealthy people, "At least that's a side business I want to start."

"That's cool." She notices flecks of paint beneath his worn cuticles. "How's it going?"

"It's going. Great. Not so much the dog houses, not yet, but I'm always thinking of new businesses where I can make some extra cash using my hands.

The painting business is busy. Lots of construction going on in the Westside."
She nods. He tells her about growing his knowledge and business in electrical
work. "I'm also getting my license to fix air conditioners and heating
equipment"

"Good for you."

He reddens, aware that he is acting as if he needs to impress this young
girl. Therefore he resents her. He discreetly searches her face for any signs of
condescension. She is beautiful but he becomes aware to his chagrin that he is
less intimidated by her beauty because she's black. But then he says, "Good for
me? You're the one who's going to be a surgeon. Paging Dr. Robinson. *That's*
impressive." His extra years might give him an avuncular quality that he
despises.

"I'm not there yet. Not everyone has to be a doctor. I couldn't do what
you do."

"What do you mean?"

"I mean I couldn't paint or build or fix something to save my life."

"Working with things is easy. Once you learn them, and if you're
curious and patient you usually do well and then they don't change all that much.
Not like people. Very messy. In every way, as I'm sure you've found out."

"Anatomy *is* messy," and she tells him about the work with cadavers.

But he corrects her, "That too, but I mean as a doctor you have to try and
understand people. Some people don't want to just take your advice because
you're the doctor" and they speak of this and that and the conversation seems to
slow but Jade does not seem to mind and she looks at him and asks,

"So, Rolfe. Are you married?"

"Married. No. I would not be here right now if I was."

"Just checking."

"I might have said hello," he smiles, "Especially with Benny here. But
no, I would not have sat down."

"Is Benny like your wing man?"

"Benny is the best."

"Were you ever married?"

"I was. But I'm not," and he rubs Benny's head.

Jade leans back archly, her arms supporting her from behind. "I seen
you here before, walking Benny."

"I've seen you, too, Jade. Studying in the sun."

"Every Sunday I'm here."

"Always alone. I told myself and I told Benny, I said let's go meet that
nice dog and that pretty lady."

"In that order?"

"Well, I was talking to Benny you know."

She laughs. "It took you long enough, Benny....Let me ask you something, Rolfe." He nods, petting his dog. "You said working with people was messy. Are you saying you find relationships messy?"

Rolfe smiles again. "You're very forward. I like that. But I'm not saying that. I just mean you can't treat a person with the same certainty you can as something you want to build or paint with your own hands."

"Well....I should think not."

"Of course."

"You're not afraid to get your hands a little dirty, are you?"

125. 1989

Planting is his favorite part of the job, though he has learned to love nearly every part; even the removing and hauling of stones. Now that he has experience, he leads most of his own jobs, or works alone, and he works at his own pace, methodically and at ease, as if he were tending to his own estates. It is less money than he had planned on making at this time in his life. His children will have to settle for community college unless they are great scholars. They might have to take at least part time work, but there is no shame in that. Tuesdays and Fridays, the quiet curvy green streets are full of gardeners like himself as well as ordinary laborers; cutting lawns, blowing and raking leaves, and every year pruning and sawing and hauling away the mulch of the winnowed woods of San Marino. Today he lays out the soil and carefully plants sapling rose bushes. He likes the feel of the wet earth on his hands and he loves the days of warm sunshine though he learns to wear a straw hat to protect his neck and head.

His children are growing tall and strong and Guillaume has skipped a grade to the chagrin of his older sister. His epilepsy is well controlled for now and the man thanks God, Lord Jesus, for his many blessings, and for the life he lives, which he realizes must be far better than his own plan. He and his family moved to El Sereno to be closer to these people's homes. Life is good and everything, just about, is in its place. "Senor! Senor Ramirez!," a voice calls out to him. "Please. Over here," the voice calls again in Spanish. Senor Ramirez frowns, wipes his hands on his work trousers and walks towards the gate where a gray looking man, short and thin, insubstantial, someone who might have blended in with the gate, awaits him. The man possesses dreary familiar features, only sharper, more wizened, wearing a filthy cap and eye patch. He resembles an aged and decrepit version of someone whom Senor Ramirez had once discarded from his life. Sensing trouble but feeling unable to ignore the man or to chase him away from afar, Perry charges awkwardly down the grassy knoll, scowl fixed upon his face.

"Who is it? What do you want?" he replies in English.

"Senor Ramirez, I am sorry to disturb you. I was a friend of Francisco Mayor." Perry just stares at him. "Paco Mayor."

"I know no such person. Nor was he ever a friend of mine."

"I am Luis Arturo Batista. I used to live across the street from you." Perry pulls up to within a single stride and stops short as if another inch might expose him to infection from the man on the other side.

"Wilson Batista."

"Yes, senor." He takes off his cap out of some sort of gesture of propriety, revealing his rapidly thinning, greasy matted hair. "I have come to speak with you. Please, I only wish a few minutes of your time. And then no more."

Perry squints at him. "Why would I have anything to say to you?"

Wilson looks down at his cap as if ashamed of how dirty it is. "Please. I won't take up much of your time."

"What on earth could you possibly want from me?" Perry thunders in Spanish. "You are like a pestilence, Wilson Batista. You bring darkness and dread to me. And now, how dare you track me down where I work! This is an insult."

"Senor. Please. Hear me out only a little."

"You want money? A job, perhaps? A new start for your miserable life? You want to suck my blood?"

Wilson merely looks down at his hands. "No, senor," he quietly responds.

"I swear, Wilson Batista, if I ever see you or hear about you near either of my children ever, I swear I will cut off your worthless head with this!" and he throws his tool down to the ground where it sticks into the earth beneath the sloping lawn. Perry privately grimaces at the scar in the grounds this is likely to leave. Wilson's eyes widen at the sight of the great shears stuck in the earth. A thin ribbon of shame suddenly peels down Perry's back, for he realizes his vehemence grows in relation to his erstwhile adversary's increasingly evident weakness.

"Senor. I meant no disrespect. I only came here because I did not dare to try and find you at home. Please, Senor, I was truly frightened to come, but I felt I had to if I would have any peace."

"Were you talking to my wife?"

"I was in the hospital. Maybe for two days. I saw Senora who was working there.....So I asked her for her forgiveness. Then I asked her if I might come to see you. And she told me where to find you."

Perry says as if to himself, "It was not for her to say. Why does she speak for me?"

"Senor Ramirez, I came to ask you for your forgiveness. That is all."

"You what?"

284

Wilson closes his eyes, intently reciting, "I will gladly say if you wish to hear, all the things I have done that I would like you to forgive me for. And I would gladly hear from you any additional ways that I have harmed you and your family or anyone you care about. And I would gladly hear if there is any way I can try to repair the damage I have caused. Only after all this would I ask you to forgive me."

Perry looks Wilson up and down. "You think I have all the time in the world for all that?"

"I would gladly meet you wherever and whenever you please. Of course it does not have to be right now. I only came to ask for the opportunity. You are, of course, a working man."

Perry stands for a long silence before asking, "And what will you do if I refuse?"

"Then I will leave you my number and I will leave. You can call me if you ever change your mind or you can throw the number away. I do not want to be a burden. Also.....God will forgive me if you refuse, but not if I do not ask. What else can I say?"

Perry takes off his cap and he wipes the sweat from his forehead. "Why are you doing this, Wilson Batista? Are you dying?"

"Not that I know of. But perhaps, Senor. It could happen at any time after all I have been through. And I want to be ready. And I want to stay in my right mind. You see, I used to take drugs. I used to drink vodka. I used to smoke marijuana."

"You took those filthy blue pills."

"Yes.... Yes senor. I took them. I stole them. I sold them. Yes senor. It is the plain truth. But I don't anymore. It has been over two years now and I don't want to go back to it. So if I don't want to drink or to take drugs, I have to come to you and to others and I have to do what I am doing now."

He stops and Perry waits so neither speaks again at first. Perry looks around and he spits and he looks again at Wilson, grimacing. He sighs and he says in English, "You swear that you will never ask anything else from me. Ever. No money, no job. Nada."

"Si Senor. Never."

"And you will speak of this meeting with no one. No one at all."

"As you wish. Only to God."

"You swear you will never, I mean never, *ever* contact me or bother any member of my family ever again."

"I swear. If ever I happen to see you or anyone in your family I will turn and run or drive away and pray for you or for them only."

"Save your prayers if they are on our behalf. Do you understand?"

"Si Senor." But Wilson reserves the right to pray to God in any way he needs to. No one can dictate conditions on that relationship.

Perry looks at Wilson and though he shakes his head at him at first, in the end he permits a single, almost imperceptible nod. He looks at his watch. "I'll give you five minutes, Wilson Batista. And I guarantee you nothing. Starting right now."

"Bless you. Thank you, Senor. Thank you…..Here are the harms I have caused you that I can recall. Thank you for hearing me," and Wilson Batista continues to speak.

126.   1990

Every Wednesday, the care giver takes Mrs. Caleb to the German restaurant at the foot of the hill that leads to lovely Rancho Hills estates where Mrs. Caleb continues to live by herself. The care giver looks forward to these outings as one of her favorite parts of the week because Mrs. Caleb treats her almost like they are actually friends or even family members going out to lunch together. Even though it's just pretend.

Mrs. Caleb's daughter visits every week and fusses, first with her mother and secondly with the care giver but the care giver reasons that the daughter is only compensating because the daughter is spending so little time with her own mother. Only a few minutes here and there to make sure the house is in general order, the house that the daughter stands to inherit. The daughter goes through the motions of asking about her mother's eating, her medications, and her bowel movements.   She then dispenses unnecessary directions and advice which is promptly ignored by both mother and care giver. Mrs. Caleb is physically frail but mentally sharp. The caregiver reasons that the instant Mrs. Caleb begins to decline, she will undoubtedly be moved into some wretched nursing home, so it seems, just like the one where the care giver herself used to work.

Mrs. Caleb likes to dress up and so both of them are in fashionable dresses and coats, at least dresses that were somewhat fashionable, fifteen or twenty years ago. Most of all, the care giver likes to wear nice and shiny black shoes with a short heel, because she feels pretty and grown up in them, although she secretly doesn't like to wear them for very long because her feet always feel too big and uncomfortable in them. The old woman pretends at first to not notice what her care giver clearly notices; the homeless man lying stretched out upon the bus bench, his coat shiny and thin with grime and despair. The old woman merely shakes her head clucking her tongue beneath her breath. Her care taker reads beneath her matron's disapproval the signs of secret fears of such inconvenient suffering in her midst. They stand together by the hostess table. There is always a hush of old world environ, uncommon, alpine wood beams, shiny decorative beer steins festooned with scenes of drunken peasants. "Are you sure I look alright, Mrs. Caleb?"

"You look lovely, Caroline. I told you."

"Thank you," and she smiles and almost curtsies.

"Just a thought, dear. You might wear a hair clip to keep your hair out of your eyes."

"Yes, ma'am," and she pushes back the locks of hair that keep falling forward.

"Never mind, dear. It won't stay out without a hair clip. Next time."

Mrs. Caleb allows Caroline to eat the remains off of her plate. Caroline always asks for more free rolls and black bread with as much butter as she wants, despite Mrs. Caleb's gentle remonstrations against eating too much dairy. She is a congenial listener and Mrs. Caleb likes to talk, sometimes about her past, sometimes about politics of which both women understand nothing and quite often about her own children, usually in disappointed undertones, and Caroline cannot help feel both special for being taken into the old woman's confidence as well as utterly baffled by what she hears. "If I knew my mother, I would want to see her every day and take care of her and hold her and kiss her all the time." Caroline is completely sincere and because she is nothing but frank, Mrs. Caleb is mystified and so she responds indifferently, sensing a hint that Caroline is angling to be treated like family in Mrs. Caleb's will. At the meal's conclusion, Caroline offers, as always to bring the car around to the temporary parking spot right in front of the restaurant's entrance.

She acquired her driver's license less than a year ago and she doesn't like to drive much but she knows this is necessary for her work as a home aid. As it is, she takes the bus to and from Korea Town every day where she rents a room sharing an apartment with a Chinese family and an elderly rumpled man smelling of onions and tobacco, a man of vague east European descent. She had tried to speak to this man to see if they were indeed from a similar part of the world, but he is a doggedly grouchy and frightened creature who speaks only to shush the children or argue with the parents. Once, however, the old man entered her room at night, whispering in some language that she did not understand. She stood up and shouted, "Get out!" and the man quickly slunk away and never came back and neither ever spoke of the incident. Her time on the bus was one of her most private times. She listens to music through headphones hooked up to a little tape recorder, which was also a radio. This is her time to daydream and the headphones and recorder were amongst her most prized possessions. Another private time for her, even more coveted, is when Mrs. Caleb falls asleep in front of the television, during which time Caroline wanders gently through the house, pretending that she lives there and occasionally dousing herself lightly with neglected perfumes that she knows where to find in the bedrooms and bathrooms. Mrs. Caleb often comments that she smells so nice but she seems to have no inkling that the scents are from her own collections, her own frozen past.

Although Caroline secretly aspires to inherit the house herself after Mrs. Caleb's passing, she would have sincerely and vigorously denied any such notion had anyone suggested it to her. Such a wish presented itself as unseemly and therefore was unknown to her. Consciously, however, she did allow that she fantasized about being allowed to live in the house and to have her own room as she continues to take care of the old woman. She could then sleep every night in a clean smelling room and wander in the early morning hours though the rolling, safe, yet mysterious streets and sometimes as far as Rancho Park itself. In the meantime, Caroline lives in her own little room in Korea Town, but sometimes the young children go into her room during the day and she can tell because her stuffed animals and pictures that she has drawn herself have either been moved or else go missing. Perhaps the old man himself goes into her room and she notices that her underwear and sock drawer sometimes seem a bit out of place, items piled more than she remembered on one side or another. She tries to put this thought out of her mind; if she ever catches the old man, she swears she will clobber him with no compunction, but she stops short of laying any plans to try and catch him in the act.

Since the restaurant has no back entrance, Caroline exits the front. She starts to pass the homeless man as she has often done before. This time for some reason she stops to notice that his feet are bare and blackened and scabbed and she stares for a moment as if mapping the lines of his scaly dried skin. Something makes her step around to try and see the man's face. In her head, she begins to talk to him, telling him that she understands and that she is sorry that she cannot do anything for him and that she cannot bring him a pair of shoes, or even a pair of socks. Instead of spoken words she hums a kind of lullaby under her breath, something she imagines that the mother of her dreams would have sung to her. Mrs. Caleb can wait for just a moment. Caroline peers over, sees the mop of curly hair, flecks of dried leaves lost upon it. She sees the rashes of angry looking acne on the back of his seemingly untouchable neck. "What happened to you?" she whispers, half scolding, half with heartache. And she peeks over to make out the man's brow, the curve of his lips and the bulb of his nose and she suddenly pulls back as if from a hot flame, putting her hand to her mouth, as if to keep herself from crying out. "Oh God," she says aloud and then she whispers, "No. No, no, no...." again and again. The man stirs but does not awaken. "Sleep. Sleep," she whispers, half aloud, half within herself. Dream well. I will find you again. I will take you to that place, like I promised. And I will try to bring you some shoes or at least some socks. But she dares not say any such thing out loud for she has no idea if she can still do any of that. So she turns away from Eugene and she rushes to the car, hoping to bring it around in time before Mrs. Caleb becomes visibly impatient.

127. The Anteater - 1991

A thin, rakish man with a short trim beard, sharp blue eyes, and a woolen newsboy cap pushes a woman in a wheel chair up a steep incline. The sky is white and the air is fragrant with roses and mulch as they pass by a very long and towering hedge towards another row of rose bushes. The woman is heavy set with prematurely white hair and bright gray eyes. "I got it from here," she says, as they crest the little hill and she presses the button to steer her chair. "Damn. This thing is just no good uphill." He walks slowly besides her, hands in pockets. "Thanks for not saying it's because I'm too fat." Everywhere there are rosebushes, trees, and freshly cut lawns. The two settle in front of a pond and they talk further amongst themselves about their work, their past, themselves, as well as ambling and random opinions and private jokes.

There's not a lot of talk about the future until the man in the newsboy cap says, "I still think we could do one more."

"One more what?"

"What do you think?"

She doesn't respond at first. "I'm happy with the two we did. You, you'll make a whole lot more records. That's you. I love your stuff. You and Louie together; you guys are such silly, brilliant fucks."

"Ours are my favorites, the three of us. Dictionary. Let's record another Dictionary record."

"I don't even know what you're talking about, Andy. I can't fuckin' play anymore, so you're makin' me crazy."

"You can still sing."

"Not much. And anyway, that's not what I really do."

"They love you in Japan. You're huge there."

"I'm huge right here, in this chair."

"You made the Karoake rotation with Screaming Jay in that club by the train station. You've got six fans in Yugoslavia. At least. There's that dude in Arkansas who asked you to marry him. There's the hippie couple in New Zealand that buys from us again and again the same records to give to everyone they know."

"All true. What a silly you are," and she touches his face.

"It *is* true. People listen to those CDs all over the world. We're international stars. We should go see them."

"I love you, Andy." He takes her hand and kisses it. "I wish I could see you every day. Or at least every month."

"I'll stay for awhile."

"Like a week?"

"Maybe more."

"You don't like it here anymore."

"Right here, right now I like it fine."

"You're the one who needs to go out and meet the dozen or so people around the world who love us."

"There's more than that actually. A lot more."

"I love that you're happy enough for both of us. You go and do that for me. Go out and find them."

"Let's first go see some savage beasts." The petting zoo, adjacent to the public gardens, had been a favorite of Maggie's ever since she became confined to a wheel chair. November was a good time to visit. The animals were livelier and the stench was milder as well and there were fewer children, hardly any on a Tuesday morning. Andy had been a little surprised at Maggie's fondness for the animals. She is germaphobic but also genuinely prone to colds and flu, so she wears a mask and she always washes her hands immediately after petting the animals. Andy carries antiseptic wipes that he hoards from fast food chicken restaurants, specifically to give her.

"You know you can just buy the fucking things at the store," she once says to him.

"Look who's a big spender," he says. She loves to pet the animals and to watch their stupid contented faces. Sometimes she looks sad like she might cry amongst the dirty little goats and sheep, but it is at exactly such moments when she is most content.

Before actually visiting the animals they stop at the little office shack where their friend is waiting for them. He has gained weight from the last time they saw him six months ago but he looks content and happy. He wears khakis and white socks and a lightly stained polo shirt tucked into his pants and a thin blue windbreaker. He is already quite gray though his face is still florid and youthful. The three friends greet and embrace, sauntering to a nearby bench in front of the soft serve vanilla cones. "Max, you think maybe you should paint this little place. It's really peeling." And it was. It had once been painted a solid powder blue. "Know any painters?"

"No. But I'll get around to it, or find someone." A moment later he says, "I love these soft cones. Don't you?" Both Andy and Maggie agree. "You picked a real good day. Real quiet. We might even start closing on Tuesdays."

"I hope you're making money."

"A little. Not a lot. Shirley's not worried." They talk a little about the different animals, their temperament and upkeep, just like they often do when they meet. They all sit together at a picnic table.

"Max," Maggie says, deciding it is time. "We have something to tell you."

"Oh no," Max says. "Is it bad?"

"Yeah, sweetie. It's Samuel. He passed away last month."

"Ohh." He looks sad but he seems to take it better than they had feared. "What happened?"

"He was just sitting in his chair by the creek near the cabin, like he always does. And that's where they found him. He was reading a book when he fell asleep. He just didn't wake up."

"Oh. That doesn't sound too bad."

"I'd like to go like that," Andy says. He remembers Maureen and their first dinner together.

"What book was he reading?"

"Honey, I don't know. You know he had all kinds of books."

"I know. I just wanted to imagine." The truth, Andy recalls, is a bit more complicated. Indeed, Samuel was found on his property outside, near the creek. There was a hammock that he rarely used. One day, though, on a whim, he decided he wanted to take a proper nap near his beloved creek. The hammock was small and not in the best repair and somehow he had ejected himself onto the ground. After, he was unable to get up again and that is where they found him, face up at least and staring at the sky. He had lived much longer than they had expected him to and he had been able to live comfortably enough from his small pension and social security. He ate little and rarely bought anything and hardly left the place except to stock up on staples. He had let his hair and beard grow wild once more. Minutes after he had come face to face again with his adopted daughter he silently drove Tim back to his apartment. Over time there were letters and phone calls exchanged, though rarely, and months would go by and Samuel had been seemingly forgotten altogether. Eventually, Maggie began to dutifully call him and on two occasions, she and Andy actually visited him. She came to like Samuel but she never felt that he was ever in any way her father. He was like from another planet to her, lovely and interesting to contemplate in its own way, but not in her realm. She remembers being given piano lessons and retreating deeper and deeper into music until everything else was a dream. All she ever felt towards Samuel was some dutiful gratitude towards a remote public figure that enabled her to dwell more freely in the sufficiently awkward present. He had gifted her music.

Elizabeth had forwarded Samuel's letters to their other children. A few weeks later he received replies, first from Joan and then from Adam and he remained in regular contact with both of them, particularly Joan who called him every Sunday. It was Joan who suspected something might be wrong when she failed to reach him all day. She had asked the Wasequa police to please go visit him and it was then that he was found, but the body was already cold and he was thought to have been dead within an hour or two after having fallen, having no doubt aggravated some pre-existing morbidity already ailing him. Weeks later, after Joan and Adam had arranged for his cremation, they also put up his cabin for sale and settled his remaining affairs. Adam contacted Maggie, whose number was amongst Samuel's entries in a notebook. Maggie was now in touch with her two step siblings.

Tim was already dead. He had died within a year of the day that he met again his only child, his daughter. He was greatly weakened from the accident, always tired, and was very soon thereafter diagnosed with late stage lung cancer. Maggie visited him every week until he became very ill. She visited him in the hospital and in the nursing home. Predictably, Tim became more and more withdrawn, but he made his best efforts to be sociable and interesting whenever Maggie came to see him. They watched baseball on television, together. She never brought Louie or Andy with her on her visits, but she talked about their accomplishments together, their small but international following. It took Tim awhile to grasp the fact that they hardly made any money from their record sales. He nevertheless came to understand what they were doing and why. "It's your art. Isn't it? This is like art. You made it. You have to do it."

"Yeah, Pops. That's it." She started to feel more comfortable calling Tim by a paternal endearment. "Like your poetry."

"Yeah. Well. I guess. You took your stuff further than I took mine."

"It's not a contest you know."

"I'm just saying. You done good, baby."

"Thanks."

"I admire your music a lot."

"You don't like it much, Pops," she says with a smile. "You hate it."

"No. I never hated it. Not ever."

"You didn't like it much."

"Listen to me. I just didn't understand it. Not at first. It was too new. But I listened to it again. You have to really listen to your stuff. It's not background music, I'll give you that. I used to know some of the greatest music in the world, the big bands, the jazz bands. That's what I know. It was really good, you know, and so alive. Your stuff is nothing like that, so I don't recognize it. But I listen. I still don't all the way understand. But it's really got something going on. Color or something. It's like one of those paintings I don't really get, but I know it's rare, it's not something you could ever say, 'Oh, I could do that'. Because no one else ever could." She realizes that this was about as magnificent a tune of praise as she would ever get from him and she decides to gratefully accept it. And the more she thinks about it, the less condescending and the more sincere he was being, not just to please her but in an effort to genuinely hear and feel their music.

"I wish I could see the stuff you wrote," she told him.

"It wasn't much," he said in a low voice, a gravel of shame in it.

"I still would like to see it."

"Maybe. Someday." But that day never came while he was alive. She found old notebooks amongst his meager possessions and she found the things he wrote which he had not destroyed. At first, to her chagrin, all she found was doggerel and she felt shame not only for her father but also towards herself for judging him. But she managed to read on and she found candid, restless pieces

292

about scenes from his native New York City and the hidden lives and recesses and corners from block to block and how the city was somehow so small and intimate compared to L.A, like going from millions of bedrooms and parties to a vast unprincipled desert of far flung strip malls. He wrote of friendships both sublime and forsaken, connections over a single beer or a full moon or a woman in passing. Poems about the moon particularly arrested her attention and she kept on reading. He wrote of unrequited love of many kinds, of requited love oft regretted, of regretted love reimagined, and of a thousand romances of the imagination, so many conceived while walking down a single spring avenue or lying wide awake at night staring at the ceiling, imagining your own private moon staring back at you. Everything Tim had ever written, clumsy or graceful, nuanced or obvious, all suggested longing and loss and loneliness. Any hint of hardness had a touch of boisterousness but without bitterness. Longing was an experience, a feast of life not to be avoided nor missed. There were poems about her as well, Maggie. This was the voice of a father she could understand, not the sullen and eternally disappointed man who retreated into boredom, but a man who clearly regretted anything less of life than fully lived. He wrote of simply loving his daughter. She also discovered simple prose of being ashamed of his weakness and his alcoholic wife, a man who had not yet abandoned his dreams altogether, but who cursed himself for giving up his daughter. And she felt in the reading of these things angry and resentful and peaceful and reconciled by turns.

But now her own body deteriorates and her options are limited and she doesn't want to think about it and the worst part of all is the loss of her own music. If only Andy would live with her and love her and take care of her so she could depend upon him and perhaps blame him for everything and she smiles at herself. She lives in a group home for those on disability and she receives a stipend and Louie comes to see her at least twice a week to take her out. Maggie works part time doing customer service, phone work, for a company that makes industrial fans and cooling equipment. She likes the work and the people though it is difficult to get to and from the office. An inside salesman named Roy gives her rides so she is rescued from having to spend most of her days in idleness. Roy likes her but she hesitates to take it further. She spends her off time reading science fiction and fantasy and listening to music, music, and music, especially Andy's which is prolific, even if only sold in the most modest quantities. Andy only comes once in a while for he lives everywhere and nowhere, and now he is moving to Vermont and she wants to go with him but he has not asked her this time to go with him and sometimes she longs to be dead so she will no longer envy the living and she is ashamed of that thought and it makes her angry to feel that way. Sometimes she misses her father.

Andy is here now and he plays his guitar and they often sing kinder more gentle folk songs and old songs and she had even tried with Andy to put some of her father's poems or fragments of them to this kind of music and she wishes she had thought to do this while he was alive and it surprises her how much she misses him and it makes her sad to think of all the time she has lost and she remembers the moon outside her little room in Gary and she imagines going back there, for time there never seems to move.

"Maxie. Louie says 'Hi'. He wants me to give you a kiss from him. A friend kiss he says. I'll give it to you later. One from me, too." She is too tired to do it now and to see Max blush, clearly he is in no hurry to receive either one. They exchange routine inquiries about their health and how they are all getting on. Max looks sad to see Maggie in her wheel chair. A tiny woman appears with thick glasses and long gray red hair down the middle of her back, yellow at the edges. She wears a fatigue jacket far too large for her and she barely fills out her child's sized blue jeans. Her name is Shirley and she throws her bony arms around Max from behind and hugs him fiercely, kissing him on the cheek. Max blushes. Happily. Shirley owns the petting zoo. They met four years ago while she still worked at the city zoo. Max frequented the zoo on days when he wasn't working in a mattress store. He would stand and gaze and talk to his favorite animals; zebras and rhinos (much gentler than they appeared) and gorillas (same thing) and tapirs and strange little wart pigs and peccaries and of course, his beloved anteater, lonely and magnificent and nameless. Shirley initiated a conversation with him and she encouraged him to visit on Tuesday mornings while it was cool and after a while, they would plan to meet every Tuesday at 10:30 by the zebras. It was Shirley who invited him to join her for dinner. She was like a being who one day had transformed from being a very young girl for a very long time to suddenly skipping prime adult hood and becoming straight away an old woman. Her tiny features are wizened and shriveled and her hands are thick and leathery though small. But her eyes are still a bright blue, young and impish with humor and affection. All her life she had been saving for something and it was the petting zoo that is now her life. But she had also been saving for Max, who is both her companion and the child she never had.

Maggie pets them and fondles their ears and the loose skin above their necks, the placid sheep and baby goats with the wide gold tiny eyes, filled with gentleness and stupidity, who sidle slowly up until they make her laugh. The animals are drawn to gently sit beside her or to proffer their necks to be pet, their eyes blinking with satisfaction, their endless grazing momentarily forgotten. Later they feed some ducks and geese, watch and laugh as chickens cluck, and they feed and pet an alpaca. Maggie is forever in her surgical mask. Max who had been running chores, mucking, feeding and watering, comes back to them.

"You wash your hands?" Maggie says.

"Yeah. I did. Shirley asks me that, too."

Andy asks, "Max, Why no anteater?"

Max blushes again. "They're really hard to come by you know. They're rare and expensive. Also..."

"Yeah?"

"They have no place in a petting zoo."

"They don't?"

"They're wild and children could never get near them. I mean they have silly, stupid heads but they're large and dangerous. Not aggressive, but it's too risky. Have you seen their claws? Huge!"

"Makes sense." A moment later Andy asks, "Max. Are you still even into anteaters like you were before?"

"I still like them. Sure. They're noble creatures and I find them beautiful and other worldly like."

"But do you love them, Max? Do you still want to *be* an anteater?"

Max grins, "I never wanted to actually be an anteater. Not really. I mean, that's just silly."

"Well I know you didn't expect to actually become one. But you fancied it would be nice if you were."

Max blushes and says, "They just... Their lives just seem simple enough. They're not afraid. They don't have to be. They just walk around, eat ants you know. Other bugs. They don't care. That's what I always like about them. Of course they're ridiculous looking but they don't care because they're actually who they're supposed to be. I guess that's really true about all animals, which is why I admire them."

"Maybe you already are an anteater, Maxie."

"Anteaters would be out of place here, wouldn't they?"

"*You're* not out of place here. You're exactly where you're supposed to be. You seem happy."

Max seems to think about this. "Yes. There's a lot of things that if I think about them too much they start to bother me. Somehow I manage not to think about them. I don't know if that's good or bad. I know there's a lot of bad things in the world." He stops and looks out at nothing, hands in pockets. "One day, Shirley says she wants to take us to South America or maybe southern Mexico. To see....well that's where anteaters and creatures like that all live. I don't think we'll really go though. I think this place is happy. That's enough for me."

After they take leave of Max and Shirley and the gentle creatures, they return to the rose garden and they sit on a bench that overlooks the duck pond and there are scattered flecks of leaves upon the placid waters. They huddle together amidst the beauty of the greenery and the milky sky and the brilliant green necks of the mallards. They huddle heads down, facing each other, hands locked together, locked in their own rhythm and thoughts. "Andy, listen. I know you're such a player all over the country. You're a goddamn Casanova."

"Not really," he whispers back.

"Shut up," she teases. "Of course you are. I'm happy for you, if that's what you want. I know you don't waste much time thinking about me."

"That's not true. You're my best friend."

"Well Louie is *my* best friend. You're something else." She squeezes his hands. "Before you go off to Vermont to go make love to a maple tree or what the fuck," she says, still whispering. "Or wherever you wander off to, I want you to save a bit for me. If you can do me a solid. I mean, I can still get a man, believe it or not. But...."

"I believe it."

Maggie is not so sure she believes it herself, or would want anyone who wants her. Then she remembers Roy. She squeezes Andy's hands again. He hears her soft voice and the voice of water streaming from a distant fountain. Music.

128. Epilogue - 1985

He drives the 101, though the 5 is faster. But the 101 is peaceful and full of hope as he watches the halcyon rolling hills. His heart is weightless. He tarries for a night amongst the Avenue of the Giants, aptly named, admiring the redwoods, his modest belongings easily fitting in his trunk and his wallet on his person and the bulk of his modest funds already transferred northward. He knows he is weak and utterly alone but he feels energized to have done what he has set out to do with no regrets. His brief and unpleasant meeting with his daughter merely confirms that he is meant to stand aside, but still there are no more regrets. What will he really see when he gazes upon that mountain top? The night before he knows he will arrive, he drives upon an open dirt road in northwestern Oregon, a mile or so off the highway and before he curls up in the back seat of his car, he steps outside and he gazes at the huge sky vaulted over the grassland and he reclines upon his hood and stares up, laying his head upon his hands and elbows, knowing he will soon feel stiff. At first he tries to locate and name the constellations and local stars. There are so many tonight for he is far from any city and the night is blessedly clear. The stars are beautiful and nauseating in the incomprehensible space and time and silence in which they dwell. But this is why he seeks them; peace in the nauseating vastness of existence, serenity in seeking his own smallness. In his head, there is no music. Only silence.

From time to time, he is treated to the sight of a shooting star, but of course he knows that shooting starts are merely fragments of ice and rock, loosed from untold recesses of the cosmos, travelling for stupefying eons until finally they flash for an instant before Samuel's eyes, only to disappear forever into the nameless valleys and oceans, nevermore to be seen or remembered ever again.

AVAILABLE NOW ON AMAZON! THE WAY TO NOD - Short stories and novelettes from the edge!

A young man fights the insane urge to throw champagne into the face of his beloved's father; a woman at work copes in paranoid ways; an underling's misplaced resentment towards his boss pushes him into a deadly street confrontation. The title story follows a desperate escape from a nightmare dystopia in quest of a peaceful land that no one knows for sure really exists. Enjoy these and other tales from the edge. **Only $6.95 in paperback.** *Only 99 cents on Kindle!*

AVAILABLE NOW ON AMAZON! **FOG** - *An idyllic tale of mayhem set in the California Redwoods.*

Ari Fisher lives the perfect life in the most beautiful place on earth. As the semester ends at the college where he teaches part time, Ari has but one unexpected task to perform; to entertain one of his school's most important donors. In an escalating game of cat and mouse with his charming and unexpected new adversary, Ari's life threatens to come completely unraveled over the course of a single evening as his inner demons are suddenly and violently unleashed.

Only $8.95 in paperback on Amazon. (154 pages) *Only 99 cents on Kindle!*

Edan Benn Epstein lives in Southern California. He can be contacted at ebepstein@sbcglobal.net. His other novels include Empty Sky (1997),

Subterranean Green (2011), Fog (2012), and Afternoon of the Faun (2015), all of which will be available through Amazon before the end 2016. For further updates like us on Facebook at Edan Benn Epstein.

www.ingramcontent.com/pod-product-compliance
Lightning Source LLC
Chambersburg PA
CBHW062129170626
46813CB00002B/627